SUDDEN BLOW

A JANE YEATS MYSTERY

SUDDEN BLOW

A JANE YEATS MYSTERY

by

Liz Brady

CANADIAN CATALOGUING IN PUBLICATION DATA

Brady, Elizabeth, date
Sudden blow

A Jane Yeats mystery.
ISBN 1-896764-05-3

I. Title.

PS8553.R24S92 1998   C813'.54   C98-930768-9
PR9199.3.B72S92 1998

Copyright © 1998 by Liz Brady

Printed and bound in Canada

Edited by Mary Adachi

*Second Story Press gratefully acknowledges the support of the
Ontario Arts Council and the Canada Council for the Arts
for our publishing program. We acknowledge the financial
support of the Government of Canada through the Book Publishing
Industry Development program.*

Published by
SECOND STORY PRESS
*720 Bathurst Street, Suite 301
Toronto, Ontario
M5S 2R4*

Acknowledgments

I am grateful to Peter Robinson, who brought his wit and superb craft to bear upon an earlier version of the manuscript; to Medora Sale and Howard Engel, for their words of advice and encouragement; to Mary Adachi, my fastidious editor, whose more ascetic prose sense tempered my flamboyance; and to Second Story Press, my publisher, for their persistent generosity in bringing new voices into print.

And I am ever indebted to Bob Brandeis, who first believed.

A sudden blow: the great wings beating still
Above the staggering girl, her thighs caressed
By the dark webs, her nape caught in his bill,
He holds her helpless breast upon his breast

....

            Being so caught up,
So mastered by the brute blood of the air,
Did she put on his knowledge with his power
Before the indifferent beak could let her drop?

                    — W. B. YEATS
                        "Leda and the Swan"

CHAPTER 1

M AX INSTANTLY took to the uninvited woman standing at my door, so I asked her in. My dog trusts strangers to the degree that they resemble his mistress. This predilection translates into a knee-jerk affiliation for women with a casual disregard for fashion. Guys in suits don't stand a chance.

"I'm Simone Goldberg," she said, offering her hand. I accepted it, forgetting to introduce myself. To understate the diagnosis, you could say I was hung over.

She stepped inside the door, gingerly bypassing a leaning tower of empty beer cases. Shakily, I gestured toward the sofa at the far end of my studio. Max, his unkempt rag of tail wagging so vigorously it made him swagger, followed the attractive stranger across the room. I prayed that he wouldn't jump up on her and expose the startling extent of his welcome. Introductions are awkward enough, without canine erections getting in the way.

I followed in their wake, absorbing her details. She was short, by my standards compact, trim and tidy. Cropped black hair shot with grey curled naturally around an unembellished face. She wore an Irish tweed jacket over a Norwegian sweater, black wool slacks, well-bred leather boots. No jewellery — unless a thin gold wedding band counts. Understated, but conveying that impression of rustic elegance I rarely manage to contrive, in spite of my frequent perusals of L.L. Bean catalogues. I guess you have to actually buy the gear to gain the look.

My intruder lowered herself onto my distressed sofa, discreetly nudging aside a heap of newspapers, magazines, flyers and sundry research notes. Her green eyes were alarmingly keen. I half-hoped my notes imparted an aura of intellectual respectability to the rest of the print detritus, which included the *National Enquirer, Spotlight on Crime, The Toronto Sun* and the sheet music to "Three Cigarettes in an Ashtray."

I swooped over to clear the coffee table of some empty beer cans and a noxiously full ashtray, then executed a quick two-step to conceal my loss of balance as I straightened up. By way of encore, I deposited the garbage into an oversize terra-cotta flowerpot, long bereft of living foliage.

When she shifted on the sofa, her sudden grimace told me she'd landed on one of the overtaxed springs. "Do you mind if I smoke?" she inquired, drawing a pack of Player's from a woven bag as if she were accustomed to getting permission, or didn't give a damn. "I know it's incorrect."

"Lady," I replied, "this place is a temple to deviation. So smoke."

Max plopped himself down at her feet and moaned. I could relate to that.

I refused her offer of a cigarette. Recently I've managed to confine my smoking to when I drink — which limits me to a pack a day and none before noon. Fitness is a bitch.

Her cigarette drew quick carcinogenic life from a silver lighter. She inhaled deeply and relaxed a bit. "I'm sorry to crash in on you like this, but I'm desperate. I need your help. You are Jane Yeats?"

That nod in the affirmative really did me in. My head retaliated with an exquisite *frisson* of pain that etched its way straight across the top of my skull. So I gave this Simone time to explain her presence, while I idly wondered if my vocal chords still worked.

I retained a fuzzy memory of straining them the previous night on the stage of my mother's country juke joint, belting out Patsy Cline golden oldies. My mother must not have been there. I must have been pissed as a newt. I can't even begin to nudge a tune off the ground, let alone carry one in any recognizable way. Still, four beers and I fall to pieces. Six and I'm k. d. lang. Eight and I'm reckless with talent, scanning the audience for Nashville scouts.

It must have been an eight-beer night. But I don't remember having been discovered.

As she leaned over the coffee table to flick her cigarette ash into a souvenir ashtray, I furtively ran a few trembling fingers through my hair and attempted an encouraging smile. All I could think of was getting back to bed, making the world go away for a few more obliterated hours. Her next remark startled me like summer lightning.

"My brother was murdered Friday night. Susan Birney gave me your name. I want you to find out who killed Charles." With that in-your-face declaration she butted out her cigarette with more energy than the task demanded.

I shuddered, remembering something I'd heard on the radio when Max woke me up this morning — something that really hadn't registered at the time. Charles Durand, one of the wealthiest men in Canada, had been found dead in his penthouse office on Bay Street.

For all its infatuation with gigantism and world-class status, Toronto logs only about one murder a week. Vietnamese gang killings in Chinatown, sundry skirmishes over drug turf, a few Mob hits in the suburbs, a scattering of home invasions and some shoot-outs at booze cans nudge up the routine tally of domestic violence. People are still safe as houses — safer, in fact, if they remain on the streets and out of their own houses. Durand's murder must be creating a media feeding frenzy. I had followed his mercurial climb to fortune with more than my usual academic interest. In this country, when wealth and power are not synonymous, there has to be a curious fault line in the system: race, ethnicity, gender, sexual preference, class. In Durand's case it had been the latter — his lack of social acceptance, his *nouveau* lust for it.

"But surely the police can handle the investigation — ."

She can't have failed to detect the insincerity in my voice. Lately I've been working on mendacity. I figure it simplifies relationships. But it takes real practice to pull off.

Simone Goldberg abruptly cut me off. "If this investigation is left in the hands of the police department, there's not a chance in hell that whoever really killed Charles will be caught. Nobody knows that better than you do. That's why I want *you* to find out who did it."

More by chance than design, I've become an expert on corporate élites, especially those areas where their dealings shade into criminal activity. That covers a lot of ground. But hell, I wrote about true crime — I didn't investigate it. Even licensed PIs rarely work a murder case and they're only retained after the initial homicide investigation has dead-ended. *Why was she hitting on me?* She had mentioned earlier that Susan Birney, an old sorority pal of mine from university days, had referred her to my door. The last time Susan and I got together, some five years ago, was to celebrate her third marriage. I must have committed a social *faux pas* at the nuptials sufficiently grave to warrant this kind of retaliation.

Already the situation had grown far too complicated for a Yeats-style Sunday morning. "Can I get you something to drink?" I asked.

She looked mildly alarmed. If she protested with anything like "Oh no, it's too early!," I'd promptly give her the bum's rush.

My escape hatch banged shut when she brightly replied, "I'd love a coffee, thank you."

Simone followed me through my studio to the few square metres I'd blocked off as kitchen space, and perched on a bar stool at the counter. First I released a small avalanche of Science Diet into Max's bowl. If labels are to be believed, my dog's diet is far more balanced than mine. So is his head.

I opened the door of my pre-war Kelvinator just far enough to fit my arm in, hoping to conceal its sordid contents: some elderly dairy products, a romaine lettuce wilted as me and a neat row of beer cans. Next I toasted two waffles, dumped over them a few dollops of sour cream, topped off with some distinctly fuzzy blueberries, poured Simone a second cup of Continental Dark, grabbed some cutlery from a recycled pork and beans tin, and a can of warm Perrier. She declined my offer of food.

Throughout my culinary preparations she had remained silent, perhaps respectful of my need to concentrate all my frail resources — more likely, enraged at my evasiveness. I sat down on the stool facing hers. "Please go on," I muttered, stuffing my face with the creatively salvaged leftovers and not giving much of a damn what she chose to go on about.

In the background, Max happily scrunched away. I envy dogs. Hey, I particularly envy my dog, upon whom all my co-dependent instincts have come to nest.

"Have you seen yesterday's paper?" she asked. "It would be easier for me if you read the article about his murder. It's on the front page."

From the recycled drywall compound bucket that served as my wastebasket I dug out yesterday's *Post*, its fat roll still secured by an elastic band. Underneath a studio portrait of the victim ran the following article:

Durand found slain in office
by Sam Brewer
TORONTO POST

Charles Durand, 55, Chairman of Durand Corporation, was found dead in his penthouse office Friday evening.

The body was found in his 43rd-floor office in the Enterprise Tower, which he built 6 years ago to house the central offices of the Corporation.

Metro Toronto Police said a cleaning lady discovered the body. She alerted a security guard who called police to the scene of the murder.

It was Metro's 13th homicide this year.

"The victim was sitting slumped across his desk," Sgt. Norm Cooke of Metro's homicide squad said.

Cooke said Durand, clad in business attire, had suffered severe cranial injuries.

There was no sign of robbery and no weapon has been found, he said. Both the cleaning lady and the security guard underwent questioning by police last night, but could not provide much information to help detectives with the murder investigation.

There were no other people in nearby offices when the victim was attacked and police have not been able to find any other people in the building who heard any sounds of a commotion.

The body was taken to the Toronto Forensic Laboratory for an autopsy to be held today. Police would not reveal if their preliminary investigation indicated the cause of death.

Durand Corp. employees and family members were not available for comment.

Over the past few months the real-estate and telecommunications tycoon had been struggling to save his $40-billion empire from bankruptcy.

As soon as I looked up, she began speaking. "This is odd. I don't know where to begin ... given your line of work, you probably know more about Charles than I do. I haven't seen him for at least seventeen years." As if in search of a clue to their distance, she peered into her coffee mug.

It was easy to toss a guess at why she'd separated herself from her brother for so long. By all public accounts, he was a pentathlon jerk. But I wasn't sure why she thought I knew more about him than she did. If shrinks can be vaguely trusted (and that's a stretch), being family sets you on the insider's track, even when you've chosen a divergent path. After all, you were there right from the beginning through the malformative years. *So what did she think I knew?*

"I know only the basic facts about your brother's career — the business side of his life." I did a passable imitation of Jack Webb. "Just the facts, ma'm." Reacting to Durand's murder like I cared was a performance I just couldn't manage.

Her silence in the face of this witty nudge beamed me a message: the lady doesn't do tricks on cue. I cleared my throat of a nicotine-related obstruction and donned my professorial face. "I'm only familiar with the kind of material that my research unearths — and that's mostly all public record by now."

Scarcely a day had gone by in the past five months when her brother's stunning slide into bankruptcy hadn't been documented by the media. Journalists cluster like black flies on reversals in the fortunes of the rich-and-famous.

"He was flamboyant and disingenuous, sure, but I always figured that was simply part of the game he played with the press. He managed to keep his private life pretty much out of the limelight."

Simone lit another cigarette. "You're right there. Charles had a mania for secrecy but, as far as I know, his personal life really wasn't noteworthy. The closer you come to it, the further away you'll be from understanding why he was such a privacy freak," Simone said.

As she spoke, her eyes took on a furtive cast. *Was she practising mendacity?* Something didn't compute. "How can you make assertions like that with such assurance — when you haven't seen him for years?"

"I have my sources," she replied humorously.

I persisted. "But I would need to know more about him, probably far more than I could ever ferret out, to connect the dots." *To compile a list of suspects*, I really meant, but I didn't want to let on how intriguing her proposition was becoming. My baser instincts smelled a fat investigative fee, possibly another book.

Her control broke. "You mean to figure out who might have killed Charles … who his enemies were." She laughed bitterly. "I can give you the short list: anyone who ever met him."

I wanted to ask *including you?*, but I couldn't muster the energy it would take to get beyond her defences. Her abiding rancour and apparent absence of grief told me she was holding a long grudge. What had her brother done to merit it? Still, she wasn't exaggerating his unpopularity. Charles Durand was globally reviled. Creating a suspects list would be limited to searching for means and opportunity. Motives for his murder were legion.

I finished my brunch. Max refused the remnant of soggy waffle I tossed his way.

I was puzzled. "You said that you haven't seen him in seventeen years — and with good cause, I'm sure. Then why are you here? Why do you care who killed him? I mean, people usually want the perpetrator of a crime discovered so he can be punished for having victimized somebody. If Durand was such an S.O.B. that he alienated everyone he ever met, you might say his death was merely the happy outcome of an informal class action suit."

"You actually consider what was done to Charles to be *justice*? Surely even the most summary form of justice in any civilized society demands a trial. Shit, I don't even believe in capital punishment — let alone lynch mobs."

Someone had uttered a profanity before I did, a conversational first. I scurried to make amends. "I'm sorry. You're right, of course. I must have sounded totally unsympathetic and insensitive." My apology came as close to authentic as I can get on a serious hangover.

"You probably think the plight of some Third World child is more important than what happened to Charles. Am I right?" This lady was persistent.

What the hell, I might as well come clean. In my experience with people — lovers excepted — honesty is the easiest policy, even though it allows so little scope for the imagination. "Yes, for the record, I do. Charles Durand created the conditions that led to his own downfall. The man had fabulous wealth, far more of it than any individual deserves. For all I know, maybe he even created the conditions that got him dead. Starving kids can't be blamed for their empty bellies."

"And I suppose you also think men like Charles are responsible for the oppression of those kids?" she demanded.

"They make generous donations to the problem. No question about that. And it's obvious from your brother's lifestyle that he was his own favourite charity." My candour was about to cap the lid on this potential pot of gold, but I'd been here before. Putting my cards on the table at the outset usually saves future grief — or so go my *post mortem* consolations.

She fell back on the sofa and laughed. "Susan Birney promised me you could be trusted to speak from the gut! As it happens, I agree with you. I live by choice in a world light years away from the one Charles built for himself. Sure he was a bastard … but I do feel that he was already getting the biggest punishment he deserved — bankruptcy and public humiliation."

My candour had loosened up her restraint. "Now I know your politics are sound, I can tell you the much more compelling reason I want you to find out who killed him. You asked me earlier how I knew about my brother's private life when I haven't seen him for so long. The answer is simple: I've always maintained a close relationship with his son, William. I love my nephew as much as my own daughter. And I'm terrified that the police are going to arrest him for Charles's murder. So will you help me?" Genuine pleading informed her voice, as well as passionate conviction — a tough combination to fluff off.

"I'm beginning to want to. But tell me why you think the cops might arrest William? Didn't he lose a court battle to his father a few months ago?"

"That hardly amounts to serious motivation to kill him. William had every right to take Charles to court. All he was trying to do was get permission to sell off his shares in the corporation before his father drove it into bankruptcy with his craziness." She leaned forward. "Trust an aunt's intuition — and an experienced social worker's insight: my nephew is incapable of killing anyone."

She must know more than she was revealing. "Then why

are you worried about the police suspecting him?"

"I know that William was in his father's office the night he died — he phoned me Saturday just after he learned about the murder."

Tricky. I needed to back-track a bit. "Simone, what makes you think I can do the job? I'm a writer, not a private investigator."

"You're a writer who already has a sound — and appropriately cynical — knowledge of the business world. You know how to sniff out a story, dig for background, separate the inconsequential from the significant. I know that to be a fact: I've read many of your articles. And Susan said you're fair, that you don't let personal politics get in the way of your judgment, that you're difficult to intimidate. She told me you'd lost a good job and had your life threatened as a result."

"I didn't have my life threatened. I merely had the shit beaten out of me."

Simone continued, "That all adds up to pretty sound credentials, in my view. The fact that you're *not* an investigator should be a distinct advantage." She was doing a very effective job of selling me on myself. That's hard work. Still, I resisted.

"Most corporate rulers are near-paranoid about having their privacy invaded — by the media as well as the law. Last year a friend of mine dared to write a piece about the Farrah family's wheelings and dealings. Maybe you read it in *City Lifestyles*? She wound up in court, with all her manuscripts seized! Even though the Farrahs hired a New York private investigator to reinterview her sources, they still didn't manage to undermine her credibility." I didn't bother to add that another fine business journalist had her book killed before she'd even delivered the completed manuscript: her publisher had received a warning letter from a high-profile lawyer. These days libel chill competes with exhaust fumes for the pollution prize.

She had another card up her sleeve. "Look, this may not be your typical murder investigation. My gut instinct tells me that Charles was probably killed by someone in the corporate world, possibly a *very* influential someone. A rival even more ruthless than he was. Someone so powerful, so well connected that the police will probably be instructed to pussyfoot around him. That's why I think they'll jump on William as the quickest route out of pushing their investigation into the upper ranks of the business establishment. Jane, you know damned well that how — even *if* — they knock on your door depends on your address. And the people you'll need to check out at that level might be much more inclined to talk to a woman who's researching a book about a man they loathe — not investigating his murder."

My nerve endings resonated in sync with her disillusion. In recent years even the most gullible Canadians have lost their virgin faith in the criminal-justice system. Belated, very public inquiries into a number of wrongful murder convictions obliged many reluctant citizens to admit that there are different tiers of justice: where you land very much depends upon where you're falling from. Ask any young black man. And the investigative route from crime scene to courtroom can be littered with fatal delays and incompetence.

Durand's breed of tycoon is a class unto itself, able to operate beyond the law because it is governed by no code of ethics and accountable to no one. Even lawyers have a self-regulating body, although it seems to have forgotten its mandate.

I decided to muster one last effort at resistance. I hate being seduced. My inner therapist says this derives from my being the adult child of an alcoholic father: I always need to feel in command. This instance had much more to do with my plans to celebrate the recent publication of my last book with an extended vacation in Barbados. Nothing could get in the way of that — neither love, nor money, power nor revenge. None of the stock motivators.

What I omitted from my reckoning was curiosity, which in my case often is tantamount to revenge.

Simone asked if she could trouble me for a beer. I glanced at my Swatch, but its hands were too small to tell me anything significant about the sun's location. Still, her request sunk my defences a notch lower. While I crossed the studio to fetch a can of Newcastle, she lit another cigarette. I reverently poured the mahogany suds down the side of a chilled glass mug and set it on the coffee table. Sipping it with obvious enjoyment, she thanked me. I was beginning to like this woman.

Max shifted on his favourite rag rug beside the sofa without breaking his snore.

Her final argument nudged me close to paranoia. Maybe she'd been talking to my inner shrink. "Look," she began, her fine eyes piercing my psyche, "if the Durand family commissioned you to write Charles's authorized biography, you'd have an instant passport to investigate."

On the instant I knew she was right. My resolve rolled over like Max in his most seductive mode. But I couldn't quite bring myself to say "yes."

"I don't know how much it matters," she added, strategically pausing to sip her brew, "but I'll pay you very well. Let's say the equivalent of a year's modest salary, even if it takes you only a few weeks to identify the murderer. Forty thousand? And I'll give you a two-thousand-dollar advance to cover your first two weeks and your expenses." She laughed, as if to discount the monetary significance of her offer. "Think of my offer as being like junk bonds — Charles's preferred method of financing some of his crazier buy-outs — high risk, but more chance of a high return!"

"I wouldn't push the analogy too far," I retorted. "Junk bonds contributed to his downfall."

"I can afford to pay you well," she persisted. "Years ago Charles set up a trust fund in my name. Need I say, it was one of his tax dodges, not benevolence. I've never touched a cent of the damn thing. Your fee will be the first withdrawal."

"Simone, forgive me for prying into an area that may have nothing to do with the case, but I'm curious about why you've kept the trust fund when you consider it tainted money."

"Given what I suffered being his sister, I could regard it as compensation." For a moment she looked as if she were going to elaborate on that theme. She paused, then spoke less bitterly. "I decided to turn it to good use. I've been keeping it in trust for my daughter, Rebecca. Robert, my husband, and I both have modest incomes, so she won't inherit much from us. And I plan to donate a portion of it to a women's shelter. Charles would sooner have burned his money than see it go to such a place."

I was ready to yield. Forty thousand dollars plus expenses. With that kind of money I could read and write whatever I wanted for a whole year without worrying about the rent and Max's Science Diet. I could go to Barbados for a month — and trade in my geriatric Harley on a new bike. Last weekend I'd gone to the annual Motorcycle Show in the Automotive Building at Exhibition Place. Love at first sight: gleaming on a pedestal like a northern lake at sunrise was a stunning red Ducati 851 Sport, aptly nicknamed the "Ferrari" of motorcycles. The last hand-built bike in the world, crafted in a limited edition, with a computerized fuel injection system. "Ravish me," I prayed. I'd keep it next to my bed. Hell, I'd keep it *in* my bed.

She rose from the sofa and pulled on her jacket. "I can see you need some time to think this through. There's no need to commit yourself today. But I do have to leave now. I'll call you tomorrow morning, shortly after nine."

"Yes," I said, with no less passion than Molly Bloom. *Yes,* I said, *yes.* I wanted to do this weird thing. Like the proverbial hounds hot on the fox's trail, my wits were off and running.

She made for the door. "If you decide to accept, it might be a good idea for you to attend the funeral. I can give you the details in the morning, after I hear from Charles's widow."

"Thank you. And Simone, if it means anything at all, I'm sorry for what you're going through."

She turned back to me, eyes soft with gratitude. "Thank you. It does mean something. He was my brother. I guess we always hope that family relations will work themselves out in the long run — before death intervenes." She paused, then flashed a leavening grin. "And on a lighter note, let me say that I'm impressed that you didn't apologize for your housekeeping transgressions. Most women would," she ventured.

"Most women use vacuum cleaners. I rent a fork-lift."

She laughed and walked down the hall to the freight elevator.

I closed the door. Max sniffed at his empty bowl, chased his tail for a few rounds, then flopped down in a defeated heap beside the sofa. He was depressed.

I made a bee-line for my research files.

CHAPTER 2

ON MY PLANET there are two categories of hangover: those I get from too much beer and the unavoidables that derive from information overload. The latter are usually more productive.

After Simone's departure I immersed myself, first in a hot bath, then in the contents of my file cabinet, which her visit had transformed from a research depository into a potential gold mine. A sensible librarian would catalogue most of my curious information-hoard under the rubric "business." I designated it "corporations, cash, class, crime and sundry other corruptions." The upper two locked drawers contained every bit of paper relevant to my published books and articles: newspaper/magazine clippings, research notes, interview tapes, my manuscripts and backup copies on floppy disks, notebooks full of hunches, guesses, suspicions, allegations, hints, rumours — all the undocumented minutiae that really fuelled my lunatic occupation. The stuff that kept me at my solitary computer when normal people are genially circulating in climate-controlled offices, sharing tales of lovers, therapies, new diets and interior decorators over mugs of decaf, revelling in their dental benefits and pension plans (or so I imagine).

By early evening I had over-dosed on the Canadian power élite in general, Charles Durand and his corporation in particular. Before I hit my duvet, I took Max for a long run through High Park to work out his cardio-vascular and rest my cerebral. He ran, I walked. I'm depressed, not suicidal.

A bitter wind hammered our tails as we entered the park from the northwestern corner and followed a winding wood-chip trail down the slope toward Grenadier Pond. Clouds overcast the anorexic face of the crescent moon. I couldn't see far ahead. The thick bush on either side of the hilly clearing enclosed me like dark parentheses. Suddenly I got scared. I whistled for Max. He didn't return to my side, which only confirmed what I already knew: my early efforts at doggy dominance hadn't worked.

I got my mounting panic under control by switching my memory track from the terrifying murder-in-the-park scene that opens Antonioni's *Blowup* to a snapshot of my "career" — always good for a relaxing laugh. Maybe I'd find something more morally uplifting than money to rationalize my decision to take up Simone's offer of employment.

Twelve years ago I began grown-up life, which coincided with my graduation from journalism school, as managing editor of the progressive magazine *Up Yours!* For "progressive" read: non-profit, circulation of two thousand politically disaffected souls, monitored by the RCMP for left-leaning bias, and as threatening to the system as a toothless Chihuahua.

My nine-month upsurge from an entry-level position as administrative assistant to managing editor had been facilitated by certain unfortunate ruptures in the group due to a serendipitous pregnancy and a drug bust. When I complained to a journalist friend about the tax-bite the Feds munched out of my meagre pay cheque, he advised me to claim self-employed status. To qualify I merely had to scribble a few book reviews a year. He obligingly tossed me some new murder mysteries. I greeted his throwaways like I'd died and gone to that corner of heaven where Nancy Drew always makes her dad proud.

Two years later, when the *Post's* Saturday Supplement crime-books columnist succumbed to a terminal liver problem of known origins, the editor of the newspaper proposed me as his successor. I couldn't afford to refuse the job: *Up Yours!* had recently succumbed to terminal circulation problems.

Near the end of my first year into that impersonation, I was elevated to crime reporter — on condition that my first assignment be an investigative series on corruption in the Toronto police force. Evidently all the experienced staff reporters, who valued their careers, had declined the challenge. I couldn't afford to refuse the job: I'd just mortgaged my life for a reconditioned vintage Harley-Davidson FLST Heritage.

Survive the assignment I did, long enough to get a series of nine investigative articles into print. For my Herculean efforts, I won a national newspaper award — and lost my job. Apparently I'd done my research too thoroughly. A spate of upper-echelon resignations from the police force testified to that. And it became clear from my subsequent dismissal that ours is not a free press. No big surprise to me: Canadian illusions fall hard on their despoilers. Because I hadn't been able to marshal enough hard facts to point a censuring finger at the Chief of Police, the Police Commission and the Mayor's Office, I merely gestured extravagantly in their direction, letting my readers draw their own sordid conclusions about where the buck stopped. The publisher of the paper, who regularly lunched with prominent local politicians at a posh private steak house, concluded that my continuing services in his employ would constitute more than an embarrassment. I forgave him. Covering your ass has become an executive lifestyle. And hey, a journalism prize trophy graced the top of my toilet tank.

Truly self-employed, I set to work on a book about the recent murder of Diana Bancroft, a prominent judge's wife. Right from the day the story first broke I'd smelled a rat and had suspected that the rodent had a law degree from a good university and was the violently deceased lady's main squeeze. Research, between and beneath the covers, confirmed my instinct. By the time the police had nailed their conviction, I was ready to hit the bookstands with the dirt that braced their investigation. I had a best-seller on my hands, filth under my fingernails, sawdust on the floor of my heart — and an attempt on my life to add to my toilet-tank embellishment.

Too perverse to be intimidated, over the next four years I followed up with several non-fiction crime articles; a book on stock-exchange fraud and insider trading; and a third book on the history and operations of the Toronto Police Department Homicide Squad. I won more enemies in high places, a couple of friends on the police force and another toilet ornament. Most important, my Harley was paid for. A tough agent negotiated American and British advances on my next book.

About my next book: I shamelessly fabricated the proposal out of air thin enough to make a canary croak. To my credit, I refused my publisher's offer of an advance sufficient to maintain my poverty-line lifestyle for six months. In my writerly guts, I knew I'd never deliver the damn book. The concept was too complex to schedule, I told my agent, inviting her to imagine Plato being given a deadline to produce *The Republic*. Backed into existential corners, I become a very tacky woman.

The truth of it was, I was tired of writing and tempted to call my fatigue "writer's block." Or maybe almost ready to shuck the more-or-less protective cocoon of words in which I'd encased myself. As good a reason as any to pursue a fresh career path.

Max returned to my side well after my inner shrink whispered that my sudden panic about goblins in the park came from my fear of making any changes to my stagnant life.

Monday morning I called Ernie Sivcoski, a detective on the Metro homicide squad. I was surprised to find him at his desk. Although he always accepts my calls, I had expected him to be caught up in the Durand investigation.

Ernie got right to his point. "You called to ask me for a date, right, Jane?"

"Wrong, Ernie. You know I don't do dates." Before I met Pete, Ernie and I had gone out together a few times, mostly to jazz clubs, but our relationship had never taken flight. Maybe cops and writers don't make a good mix. Ernie has a fine heart and he is a damn good homicide detective. But he spends too many of his working hours dealing with women who are messed up with prostitution and cocaine to know how to adjust in his off-hours to women who aren't. In his universe, every broad is on the make.

We'd first crossed paths when I was researching my book on the Bancroft murder. From the start, Ernie had choreographed his investigation as intricately as a ballet. His prime suspect was one of the best-connected lawyers in the city. Ernie knew that if he made one false step his career was toast. He played it like Balanchine. And he got his conviction.

Afterwards he readily consented to my request for an interview. He provided me with much of the inside detail that made my book an authoritative, riveting read. And he did that *after* I told him I wouldn't sleep with him. But back then it had been safe for him to confide in me: the Bancroft case was closed. I wondered how he would react to my questions about an investigation very much in progress.

I entered the conversation *en pointe*. "I'm surprised to get hold of you so easily, Ernie."

"You have a hunch that I've been assigned to the Durand murder."

"Thanks for confirming it. So how's it going?"

He drew a deep breath and pushed it out like a weight-lifter. "Well, as a matter of fact, I'm sitting here at this very moment because the coroner's report landed on my desk about twenty minutes ago," he said, sounding like he'd sooner be sailing.

He'd given me permission to take another step. "Let me guess, Charles Durand died because he stopped breathing."

"Why would you want to guess? Why are you even interested?" he snapped.

"Okay, Ernie, I'll level with you. For the past few months I've been working on Durand's official biography." I didn't tell him that the project began yesterday, that I hadn't written a single word and never intended to. "So I have a special interest in the circumstances surrounding his death."

"And now that he's splashed all over the media you're hatching another best-seller," he commented sourly.

That vexed me. "You know me well enough to trust that I won't wrap up the book before I'm satisfied with it — whatever pressure my publisher puts on me." In my limited experience of my own character, mendacity invariably breeds self-righteousness.

"Yeah, I do know that. So I'm sorry. Look, this case has got me really frazzled. There's a lot of heat coming from upstairs to make a quick arrest."

"So you've got a suspect?"

"*A* suspect? They're coming out of my ears! But are we ready to make an arrest? Not quite."

"How much can you tell me, Ernie?"

"I can trust you to keep your mouth shut, right?" I was pleased that he didn't wait for an answer. He knew from experience that I'd go to jail before I'd reveal a source. "Well, I'm going to disappoint you. Basically the preliminary coroner's report adds up to saying that Durand didn't kill himself — which wouldn't have been a surprise, given the flak he's been dodging for months, eh?"

"Three high fliers associated with the Vancouver Stock Exchange have committed suicide recently, so the phenomenon is not unknown. Guys facing personal ruin, lawsuits, wives walking out. But Charles Durand wasn't the suicidal type, Ernie. He wasn't a victim, he was a prizefighter. He's been knocked down before, and every time he got up before the count."

"You're right about that. Anyways, it says here *the victim died as a result of massive cerebral damage caused by repeated blows sufficient to smash through the skull and decimate a major part of the brain.* Hey, I was on the crime scene. We didn't need the experts to tell us why he croaked: the left side of his head was caved in like a rotten pumpkin. Half his head was pulp. Not a pretty sight. I mean, his desk blotter was totally soaked in blood and there were clumps of brain tissue and pieces of fractured skull all over the desk."

As my breakfast began to resist gravity, I was tempted to

tell him to spare me the information. But I knew that if God wasn't in the details, the perp was.

Ernie droned on like he was doing a play-by-play for a hockey game. Maybe the gory mantra helped him block out the scenario. "His attacker must have been totally over the top — I mean, he must have kept hitting and hitting him after he was dead already. Report says *at least sixteen blows.*" Coroner speculates that the first blow hit him from the front as he was getting up from his chair, knocked him unconscious and caused him to slump over the desk. All kinds of fracture lines radiating out from the first penetration. The remainder of the blows were delivered after his head was resting on the desk. You could say it was overkill."

"Any idea yet what the weapon was?"

"Nah, apart from it being a not-so-blunt object. Coroner couldn't match up the skull perforations and fractures with any tool he's familiar with. Just says that it had at least one flat surface, irregular sides and top, several sharp points. That was all he could determine. Whatever the hell it was, the killer must have taken it with him — or at least removed it from the office. We'll be checking the rest of the building until we're sure it wasn't dumped on site. You can imagine what a job that is. Fucking tower's got forty-three floors."

"I gather from the press report that you've already done some interviewing."

He nodded. "Yeah. First, a cleaning lady who discovered the body. Given the time lines — Durand passed on to the Great Stock Exchange some time between four, when he was last seen alive, and eight, when she found him — she could have been on the same floor when it happened. But she didn't see or hear a thing. Poor old broad's a basket case. Portuguese. I had to call in a translator for her interview. She found the body as she was making her usual rounds. She did say, though, that Durand wasn't in the habit of using his office on Friday nights."

"And the security guard?"

"I got nothing from him. Dumb bugger with a serious

history of assaults. Used to be a bouncer at the El Mocambo 'til he got sacked for causing more fights than he cured. The night Durand got killed he was working his way through a six-pack and watching a hockey game instead of the surveillance monitors in his cubby-hole on the main floor. Security at the Tower is token after normal business hours anyways."

"That surprises me, Ernie. You know, the security industry thrives on paranoia — and Durand regarded even dust mites as personal enemies. I'd have guessed he had the building protect-ed by state-of-the-art equipment monitored by guys who'd die for him."

"Yeah, and the media's got some people so scared about violent crime we find old ladies who've been sold enough gear to make the prime minister envious. But I guess Durand fig-ured there was nothing to steal in there, unless you're into tropical plants or high-tech office furniture. All the important computer systems were safe-guarded. He had a few cameras placed at the entrances and exits, enough fire alarms to meet the code. But nothing else — didn't even have any cameras in the underground parking lot. In any case, even the best sys-tem's only as good as the guy monitoring it. And the security industry isn't properly regulated — a lot of their personnel are the kind of people their customers are paying through the nose to keep out! The guard's main job at the Tower was to let the night-time cleaning staff in and out, and eyeball the monitors. He couldn't even get it up to do that much responsibly. We found a rear service door open. The jerk hadn't checked it out when he came on his shift. Anybody could enter and leave that building after hours easier than the Metro Library."

"And Forensic? Have they got anything to analyze … hairs, fibres? Particles in the wound? Assailant's skin under his fingernails? Fluff in his navel?"

Ernie laughed. "You've been watching *Quincy* reruns, Jane. Sure, some prints — but mostly Durand's. The rest probably won't match up with anything we've got in the computer. Lots of blood — but so far all of it's Durand's. The suspect's clothing must be covered in his blood — but we haven't apprehended a suspect, who's no doubt ditched or destroyed his tell-tale threads by now. You know the routine: whatever you got, you gotta have a match for."

I persisted. "Have you got *any* other evidence?"

Silence on the line.

"Ernie, how in hell are you going to be able to make that speedy arrest the Chief is screaming for?"

He spoke reluctantly. "Apparently there were some funny-looking chips and particles embedded in his head that haven't been identified yet. And there's something else, not as tricky as bits of whatever. An empty book of matches left beside an ashtray on the coffee table in Durand's office. The man didn't smoke."

"But he must have had a lot of visitors who did."

"No, not many visitors got into the inner sanctum. His secretary, Ruth Porter, made sure of that. She protected Durand like a mother bear — and she looks like one, too." Men like Ernie made depilatories an essential feminine product, that is if you want to bag a man like Ernie.

"So what can you tell me about this book of matches? Do you know where it came from?"

Pregnant pause at the other end. "You didn't hear me say this, right? How about from a gay bar?"

I held my breath. "Which gay bar, Ernie? The city's got dozens of them." I tried not to sound too eager.

"I can't tell you another goddamn thing, Jane. I've already told you too much." Ernie's voice closed down. No point in pushing him any further.

Then he added an afterthought. "When someone as big as Charles Durand gets killed, it causes a lot of ripples."

"It causes tidal waves, Ernie. Keep your head above the water, eh? And thanks. I owe you."

"Sure you don't want a date?"

"I'm sure. My dog is a possessive beast. Bye, Ernie."

. . .

I opened a can of beer and flopped down on my armchair. For five minutes I stared through the uncurtained windows that ran the full length of the east-facing wall. Bright winter sunlight illuminated to sordid intensity my sins of housecleaning omission. So I swept into action, reverting to an old female survival routine: when the head is cluttered, organize your space. I tossed back the remains of my beer and began to pilot my shop vac over the disaster zone.

I rent fifteen hundred square feet of a converted coughlozenge factory that now houses indigent artists, writers, aspiring rock musicians and sundry other unappreciateds — like me. This is the site where I've incarcerated myself since Pete's death. So I put a lot of work into making it agreeable. The view only a land mine could alter. My window wall overlooked the garbage-bedecked roofs of other factories, a huge rear parking lot resembling a museum of transportation discards (cars, pick-ups, motorcycles, bikes, wagons and a lone sailboat), interspersed with derelict stoves and fridges, littered with spark plugs, Coke cans, Chinese cooking wine and bitters bottles, car-ashtray contents and spent condoms. A ravine bounded the east side, terminated by a Berlin Wall of old tires and overpassed by a bridge deafeningly crossed by the Dundas West street car and the VIA Rail train.

The window view onto my studio, accessible to anyone who scaled the fire escape to the third floor, afforded a different picture.

Shortly after Pete died, I rechannelled my dumb grief into patching and painting walls, sanding and varnishing the old oak-strip floors, slapping fire-engine red enamel over all the industrial steel beams and pipes, refinishing some old furniture Pete and I had bought at country auctions. I was left with a huge, well-lit open space, sub-divided into different functional areas, brightly accented with prints, posters, exceptionally hardy tropical plants, silk-screened fabrics collected on three trips to the Caribbean. Cheery — yet empty as a cathedral on a midnight that wasn't Christmas Eve. All my restorative work hadn't brought him back.

I retaliated against fate by turning myself into a reclusive writer who scribbled obsessively, read three or four books a week, socialized rarely, and hung out on weekends at her mother's bar. There I camouflaged myself by drinking too much, singing the occasional country tune, and pretending to manage the place whenever Etta took off on one of her weekend jaunts to Nashville on a bus tour package that included two nights' accommodation in a tacky hotel, reserved seats at the Grand Ole Opry, a tour of the town, transportation, baggage and taxes. All for $292 Canadian funds. Etta always bought the twin package because she always had a boyfriend in tow.

As I tugged my studio into a semblance of order, I tried to marshal some stray anxieties. When I thought about it, it still seemed odd that a woman estranged from her brother for most of her adult life would want to invest serious money into having his murder investigated. Had Simone Goldberg been telling the truth when she said that her real motivation was to protect her nephew William — who probably had even less reason to mourn Durand's passing than she? Or did she really want to enlist my aid in flushing him out as the prime suspect? What had she been withholding?

I popped open another can of beer and flopped onto the sofa. My housecleaning seizure hadn't dispersed my depression. Why not take up Simone's offer and use the investigation to keep my inability to deal with Pete's death on the back burner a bit longer? No reason, I thought, unless I cared about my own life enough to want to avoid any possible encounter with Durand's killer.

At least sixteen blows, the first few delivered with enough force to render the remaining baker's dozen redundant. Rage purer than that you couldn't find. A presumably unarmed person had used an unconventional weapon — maybe whatever was within reach when he lost it — to exhaust that rage. What could Durand have done to provoke such a manic attack?

To look on the bright side, maybe the killer was just an ordinary person somehow pushed right over the top by his victim. Anyone past the diaper years knows what a homicidal impulse feels like. So maybe most of us are just lucky that nobody's ever pressed the right rage buttons at the wrong time. But stepping over that irrevocable "shalt not kill" line must change a person — like make him capable of doing it again to save himself from discovery.

The phone was ringing.

"Hello, Jane? It's Simone Goldberg."

Commitment time.

My sex life was less active than the Senate, my writing life in a deep sleep. Maybe I was turning to danger for the edge I needed to make breathing a worthwhile exercise.

CHAPTER 3

"HI, SIMONE," I said, careful to erase the slightest hint of anticipation from my voice. "How are you holding up?"

"Surviving, so far without tranquillizers. Thank God I got a good night's sleep. The visit to the funeral home was pure Monty Python. Have you ever been through that routine?"

"Yeah," I muttered, reluctant to divulge any particulars. "A few times, in fact. I sympathize. I've always felt that funeral directors are the guys who lost out on Vincent Price roles or didn't get into dental school."

She laughed. "Or ex-finance ministers."

"You've got my drift," I returned.

"His wife chose a casket fit for a prince. I couldn't help thinking that it was a terrible waste, given that Charles is being cremated." She sounded as cold as he'd be hot.

So I commented with equivalent sensitivity, "Yeah, they should just rent the things. They probably switch them for a cardboard box anyway just before they hit the oven."

"Oh well, I'm sure the corpse doesn't give a damn. Jane, the funeral is at eleven tomorrow morning, from St. Michael's Cathedral. There's to be a wake afterwards at his ... " She hesitated.

No way could she call his residence a mere "house." And she seemed too unpretentious to say "mansion." So I filled in the blank with "... place?"

"Yes, at his place on Swindon Path." Swindon Path was a private enclave of monster edifices erected for the *nouveau* rich-and-famous. "Can I count on you to be there?" she asked.

"I'll be there," I affirmed, with all the authority I could muster.

"Then you are willing to investigate Charles's murder?" She sounded eager as Madonna confronted by an opportunity to get offensive.

"Yes, I am." Visions of that red Ducati danced in my grey cells.

Ma Bell amplified her sigh of relief. "Thank you. That matters to me, Jane. I appreciate your support."

"Look, Simone, this isn't exactly foreign aid. Yesterday you managed to appeal to most of my base and cunning instincts. I'm not Mother Teresa, you know."

"Maybe Mother Teresa wasn't either!" I loved it.

"Yeah, who knows who anybody really is any more, after the spin doctors are done," I said. "Do you mind if I bring along a friend tomorrow? I need someone beside me who can identify the mourners."

"No, of course I don't mind. Most, if not all, of the alleged mourners will turn up only out of a sense of propriety or just to gloat — not because they feel any personal loss," she replied, reaffirming my sense of her candour. "Who are you thinking of asking?"

"Portia Sherman, another old friend of mine from university days, like Susan Birney. She's a stockbroker, married to a Bay Street investment counsellor. Between them, they know the corporate world inside-out," I said.

"No problem. And Jane, when it comes to introductions, why don't we agree to present you as Charles's official biographer? Perhaps it would be more credible if we let on that you've already been at work on the project for a few months."

"Right," I confirmed. Odds were that at least one publisher had picked up his phone shortly after news of Durand's murder hit the media and commissioned some hack to scribble an instant book.

"For the record, Simone, does anyone else know why you've hired me?"

My survival antennae were quivering. There was danger in this job, that much I knew for certain. Investigating powerful white boys' dirty tricks had already rewarded me with a fractured shoulder and a broken leg. Self-help books never cite murder as the quickest route to conflict resolution, yet it's a very popular option.

"Only my husband, Robert, who's as far removed from the power élite as a welfare mother. Oh, and maybe my daughter, Rebecca. She could have overheard me and Robert discussing it. But I doubt it — she's hardly left her room since we got news of Charles's murder. You know, the whole thing seems to have really freaked her out. She's in that hormonally unstable stage that makes her hypersensitive to everything. Anyway, a day or two after the funeral we should get together over lunch. I can fill you in on some of our family background to get you on track. Can we arrange that when we connect tomorrow?"

"Sure. In the meantime, take care." Unlike me, she seemed to know how.

"Thank you, Jane. I will." She hung up.

I needed to get myself on track before the funeral. Several dustballs short of a clean flat, I retired the vacuum cleaner and set about disposing of litter and fluttering a feather duster. Max, no tidy freak, farted from a disdainful distance.

I mentally reviewed yesterday's foray into my file cabinet. I had been right on target when I commented to Simone that compiling a preliminary checklist of murder suspects would be easy. Much more problematic would be narrowing it down to a number small enough for me to investigate in time to get me off to Barbados with only a slight hitch in my original schedule. Since Pete died, I prefer to think of events in my life as mere glitches on the screen, fugitive obstacles in my path to stopping the world long enough to disembark.

A convincing excuse for interrogating these people was crucial. As well as being sufficiently motivated to murder Charles Durand or to enlighten me as to why somebody else did, they had to be obvious biographical sources. If my cover story wasn't believed, I might not live long enough to enjoy the benefits of a Ducati's computerized fuel injection system.

It took only a damp day to remind me that the city of my childhood was not benign. My right knee joint hadn't properly repaired after my beating. On rainy days I have to struggle to keep Harley upright when I brake to a stop. I resent that. Only Max would notice if some thug decides to "terminate me with extreme prejudice." My mother, Etta, would log at least a dozen daily monologues on my answering machine before it occurred to her that something might be amiss. Reciprocity isn't one of her virtues.

That thought did not comment well on the current status of my relationships. My reclusive ways were quickly losing much of their glitter.

I left a message on Portia Sherman's answering machine, asking her to get back to me on urgent business. I really did need her beside me to identify the rogues gallery at Durand's funeral.

Not for the first time in my writing life did I ask the rafters why I hadn't stumbled upon the stock murder scenario — you know, the familiar impulse one in which the crime is domestic and always gets solved. A nosy neighbour overhears a violent dispute between the wild couple next door. She calls the cops, who arrive on the scene to discover a drunken husband holding a still-dripping kitchen knife over his spouse's warm body, sobbing "I told the bitch a million times not to feed me Brussels sprouts." Garden-variety crimes don't require the deductive expertise of Loveday Brooke, Lady Detective — only a cast-iron stomach.

This was no dripping-knife case. To complicate matters, the cops weren't likely to overtax their resources grilling the Barons of Bay Street.

The phone rang again, echoing through my isolate vault like the hour of the wolf at the city morgue. Etta's bus wasn't threatening to be back from Nashville until close to midnight.

"Hi, Jane. It's Sam." Smooth as Coltrane's sax, his velvet, bluesy voice caressed my eardrum.

I know only one Sam, the *Post*'s veteran crime reporter. We'd been colleagues back when I did the books column and often used to drink together on Friday nights. When we first met, Sam Brewer was in his mid-forties. His wife had died from breast cancer shortly before Pete was killed. We quickly became friends, bonded by the brutal fact of a desolation we shared but silently agreed never to speak of. Although we've kept in infrequent touch since I got sacked, we remain useful to one other, exchanging information and rumours garnered in the course of our work. More important, we really enjoy one another's company.

"Sam, it's good to hear your voice. How are you?" Sam is the kind of guy who answers that question truthfully. Now that's un-Canadian: the rest of us are always "fine," as if being evergreen were part of our collective identity.

"In a word — screwed. I'm on a tight deadline. Got to deliver a big chunk of copy for tomorrow's front page — you know, Durand's murder — and I'm hellishly short on background. That's why I called. Can I pick your brains?"

Sam's article in Saturday's paper hadn't gone beyond the bare bones of a terse police press release. Small wonder he needed help fleshing out his story.

"I gotta warn you, Sam, that could be as productive as picking the skull of one of Georgia O'Keeffe's cows. So what don't you know?"

"I'll tell you when I see you. Look, will you meet me at Delaney's — in half an hour say, at one?"

"And don't tell me, you'll pay for the beer. Right?" I teased.

"You're a mind-reader, Janie. I'll even throw in some chicken wings."

"Now I know you're desperate. See you at one, Sam."

Sam's friendship over the past, rough years had earned him an hour of my time, any time. And no one in the city was better placed to pick up the behind-the-scenes buzz on the Durand murder. Even the cops trusted Sam: he was that fair. Never lunged at the sensational aspects of a story, always double-checked and cross-verified his sources, didn't make allegations he couldn't support. In a past life, if New Agers are to be trusted, Sam must have been a history scholar.

In case she got back to me while I was out, I left a second message on Portia's answering machine, then pulled on a pair of clean jeans and a heavy sweater, grabbed my leather jacket, gloves and helmet on the way out the door. Max sunk into terminal depression when I didn't pick up his leash. I apologized. Parenting has its heavy moments, and they're all guilt-ridden.

CHAPTER 4

I SPED EAST ALONG Queen Street, regretting that the sullen sky
leached even this lively part of town of its vibrancy. When the
weather is less hostile, the street's raucous jumble of businesses
and eclectic sidewalk traffic rarely fails to divert me. I turned
into a laneway and parked my hog in the lot behind Delaney's,
right by the rear exit.

The bar had retained its regulars by clinging to its cheesy
pre-World War II décor as a tidal wave of renovation engulfed
its neighbours. I walked in through the back, stopped at the
bar to say hi to Frank, who nodded his flawlessly parted,
Brylcreemed head in the direction of a table against the far
wall, where my anxious-looking friend was seated, working on
a liquid preamble to lunch.

Sam rose from his chair and made his way around the
chipped Formica-topped table to greet me. I don't let many
men hug me — only the few who don't incite my territorial
ferocity. Sam's hug I returned with great warmth.

"Hey, lady, it's been too long. Have ya been okay?" he
asked, concerned. He stepped back to check me out, nervously
fingering his bow tie to ensure its trademark crookedness.
Sam's face is as crinkled as the baggy grey trousers he was born
in. The rest of his power wardrobe includes a pair of brown
Hush Puppies, worn into geriatric dogs years ago; a crisp white
shirt; and a navy wool cardigan strained to a few strands at the
elbows. His clothes hang on a frame so close to skeletal you
wonder what's holding him upright, apart from his innate
sense of distressed propriety.

"I'm okay. Time passes, Sam," I shrugged. Feminist literature claims that it's rare to find a woman as emotionally unforth-coming as most men. That makes me extra rare.

"Yeah, but does it heal?"

"Let's not get off topic, boy," I warned.

"Frank, will you bring this woman a pint of Guinness?" Sam bellowed, following up his order with an apologetic gri-mace. We both knew better than to ask for Newcastle Brown at Delaney's.

We chewed the fat for a few minutes before he interjected, "All right, Janie, I'll get straight to the topic. I got a deadline. Charles Durand got himself whacked Friday night, so Armstrong assigned me to cover the story." John Armstrong was a senior editor at the *Post,* who took his directions straight from the publisher.

Frank banged my Guinness down on the table. The head kept spewing like a lazy volcano.

"We both know that Armstrong's an asshole, but not the kind you can have arrested on a charge of indecent exposure. So I couldn't say no, in spite of the fact that I know zilch about the corporate scene. Durand was such a privacy freak, even the archives don't tell me much," he explained.

"I can guess why he chose you, Sam. This one's sensitive as a baby's bum. He trusts you *not* to go after the sleaze factor."

"Yeah, yeah, that's fine, but I don't know where the hell to begin. I mean, the guy had enemies falling off him like roaches from a tenement ceiling. You must be a walking bloody ency-clopedia on the guy. Can you give me some background?"

"Okay. Here beginneth the potted saga of the rise and fall of an empire." I sucked another inch from my mug. "In the early '60s, a poor French-Canadian boy from Noranda took a construction job here in Toronto, which was well into its post-war suburban growth spurt. Built himself a modest house in Toronto big enough to hold himself, his wife and their little kid, but too small to contain his ambition. As he laid bricks in one new suburb after another, he began to dream big — about throwing in the trowel and developing his own suburbs. When he'd done that for a few years, he got bored playing LEGO.

"His original vision inflated. He shifted his energies to the downtown core, which by then — we're talking the late '60s — needed towers to house the central offices of the new corporations. So he piled the bricks higher and higher, until by the end of the next decade of his career he had built fifteen of the city's biggest office towers, in addition to the twenty thousand boxes housing the drones who slaved in the towers. Again, he grew bored." I interrupted my narrative to finish my Guinness.

Sam guffawed, then transferred most of the beer froth garlanding his upper lip to a paper napkin. "Christ, I'm still paying off the twenty-five-year mortgage on a bungalow in Etobicoke. I won't be bored when I own the joint. I think we're talking about a different kind of creature here."

"For sure we are," I nodded. "This country's only seen a handful of his species, beginning with the boys who engineered the fur-trade routes with a little help from the Natives, followed up by the ones who shoved the railway west on the backs of the Chinese navvies. But you know, Sam, I'm not sure how many more of his kind we need. You could argue that there are better ways of building up a country."

That's a shortcoming of mine: I can't talk for long on the subject of capitalists without tossing out a renegade grenade on behalf of "just folks."

Sam groaned. "Just this once, love, spare me your socialism. It doesn't make good copy — especially since the buggers ran Queen's Park into the ground. The paper can't sell it to the masses," he jibed.

"If you want apolitical," I bargained, "you'll have to oil my vocal chords with another pint." He nodded at Frank, who headed for the tap. I'm always meaning to check into having a draft keg installed under my kitchen counter; it could save me serious dollars.

"The facts. Marx knows, they're unsavoury enough to convert even you to the NDP!" Past arguments at Delaney's had taught me that Sam voted Liberal. He couldn't disabuse himself of the notions that basic decency would finally prevail over rapacity, that free enterprise, guided by the ghostly hand of John Stuart Mill, would give capitalism a kinder face. Sure, says me, and guys with the kindest faces bankroll the election campaigns of politicians who later eat from their greasy corporate hands. At that point, we always check-mate one another.

"Second round of major boredom and Durand-built towers spring up in Vancouver, Edmonton, Winnipeg, Ottawa, Montreal, Halifax, St. John's. The guy's on a roll. So he builds the ultimate monument to himself, a forty-three-storey tower at the foot of Bay Street, one storey for each year of his life. With a truly awesome penthouse office for himself at the top. Durand Corporation is installed like a giant zit on the chin of commercial Toronto. Still, the Emperor broods in his perch atop the city. The old Establishment is still laughing at his new clothes. For all his crowning glories, they still haven't let him into the inner sanctum of Canadian corporate respectability. He sits up there, a solitary eagle plotting his next kill."

Sam interjected, "But your eagle can't still be hungry."

"He's so hungry his guts are shrieking. Over the years he's acquired enough assets to discharge Brazil's entire foreign debt, but in his guts he knows he doesn't have the kind of power, the entrée, that the sons of the Establishment were born wielding. In his heart he's still the poor Frenchie from Noranda, flamboyant, vulgar, an *arriviste*. So eventually he decides to buy what they hold over him — a handsome bite of control over the financial purse, from one of the institutions that decree who gets the bucks to underwrite their schemes. He makes a surprise bid for Imperial Trust. A sound bid, backed up by gilt-edged securities — not the kind of crap-leveraged buy-out that was in vogue those days. The old-guard financiers closed ranks tighter than Preston Manning's buns and shut him out."

"That one I remember," said Sam. "And didn't they cut him off at the pass in ways that weren't strictly *ethical*?"

"Ethical, hell, they pulled manoeuvres that were barely

legal! They got their wrists slapped by the Securities Commission, but nothing more," I said. "It's at this point in the story that even I begin to feel for the guy, Sam. Durand started to engineer his own downfall. After the Imperial bid his behaviour became as unpredictable as a drunken gambler's. For the first time in his career, he made some takeovers and buy-outs that were debt-financed. When real estate took a down-turn in the late '80s, in order to recoup his losses he decided to venture into what was, for him, virgin territory. He wound up digging himself into a hole so deep he couldn't have done worse in a casino."

"Is this a fable that ends with the moral *small is beautiful*?" Sam asked.

"No, I think it's a moral about class, that your working-class reach should never exceed your master's grasp," I said, drawing deep on my Guinness to drown the rest of my Marxist Institute script. "Hey Sam, about those chicken wings ... I reckon I've already earned a coopful!"

"Frank, two baskets of wings, suicide sauce," he bellowed compliantly.

"When the Imperial bid screwed up, he lost his judgment. He knew real estate like God knew the Garden of Eden. But then he wandered further afield and acquired ComTech: telecommunications was an area he knew nothing about. He deluded himself into believing he could manage the company himself and let ComTech's best man go. With a more astute CEO at the helm, ComTech would have been beautifully posi-tioned to become one of the country's leading high-tech corpo-rations. But just when such companies needed massive invest-ment — especially in R&D to keep pace with all the rapid tech-nology changes — he slashed everything in sight in an effort to boost short-term profits. He alienated major customers by offering really shabby tech support when their equipment kept crashing due to faulty software. Employee morale was so low his brightest people left. They were fed up with never being consulted, forced to sit on the sidelines and watch what had once been a terrific company with a hell of a lot of potential virtually self-destruct.

"So ComTech took a nose-dive. Durand had paid too much for what he had acquired in the first place, had financed the acquisition poorly and overestimated revenues. Overall Durand Corp. wound up with a multi-billion-dollar debt and almost a billion in annual interest payments. In the end, his ego was his worst enemy — not any power élite.

"Just before he was murdered, he'd been running in ever-diminishing circles trying to buy time to reorganize, sell off the less-profitable real estate, find a partner to advance enough capital to stave off the banking syndicate that was calling up his loans, and soothe the shareholders. His impending bank-ruptcy would have driven several thousand employees onto the street — a tragic fact that didn't seem to preoccupy him in the least. Rumour has it that he was frenetic as a bug in a bottle, Sam. There was no way he could repay his creditors on time or secure a partner. He just ran out of resources and time. Death must have come like a reprieve."

I paused to attack my basket of wings, zapping the stings from the suicide sauce with gulps of cool beer. Delaney's fries are the best in town: I'm an authority, but no snob. McDonald's fries are good, sure, but Delaney's come cut in thick wedges, peel intact, unsalted.

As I licked my fingers, Sam asked, "If you had to do a shortlist of Durand's enemies, who'd be on it?"

"It would be as short as a roll of toilet paper, man! Anyone who ever met him would be on it, including his family," I quoted, without acknowledging my source. "Perhaps excluding his dogs and ponies."

"Off the record, Jane, throw me a few names." Sam always pumped his sources dry.

"Throw me the phone directory, Sam." I sipped my Guinness, very slowly. "In recent months, I guess the list would include those who stood to lose the most if Durand Corporation went belly up. His son, William, has already gone to court to try to salvage what he could of the family trust fund that's been leaking value like the Titanic. Two months ago Durand fired his two top CEOs: either one, or both, could be nursing a big grievance. The people thrown out of work as ComTech lurched toward bankruptcy: it wouldn't be the first time an angry shareholder or ex-worker took out the King of the Castle, would it? Several others, including the bankers, stood to lose significant bucks and face — but they can more or less afford it, and they're not likely to resort to murder as a bottom-line salvage strategy! You could throw in the irate thousands caught holding stocks worth only marginally more than the paper they're printed on. And, what the hell, what's left of the Establishment. They've been on his case since he first attracted their attention, trying to block every new deal he was making. Even the venerable Dawson — "

"Surely not *Dawson*, for Christ's sake," Sam interjected. "He's been at the top of the corporate heap for a quarter of a century. He created the conglomerate build-up before it became a frenzy. Wouldn't Durand be a flea on his rump?"

"Flea bites get infected, Sam. It's no secret that Dawson masterminded the Imperial Trust shut-out. Apparently he was obsessive about ruining Durand — in which case he's probably disappointed that his target got bumped off *before* he got hit with a ball-crushing bankruptcy."

"And his personal life? Did he have one? Most of these tycoons seem to consider that wasted time," Sam remarked.

"Yeah," I agreed. "Durand had two wives, one kid by the first wife, a kennel of Rhodesian ridgebacks and a stable of horses. A younger sister he hadn't seen in years. If there was an underbelly —mistresses, illegitimate offspring, call girls or rent boys, coke parties — who's to know? He didn't have any friends. Didn't drink or smoke. Was as furtive and as nuts about secrecy as J. D. Salinger," I said, reaching for a Rothmans. SMOKING CAN KILL YOU, screamed the package. I defiantly lit it.

"He courted the media when the publicity was good for

one of his deals, but when it came to actually revealing anything about himself, he was tight as a zebra mussel. Sorry to be so unhelpful on that one."

"No, you've been really helpful, Janie. I only asked the question about his personal life out of curiosity. This assignment came from Armstrong with some pretty explicit instructions — warnings in fact — that all the paper wants is primarily background. Nothing *investigative*. Because of Durand's notoriety, the story has to be front-page, but so low-profile it won't give the élite a belch of discomfort."

"Did Armstrong hint at where the pressure was coming from?" I asked.

"Hell no. When he talks in his sleep, you can be sure that his poor wife doesn't learn a thing. So before I called you today, I phoned Ernie Sivcoski." I kept quiet about having punched the same buttons this morning.

"Even Ernie was discreet. All I got out of him is that the Chief of Police received a couple of very heavy calls from Ottawa, and a personal visit from the Attorney-General."

I laughed to conceal my growing panic. "So the boys upstairs are praying that the office cleaning lady did it."

"They must have reason to believe that someone who pays more taxes than the cleaning lady terminated Durand — Jane, you've turned whiter than a carp's belly. Why should any of this bother you?"

I prevaricated. Much as I trust Sam, I wasn't prepared to tell him about Simone's offer, which I'd accepted just two hours ago.

"Oh, I guess the whole thing just triggers memories of how I lost my job at the *Post*, Sam. Sounds like the same can of worms. Make sure you keep your butt covered, eh?"

"Janie, until that mortgage gets paid, my butt's sealed in concrete," he assured me.

"Never forget, Sam, concrete is how the Mob disposed of their enemies. Like the fabric of the month. Jimmy Hoffa's shroud."

He finished his drink and shrugged. "I'm an old hack. Don't worry about me." Had I been honest with Sam, he'd be worrying about me.

We hugged, he thanked me and said goodbye, promising to keep in touch.

On my way out I picked up a rack of ribs for Max. No fries.

Lunch with Sam hadn't been a great launch for my detective career. Investigators are supposed to collect, not dispense information. All I got in return for Sam picking my brains cleaner than a saint's conscience was having the fear of the Ayatollah thrown into me. Still, he now owed me a favour, and I'd probably wind up collecting.

CHAPTER 5

WHEN I GOT back to my studio after lunch with Sam, I tossed the ribs into Max's gargantuan bowl, then retrieved Portia Sherman's phone message. She was home when I returned her call. I quickly filled her in on my assignment from Simone Goldberg. I told her the truth — that I had been hired to find Durand's killer — and swore her to secrecy. Portia, who has a gossip columnist's nose for intrigue, readily agreed to accompany me to the funeral. Stockbrokers need all the comic relief they can find, she quipped.

My answering machine is state of the art, all bells and whistles, more buttons than a set of long johns. But its cunning designer hadn't included a button you could hit to mute recorded messages. I forgave him: he'd never met me.

I bought it just after Pete's death. At first I left it on all the time; this gave me a necessary illusion of control. During those first few self-obliterating months, I never once picked up the phone when it rang. The only person I wanted to hear from was dead. Then I started answering it selectively. More recently, I've been responding almost every time it rings, leaving the machine on only when I'm out of my studio, in the shower or writing. Maintaining this routine occasionally becomes a major discipline. The taped message that followed Portia's was a prime example of why I found phone avoidance so appealing. Another female voice sounded, straining under the pressure of knowing that my tape can accommodate only two-minute information bites. Etta is much more comfortable with marathon-stretch soliloquies:

Hi dear it's your Mom. I'm back from Nashville and have I got stories for you. Slim — did I tell you I took Slim with me? — anyways me and him loved the place so much we're planning on going back on the Easter tour package. You won't believe this but we saw Randy Travis and the Oak Ridge Boys at the Opry and Slim is sure it was Dolly we saw at this take-out chicken joint, this broad was just as stacked and them hooters weren't falsies, though what she'd be doing there when she could send a servant I can't imagine. We also got told by a waitress at the hotel we was staying at that Kitty Wells has got piles so bad she can't be on stage for more than five minutes, ain't that a bitch. We had a real nice time all in all but that was wrecked when I got back to Sweet Dreams and heard about you cutting up on Saturday night. What you need is a boyfriend you know. You wouldn't have time to think and drink so much if you know what I mean. When you meet Slim for sure you'll know what I mean 'cause the guy's hung like a rhino. Hey this tape must be running out so call me as soon as you get in okay. Oh yeah, did I say it was your Mom calling?

Etta's voice, running full-tilt like Max on a rodent chase, distinctive as DNA. I can't believe that she found it necessary to identify herself twice. On second thought, I can believe *anything* about my mother, who is as unpredictable as sunshine on the West Coast — and just as hot when she shines. By any conventional medical reckoning, Etta's totally politically incorrect lifestyle is a prescription for premature death. Etta is sixty-three (although the date on her birth certificate makes her sixty-five).

I returned Etta's call and cut short her torrential Nashville narrative by telling her that I had to get ready for a funeral. I didn't bother adding that the funeral was tomorrow. That bit of information got her off on a jag about how it was time I started hanging out with people who didn't up and die on me. She didn't bother to ask who had croaked, and that was a genuine shame because I had planned to tell her it was the premier. That would have cheered her up.

Her harangue left me with nothing to say. Etta always leaves me with nothing to say. I managed to get off the phone by promising to come to Sweet Dreams on Tuesday night to meet Slim. Etta runs through boyfriends like shit through the proverbial goose, so I had a pre-scripted rap in reserve whenever she flaunted a new model.

I was definitely sliding back into a depression. Etta's prescriptions for how I can get my shabby life together are always wildly off the mark. But I know her diagnosis is fundamentally sound. I'm just not prepared to act on her remedies.

Once I kicked my mind into gear, it started ticking over faster than a Toronto taxi-cab meter. Ernie had told me about the cops finding a book of matches from a gay bar at the crime scene. I riffled through my mental Rolodex of gay and lesbian friends and went straight to *Maracle, Silver*.

I dialled her number. "Silver, it's Jane. Can I come up for a drink?"

Silver Maracle is my best friend. She lives a floor above me. "Sure, white woman. Be up here in five."

We are well matched, far more often than not, complementing one another's alternating needs for detachment and intimacy. But something in her tone of voice turned my request into a command appearance.

Silver opened the door onto her studio, which always reminded me of the interior of Jonah's whale. All ribs, unadorned, totally given over to function. Silver is an artist. The naturally illuminated area in front of the huge east-facing windows was where she painted; the surrounding walls propped up her canvases. Somewhere off in the far corners she ate and slept, as though bodily functions were mere parentheses around her work.

Inside the door we embraced and kissed one another's

cheeks. Rather, I kissed Silver's cheek and she kissed me full on the mouth, drawing my body into what with anyone else would have been a lover's embrace. Silver has no time for what she calls white man's "teepee" hugs. If you don't want to draw people close to your fire, you don't hug them in the first place, she says. Silver is a Mohawk.

She went straight to the fridge and pulled out a can of Blue for me, a Coke for herself. Silver never drinks alcohol. I'm always reluctant to share my belief that Coke is even further removed from the Creator's health food legacy.

Any other friend with a loaded agenda probably would have spent a minute or two observing the niceties of seeming concern for what was transpiring in my life, especially since I had requested the meeting. Not Silver. She never wastes any time getting directly to her point. I followed her to a woven carpet that rested on the floor in front of a large canvas on an easel. The face of the canvas was turned away; Silver never lets anyone see a work-in-progress. She holds to some notion about protecting its spirit. I could understand why she felt a bit paranoid about losing the things she treasured. I sat down on the carpet across from her.

She is a very large woman, close to six feet tall and two hundred and fifty pounds. She wears her raven hair in a single, thick braid that reaches down to her waistline. Her black eyes are set in a wide, high-cheek-boned face; they open and shut as definitively as her moods. Tonight she was wearing a paint-smeared T-shirt, blue denim overalls and a gorgeous pair of fire-engine red snakeskin boots she'd smuggled back from a recent trip to San Francisco.

Scrutinizing my face like she was reading a medicine wheel, she barked, "You know that show of mine you came to a couple of weeks ago? It sold out." She sounded disgusted.

"So why are you angry?" I looked across into her eyes. "That's why you exhibit, isn't it — to sell?"

Her reply was so swiftly launched I felt like a snag of driftwood caught up in white water. "Yeah, that's why I *exhibit* — not why I *paint*."

She pulled on her Coke, like she had nothing more to say. Silver often lapses into silence when she's in one of her anti-imperialist moods, as though she's challenging me to fill in the colonial blanks. And that scares me, because I always feel that if I don't provide the correct answer she's withholding, I might get relegated to being just another white person. But I refuse to play that game: I am white, and no amount of guilt-ridden, liberal concessions can ever erase that accident of birth and privilege. So I said nothing. The silence between us ballooned to fill the studio.

Finally her drive to explain herself overwhelmed her need to guilt me. "Why I paint — why I *painted* — is to make a record of where my people come from. I must have filled a hundred canvases with our moccasin tracks. But I was always trying to make symbols of what the Elders taught us, stories about how we got here and what we had to do to stay here in a good way. And you know, I actually thought I was doing what I was sent here to do — until that opening at the gallery. For the first time, I really looked around … and what I saw were all these designer-dressed WASPs buying up my stuff like it was so much Indian wallpaper. The ancestors of these trendies dedicated their lives to wiping out my people's culture, and here their relations are buying up what I can recall of the remnants. Jane, that really totalled me. I mean, it sucks so bad — and all along I'd been playing into it."

"So what did you decide to do?" We hadn't talked since that night.

"First thing I did was take my cheque from the gallery and sign it over to the Native Women's Resource Centre. They were about to go tits-up because the Feds cut off their operating grant. Second thing I did was go out and get laid. Third thing I did was give up being a so-called artist." Silver is a storyteller: she knows how to create cliff-hangers. She paused.

I responded on cue. "How long did giving up your vocation last?"

She dumped the remainder of her Coke down her throat

so vigorously a wayward stream trickled down the front of her T-shirt, soaking a fresh hue into the stained fabric. "About a week. I went back to the rez and spent a lot of time with Marie, the old woman I told you about. She asked me why I painted the way I do. So I says, 'I paint it like I see it.' Then she tells me, 'No, you paint it like you *think* our old people remember it, like their old people saw it. You're not painting what *you* see.' She wouldn't tell me what I see, eh? I come back to the city. Soon as I step foot in the door the phone's ringing. It's Gertie, telling me to get my butt over to the Silver Dollar because a bunch of Indian women are fighting, and she thinks my sister's in the middle of it. She wants it broke up before the cops start arresting every bimbo in sight. Some argument about a fucking man. So I tear off over to Spadina, break up the fight, and drag my stupid sister to a table. She's sitting there, sniffling and grumbling, ready to pass out or throw up, whichever comes first, when I take a look around the bar. Then it hits me like lightning: *what I'm seeing is what I should be painting.*"

She stood up and walked over to the easel, turned the canvas to face me. Her painting looked nearly finished. It was a huge, darkly coloured acrylic. A grittily realistic picture of three Native women slumped in three drunken solitudes along a bar counter, facing a mirror that reflects three Native women slumped in three drunken solitudes in front of a bar counter. The only aboriginal reference was a large raven perched at one end of the bar. The mood was desolate, liminally menacing.

I turned to my friend. "You've found a new path."

"Yeah. Do you think I'll get dumped on for appropriating the raven from Emily Carr?" she chuckled. "So, my moccasins are moving onto a fresh path ... where are your Reeboks taking you these days?"

I told her the straight poop about my latest job offer. Silver knows the four directions; she won't abide indirectness.

"Sounds like trouble, girl."

"Sounds to me like a new Ducati and time to write

another book — or something," I countered.

"Why are you really doing it? Ain't you had enough trouble already without rooting around for some more?"

"The money's good, Silver. And I'm curious."

"Curious landed Christopher Columbus on our shores. Curious brought your ancestors here. Curious killed the cat. Curious got you beat up real good once before — and there's lots of books out there waiting to be written that don't have to get you involved in grief."

I gave up. "What are you telling me?"

"I'm telling you I think you decided after Pete died that if you buried yourself in enough work — maybe even danger — then you'd never have to stare down the big hole in your world. Girlfriend, one day soon you're gonna have to put aside the writing, the booze, the hiding out, and really let yourself *feel* his loss. But the path you've chosen is none of my business, is it?" She crushed her Coke can.

Before I let her wise counsel sink into my brain, I said, "Look, I really need your help on this one, Silver. Can I count on you, in spite of what you just said?"

Love and exasperation danced a tight two-step across her eyes. "Can you count on me, woman? Do bears shit in the bush? Do Indians overpopulate our prisons? Could I count on you last year to give me that bail money for my sister?"

I crossed the carpet and pulled her close. Hugging Silver is akin to entering a virtual womb. After a minute or two of holding me, she gave me a playful shove. "Hey, any more of that and I might get distracting notions!"

"Silver, you are a hopeless case! I mean, I don't even *think* about sex any more," I protested.

"Now that's what I call terminally hopeless. What do you need, Jane?"

"I need to know about gay bars in the city — in particular, the kind of gay bar that an acquaintance of Charles Durand's might hang out at."

What I expected from Silver's extensive hands-on knowledge

of the scene was a shortlist of possibilities. What I got was dynamite.

"Leather Boys."

I was speechless.

She smirked at my astonishment, then shrugged. "You threw me an easy one, Jane. Durand's son, Billy, is gay. And the fact that his father is who he is makes our small queer world even smaller. A good friend of mine from the rez, George Potts, owns Leather Boys, so I get all the gossip."

"What do you know about William, Silver?"

"Not a hell of a lot. I do remember, though, that last year when the media were all over the story about him taking his old man to court, some Queer Nation types who hang out at Leather Boys were talking about outing Billy — like, to show that even rich white celebrities have queer kids. Apparently the lavender fascists decided to leave him in the closet 'cause they figured having Charles Durand for a father made him enough of a martyr already. George can probably tell you lots more about him."

"Will you take me to Leather Boys?"

"Sure, and if you ride your Harley and wear your leathers we won't even have to explain why we're there!" she cackled.

"Can we go tomorrow night?" I asked, in my excitement utterly blotting out my appointment with Etta at Sweet Dreams.

Silver assumed a mock solemn face. "No. Tomorrow night I got a heavy date — even heavier than me." She slapped a generous thigh. "How about Wednesday?"

"Wednesday's great. Meet me downstairs at nine?"

"You got it, honey. We should be out of bed by then."

At the door I turned back to her. "I hope your date goes well."

She grinned. "Yeah, me too. Meantime, watch your white ass."

I felt genuine delight about her new vocational direction — and equally distressed about my own.

CHAPTER 6

TUESDAY MORNING I awakened to a peculiar noise coming from the floor close to my futon. As soon as I opened one eye, my dog, tail wagging so hard it set his toenails tap-dancing, started licking my face. I opened my other eye.

A kitten-size rat, conspicuously departed this vale of tears, lay about a foot from my head. Max's soulful brown eyes beseeched my thrilled approval of his trophy.

Just after I met Pete, I began dreaming of waking up to dawn love-making, shared hot showers and back-to-bed breakfasts of cappuccino, hot croissants, strawberries and cream. For twenty-three short months my dreams got real. This morning's reality, light years removed from my time with Pete, was a rude contrast. I had a small corpse to dispose of, in a manner that wouldn't offend my current house-mate.

I closed my eyes to figure out the scenario. If I stepped off the far end of the futon, fetched a pair of rubber gloves, the barbecue tongs and a green plastic garbage bag from the kitchen, then I could pick up the rat by the base of its tail with the tongs, drop it in the bag, quickly seal the bag with a twist-tie, and temporarily deposit the sorry bundle on the landing of the fire escape — all the while, of course, lavishing great praise and gratitude upon my canine hunter-protector, and rewarding him with a Milk Bone. This was beginning to feel like marriage.

I opened my eyes and looked more closely at the rat. Max might not be so hungry for the Milk Bone after all: my gift was missing its tastier interior bits.

I efficiently disposed of the rat according to plan. My decision to skip breakfast seemed preordained. Something had depressed my appetite. So I threw on my sweats, put Max on his lead and headed off to High Park for a canter. As I turned off Roncesvalles onto a short residential street blessedly free of traffic, the crisp February sun lit up the scene like creation's first morning.

What a contrary damn city I live in. Much of the time I hate Toronto — its traffic congestion and pollution, its overcrowding, noise and impersonality, its progressive erosion of neighbourhoods by office towers, condos and high-rises, its adolescent striving for world-class status while it busily cosmeticizes the disfigurements of poverty and shuttles out of sight its street people, the disaffected and dispossessed, whenever we're hosting an international event. I never expected Toronto in the '90s to resemble the city of my childhood, but I still have a lot of trouble accepting what our city fathers have warped it into.

I often escape these black perceptions into fantasies of buying a hundred acres in the country, with an old Victorian farmhouse and a few outbuildings I can restore, a pond that is home to ducks and geese (dare I dream that blue herons come this far north?), a garden plot sufficient to feed me, a trail through the bush for cross-country skiing, silence enough to hear an acorn drop and a squirrel's scratchy retreat, maybe even birdsong, my own thoughts …

Yet on mornings like this, Toronto can still catch me by surprise. We jogged into the four-hundred-acre park, which opened up to us like some great wartime-forsaken cathedral, shorn by winter of its showiest decoration, but still grand and as near to solitude as you can get in a city of two and a half million people. And this was the same park that, in its nighttime aspect, had frightened me witless just two days ago. Maybe my serotonin is kicking in.

Released from his lead and darting well ahead of me, Max bounded across the gently rolling terrain in ecstatic streaks punctuated by tail-chasing circles of delight. If dogs could vote, Toronto's green spaces would be protected in perpetuity.

Later today Charles Durand would be reduced to ashes;

presumably a mausoleum fit to rival Versailles would house his powdered bones, now on a par with the proverbial pauper's. As I loped along at a non-punishing pace, I remembered back to when I was a kid, to an old great-aunt commenting on the morning of another ancient's burial that "it was a lovely day to be buried." And I remembered thinking that a dead body had to be indifferent to weather. Pity, Durand was missing a great day.

It had snowed the morning of my father's funeral. Pete's casket got rained on.

As I wound down, so did Max, who fell back to pacing me. I still had lots of time to shower, dress for the funeral, and meet Portia outside St. Michael's Cathedral before the service.

I took a taxi to St. Mike's: even I know when a Harley transgresses basic decorum.

Mist did not shroud the Gothic towers, nor did it muffle the steeple bell's tolling. Indeed, brilliant sunlight illuminated architectural detailing and sharpened the iron's normally leaden acoustics. If God was sad about Durand's passing, he wasn't using any cheap rhetorical devices like onomatopoeia to dramatize it.

Half an hour before the Mass of Christian Burial was due to begin, we entered the Cathedral. So we wouldn't have to crane our necks taking in the arrival of the mourners, we sat at the end of a pew close to the back.

Charles Durand's penultimate residence was mounted like a fine art exhibit in front of the altar. Resplendent on a silk-draped plinth, it was a masterpiece of corporate wealth on rare display. Mahogany with maple inlays, gold hardware and dovetail joints. It seemed a crime to incinerate it: up-ended and fitted with a few shelves it could happily grace a Rosedale drawing room. Only one floral tribute had been allowed into the Cathedral. An exquisite spray of rare orchids (no doubt flown in from one of the Amazon rainforests Durand and his corporate colleagues pillaged) rested on top of the casket.

Those mourners familiar with the late tycoon's obsession with privacy might reasonably have assumed the coffin was closed because its occupant hated being placed under close observation, especially in a scenario he couldn't hope to control. The real reason was less complicated: even the cosmetic wizardry of Thomson-McKinnon Funeral Home Ltd., morticians to Upper Canadian gentry since before Confederation, couldn't conceal the woeful damage to his head. That was a job for Madame Tussaud's.

I glanced sidelong at my friend. Elegant and unself-consciously beautiful in a charcoal-grey silk suit with a soft pink scarf at the neck, she must have been born wearing eyeliner and panty hose.

Beside her I looked like I'd assembled my outfit from Budget Rent-a-Dress. I don't have much occasion to get tarted up, so my wardrobe includes only two dress outfits. One I was wearing today, a basic black skirt and jacket I bought at the Bay five years ago to wear to my father's funeral. It was as cheap and under-stated as his life. The other was a wild green dress Pete gave me, which I should have given away along with his clothes. I hadn't worn it since he died. Never mind, Durand's gorgeous casket was the centre-piece of this occasion. I reminded myself to hold my knees together: if I don't concentrate when I'm wearing a skirt, they wander off like weak eyes in search of a focal point.

Portia sat erect and sedate beside me. Only her eyes, roving the Cathedral with the probity of the TV cameras we'd passed outside, betrayed her keen interest in the mourners filtering inside. I asked her to identify the faces I didn't recognize from *Prime Time News, The Globe and Mail, The Financial Post* and *Maclean's*.

Members of Charles Durand's family arrived first. Simone, accompanied by a stout, bearded man who reminded me of Allen Ginsberg *circa* 1980, and a tall, stunning teenage girl, presumably her daughter, Rebecca. She was slender, but appeared fit and athletic. Fair skin, delicately featured face and artfully "untended" long, curly blonde hair, she seemed a strik-ing combination of strength and vulnerability. A Botticelli Venus head seamlessly grafted onto a track star's body. As soon as the Goldberg trio were seated in the front row, the girl, looking very agitated, turned to her mother, who put her arm around her. By my calculations, Rebecca had never met her uncle: perhaps she shared my funeral phobia.

Shortly after their entrance a very thin, anxious-looking, grey-haired woman tottered up the centre aisle with a wan, handsome man I recognized as William, Durand's son. His genetic script certainly deconstructed his father's hearty sports-man image. His bearing echoed a young Sitwell, elegant bones animated with the effete grace of a race-horse. I bet his father hadn't found him manly enough.

I assumed that the mousy woman beside him was his mother, Durand's first wife, Helen. As soon as they sat down, she started chattering away at him without a cursory glance at the coffin. Maybe knowing who occupied it was enough to sat-isfy her. Durand had sprinted out on her twenty years ago, leaving in his wake a divorce settlement that left her a very rich, proportionately embittered woman. She had moved back to Noranda.

William sat like a six-year-old boy in Sunday School, evi-dently attentive to his mother's words while he stared at his father's coffin like it was the Starship Enterprise. I wondered what Durand's death would mean to him financially. He'd recently lost a nasty court battle to sell his shares in the family trust before they got recycled as toilet paper. What, if any-thing, did he do for a living?

As more mourners filled the back pews, the deceased's sec-ond wife entered, alone. Judith Durand looked just like she did in all her press photographs, utterly refined, utterly com-posed and utterly vacuous, every considered inch of her betray-ing the ex-model and game-show hostess she had been prior to her marriage to Charles. She made an effective entrance, strut-ting the cathedral aisle like a catwalk. She did not appear to be distraught. No widow's weeds for Judith: cosied beneath the regulation mink, her dress bespoke charity ball. I wondered what that meant. Widowhood is not always synonymous with grief, but even Etta was gracious enough to fabricate a brief weep at my father's interment. (At the wake my mother admitted that the tears were prompted by thinking about what it was costing her to stick the bugger into the ground.)

At the front of the Cathedral the current Mrs. Durand genuflected before the altar, then seated herself next to Simone's family. Simone smiled politely across at her, as did her hirsute husband. Durand's first wife darted a curare-drenched glance between Judith's shoulder blades. I guess you don't have to love a man to hate the woman who replaces you.

Durand Corporation employees made up the next tier of mourners. Prominent among them was Norman Jameson, his current CEO, Fay Davies, the company spokesperson who for months had been adroitly running interference between her boss and the media, and — to my surprise, seated with them, the two executives Durand had fired three months ago when they disagreed with his strategy for retaining control of the corporation. Clustered around them were several people I assumed were also on the payroll. Portia pointed out two top executives from ComTech. Due as much to their boss's mismanagement of his empire as to his murder, quite a few of these people must be "between jobs."

More powerful men and their suitably attired wives were there, non-WASP types not directly attached to Durand Corporation. The two Farrah brothers, Samir and Karim, were seated only a pew away from Jean-Luc Hébert, Durand's one-time partner, and for three decades a major force in the Canadian resources industry. Durand had his first nervous breakdown after their partnership ended up in court. Like Durand, Hébert was French-Canadian, and had never quite made it into the inner circles. Nor had the Farrahs, in spite of their extensive corporate reach into England, Russia and Japan. Wealthy Anglo-Canadians are not overtly racist: they simply carry on discreetly maintaining certain exclusionary practices.

The ruling class turned out in full force. Portia identified most of the faces I couldn't place. I didn't need her to point out Gerald Dawson, dean of the Canadian business élite, looking more distinguished than the Governor General and a damn sight more authoritative. He entered the Cathedral with a small entourage. If someone threw a grenade into St. Michael's this morning, most of the country's boards of directors would be decimated. Dawson must have decreed it poor form not to show up.

A number of reporters were on the job, identifiable by their underdressed, underpaid, hung-over and bored demeanour. And I knew that Ernie Sivcoski, along with several other members of the homicide squad, must be lurking about in plainclothes, but I hadn't spotted him. Perhaps he was disguised as a choirboy.

When the service began at eleven sharp the Cathedral was packed to its august arches. Thomas, Cardinal Callaghan, resplendent in robes you had to die for, celebrated the Requiem Mass. The man wielded power like an incense burner; he had more clout than any elected member of the Metro Council — or any member of the Provincial Legislature, for that matter. Several years ago the Pope's visit to Toronto had revealed how very many of the city's voters were registered, if not ardent Catholics. Shortly after His Holiness returned to his modest abode in Rome, the premier announced that his government was prepared to throw its belated support behind separate school boards. That struck a lot of concerned people as a regressive move, but it went ahead without a hitch. The Establishment didn't let out a whimper: they sent their kids to private schools, where they dictated the agenda. Rumour had it that Callaghan had simply informed the premier how many votes the pulpit could direct his way.

Had he chosen a stage career, Callaghan might have rivalled Gielgud. The Mass was a great piece of theatre — processional candles, clouds of incense, all that chanting and bowing —

powerful enough to make me nervous about not having been to Confession since my parish priest had shown so little sympathy when I confessed to having necked with a Protestant at my grade-eight graduation party. If memory serves, he had over-reacted terribly, flinging penitential Our Fathers and Hail Marys at me like wedding rice. And I hadn't even gotten around to confessing that it was a girl I'd been passionately kissing.

Just as the show was winding up, there was a brief disturbance not far from the coffin. Simone and her husband jumped up, then disappeared from sight as they dropped to their knees and bent over. Figuring no one but God could see me, I stood up to take in what was happening. It looked like Rebecca had fainted.

Callaghan concluded the service without missing a beat. We followed the coffin outside to the waiting hearse. It was borne by Durand Corporation executives, forced by custom into their first experience of manual labour. The mourners quickly dispersed, most of them to chauffeur-driven limos. I wondered how many of them would show up at the wake. There was no graveside service. Simone had told me that Durand's ashes were to be sealed in a vault on the grounds of his villa in Montreux, overlooking Lake Geneva.

Portia drove along at a leisurely pace in her silver grey BMW, cruising through residential streets to avoid the expressways. We didn't want to be among the first arrivals at Swindon Path.

I reached into my bag for a cigarette, then thought better of it. Portia's lifestyle was as clean and crisply organized as her career and her wardrobe. Our differences made Siamese twins of apples and oranges. The years following our undergraduate friendship had sharply accentuated personal traits less obvious when we were nineteen. Yet our bond had survived, thanks to mutual tolerance of divergent ways. (If vulnerability didn't drive me into instant palpitations, I would simply declare that we love one another.) But clouds of tobacco smoke in her closed car might strain things a bit. I tucked my Rothmans back into my purse.

Portia had noticed my nicotine push-pull. "Light up if you must, Jane."

"*Must* implies a lack of choice," I snapped. As conversational styles go, tight-lipped is my least favourite. "You sound like a head mistress."

"How would you know what the hell a head mistress sounds like?" she sweetly queried.

"I must have watched *The Belles of St. Trinians* a dozen times ... and don't be so smug, Portia. You must have at least one filthy habit." I devoutly wished I could name it.

"Darling, of course I do — but it doesn't clog up my lungs," she grinned lasciviously.

"May you breathe your last in the midst of a multiple orgasm."

"Is that a curse or a benediction?" she asked.

"Portia, you must have guessed how long I've been celibate. That makes it a curse!"

She glanced at me. "Now that you mention it, I would guess that you've been celibate since the last time you made love to Pete."

I'm skilled at blocking. "Hey girl, if this was a game show, you'd be walking away with a microwave or a trip for two to Disney World." I loathe myself when I smart-ass my friends, but who needs another Inquisition?

"And if I were your therapist, I'd tell you to take a walk until you overcame your flippancy addiction."

I really needed a cigarette. "You're telling me to get real?" I asked.

Portia moved her right hand from the steering wheel and squeezed my clenched hands. "Jane, I've always loved you precisely because you're so damned real — by which I mean true to your own lights. You sometimes make me feel like one of those cardboard dolls we cut out and dressed up when we were kids. So if I'm suggesting anything, it's that maybe you could begin to end your mourning for Pete."

I reverted to the kind of verbal sleight-of-tongue that keeps me insulated and isolated. "Pete's death ended my mornings." My pun received the inattention it merited. "What can I say? I'm working on it, Portia. My therapist gets ninety-eight bucks for forty-five minutes a week of tolerating what I wouldn't dream of subjecting my friends to at any price. In any case, Silver took it upon herself to tell me that I haven't even begun to mourn Pete because I've found too many ways to block the fact that he's gone."

"Fair enough, Jane. Just know that when you're ready to talk, you've got a friend. Meantime, tell me: will this be your first sighting of the Durand mansion?"

"Yeah," I said, thankful for her reprieve. "I've seen a few photos of it in magazines, but for some inexplicable reason I've never attracted an invitation."

Portia laughed. "You have, though, heard about the infamous housewarming Charles threw to christen the place five years ago?"

"Again, only hearsay. Tell me about it," I urged. Portia and her husband had been on the guest list of five hundred drawn up to celebrate Durand's attempted installation into Toronto.

"The mansion itself is beautiful — as you'll see for yourself in a few minutes. And, you know, it really does symbolize so much about Charles Durand. It's beautiful but *inauthentic,* like a facsimile printing of the *Book of Kells.* Apparently after he decided to relocate the corporation, he travelled to Europe to tour the great houses. He finally spotted the one he wanted in Somerset. When he got back he hired an architect to replicate it stone by stone, right down to the statues and gardens, like a contemporary Casa Loma."

"You're so right about it being symbolic, Portia. The subtext of the man's whole career is about striving to *buy* credibility, respectability, legitimacy — even ancestry. The Establishment always regarded him as contemptible. Maybe now he's dead, they'll be content with seeing him as merely pathetic. Imagine him having all that talent and energy, and still craving for Daddy's approval!"

Portia nodded her head. "The social code is fascinating, isn't it? I mean, however loathsome it may sound, when we were in the Cathedral I felt a bit like an anthropologist. There was Big Daddy himself, Gerald Dawson, still the pack leader, herding the rest of the old guard and his own minions into place to observe the last rites for a man he's been obsessed with keeping in his place since Durand first showed his upstart face. You know, Jane, without Dawson's *imprimatur*, St. Mike's would have been close to deserted. I think he staged their presence like a victory parade. Look Ma, no hands: the wannabe is dead. Long live the King."

"Two undergrad psych courses never prepared me for this analysis, Portia. Why did Dawson care so much about cutting Durand off at the pass?" I asked.

"Durand represented the first wave of a new breed of entrepreneurs in this country. He *counted*, in stock-market language — Dawson's mother tongue. But he came out of nowhere. He had no notable roots. And without the help of the Old Boys' network, he still managed to amass enormous wealth and considerable clout. In Dawson's eyes, that made him a real threat: if the Establishment meant anything, it meant that non-members were excluded from the benefits of belonging. So the Old Boys still clung to the one thing that Durand, for all his brilliant renegade wheelings and dealings couldn't acquire — legitimacy."

"Maybe the mansion was an attempt to give himself ancestry," I suggested.

"No 'maybe' about it. And as for the housewarming, I guess it only went to prove that you can't warm a castle! God knows it was lavish enough and he got every detail correct, but the whole event felt, well, *staged* — as though it had been constructed by following to the letter a 'how-to-host-a-great-event' manual. The guest list was enormous. Durand must have consulted *Who's Who* to draw it up. Let's see: the PM was there, a few cabinet ministers, a Supreme Court judge, the premier of Ontario, most of the corporate élites (who gave every appearance of having attended out of curiosity), some high-profile cultural types — actors, dancers, entertainers, writers, a few media names. He didn't miss a base. But Durand and Judith actually *knew* only a few people there. The man didn't have any real business or social connections in Toronto. Perhaps because he didn't have any friends, I don't know."

"Portia, I've always wondered what the hell people *do* at that kind of non-event."

She laughed. "Nothing, for God's sake, otherwise it would be an event! You sip a cocktail, nibble an *hors d'oeuvre*, and mingle. It's considered bad form to do deals, of course. Oh, I remember one odd thing: security was tighter than you'd find at a Cuban holiday resort. Uniformed guards were posted everywhere, on the grounds and inside the place. That offended his guests. I guess they thought Durand was paranoid about someone stealing the silverware."

I interrupted her with a sarcastic chuckle. "Surely you can see why. You know the line 'even paranoids have real enemies.' Durand could be forgiven for thinking he might be robbed. The Old Boys *had* stolen his first big grab at legitimacy when they blocked his bid for Imperial Trust."

Portia nodded her beautifully coiffed head, making me wonder for the thousandth time how she trained every one of her hairs to stay in place. She'd drop out of the end of a wind tunnel looking composed. "Perhaps he meant to offend with the security guards. Certainly the entertainment he laid on suggested mischievous intent. He brought in Robert Charlebois, the singer who's probably contributed most to the spread of sovereignty in Quebec. Charlebois lead off his performance of political songs with "Qué-Can Blues." No one was amused, except Durand. Oh yes, although I suppose one shouldn't consider him part of the entertainment, strictly speaking, Cardinal Callaghan was on hand to formally bless the mansion. He didn't sing, though," she giggled.

"I bet His Eminence got his supper anyway, girl," I muttered darkly.

"The whole thing was tense as hell. Everyone knew it was a set-piece, a vulgar bid for acceptance that hadn't raised Durand's social stock a single point on the Establishment exchange. I remember thinking how bloody lonely he looked, surrounded by all the trappings of his success, yet somehow orphaned."

"Now that's an achievement."

Portia shook her head so vigorously she came close to disturbing the placement of a hair. "Jane, don't let your politics fog the lens — not if you want to find out who killed Durand. Maybe this is about psychology as much as economics or class. Right to the end of his life Durand was like a poor kid loitering outside the SkyDome. He wanted into the ball game so badly he could smell the catcher's mitt, but he couldn't get his hands on a ticket."

She swung the car onto Swindon Path, while I worked hard at feeling sorry for rich white boys.

The prospect that confronted us didn't help.

CHAPTER 7

WE PULLED INTO a short driveway. Portia stopped the car at a gatehouse, from which a security guard promptly goose-stepped to her window. He looked like the *Top Gun* version of Tom Cruise. I decided to keep my mouth shut. Uniforms make me belligerent. Portia graciously obliged him with our names. He scanned the list on his clipboard. When he asked for her licence plate number, though, she gestured with an air of *noblesse oblige* I rarely saw her affect, signifying that he could read the plates for himself. Just one of our many differences: by way of protest, I would have given him my middle finger. This may have something to do with why my friend wears silk and I'm locked into denim.

"Just drive your car up to the front entrance, ma'am. Someone will be there to park it for you."

He went back into the gatehouse and punched some keys on a computer console. Two elaborate wrought-iron gates glided soundlessly into their stone envelopes. As Portia accelerated, I turned my head and saw the guard speaking into an intercom. This sure as hell wasn't any part of the Toronto landscape I was familiar with.

Portia negotiated the BMW down a birch-lined avenue as long as an inner-city block. The repro fifteenth-century mansion we were approaching must have been modelled after one of the most beautiful estates in the West Country. It was gabled and buttressed, with mullioned windows and limestone walls. Even on this late February day, the surrounding gardens hinted at their summertime splendour. Come June, I bet the evergreens got sculpted into likenesses of their owner.

When she brought the car to a halt outside the entrance, another Durand-liveried retainer approached, smooth as an in-line skater. He opened first her door, then mine.

The front door of the house was opened by another uniform, this one from the butler academy. When he took our coats I reckoned that he'd choke on my Bi-Way label. But this guy was no slouch. He cocooned my pathetic garment inside Portia's politically incorrect but socially right-on mink.

We stood only briefly inside a foyer bigger than my studio before Judith Durand detached herself from a cluster of earlier arrivals to greet us. She had changed into a suit. Its near-mini black skirt, tailored with considerably more finesse than mine, and pink double-breasted jacket with black collar, cuffs and pocket flaps rang a fashion bell. Portia whispered, "It's a Chanel — Jackie Kennedy, remember?" Who of our generation could forget that blood-spattered garment? Surely the second Mrs. Durand wasn't intentionally echoing fashion history?

As she approached, my mind did one of its unsolicited flips to the past. I recalled her earlier incarnation as hostess of the TV game show "Canada Wins." She was all perfect teeth and tits, smiling brilliantly, extending a hand pale as one of Dracula's brides. "You must be ...," she stalled, I guess hoping God would promptly fill in the blank.

I beat Portia to the draw. "I must be Jane Yeats, but I'd sooner be the Queen." To her credit, she laughed.

Portia quickly moved in with her extended hand. "I'm Portia Sherman of Thomson Sherman Edgeworth. Jane is ...," pausing only for the time it takes a mosquito to mate, "... a colleague of mine. I'm so sorry for your loss."

An expression grazed Mrs. Durand's face that suggested Portia's condolences had jolted her back into the Official Widow role. Even the deceased's wife seemed to find grieving him put a major strain on her thespian resources.

An earsplitting fanfare of shattering glass sounded at the far end of the foyer.

Our eyes darted to the origin of the noise. William

Durand was standing holding the severed neck of a Glenfiddich bottle he'd just smashed against an enormous painting. We stood momentarily shell-shocked as he proceeded to slash the canvas with the jagged fragment.

Had my legs not been confined by a skirt, I could have moved much faster. Just as he made a third enormous gash in the painting, I brought the heel of my right hand down across the back of his wrist. The bottle neck shattered on the marble floor. When he spun around to face me I had already assumed a defensive position.

As the mask of rage contorting his face fragmented, his shoulders slumped from hostility into submission. He staggered slightly, regained his balance and tried to focus on my face through dilated pupils. Just as two burly security guards entered the foyer, Judith ran up and threw her arms around him.

I relaxed and switched my adrenaline into observation mode. Judith consoled her stepson as though he were a disobedient schoolboy. The two guards gently strong-armed him into an adjoining room and closed the door.

By the time Judith reappeared a minute later, a maid was already cleaning up shards of glass and spilt Scotch. The widow spoke to her *sotto voce*. "Mila, please ask Joseph to come and remove this painting immediately." As God is my witness, Mila curtseyed before exiting the foyer.

I studied the painting, a huge formal portrait in oil of Charles Durand. Like his mansion, it was a direct reference to a work from the past. Its style and details seemed to quote Holbein's painting, *The Ambassadors*. Durand was majesterially seated in a Louis XIII armchair, gazing authoritatively at the spectator like the seigneur of a manor. He was wearing a Hugo Boss suit; a Cartier watch gleamed gold and diamonds from the cuff of his shirt. On the ring finger of his left hand, which clutched a leather-bound book, was a thick gold ring. The chair rested on an Aubusson carpet. Accenting the wall behind him was a Lawren Harris wilderness landscape. An architect's model of the Enterprise Tower rose from a Louis XIII side table.

The portrait was a hymn to commerce — which the cultural *objets* somehow failed to legitimize. In the end it only served to buttress Durand's view of himself: this is who I am, what I can build, what I have bought. I am the proprietor of all I survey. *True enough*, I mused. If corpses can see, he was now the proud boss of an urn.

Just as Judith approached us, I was peering intently at one decidedly unpainterly detail. The sitter's crotch hung in shreds like the knees of my favourite pair of vintage Levis. In spite of his evident impairment, William had succeeded in slashing the family jewels to ribbons.

She glanced nervously at the front door, evidently praying that no one would arrive on the scene before Joseph removed the genitally challenged likeness of his late master.

She smiled an explanation. "William, as you can see, is simply overcome with grief."

Everything subsequent to William's freak-out was anti-climactic, making me feel that we had stumbled backwards onto the set of a Shakespearean tragedy well into its final scene. Had William escaped his cell off the foyer, he might have managed an encore.

For an hour I sipped a Scotch (no beer on hand), munched *hors d'oeuvres* to compensate for the lunch I'd missed, and stuck like Boston ivy to Portia as she circulated. She introduced me to a gaggle of people I'd later need to interview, careful to present me as Durand's official biographer.

I concluded that Judith, for all her schooling-come-lately in aristocratic ways, simply hadn't inherited the genes required to organize a wake. I thought back to the one Etta had hosted for my father. We sang — yes, even "Danny Boy," we reminisced, we got pissed, we laughed and we wept. Dad's only literate friend even read from *The Dubliners*. By the time the last mourner staggered out the door at four a.m., the only thing any one was left mourning was that Seamus himself had missed a great party. For once, he was blameless. We'd fired him off to glory like a rocket.

From what I had seen so far, Charles Durand went out with only the velocity of a social hiccup — after his skull caved in.

I grew anxious to leave. I'd pick up a lot more background information at Portia's, where she'd invited me to share supper.

Before we departed, Simone Goldberg and I managed to connect in a quiet corner.

"How is Rebecca?" I asked, remembering her swoon in the Cathedral.

Her expression tensed. "Thanks for your concern. Robert drove her home after the service. She's been very high-strung for the past few months, but Charles's murder seems to have brought her close to the breaking point. I don't understand why she's so affected." She passed me a quizzical wee smile.

I looked at her sympathetically. "Perhaps it's just her age. I was a bundle of nerves throughout my mid-teens. And family funerals are so emotionally fraught — no matter what the nature of our relationship to the deceased."

"You're right, Jane. Perhaps I really shouldn't worry so much. Maybe I invest her moods with a significance they don't merit. Rebecca is always telling me to leave my social working at the office." Her face told me that my words hadn't alleviated her anxiety. We confirmed a Thursday luncheon date at her place north of King City. She gave me instructions on how to get there.

As my buddy and I drove past the gatehouse, I threw a lewd wink at Tom Cruise. He ignored me.

Lennie Sherman had just arrived home when Portia opened the door to their condo. Her husband was a great advertisement for the health benefits of a successful career and a contented, child-free marriage. He was well over six feet tall, on the thin side, and just recently Club Med-tanned. His face, with its high cheekbones, deep-set dark eyes and sensual mouth, was rescued from extreme handsomeness by an irregular nose. He claimed that a jealous girlfriend had broken it back in his high-school days. Portia once confided to me that he had stepped on a rake.

He greeted me warmly with a brotherly hug, then excused himself to take a quick shower. He returned in a canary yellow cotton sweater and black jeans, somehow managing to look as dignified as he had in his suit. Handing me a Newcastle in a stone mug, he went over to the bar to mix himself a martini and pour a glass of Harvey's Bristol Cream for Portia. For the thousandth time, I refrained from asking her how she stomached the potion.

"So, Lennie, how's tricks?" I asked.

"Getting trickier every day, Jane. Thanks to the Bre-X Minerals fiasco, the market's fluctuating almost as badly as it did during the Gulf War. Some days I feel like I'm tossing darts at a moving target." He paused to sip his cocktail.

"You're too modest. I bet your clients are still profiting handsomely from your darts," I chuckled. Lennie was one of the best investment counsellors in the country. He anticipated tremors on the financial Richter scale well before any quakes struck. His colleagues nicknamed him the Nostradamus of Bay Street.

He was squinting at me, Clint Eastwood-style, over the lip of his martini glass. "I've got a hunch you're here to talk murder, not the economy. Portia told me about your new assignment."

"You're right, and first I'd like to ask you a question — and I want a totally honest answer," I urged.

"I always give you totally honest answers, Jane, because I know you always listen carefully, then do precisely what your obstinate heart dictated in the first place!"

I pulled on my Newcastle and regarded him with mock anger. "You wanna know the most appalling aspect of friendships that go back as long as ours, Lennie? You can always count on your friends to cut straight through the bullshit."

He grinned. "If the bullshit industry drew upon you as its

primary resource base, Ms. Yeats, I wouldn't invest a cent in it. So what's your big question?"

"Do you think I've got a snowball's chance in Barbados of figuring out who killed Durand?"

"Yes, I do, if brains and persistence and Celtic cunning are called for. But what I don't know, old friend, is if you'll *survive* your enquiry. Do you really know what's at stake in this whole mess?" He set down his empty glass on the mahogany coffee table and looked at me with enough solicitude to melt my chilliest defences.

"No, not really. Lennie, I feel so far out of my element. I mean, these days my life revolves around my studio, the Internet and Etta's bar. My brief sniff of the refined air of corporate Toronto and Swindon Path has left me gasping for lower altitudes."

Like one of Max's fleas to my arteries, Lennie honed right in on target. "Why, then, for Christ's sake, are you doing this?"

"When my friend Silver asked me the same question, I said 'curiosity.' She made short work of that answer, which provoked me to flounder around in my psyche for the real reason. What I've come up with isn't particularly palatable. Setting aside for the moment the profit motive, Lennie, I think I'm doing it out of revenge."

He shook his head. "Revenge for what?"

"Deep down, I think there's a strong possibility that someone in very high places murdered Durand, and my vindictive heart aches to bring him down, maybe as a sop to my political anger."

Lennie studied my face. "Or maybe as a sop to your *personal* outrage?"

He was lucky he phrased that probe as a question. I felt my blood pressure surge anyway. "What the hell does *my* motive matter, as long as the murderer is brought to trial?"

Lennie wasn't easily intimidated. "If you're setting yourself up as a detective — and a target — you'd better stop discounting the importance of motives."

I backed down. "I'm sorry I bristled, Lennie. I don't want to fight."

"And I don't want to attend your wake, love, much as I enjoyed your dad's! And you intend to go ahead with this anyway — no matter what your friends counsel, right?"

"You've got it."

"Okay. Your guts tell you that someone in Durand's business life may have killed him. I don't know much about his private life, but if he enjoyed the same popularity on that front as he did in the corporate world, your search might nudge my candidates out of place and end up right in his own backyard."

"Toss me a few names. Who, that you know of, might have had sufficient reason to wish him dead?"

Lennie got up to refresh his martini. "I didn't know the man socially — who did? But I do have some inside poop on some of his business deals. A few of the biggest shake-ups in Canadian stock-exchange history emanated from him. Off the top, two names come to mind for your enemies list: his first partner, Jean-Luc Hébert and, of course, GOD."

"God," I shrieked, "surely Durand wasn't that big a threat to the planet?"

Lennie laughed. "GOD is what we call Gerald Dawson, behind his well-upholstered back, need I say. His middle name is Oliver," he explained.

"Can we start with Hébert and work up to GOD?"

"Sure. You couldn't find two personalities more unlike than Hébert and Durand — except that they shared similar class and ethnic backgrounds. Only Hébert thought that their backgrounds would act like Crazy Glue in their merger. Hébert grew up a poor francophone in Thunder Bay at the same time Durand was growing up even poorer in Noranda. Their paths didn't cross until the early '70s. By then Hébert was sitting at the top of Shield Corporation; he had acquired control of some of the most important resource, transportation and manufacturing bases in the country. He was beginning to move the corporation into property and development. He needed real-estate expertise and he knew where to go to get it."

I added, "Straight to Durand's door."

"Exactly. At the outset, it looked like a marriage forged in corporate heaven. When Hébert came knocking, Durand had a huge asset base and suburban land bank, but he couldn't continue to grow at the cancerous rate he wanted to without a large infusion of capital. So Durand needed the cash pool Hébert could provide; Hébert needed his property smarts. In 1973 Hébert bought controlling interest in Durand Corp. The terms of the merger dictated that all of Hébert's realty assets were exchanged with Durand for shares in Durand Corp. After purchasing other shares from the Corp., and acquiring still more on the open market, Hébert wound up with fifty-three per cent of the voting shares. In short, the deal gave control of Durand Corp. to Hébert."

I was puzzled. "But Durand was a total control freak. Why would he have agreed to such a deal, Lennie?"

"True, Durand was a control freak. You've been doing your homework. But he thought that having the Hébert name behind the corporation would open doors to more cash and ultimately more control. As it turned out, he was mistaken. He expected to get his financing from Hébert's subsidiaries at preferential rates, but wound up discovering that he was in a worse situation when it came to acquiring financing — and he'd lost control of his corporation in the bargain!"

"I don't get it."

Lennie explained. "Shield Corp. had always set strict legal limits on inter-corporate dealings that prohibited major internal financing or cross-guaranteeing of loans to other subsidiaries or divisions."

"But isn't that they very sort of thing that Durand's lawyers would have sniffed out prior to Durand signing the deal?"

"In the normal run of events, yes. But think back to another of Durand's character quirks, Jane. He often ignored the good advice of the people around him whom he paid dearly to advise him. In fact, that's the very reason he lost his two top CEOS just before he was forced into declaring bankruptcy."

"Perhaps that was his tragic flaw as a mogul, Lennie — he couldn't admit that his brilliance wasn't the same thing as omniscience, that other people might know something he didn't."

"You've put your finger on the root of his paranoia. The man could never bring himself to trust anyone but himself. He was a lone wolf on the scene. Ultimately that was his undoing."

"Based on what you've told me so far, Durand had more reason to hate Hébert than vice versa."

Lennie nodded. "That seems even more apparent when you look at the outcome of their partnership. Two years later, after some fancy financing with Swiss bankers, Durand managed to buy back his own company. Hébert walked away with a net profit of more than six million dollars. Durand only succeeded in regaining control of his own firm at an enormous cost in money and ego."

"I still don't get it. Hébert didn't get burned — in fact, he came out the winner. So why should he carry a grudge against Durand?"

"This is where psychology comes into the picture, Jane." I glanced at Portia, who smiled at me sweetly, but had the grace not to utter an "I told you so." Lennie continued, "Apparently Hébert needed a partner more than he needed expertise. Because they shared similar backgrounds, they were both outsiders — so Hébert thought he had a comrade in Durand. *Mon semblable, mon frère.* Life is lonely on the periphery. When Durand sheared the corporate umbilical, he negotiated the whole severance through his lawyers, without once meeting face to face with Hébert. He just cut his losses and scurried back down his rabbit hole. He had no instinct for friendship: the only alliances he ever forged were marriages of temporary convenience."

"Lennie, that all happened over twenty years ago. Is there any reason to think that Hébert still hadn't buried the hatchet?"

Lennie nodded emphatically. "Yes, there is. Years later he

briefly joined forces with GOD — an unholy alliance if ever there was one — to block Durand's Imperial Trust bid. And the Bay Street grapevine buzz has it that Hébert moved in behind the scenes to help screw up Durand's recent efforts at refinancing."

Something still didn't compute. "Surely that's how these men get even with one another, by screwing up deals, attacking one another where it hurts — in the bonds? But murder? I mean, why bother? Surely you're as good as dead in that world when your corporation has gone belly up?"

It was Portia's turn to enlighten me. "Jane, old buddy, am I detecting an unbecoming whiff of élitism in your bewilderment? You don't honestly think that the ruling class is exempt from the nasty motives reputed to drive the masses to murder their enemies?"

There was a scorpion's tail of truth in her teasing. She salved my humiliation by fetching another pint of Newcastle.

"Okay," I conceded. "Hébert is now on my list. But GOD — surely even you two sorcerers can't stretch my credulity that far." I paused for refreshment. "What do you know about the Imperial Trust bid I don't?"

Portia said, "Probably at least enough to persuade you to add GOD to your roster." She turned to her husband. "Lennie, the floor is yours. Excuse me, I'm going to prepare something for us to eat. Any more booze sloshing around on empty stomachs and we'll be comatose."

Just as Portia rose from her chair, the answering machine woke up. The caller's voice was unmistakable. "Portia? Lennie? It's Etta Yeats. If you're home, PLEASE PICK UP THE PHONE. Is my Jane there? THIS IS AN EMERGENCY!"

My neck hairs bristled, but only moderately. Although Mom's voice vibrated urgency, I can't remember when it didn't. Her most recent emergency occurred one night last month, when the lights and the electric guitars at Sweet Dreams went into cardiac arrest during an ice storm.

Nonetheless, I bounded to the phone before Portia could

reach it. Good friends deserve my protection. "Mom, it's me. What's happening?"

"This is your mother speaking," she said.

"Yes, Mom, I know that. This is me speaking — not a machine."

"So how can you tell these days?" she asked indignantly. "I need you at the bar. Like fifteen minutes ago."

Etta never apologizes for interrupting me at anything. She feels entitled to my attention, whenever, wherever. The last time I was foolish enough to complain about this, she volleyed "I wouldn't interrupt if I thought you was in bed with a man. But fat chance of that, eh?"

"Is it something that can wait an hour or two? I'm in the middle of an important conversation."

"Sure it can wait — if a daughter doesn't care that her mother will be drowned or electrocuted by the time she gets here." Etta rarely leaves me with anything that could be mistaken for an option.

I firmed up my tone of voice. "Mom, has the toilet in the ladies' backed up again?"

"I'm up to my goddamn knees in —"

I hastily interrupted. Compared to Etta, I'm a paragon of decorum. "I'm on my way."

She slammed down the phone without thanking me. "Goodbye, Mom. You're welcome," I muttered into the dead line.

"Etta just reshuffled my priorities, folks. I'm sorry. She desperately needs me to fix the toilet."

My friends burst out laughing. They know Etta.

I thanked them both for their help. "It beats work," Portia said.

"Hey, for me it is work," I reminded her.

"No problem, Jane," Lennie assured me good-humouredly. "We can pick up the threads in a day or two. Listen, a guy at my firm worked for GOD when Durand made his bid for Imperial Trust. He knows a lot more than I do about the behind-the-scenes moves — and he owes me a favour. Why don't I set up a lunch date for the three of us for, say, early next week?"

"Lennie, that would be terrific," I agreed appreciatively.

I hugged them both goodbye. The elevator let me off at the lobby. I passed by the doorman, whose practised eye dismissed me as a down-at-the-heels hooker. Hell, maybe he's a Bi-Way shopper too.

I grabbed the first cab that came along Avenue Road.

CHAPTER 8

I N A FEW SHORT hours I had descended from Swindon Path to Etta's basement washrooms.

Five minutes earlier the cab had delivered me to Sweet Dreams. I could say that the exterior of the joint isn't promising, but that might mislead someone into thinking that the interior is. Shortly after my father's death, Etta bought this two-storey barn on the Danforth just east of Broadview with the proceeds from his insurance policy. The outside was, well, unpretentious: pollution-stained red brick with four main-floor glass-block windows set well above pedestrian viewing height — in accordance with the liquor laws which once decreed that drinkers should neither be seen nor heard practising their sinful craft in the province of Ontario.

"Your grandfather always said, may his soul roast in hell, that people were better off during Prohibition: booze was cheaper, easier to get and more fun to drink," Etta once told me. "Now Prohibition's one crime they can't blame the Irish for," she added, "it was those bloody Methodists." Mother likes to keep the family oral tradition alive.

Above the entrance a large hot pink neon sign flickered SWEET DREAMS. The stem of the "T" in "SWEET" was capped with a Stetson. On the west side of the bar was a drug store with two display cases in the front window. One held a winsome selection of trusses; the other, large detailed drawings of house pests, from ants through roaches. A Greek restaurant, The Last Temptation, occupied the other side. Etta blamed its *dolmádes* and *mousaká* for having driven hordes of worthy Greek immigrants back home or to the Burger King. I blamed the *ouzo* which Nikos, the proprietor, claimed was homemade. I believed him.

As soon as I entered the bar, I knew that Mother wouldn't be easily mollified: Dolly Parton was tremulously warbling "It's my coat of many colours that my Momma made for me" out of the speakers. That was no coincidence. One of Etta's many unendearing traits is to let country classics convey her plaintive themes when fury renders her the closest thing to inarticulate she'll ever get. For sure she was playing this one deliberately, to guilt-trip me for filial ingratitude, for not being on the spot when the toilet overflowed.

She was nowhere in sight, so instead of looking for her I sat down at the bar out of sheer petulance and asked Kenny-the-bartender for a coffee. He could tell I was in no mood for conversation. Tonight the place depressed me. Etta had decorated it like her notion of Miss Kitty's Long Branch saloon. The walls were panelled in authentically wormy barn wood, plastered over with posters and album covers featuring country music stars, most of them autographed in real ink. Etta is something of a scholar-archivist in her field. If universities offered courses in Country, she'd be a Professor Emeritus. She even has photos of the Dixie Clodhoppers and the Fruit Jar Drinkers. The room was dimly illuminated by wagon-wheel light fixtures. A variety of beat-up instruments — an autoharp, guitars, banjos and fiddles — hung from the walls. A huge ten-gallon hat, which Etta claimed to have been taken straight off Hank Williams dear dead head, resided in a Plexiglas display case set into the mirror-tiled wall behind the bar. The wall facing the bar Etta had christened the Girl Warblers Gallery: they were all there to greet you — from Mother Maybelle Carter to Shania Twain. Last year we had a big fight when she refused to hang my k.d. lang poster on the grounds that the vegetarian renegade only sang country music so she could poke fun at it and anyways she looked like a he and furthermore could no more imitate Patsy Cline than I could do an impression of a lady. That's when I stormed out, when she got to the lady bit.

The tables and chairs were '50s chrome, Formica and padded plastic. Etta refused to update or renovate. "What goes around, comes around," she claims. "Furniture's like dresses — hang onto them long enough and they're back in style."

She has a point. Even if she doesn't, her customers aren't the sort to give a damn. Boomer shifting tastes in quiche, sushi, tapas, salsa, arugula — all had passed them by.

Only the sawdust was missing and Etta would still be strewing that authenticating touch about every day if her cleaning lady hadn't threatened to quit over it. "Most people pay me to sweep stuff like that offa the floor," she had told Etta. "It goes or me." Etta reluctantly gave it up. "The woman's culturally deprived," she explained. "Grew up in Portugal where they never heard of Johnny Cash." I wondered how they survive.

Although the evening was still early, the bar was packed. Sweet Dreams is home-away-from-home for most of Etta's regulars. They hang out for the music and the closest thing to down East camaraderie you can find west of New Brunswick. Some were born here in Toronto — the older ones in Depression Cabbagetown, the younger in places like Regent Park. Others came from rural Ontario, where they grew up listening to country on the airwaves. Some had come here from the Maritimes, thinking they'd get better jobs in Toronto. Most of them were disappointed, and gladly would have returned to Corner Brook, Sydney, Glace Bay, Charlottetown, Yarmouth, Lunenburg, Truro, Moncton, Halifax or St. John's — if things weren't even worse back home. All her regulars are united by a genuine love for country music and their need to share broken hearts and shattered dreams with fellow-sufferers over a few cheap drafts. On weekend nights, when Sweet Dreams hosts local country singers and bands, a younger crowd swells their ranks.

Etta knows these people like she knows her music. A lot of folks love my mom, even depend upon her ever-cheeky defiance of the ravages of time and fortune to bolster their own hopes.

Hell, I love her too. It's her exorbitant demands that drive me nuts. She wouldn't dream of laying them on anybody else but me. "What's a daughter for?" she asks, whenever I show offence, rushing in to answer her own rhetorical question, in case I missed the point.

"Why the hell didn't you come straight down to the basement as soon as you got here?"

I swung around on my bar stool as Etta the Hun approached. She looks like a geriatric, scaled-down version of Dolly Parton. She's short, only slightly over five feet, slender and stacked. Unlike Dolly, the blonde hair is real — not the colour, but not a wig either. She piles it very tall on top, considerably compensating for her lack of height. Curls cascade wantonly over her bony shoulders. She wears blue, sometimes violet eyeshadow and lots of mascara. Lips fit to make Betty Boop eat her heart out. Her stubby fingers terminate in long scarlet nails that she regularly strips and relacquers. Mondays through Thursdays she wears satin shirts, stretch jeans and tooled cowboy boots. Fridays and Saturdays are dresses and high heels. Every day is a party — except when the plumbing fails.

No one could claim that Etta has aged graciously. She has defied age with granite-hard resilience. She steadfastly believes God put her here to have fun and she is true to her mission.

"Mom, why are you so bitchy tonight? It's not like you," I added, only half-lying.

"I'm bitchy because my toilet's broke and I got a bar full of customers with full bladders," she replied, reasonably enough if you ignore the fact that men empty their bladders into urinals. She sat down next to me. "Kenny, I'll have a Shirley Temple, straight up." Kenny obliged her with a glass full of non-alcoholic pink froth punctuated by a maraschino cherry impaled on a red swizzle stick shaped like a ukulele.

Etta delicately sucked an inch of froth up the plastic straw. "You're right, love, I am bitchier than usual. Just before I called you, Slim ran out without saying a word. He'd been looking a bit green around the gills from celebrating our return and he went downstairs to the can. Then he just ran out."

She looked at me, worried. "Do you think he's chasing some skirt?"

My compassion for her possible abandonment got considerably diminished by my recall of the legion of lovesick ex-suitors she's created without a pang of remorse. I finished my coffee. "Hey Etta, chill out. What man in his right mind would go looking for another woman when he had you on his arm?" *Any man in his right mind.*

That cheered her up. "You've got a point. Anyways, right after he takes off the damn toilet backs up. Can you take a look?"

"Sure." Clutching the keys to the store room, where she kept some plumbing tools and a pair of rubber boots, I dutifully headed for the basement.

Downstairs I hauled on my boots, grabbed the plunger and a closet snake. I turned into the narrow corridor the washrooms open onto. The men's door is labelled ROY, the ladies' DALE. After a few beers, customers used to get confused about which door to enter. I suggested that Etta put photographs of the famous pair under their names: no one could ever mistake the King of the Cowboys for a girl (although Ms. Evans sure as campfire beans looks to me like she's in drag).

I entered ROY. After repeated unsuccessful plunges, I gave up on the plumber's friend. I pushed the closet snake down into the outflow opening until it hit the clog. It felt solid. The snake couldn't work its way through to whatever was blocking the toilet.

I shouted up the stairs. "Mom, will you toss down a wire coat hanger?" I straightened out the hanger, narrowed the hook at the end. Two minutes later I had managed to fish out the obstruction — a pair of false teeth. I poured a bucket of water into the bowl to make sure the drain was clear.

After thoroughly scrubbing my hands and the cause of the clog, I changed back into my shoes and returned upstairs.

I sat down on the stool next to Etta's and placed the offending choppers on the bar counter.

By the time Etta stopped laughing two minutes later, a small crowd had gathered around us. Mauve rivulets streamed down mother's creased cheeks. "And here I was thinking he snuck off without saying goodbye because he was mad at me, or heading off to meet another broad," she shrieked.

"Mom, I don't get it."

"Don't you see, he must have chucked up his teeth along with all the beers he drank. I told you he looked green around the gills."

A voice directly behind my right shoulder inquired, "Do you want to turn those into Missing Persons, ma'am?"

I swung around to face Ernie Sivcoski. The crowd around us quickly returned to their chairs. Why do Toronto plain-clothes cops always look more like cops than the guys in uniform?

Etta's hand moved faster than a lizard's tongue to grab Slim's teeth. She got up, grabbed a rag and found a spot to wipe off the stainless steel sink behind the counter.

When I patted the stool next to mine, Ernie shook his head. "Can we find a table in the corner?" He nodded toward the rear wall of the room. "I need to talk to you in private, Jane."

Etta threw him a murderous glance that could pierce a bullet-proof vest. She hates being out of earshot.

After drawing a pint of draft Blue for Ernie, I led him to a back table. Etta put Johnny Cash's "Folsom Prison Blues" on the tape deck.

Ernie took a swig of his draft and remarked, "You look tired as hell."

I briefly considered commenting that he looked like he shopped for clothes with Lieutenant Columbo. I must be weary: I was getting oversensitive. So instead I admitted, "Yeah, I am. I wish I could say I had fun getting this whacked-out. How's the Durand investigation going?"

He made short work of my attempt. "Perhaps I should be asking you the same question, Jane."

I took a breath and said, perhaps too quickly, "Hey, you're the cop. I'm only a writer."

He grinned. "Perhaps in your case, the distinction gets blurred."

I got impatient. So far my day had included a funeral, a pseudo-wake, an interrupted meeting with old friends and a toilet blockage. "Ernie, it's been a long, long day. And we know each other well enough not to fuck around with word-games. What are you saying?"

"Rumour has it that you were at the Durand funeral this morning — and part of the élite group that met afterwards back at the deceased's for Scotch and sympathy."

"So what, Ernie? I told you on the phone yesterday that I've been commissioned to write the man's biography. Naturally it follows that I needed to be there to pick up on the vibes, schmooze for interviews." I sounded too defensive.

Ernie is no fool. "How long have you been working on this project? And who hired you?" he parried.

For a few moments I toyed with a variety of misleading responses, then looked directly at him. "Since Sunday morning. Simone Goldberg."

Ernie choked on his beer. "Why did you tell me that?"

"Because you're a smart man and would have figured it out soon enough anyway. Because we have a personal history — and that should mean something. Because you know if you blow my cover, you might risk my bones. And because you're honourable enough to recognize that in return I expect you to feed me with as much inside dope from the cop shop as you feel comfortable spilling. We both respect our sources, Ernie, especially when the source is one another," I said, with only a hint of pleading for confirmation.

He set his mug back on the table. "Okay — and thanks for your honesty. We won't have the forensics report for a couple of days, of course. But I've checked out that book of matches I told you about."

I couldn't resist interrupting. "Let me guess: it came from

Leather Boys." Etta always tells me I was born smart-ass.

Ernie was nonplussed. "How the hell do you know that?"

"With contacts like mine, who needs a crystal ball?" I answered smugly. "My grapevine has it that William Durand was a member in good standing of Ashley MacIsaac's fraternity. Toronto is still a small town, Ernie — especially when it comes down to its sub-cultures. It didn't take a lot of work to ferret out where he hangs."

He nodded. "Yeah, well I went to Leather Boys last night. William was there and that turned out to be a good thing, given that nobody in the joint would talk to me."

"So all you've got at this point is a book of matches from the scene of the crime that tells you that William was probably in his father's office on or about the day he was murdered," I said.

"And a son with a list of legitimate grievances against the deceased long enough to drive a saint to homicide," Ernie added. "Anyway, I got nowhere at Leather Boys. When I tried to question William, he told me to fuck off. At that point I didn't have any authority to bring him in."

I tried to keep my voice matter-of-fact. "So what do you want from me, Ernie?"

"I need to know where to look for William. This morning orders came down from the brass to question him after the wake. We sent two officers up to Swindon Path late this afternoon, but he was gone before they got there," he explained. "The current Mrs. Durand couldn't or wouldn't suggest where he might have taken off to. Under pressure from the boys, one of their staff, who has a record, told us about William mutilating the painting of his father."

"I witnessed the mutilation. But I don't have a clue about where he is now, Ernie," I said. "I haven't even had a chance to talk with him yet. And the little bit I do know about him comes from reading the papers."

Ernie leaned forward. "Will you let me know if you do find out?" he asked, sounding more supplicant than I'm sure he intended.

"Give me a break. You don't want to haul him in just for questioning, do you?" I asked sharply. "You think he murdered the old man."

Ernie was quiet for a minute. "Until we question him, until Forensics brings in their report, I don't know what to think. But he is our hottest suspect."

I hit my fist on the table. "He's your *only* fucking suspect, Ernie. You guys haven't had time to do a decent investigation."

"But you can see the attraction: make a quick arrest of the enraged queer son, against whom we've got motive and circumstantial evidence, and avoid having to cast our net into the corridors of power. Keeps everyone happy." He looked at me cynically.

"Yeah," I snapped back angrily, cheeks flushing. "Except anyone who cares about William."

"At this point he's all we've got. And there are other reasons — which I can't go into at the moment — for suspecting him," he protested.

"Look, Ernie: we both know that I'll be looking for him, too. If I find him — and my chances are at least as good as yours, given how the gay community regards the police force — I'll let you know, but *only* if I think he's guilty. And my concept of guilt is pretty elastic. It stretches well beyond your precinct walls."

Ernie turned up his hands in a gesture of resigned acceptance. "Fair enough." From past experience, he knows that when I'm pushed too far, I become downright obstreperous. As he stood up he asked, "By the way, do you *really* intend to write Durand's biography?"

"I honestly don't know. He's certainly the most compelling subject I've come up against, especially since his premature departure. But I don't really feel like taking on another book right now, Ernie — not even sure I could write one. I think I need a career change. Hell, on bad mornings I think I need a new life."

He grinned ruefully. "I know what you mean, Jane. We're

agreed to keep each other posted then?"

I nodded.

"Take good care, lady."

I watched Ernie thread his way through the crowded room to the front door. As he passed each table, the occupants turned away as if to avoid a bad smell. I don't envy cops.

Kenny-the-bartender raised his eyebrows, astute as a country auctioneer. I shook my head. "No thanks, Kenny. My system couldn't stand another drink. I'm wiped." I slipped on my coat. "Please tell Etta I said goodbye — and that she's welcome for the free toilet repair."

He laughed and set a polished glass on the bar. "You want me to call upstairs?" Etta lived on the second floor. "She took off with them teeth just after you sat down with Ernie."

"No. She's probably on the blower with Slim, negotiating the return of his missing property."

I took the Bloor West subway home, feeling even lonelier than usual. When I opened the studio door, Max bounded toward me like we'd been separated since the Ark.

I dropped to my knees and rested my face against his. "Hi guy."

I needed a walk at that time of night as much as the Pope needs another dress. But Max's bladder has its own imperatives. So I put him on the leash and briskly trotted us around the block, promising him a long run in the park tomorrow morning.

The phone was ringing when we returned home. Pavlovian, I unthinkingly picked it up.

A female voice inquired, "Hello. Is that Jane Yeats?"

"Yes."

My midnight caller at least had the smarts to immediately identify herself. "This is Helen Durand." My ears pricked up.

"I'm sorry to trouble you this late at night, but I've been calling for hours." She sounded more vexed than contrite. I glanced down at the red light on my answering machine. It was blinking ten calls.

When I didn't reply, she went on. "Could we possibly get together tomorrow — I'm returning to Noranda in the early evening."

I gently shoved Max from my side. He takes nosy lessons from Etta. "Why do you want to talk to me?" That was rude and abrupt. Fatigue had obliterated my manners.

Her voice turned coy. "I have reason to think that we could be useful to one another. Simone told me that you are writing a book about my ex-husband. I can tell you things about him nobody else knows."

Already I'd mentally snapped at her bait, but curiosity drove me to query: "And how can I be useful to you, Mrs. Durand?"

The ensuing pause lasted long enough to make me wonder if she had passed out. "I just want that book of yours to tell the truth about the bastard," she finally responded.

"So do I," I said. "Let's set a time and place."

"Would four o'clock in the Lobby Bar suit you? I'm staying at the Four Seasons. My package includes afternoon tea for two." She sounded like an upscale Etta with bucks to burn.

"I'll be there." I hung up the phone and began pulling off my clothes, dropping them on the floor en route to my futon.

As I hit the bed, an unwelcome shaft of memory pierced my exhausted brain. Just two years ago, my trails of discarded clothes were partnered by Pete's as we raced into love-making.

I fell asleep crying.

CHAPTER 9

TEN HOURS SLEEP knitted up my "ravell'd sleave of care." Just before eleven on Wednesday morning, I woke up to sunlight breaking itself into Cubist patterns through my besmirched window panes. I showered, then enjoyed brunch with Max. Afterwards we went for the long run through High Park I'd promised him.

I passed the few hours remaining before my meeting with Helen Durand reading a biography of Elizabeth Smart, with some Mozart playing in the background. Since Simone parachuted into my life four days earlier, I had enjoyed too little of the solitude I need to get my head into a passable imitation of working order. My weeping fit last night was sound proof of that. Whenever I overdose on people, I have to slow down long enough to let my hyperactive neurons disentangle themselves.

Shortly after three I got dressed. My impending tea-for-two assignation at the Four Seasons was putting a real strain on my wardrobe, to the point that I wondered if Simone's expense account could be stretched to include refurbishing my threads. When I left the studio I looked passable in an out-of-season linen skirt and daintily flowered rayon blouse.

The Four Seasons, which describes itself as "elegant without pretension," is situated on Avenue Road just north of Cumberland. Smack in the heart of Yorkville, Toronto's Haight-Ashbury during the late '60s, now a fashionable shopping district.

As soon as I entered the Lobby Bar, I recognized the thin, grey-haired woman who had occupied the pew next to her son,

William, at the Cathedral yesterday morning, now seated at a table with two high-back chairs.

She began to rise to greet me, then must have decided in mid-execution that only gentlemen perform such gallantries. In the process of hastily reseating herself, she managed to knock a pack of Cameos from the edge of the table. Because she next got suspended in mid-air between picking them up and introducing herself, I swiftly extended my hand and said, "I'm Jane Yeats."

When her icy hand clasped mine, I figured she must have circulation problems. The *maitre d'* discreetly retrieved the wayward cigarette pack and returned it to the table.

Helen Durand had received an enormous divorce settlement from her ex-husband after he left her twenty years ago. Judging from her appearance, she invested very little of it in maintaining or rejuvenating herself. She was fine-boned, gaunt as an anorexic. Sparse grey hair clung only slightly to the aftermath of a bad perm. The lines of her face seemed terminally set in a vexed, defeated mask. Her scrawny frame was draped in an expensive pearl-grey wool suit that drained what colour remained in her face. She reminded me of the aged Duchess of Windsor. Even her body language screamed shattered expectations.

Upon seating myself, I immediately decided against lighting up. She was emitting toxic clouds sufficiently dense to make even me faintly nauseated.

She told me that she had already ordered some "things" to eat. When the waiter asked me my preference in tea, I was momentarily struck dumb. Once, years ago, I had tasted the swill and found it wanting in body. "The Earl Grey is very nice, madam."

Helen stubbed her cigarette into a cut-glass ashtray and immediately lit another. I resolved to quit the filthy habit once and for all time — more for the way it so nakedly reveals one's neuroses than for health reasons.

She looked at me with glacial blue eyes quite bereft of light. "Thank you for coming. I told you last night on the phone why I wanted to talk to you. Why don't you ask me some questions?"

Already I was feeling the restraints my biographer cover story imposed. What I really wanted to ask her was *Who do you think murdered your ex-husband? Was it you?* Instead I settled for "Perhaps you can tell me something about how you met Charles, what your life with him was like, what kind of man he was?"

She looked perplexed. "Where should I begin?" Alice-in-not-so-Wonderland needed narrative direction.

"Why don't you begin at the beginning and go on 'til you come to the end." I resisted adding "then stop."

When she began to talk, an interesting linguistic change slipped into play: she reverted to locutions much more redolent of her roots in rural Quebec. "I met the bastard in school, right? I mean, I knew about his family before then — Noranda was a real small town when we was kids, you know. In high school he was in what they called the tech stream and I was doing commercial — those are fancy terms for where they shoved the kids they figured wasn't going nowhere, right? Anyways, after it was obvious that Charles was interested in me —"

She paused as if to recollect something, ran a blue-veined hand through her thin hair. "You might not believe it to look at me now, but back then I was real cute and sexy as hell. And I was dumb enough to think that he was a big catch. Not that Charles was ever what you might call popular: he was always a loner. He didn't get good grades, but you could tell he was smarter than the other boys. He was handsome, too. But he didn't do none of the stuff the other guys was into, if you don't count hockey. Didn't smoke or drink, didn't date hardly at all, never hung around the pool hall. Just showed up every morning at school, sat through the whole day like he was watching some boring movie, and went home soon as the bell rang. He always looked like he was thinking about being somewheres else, like none of us was good enough for him. That put the other kids off, right?"

Whenever people append "right?" to the end of a sentence, I'm never sure whether they're soliciting confirmation or being rhetorical, so I don't respond. Her pause grew more pregnant.

The waiter arrived with our tea, elegantly brewing in a silver tea service with individual strainers. The porcelain cups were so fine you could spit through them. At this point in the ritual, Etta would have been paralyzed with anxiety about what to do next. Mine is a different generation. In order to figure out the protocol I simply imitated Helen's moves, except when she dumped a lot of sugar and cream into her cup; I took mine straight up. Hard on the heels of the tea, another waiter appeared with a trolley of dainty savouries fanned out on a flourish of doilied plates. He set down a plate of crustless white bread squares variously and lightly enhanced by smoked salmon, prosciutto with tomato and basil, cucumber, watercress and English Cheddar. A linen-covered basket of warm currant scones with British clotted cream, tiny pots of Fortnum and Mason jams.

Helen lit up another menthol cigarette while I helped myself to a scone, dabbed onto it some cream and raspberry jam.

"Please go on," I prompted my nervous companion.

"We dated for a few months before I got pregnant. It wasn't his fault, eh? Charles never was one for sex, if you know what I mean."

I did: lately I've been suspecting that I've lapsed into the same category.

"Even after we got married he only did it when I reminded him to, like I was his mother telling him to brush his teeth or something. And when he did do it, his mind was always somewheres else — probably planning another move, you know, the next deal." Her thin lips wrinkled around the cigarette again. "You know something — in more than twenty years of marriage, I can't remember him once touching me except when we had sex — nothing just affectionate, you know."

She still hadn't eaten a thing. When I gestured to the

sandwich plate, she reluctantly helped herself to a sliver of cucumber on a piece of crustless bread only slightly larger than a loonie. I helped myself to an eclectic selection of minuscule offerings. My stomach yearned for something as substantial as Irish stew or a Ploughman's lunch — peasant fare that sticks to your ribs.

For a few moments Helen picked at her food, quickly abandoning her foraging to light up another cigarette. Not once had she asked me if I minded her smoking while I ate.

"Like I was saying," she resumed, "I got pregnant. I figured it wasn't Charles's kid — after all, I'd been doing it a lot more with other guys, but he was the only one dumb enough to want to marry me. And now that I think of it, that was so typical of him. He just assumed from the start that it was him who got me knocked up. I mean, if anything was ever happening around him, he always assumed he must have started it."

I looked up at her. "Did you want to marry him, Helen?"

"Huh — you think a girl had any choice back then? I mean, abortion was out of the question, unless you wanted to take your chances on doing it yourself with a knitting needle or bleeding to death in some old broad's back room. Anyways, we was Catholics. And my old man didn't even have to lean on Charles to make him marry me. Charles just went through with it like it was the only thing to do."

I couldn't resist probing her concrete defences. "Were you and Charles in love?"

She laughed bitterly. "You must have heard that Tina Turner song — 'What's Love Got To Do With It?' Yeah, I loved him. But as for Charles, he never knew the meaning of a word that didn't spell 'power.' We never had anything you could call a family life, not even after William was born. Charles was always too busy figuring out his next move. I'm not saying that he wasn't a hard worker right from the start, that he didn't provide for us proper. It's just that he was hardly ever around and even when he was home, he was somewheres else, if you know what I mean."

I nodded my head. "I know what you mean. My old man was like that."

My admission seemed to fortify her resolve to get on with her pathetic life-narrative.

"Anyways, we got married in the spring that year. Charles got thrown out of school, so his older brother got him a job as an apprentice machinist at Canco — you know, the big mining and smelting company. At the beginning he was earning three bucks a day. He quit when Pierre — that was his brother — got killed in an accident underground."

"Was he close to Pierre?" I asked.

"Yeah, real close. Come to think of it, I guess Pierre was the first and last person he ever got close to. He had a younger sister. You probably seen her at the funeral — the one whose daughter fainted. But Pierre was the one he adored. Charles never got over him dying and he was always saying the accident never had to happen, that it was the mine bosses' fault for taking shortcuts on safety. He got real bitter after that and even more clammed up, like he couldn't trust nobody. After he quit Canco he moved us to Toronto, eh? He got a job in construction. We were renting a real small apartment with only one bedroom, so he bought a lot and started building us a house in his spare time. I got so excited: it was a nice brick bungalow with three bedrooms and a real big backyard. But before we even had a chance to move in, he sold the goddamn place. Somebody offered him three thousand dollars more than it cost him to build it. When I complained, he told me it was the fastest money he ever made and he said that it gave him an idea that would make us rich. He was going to use the profit to buy up some farmland and become his own boss. So he wound up building a fifty-house subdivision on that land. After he'd sold all those houses, we didn't have to worry about money no more."

At that point in her narrative she paused. In the interlude I helped myself to more mini-goodies. Her next remark suggested that she must have been busy recollecting old grievances.

"We shouldn't have had no big worries after that. I mean, given how me and him grew up, back then I thought that once your money worries was over, it was going to be smooth sailing." She laughed, bitter as Angostura.

Again she lapsed into broody silence. I kick-started her story by asking, "Why wasn't it smooth sailing after that?"

"Because I wanted a family life. Charles just wanted to keep his business growing. He never spent much time with us, and when he was home he wasn't the kind of person you could just relax and do normal family things with. He only had two moods. Either he was up higher than a kite or he was down. There wasn't much to choose between them. When he was high, he'd talk non-stop about his latest scheme, never stopping to check on how me and William was doing, or how any of his plans affected us. When he was in one of his black moods, you couldn't go near him. I used to keep William out of the house as much as I could, because if either one of us tried to get through to him he'd fly off into one of his rages. The bastard might have made his fortune as a developer, but his biggest private property was himself. After all them years of marriage, Charles was a total stranger to me. I never really knew him. By the time he told me he was leaving, I felt like he'd already been gone for years. The only real difference was, he moved out his clothes."

I decided to risk provoking this embittered woman into exposing the deepest roots of her anger, which clearly had lost none of its corrosiveness. I needed to see if she hated Charles Durand enough to want him dead.

"If moving out his clothes was the only real difference his leaving made, why are you still so angry?" I ventured, wishing the teapot were big enough to offer shelter.

"Because that son of a bitch was no builder. He was a destroyer. He didn't just take his clothes away with him, he took me." She jabbed her bony right thumb at her chest. "*My self.*"

I pushed further. "Was there another woman?"

She shook her head like she was trying to dislodge a squirrel, but her perm didn't budge. "No. That's what made it hurt so bloody much. Sure, afterwards he had to get himself another broad — when you're as rich as Charles, wives are part of the scenery. No, it was *me* he wanted to dump. Having me around was like a scar on his face, right? I reminded him of what he needed to forget real bad — where he came from. By the time he walked out on us he was the biggest suburban developer in the whole city. And, as if that wouldn't have been enough for any ordinary man, he was moving into shopping malls and stuff. Even if the people he wanted to impress didn't like him, they still had to stand up and take notice of Charles — and he didn't want them noticing a tar-paper shack outside of Noranda and a wife too dumb to know how to dress and talk right."

If I worry too much about where angels fear to interrogate, I would never leave my studio. "Did you hate him enough to kill him?"

She gave a tight smile. "I hated him enough to be glad he's dead, but not enough to kill him. Hey, I'm not smart enough to pull it off without getting caught. Charles would have told you that much, eh? Anyways, it was enough knowing that he was bleeding to death from where it really hurt — his goddamn empire. Whenever I needed a fix for my hate-Charles habit, all I had to do was pick up the morning papers."

"Can you think of anyone else who might have killed him?"

"If I could, I sure as hell would keep it to myself," she said defiantly. "Whoever killed him should get the Order of Canada, not a prison sentence. Look, I ain't had nothing to do with him since our divorce. In fact, I figure that's why he gave me so much money — so he could ignore me for the rest of our lives."

"Then you don't benefit financially from his death?"

She looked directly across at me. "No, only what you might call spiritually. The divorce settlement left me with a big chunk of dough, enough to live off the interest without hardly touching the principal. It also left me right out of his will. In fact, I signed a paper saying that I wouldn't make any claim on his estate if he croaked before me."

I was quiet for a moment, wondering if she wasn't working overtime to disabuse me of the notion that she might have a motive. "But your son is now in a better position money-wise than he was when his father was alive."

She took a quick breath, only to release it as a hiss. "What the fuck are you suggesting?"

I explained disingenuously, "William's interest in his father's corporation rested entirely in his shares. It's public knowledge that your son has already taken his father to court in an unsuccessful effort to get permission to sell his shares before they're totally worthless. But isn't William also named as a benefactor in his father's will? Doesn't that give him the power he couldn't get from the court — not to mention a huge stash of cash? Charles's empire may have been in decline, but he was still worth a fortune." I didn't even know if William was a benefactor, but a full-frontal attack seemed a good way of finding out.

She looked down at the linen tablecloth, now liberally dusted with cigarette ash. "It's true what you say: William can finally put his hands on a lot of money now that his father is dead. But if you knew my son, I mean *really* knew him the way I do, you'd know what a stupid goddamn suggestion that was. William couldn't hurt a flea. Fact is, he was one of them kids who was so sensitive he used to bring home broken birds for me to fix. I remember taking him for a walk one day just after it rained, when he was about four years old. He cried all the way home because he had stepped on a bloody worm."

"Are you aware that your son is gay?" I asked, daring the knock-out punch.

Her response surprised me. Just as I was preparing myself for vehement denial or sudden death, she calmly replied, "Of course I am. I told you, I *know* my son. It was obvious right from when he was a little boy that William wasn't like other boys. I mean, when all the other kids was playing hockey and dreaming of getting into the NHL — you know Northern towns — William was asking for ballet lessons — *ballet lessons* in Noranda, for Christ's sake! Whenever Charles took any notice of him, it was only to try to make a man of him, but William fought back right from the start, like he knew he was different and he wasn't going to give that up for nothing, not even to please his father."

"Did his father know he was gay?"

"I don't think so. I'm sure William would have told me if Charles had found out because it would have driven the old man even crazier than he already was. I mean, he would have written him out of his will, totally shunned him like he was a leper or something."

As soon as that last sentence was out of her mouth, she closed up, obviously wishing she hadn't said it. From the locked-vault expression on her face, I knew I wouldn't get much further with my interrogation.

I tried one last question, couched in conciliatory words. "As you can imagine, Mrs. Durand, you and your son are the two most important people I need to interview for my book. What you've told me this afternoon will be very helpful to me in depicting your ex-husband's character. Do you know how I can get in touch with William?"

"Like anybody else would, I suppose — at his house. I'll give you his phone number." She leaned down to fetch her handbag.

"I understand that he hasn't been back there since yesterday afternoon, after the gathering at his stepmother's," I said.

"Well," she snapped, clutching her bag to her chest like it held the secret to Eternal Youth, "I don't know where you get your information from, but you might be right. He was supposed to call me this morning to confirm that he was driving me to the airport tonight. He didn't." She added quickly, "Not that it matters. I'll just call the limousine service. I mean, you can see why he'd want to avoid people right now." I could see why he'd want to avoid his mother any time of the year.

She was winnowing through her handbag. "I can't seem to find my address book. But William's listed in the phone book anyways."

"You're right, of course," I said. "This must be a very difficult time for him. Thank you for inviting me to see you. You've been very helpful."

"It was worth it if I've helped you see what a bastard Charles Durand was," she replied. "You know, I only took the trouble to come down here for the funeral because I was hoping to get a last look at him. I figured death might have wiped that smart-ass smirk off his face. But the coffin wasn't open."

"No doubt because the damage to his head was too severe," I gently suggested.

She cackled. "That's what really disappointed me. I'm sorry I didn't see it for myself."

I walked out of the Four Seasons feeling like I'd been dipped in battery acid. Helen Durand's anger was caustic enough to burn anybody within a five-mile radius. I really wished she'd shown me one scrap of dignity, some small shred of self-pride salvaged from the wreckage of her life's dreams. I charitably chose to remember her as a survivor, a woman strong enough to bear witness to her own rage.

I didn't think that she had killed her ex-husband. Yet she'd fight with all the ferocity of a she-bear to protect her son. Even — no, *especially* — if he had murdered his father. Maybe I was mistaken, but gut instinct, a capacity to read character and a good bullshit detector (no doubt inherited from Etta) were all I had to go on.

I had to get to William before the police did. Once he was in their custody he'd be beyond my reach and anybody's protection.

CHAPTER 10

OUTSIDE THE HOTEL I flagged a cab, which dumped me back at my studio just in time to effect a rapid wardrobe change. My high-tea gear gave way to blue jeans, black Harley T-shirt (a gift from my bike mechanic), hockey socks and biker boots. I combed some gel into my hair and spiked it. A glance in the mirror confirmed my image shift. No time to ponder the fault lines in my identity.

As I headed for the door, Max guilt-tripped me with doleful eyes straight out of a velvet painting. He half-forgivingly perked up when I explained my rush to meet Silver for our date at Leather Boys. I offered him a Milk Bone. If there's a canine behavioural equivalent of a gourmand being presented with a burger, he enacted it. When I placed a leftover T-bone on his plate, he promptly absolved my sins of culinary omission. On the way out I pulled on my leather jacket and grabbed an extra motorcycle helmet for Silver.

She was already in the parking lot when I got there, perched like the duchess of all she surveyed in a discarded lawn chair.

"Last night must have been a good date," I guessed.

She nodded her head. "Must have been."

Silver is amazingly agile for an enormous woman. She smoothly distributed her bulk over the passenger seat. We headed off without further conversation.

Without Silver at my side there would have been no point in my venturing into the bar. Well-known and trusted by the gay community, she co-founded a recently organized group of activists called Lesbians and Gays of the First Nations. The other founder is George Potts, who owns Leather Boys. Potts had been a very successful hairdresser prior to his present incarnation. In the Gospel according to St. Silver, only by ignoring braids can you claim that hairdressing is a non-traditional occupation; only by ignoring the history of the *berdache* can you claim that being a gay Indian is unconventional.

I sped through a viciously cold wind from Roncesvalles straight east along Dundas and onto College Street until we reached the infamous rectangle of inner city turf known as "The Track," where prostitutes of every conceivable persuasion collect to cruise and socialize. Most of them live in the vicinity, which is also home to many of Toronto's gay bars. WASP Toronto has finally admitted that it has a thriving sexual marketplace and seems prepared to tolerate what it can ghettoize — and furtively visit when vagrant hormones beckon.

Silver directed me to Leather Boys. We left my bike in the parking lot behind the bar.

"By the way," she mumbled as she swung open the door, "did I tell you tonight's Strip Night — featuring European lap dancing?"

Close to the back entrance two men in Marlon Brando *The Wild One* gear were necking and whatever against the wall. What the hell, I still felt more comfortable here than in the Four Seasons.

The interior of Leather Boys was much like any other downtown singles bar — singularly unappealing unless you're in heat — except for the paucity of women and the clientele's clear preference for leather apparel. Animal skins tailored into hats, vests, jackets, G-strings, studded jocks, chaps, boots (many with spurs). Heavy metal blared through the speakers. Sexual, maybe even emotional, desperation lay thicker than cigarette smoke in the feverish air. Prince Philip-style, I trailed Silver to the bar. Our estrogen-fraught presence didn't seem to excite much notice. The boys were too busily engrossed in seamier distractions. Or maybe they figured we were just part of the furniture. God knows, neither one of us was decked out for a beauty pageant.

The bartender, a sculpted young guy with bleached hair, a chain mail vest and a bulge in his jeans so prominent I thought maybe he should get his jewels straight to a doctor, leaned forward to give Silver a big hug. "You look gorgeous, doll, as usual. What can I get you and your girlfriend?" he asked.

Silver laughed and jerked a thumb in my direction. "Hey man, if this broad was my girlfriend you could get me some hemlock. We'll have a pint of bitter — and a Coke, heavy on the ice. And, Stevie, can you tell George we're here? He's expecting us."

Stevie pirouetted full circle. "Two drinks coming up, dear, and one George." He giggled, flitted off to fetch our drinks, set them in front of us and headed straight for the house phone.

As I took a long sip of my draught and turned around on my bar stool to survey the Bacchanalian scene, the music switched from heavy metal to bump-and-grind. Everyone was looking expectantly at a small stage against the wall where a body-builder was moving into his strip-tease routine. Given what he stepped on stage wearing — only a sheer shirt and a G-string — his act didn't threaten to run overtime. As he slithered out of the shirt, bumping and grinding like he was dead set on mating with a recalcitrant bull moose, Silver muttered in my ear, "That guy's got the most god-awful acne on his back."

I checked out the audience response. Silver was the only one in the room checking out his dermatological challenges. The pouch of his G-string strained so vigorously I thought maybe a small animal was trapped inside. An admirer at the back of the room tossed a leopard-spotted condom on stage. Our star picked it up between his teeth and started doing something with it that made me turn back to my beer with an uncharacteristic blush.

I was rescued from further embarrassment by the arrival of George Potts. After they greeted one another in Mohawk, Silver introduced me. "Jane, this is George. George this is Jane. Tarzan is on stage."

I knew Silver well enough not to anticipate another word on her part. I extended my hand to a tall, lean man in blue jeans and a sweatshirt. A strip of red leather held back his long grey-streaked hair.

As he took my hand, he looked directly into my eyes. "Hi Jane. Silver told me you want to pick my brain."

"Yeah," I said, "and if I know Silver, she also told you why — I mean the *real* reason I'm here." Silver had undoubtedly told him that my biographer cover story was a crock of shit.

George glanced nervously at Silver, who nodded her head. "Don't get mad at Silver," he said. "Our people have lost everything we ever had because of white people lying to us. Finding our way back to the sweet-grass path means that we have to try to be honest in all our relations."

I set my mug on the bar and faced him. "I gotta tell you man, straight up: moralists of any stripe make me reach for the closest mortal sin. But I can handle your script if you also make a habit of keeping necessary secrets. My health depends upon it."

His laugh broke the tension. "Hey," he replied, "I never said I mistook you for a missionary! So let's get down to business. You're here because you want to ask some questions about William Durand, right?"

I nodded. "But more than that: I want to ask *him* some questions."

"The best I can do tonight is to tell you the bit I know about William and to introduce you to his lover, who can tell you a whole lot more."

I was surprised. "His lover is here tonight?"

"Yes. I asked him to stop by after Silver phoned me. He agreed to talk with you."

"Thanks very much, George. Where is he?"

He nodded toward the end of the bar, where a young man who looked seriously out of place was intensely hunched over what appeared to be a glass of orange juice. He was very fair, had a moustache and beard trimmed to Navy precision, and was wearing a dark green leather jacket that was a closer child to an Italian designer than a biker.

"Will he wait a few minutes while we talk?" I asked George.

He nodded. "So shoot — what do you want to know?"

"Anything you think will help me understand William. How long he's been coming here, what he's like when he's here, who he hangs with, how much he drinks, what you think of him ..."

Like Silver, George was a word conservationist. "William started coming in here five years ago, shortly after I bought the place. I even remember the first night he showed up, because he looked so scared. I'm sure it was the first time he'd ever stepped foot inside a queer bar. A lot of guys hit on him right away: he's very cute. At first I tried to keep the nastier boys away, but he didn't seem to care about how he got treated — so long as he had company when I closed the place down every night. He's not a heavy drinker, by the way, but I think he powders his nose occasionally. After about a year of screwing around, he met David in here one night. Since then it's been marriage and monogamy — and just as well, these days! We've lost half our regulars to AIDS. Anyway, they come in here together about once a week, have a drink or two, shoot the shit for a couple of hours with some of the boys, and leave — always together."

"What's he like, George?" I asked.

He shrugged. "Who knows? He's tight as a clam. Friendly, polite enough, but the guy just doesn't reveal himself to any-body — except David, I guess. The only time I ever saw him get hostile was one night when some smart-ass journalist loud-ly announced who William's father was. William knocked over a table getting to the jerk and nearly strangled him. He's real skinny, but it took two of our muscle boys to pull him off." George clearly enjoyed the memory.

"Was that the only time you ever saw him angry?"

George pondered my question for a moment. "Come to

think of it, he came in here late one night last week looking like he'd like to kill somebody. David managed to calm him down." His face drew back from the implication of what he'd just said. "Hey, I didn't mean to suggest that William came in looking like he'd just bumped off his old man."

"Do you remember what night that was?"

"Yeah, it was Friday. I remember because that's the night we had The Sequins booked — they were just getting into their second set when William crashed in. Must have been about eleven."

"George, thanks for trusting me," I said, offering him my hand. "Can you introduce me to David now?"

"Sure, but why don't I seat you at a table first? The bar is a bit too public for intimate discussions." He led me to the one vacant table in the room, situated behind a large pillar that obstructed my view of the stage. Small blessings. Before seating myself, I did glance around the pillar to check out the stripper's progress. He was down to those gifts Nature gave him at birth, except there was much more of them now.

The bearded man who had been sitting over a juice at the end of the bar approached my table. He smiled nervously and extended his hand. "Hello. I'm David Walker. George said you wanted to talk with me."

His voice was soft, his manner non-invasive. I took his hand in a firm grasp and invited him to sit down. George appeared with another draft for me and a fresh glass of juice for David.

His initial sincerity — and the fact that Silver already had claimed the liberty of playing fast and loose with my cover story — obliged me to be forthright about my credentials. "David, I'm here because I've been hired by Simone Goldberg to investigate her brother's murder."

The tension lines on his face immediately relaxed. "Thanks for being so honest. It's become a scarce commodity. Homophobia forced our community into deception for such a long time. Then, just as we were beginning to reap the benefits of stepping out of the closet and insisting upon our rights, we got hit with AIDS. I'm very tired of smoke-and-mirrors."

He looked up and smiled sheepishly. "I'm sorry. I was beginning to launch into my lecture mode. I guess it's an occupational hazard. I'm an instructor and a grad student at U of T," he explained. "William is always teasing me about it."

"That's fine with me," I assured him. "I can't get to first base in my line of work without being able to separate truth from bullshit."

"Exactly what is your line of work?"

"I'm a writer. My special interest is corporate crime. But Simone has persuaded me to change hats for the time being."

"Have you published?"

I laughed. "Now that's a question I'd expect from an aspiring academic! Yes, I have. Three books, some articles …"

His face lit up. "Of course. I'm sorry. Jane Yeats — you wrote that superb series of articles on corruption in the Metro police force. I'm ashamed to admit that I don't know your books, but my field is medieval literature. I rarely read anything after *Gammer Gurtons Nedle*," he explained, like I'd get it.

"That makes us both culturally deprived, although mine is probably the more serious case. I rarely read anything written prior to yesterday's deadline."

Having broken the ice, I got down to some pointed questions. "What I need to know, David, has more to do with the kind of knowledge we come to outside of print. Are you aware that your lover is fast becoming a prime suspect in his father's murder?"

He paused before responding. "Presumably I should feign surprise. But William is such a convenient target, isn't he? His grudges against his father are public knowledge — particularly since the court case William launched to sell his shares in the corporation. And it wouldn't take much digging to reveal what a totally inadequate father Durand-the-Elder was. It all adds up to William being such an attractive candidate one might wonder why the police would even bother to look any further, especially when looking any further might lead them into investigating the underbelly of the ruling class." We both grinned in recognition of his relapse into the didactic mode.

"You've pretty well summarized why Simone hired me as an independent investigator," I agreed. "But can you give me any cogent reasons why William should be disqualified as a suspect — or point me in another direction?"

"The reason I find most compelling, and most pathetic, wouldn't hold much water in a court room. Believe it or not, William actually *loved* his father. Gaining the old man's approval was the most important thing in the world to him — not that he ever had a snowball's chance in hell of getting it!"

"What do you think it would have taken?" I asked.

"Durand-the-Elder wanted to establish a dynasty, with William as the linchpin. But William resisted all his father's pressure to get him involved in the corporation. He talked about it almost as though he feared guilt by contamination, like he felt he would wind up *becoming* his father if they worked together. In any event, William's talents are much more creative than managerial. And although he hasn't got the confidence to become an artist in his own right, he did start his own gallery. It's called Per/Visions." He sounded proud as a co-parent.

"On Queen Street, just west of McCaul?" I took a swallow of my beer.

David smiled. "Yes, have you been there?"

"No. I rarely visit galleries. They make me uncomfortable. Because I can't afford to buy, I usually end up feeling like I'm skulking around in someone's living room."

He laughed. "I know the feeling. I live on a grad student's income. But you'd feel at home in Per/Visions. William show-cases the work of new and emerging young artists and photographers in a deliberately unpretentious setting. He's done a lot for the local art community, particularly for gay artists, who often get marginalized — especially when they depict anything connected to sexuality. People love to hire us as their interior decorators, but they don't want their own interiors challenged." He paused briefly. "You know, William's father never gave him a word of praise for his accomplishments."

"From what I've heard, David, his father wasn't aware that anyone else on the planet might be doing anything noteworthy — unless it affected the Dow Jones. But running a gallery is a risky business. Didn't Durand senior give William any financial support?"

"Not a cent, and William is very proud of that. The Elder tried to keep him on a very short leash by providing him with a living allowance generous enough to support a moderately comfortable middle-class lifestyle, but not to provide venture capital. William figured his father thought that financial desperation would eventually drive him to join the corporation."

"Was the gallery a financial success?" I asked.

"Until recently, yes. It was a success in William's terms. Because all his artists are broke, he sold on a small commission and he often mounted installations and exhibitions as a community service. But sales have slumped in the art market. And, of course, there are fewer buyers for gay work simply because there are fewer of us these days."

While he paused, as if in silent remembrance, I reflected on how insulated most of us are from the realities of AIDS: we rarely get any closer to its devastations than infrequent media statistical reports. A while ago Silver told me that George Potts had been to so many funerals in the past few years he'd lost track of the number.

When David looked up, I met his eyes. He gestured toward a brass plaque on the wall behind the bar. "Did you notice our memorial when you were at the bar?"

I didn't tell him I had assumed at a glance that it was a roster of champion billiards or darts teams. Of winners.

"I'm sorry for losing track of what I was saying," he apologized. "It's just that it's hard to forget for very long. We've all lost so many friends — those of us who survive pitch between grief and terror."

"I won't say that I can imagine, David. I simply can't."

He nodded acknowledgment. "About the gallery's finances. Things were tight, but William was paying the bills and having a good time. But when the lease on Per/Visions expired last spring, his landlord raised the rent exorbitantly. William knew that unless he could raise a substantial chunk of cash fairly quickly, he stood to lose the gallery — just when a few of his shows had received rave reviews. That's one of the reasons he took his father to court."

"What were the other reasons?" I asked, keen to uncover all William's motives.

Up to this point, David had talked very freely. My last question threw a veil over his face. "William made me swear not to tell anyone," he muttered fiercely.

"David, I don't intend to share anything you've told me with anyone else. In fact, I'd like to discover some concrete reasons for exonerating William. From what I've learned about him, I already feel very sympathetic. Please trust me not to betray your confidence," I pleaded.

He made a quick decision. "Okay. You are one of the very few people on our side right now, and I have a feeling that William is going to need as many friends as he can get in the very near future. The other reason, the major reason he was trying to pry those shares loose was for *me*: two years ago I was diagnosed as HIV-positive. I've already been hospitalized twice with pneumonia. Medical treatment for AIDS is awesomely expensive, especially if you want to try some of the newer drugs the government hasn't yet approved. William is so frightened of losing me, he has convinced himself that he can *buy* me a cure."

He chuckled through tears, obviously knowing better. His hand was shaking so badly he set down his glass of juice.

I could think of nothing to say. Not much older than twenty-five, this gentle young man was facing a death sentence. Instinctively I reached across the table and took his hand. My small effort to connect triggered him into weeping openly.

I let him cry for bit before saying, "David, I know there's no consolation. But I do know something about grieving. My lover died two years ago. Some mornings I wake up envying him."

He smiled up at me through his tears. "That's just it, you see. William's the one I feel sorry for. I've got this whole support network of friends, colleagues, even family. But I'm all that William has. I'm so frightened about what will happen to him when I'm gone. He's already half-crazy with fear."

"Then he surely wouldn't do anything to jeopardize your time together — like kill his father."

As he nodded, his blond forelock dropped a notch. "Exactly. But now we're both afraid that he'll get arrested and be held in custody while I'm sick. After a year of good psychotherapy, I think I've more or less come to terms with dying, but every swan scene I can imagine includes William holding me at the end."

"Do you have any specific reason for thinking he'll be arrested?" I asked softly.

"I know that he met with his father last Wednesday afternoon and that they had a horrendous fight. That's bound to come out in the police investigation. Someone must know about it, apart from me and William."

"Do you know what the fight was about?"

David shook his head. "Not really, just that William made one last effort to pry loose enough money to keep the gallery — and me — afloat for a few more months. His father told him to fuck off. I didn't hear about it until Friday night, though. Wednesday night I was studying for an exam I had to write on Friday — one of my Ph.D. comprehensives. William didn't get home until after I had gone to bed. When I left the next morning, he was still sleeping beside me. I left him a note asking him to meet me on Friday after my exam for an early supper at Splendido — that gorgeous Italian restaurant on Harbord. I knew I probably wouldn't see him on Thursday because I planned to stay very late at school to study with a friend. Anyway, as soon as he walked into Splendido, I knew something was up. He said he could only stay for a drink. He seemed high, very high. That worried me." He stopped talking to fidget with his glass.

Something clicked. "Did William use coke?" I asked.

"Yes, but only recreationally — at least until I got hospitalized. After that he got into it in a serious way. I threatened to leave him as soon as I recognized his addiction. When I told him how outraged his drug use made me, he went straight into a rehab program. I mean, here I am with no control at all over my disease and he's working overtime to kill himself." He smiled wryly. "Staring death in the eye brings a lot of other things into sharp perspective. I told William I didn't really believe that we would be united in the Great Beyond, so he shouldn't use that as an excuse to hasten his own demise."

"But you suspected that he might be back into using when you saw him Friday at supper?"

"Only at first. But then he told me why he was flying so high. He said he was in a rush to get to his father's office because he had decided to put some new cards on the table."

I held my breath as I asked, "Do you know what they were — and if he did?"

"No. He promised to tell me the whole story later and to meet me here around ten. He didn't show up until some time after eleven — and when he did he was already three sheets to the wind. He was so uptight and withdrawn I couldn't drag much out of him. Except that they had that god-awful fight on Wednesday — and that William had just managed to persuade his father to give him his trust fund. After finally wrenching that money out of him, you'd think he would have been in a great mood. Instead he kept obsessing about his failed relationship with the old man, about how he'd seemed to really get off on humiliating William, about how now they'd never be able to heal their relationship. I'm sure it was the drink that made him so morose and maudlin. "

"But he said nothing whatsoever about why Charles suddenly decided to relinquish his hold on the purse strings?"

"Not directly, but he referred to it when I asked him why he was beating himself up when he should be celebrating. He said he'd just flushed what was left of his self-respect down the toilet by selling Charles some information. Said he felt like a blackmailer and he was sure he'd dropped even deeper in his father's esteem by doing it. Anyway, I managed to get him home intact after he drank himself into oblivion — something I'd *never* seen him do before. He passed out and was still sleeping late Saturday morning when his stepmother, Judith, phoned to tell him about Charles's death. I couldn't get through to him after he hung up. He just showered, packed a bag and left, saying he'd be in touch with me as soon as he could manage. That was the last I saw of him."

"And he hasn't contacted you since then?" I asked.

"Yes, he has. He phoned me at home last night. It was obvious he'd been drinking again — he was almost incoherent. Said something about having created a scene at his stepmother's after the funeral. I think he'd been staying at Judith's since he left our place. Even when I pressured him, he wouldn't tell me where he was. He just said that the police were looking for him and that he had to clear up some things before he saw me."

"Where's he staying now? I understand that he'd left Judith's by the time the police arrived after the wake to ask him some questions."

For the first time since we'd started talking, David didn't make eye contact when he responded. "I don't know, but it's probably somewhere outside the city. There was a lot of static on the line. I'm sure it was a long-distance call."

"David, can we make a deal? If I find out where he's staying, I'll tell you right away. If you talk with him again, you'll pass on this message — that I want to talk, even if it's just by phone?" Convinced as I was that David had lied to me about his ignorance of William's whereabouts, I nonetheless felt that my proposition offered an opening, should he and his lover decide to go for it.

He agreed. "That's more than fair. I'll give you our unlisted number." He reached into a leather knapsack resting on the floor against his chair and extracted pen and paper. He jotted down a number in an elegant script and passed it across the table.

We both stood up to shake hands, but wound up hugging one another. How much easier life would be if some of us hadn't been weaned on peculiar expectations of justice.

I walked away from the table to collect Silver, who was in the centre of the dance floor waltzing with a drag queen to a Bette Midler tune. After a moment's indecision as to whose shoulder I should tap, I lit on Silver's. "I'm sorry to break in like this, but may I have the next dance?" Sequins yielded to leather and I found myself being led around the floor to the strains of "Feelings." Yuk.

"Silver, this is ridiculous," I muttered darkly into her ear. She smiled sweetly and trotted me around the floor in an iron grip that almost lifted me off my clumsy feet until the song ended.

Still clutching my hand, she led me back to the bar. "That was not ridiculous, my friend. This is about land claims. In here you are on *our* turf, eh? Norms change."

"Okay, I get your point," I conceded. "But can we go home now?"

"And here I thought you wanted to dance the night away!"

"Shut up, Silver," I laughed. "If your date last night went all that well, then you're already spoken for — and too whacked out to perform up to my standards anyway."

As we walked through the back door, I turned to my friend. "Give me a break. A person could be forgiven for getting confused in there."

"Only if that person didn't know who he or she was *before* he or she walked in," she snapped.

Without another word we hopped onto Harley. Just as I began to accelerate, a drunk lurched forward and collapsed onto the street directly in the path of my bike. I had lots of time to bring us to a halt so we could check out his situation — except that my brakes didn't respond. I swerved so sharply in order to miss the guy that I lost control of the bike. As it slipped out from under us, I wondered if that's how figure skaters feel just before meeting the ice.

I rolled to a stop when I hit the curb. Silver was lying motionless closer to the bike. I guess she doesn't roll so fast.

"Silver," I screamed, "are you okay?"

"Fuck," was her only comment.

I pushed myself up. My bad leg paining like hell, I limped over to her. "Are you hurt?"

"While you were rolling, I was bouncing on the spot," she laughed. "But my Levis are in a real bad way — and that's gonna come straight out of your expense account. Shit, I would have been safer at Little Big Horn."

As I was helping her to her feet a volley of profanities issued from the heap I'd swerved to avoid hitting. A very old man staggered to his feet.

"Fucking broads. I always says women can't drive. I'm gonna sue the tits offa ya."

Silver struggled out of my arms. "You missed him the first time. Let me at the old turd."

"Forget it, love. With any luck at all, next time he'll fall in front of a male driver."

We pushed my disabled bike the short way back to the parking lot behind Leather Boys. I decided to leave Harley there until I could call my bike shop first thing in the morning.

I parked and locked it next to the rear wall under a spotlight. A close examination confirmed what I already suspected.

Someone had cut the brake cables.

CHAPTER 11

WHEN MY ALARM buzzed Thursday morning, I stumbled straight to the phone and called my mechanic. Hank once rode with The Renegades. Around bikes he has the instincts of a blind piano tuner.

I asked him to pick up my bike from behind Leather Boys and repair it by noon. And I needed to know where he figured the damage came from. Three hours later he called back to say that my hog was in running order again and that the brake cables had been sheared — by design.

I paid him extra for the speedy service and for affirming my diagnosis. This bill would be coming out of my pocket. In all honesty, I couldn't put it on my expense account. I had no way of connecting the severed cables to my search for Durand's killer. At least not yet.

Perhaps some jerk on a random trashing spree had hit on my bike, but that wasn't likely. Even jerks tend to avoid molesting Harleys, whose owners generally run to the sort of people who exact Rambo-style vengeance on vandals foolhardy enough to abuse their machines. Hey, it's a religion.

More likely, someone had tried to discourage me from pursuing my inquiries — and had chosen a method that could have discouraged me from doing anything more energetic than pushing up daisies, had not that obliging old sexist drunk fallen into my path before I had time to work up any serious speed.

Someone miscalculated. Fear galvanizes me into defiance.

I took my bike for a short run around the block. Hank, who'd done a fine job on very short notice, told me that it needed some body work. That could wait: my current schedule didn't allow for cosmetics. I looked at the scratches and dents, and kicked the ground with enough force to send a spray of gravel into the air. Goddamn it, I was pissed off. Mightily pissed off, in a controlled but vicious rage. By the time I set off for Simone's house, I had devised a strategy for cooling out along the way.

The sky was so overcast and threatening I would have borrowed Silver's car, had my brain been in gear. But I was in no mood to give into any further intimidation, from humans or the major guy in the sky who controls the weather. Today no one was keeping me off my bike.

With the gentle assistance of Vivaldi, delivered into my earholes courtesy of my Walkman, I managed to chill out en route, as thunder-clouds gave way to sunlight. It was too early in the year to trust these rays as anything more than tentative harbingers of spring, but I summoned up enough faith to enjoy them.

I took my own good time getting to my destination. Until I reached the city's northern limits, I flew as much like the crow as roads allowed. Then I veered onto a series of less-trafficked rural routes through a part of the country I know well. In the summer months following Pete's death, I often biked up here, finding brief solace in exploring routes too unfamiliar to trigger memories.

Simone Goldberg's house was located about twenty minutes northwest of Orangeville. Following her directions, I turned onto a poplar-lined road leading up to a beautiful board-and-batten house nestled amidst a heavily wooded property.

Well before the house, I brought Harley to a stop. The Goldberg dwelling was rectangular, with a high gambrel roof, Gothic arched gables and three dormers in front. The rear of the property sloped dramatically down to a river. Whoever had designed this place understood something important about proportions. Simone's house fit so unobtrusively into its surroundings, it reminded me of a village of stone cottages I'd seen cupped in some cliffs in the south of France that appeared to be an indigenous outcropping. A sharp contrast to her brother's ostentatious pseudo-château and gentrified neighbourhood.

Just as I raised my arm to knock on the door, I heard loud voices from within. I lowered my arm and pressed my ear to the wood. One angry female voice succeeded another, then both rose to shout in unison. A raging duet. Unfortunately, the door muffled the sounds too much for me to make out the identity of the antagonists and what they were fighting about. After sneaking around the side of the house away from the renovated barn, I peeked briefly into the first living-room window I encountered.

To my horror, I saw Simone raising her arm to deliver a stinging slap to the side of her daughter's face. I risked another peek. The girl was raising her arm. I didn't pause long enough to determine whether in self-defence or to return her mother's blow. I ran back to the front door and knocked loudly, hoping to snap them back into civility.

I hate scenes, especially when the combatants get physical. When I was growing up, my father's drinking routinely spilled over into violence against my mother. Racing between them like a human shield, I took a lot of blows intended for Etta. As I grew older and more verbally defiant, he tailor-made swats for me. I often wish my memory-triggers were as benign as Proust's *madeleine*.

About a minute after the voices fell silent, Simone opened the door. Her appearance was a far cry from the standard set by our two previous encounters. Hair dishevelled, eyes red and swollen, face flushed. She was wearing old blue jeans and a crumpled plaid flannel shirt, open at the neck by two buttons too many.

"I'm sorry if I've arrived at a bad moment, Simone. If you'd like some more time to yourself I could walk around your property for a while. It's such a beautiful day," I lamely offered.

She hesitated briefly, then invited me in. She took my jacket and ushered me into the main living area, the walls of which rose straight up to the hip of the gambrel. The interior resembled a cathedral, all light and air. It was furnished with simple, honest pioneer pieces. It amazed me that a structure so solid looking on the outside could be so warm and open inside. Had I not witnessed the scene with Rebecca, I would have thought her home was a metaphor of her being.

She wordlessly led the way to the kitchen and offered me coffee. "What I really need is a drink," she said, opening a cupboard door on a well-stocked shelf of booze. "Can I offer you a drink?" she asked, pouring herself a major splash of gin. To my surprise, she drank it neat, then refilled her glass.

"No thanks," I replied. Anyone with Celtic genes instinctively knows that gin is for paint-stripping. "My body is still processing last night's intake. But I will take you up on the coffee." She made me a *cappuccino,* then invited me to join her at the kitchen table. She brought the gin bottle with her, along with a jug of orange juice.

Running a hand through her tousled hair, she ventured eye contact for the first time. "Jane, I'm sorry you find me in such a state," she apologized. "I'm afraid you caught me in the midst of a row with Rebecca."

I quickly interjected, "You don't have to explain. I really should have called you first."

She poured herself another shot and dribbled some juice over it. If she kept drinking at this pace, I'd be delivering my progress report to the quarry tiles. "No, it's okay. I want to explain." She rose to cross the room and close the kitchen door. From the sound of the front door slamming shut, she needn't have bothered.

"Just before Christmas, Robert and I were shocked when we received Rebecca's report card. She turned sixteen last summer and was in grade eleven at the local high school. She's always been a way-above-average student — not that she works terrifically hard at getting good grades; she's just very bright.

She graduated from grade ten with an 91 per cent average. So you can imagine our astonishment when she failed four subjects in her first term this year! She refused to discuss it with us. Her teachers all reported the same thing: she wasn't concentrating in class, had failed to complete several assignments, showed no interest in her work, and seemed to have lost her confidence. She'd even started skipping class."

She paused to slake her psychic thirst with another swill of gin. "We'd been noticing a change in her personality before we got the report card. Until last fall she'd been an energetic, well-balanced kid, as good an athlete as she was a student. She was a track star — had a huge poster of FloJo on her bedroom wall. Her real passion was horses. She's won a shelf of equestrian trophies. But then she started dropping all her activities. She didn't seem to have any energy, couldn't focus on her homework, didn't spend much time talking with her girlfriends on the phone or seeing them. Even her pride in her appearance evaporated. You couldn't look at her without getting screamed at and she'd burst into tears whenever I tried to talk with her."

She looked at me with puzzlement in her eyes. "At first Robert just wrote it off to raging hormones. I was frightened that it might be the onset of my family's tendency to clinical depression."

"Simone, did you check into the obvious pitfalls for girls her age — booze, drugs, boys …?" Professional social working often stops short of one's own front door.

She shook her head, her eyes empty. "None of the above seemed to apply, at least as far as everyone we talked to was aware. And keep in mind that I trained as a social worker, so I can usually pick up on those things. Rebecca refused to tell us anything about what was troubling her and she refused to see a therapist, so over the Christmas holidays Robert and I decided to enroll her in a private girls' residential school, at least for the remainder of the school year. We thought that a change in environment and a more structured curriculum might make a difference. Much to our surprise, she immediately agreed to go. A week ago she arrived home unexpectedly and informed us that she had no intention of returning to St. Hilda's — or any other school — for the final term. I'm beside myself with anxiety," she told me, voicing the self-evident.

I expressed sympathy, hoping that I could get on with delivering my progress report. But the gin seemed to be fuelling her compulsion to talk about her daughter's acting out.

As she looked up at me from her glass, tears welled in her eyes. "I have never in my life drunk like this, please believe me. I'm really out of control. Just before you knocked at the door, I slapped Rebecca in the face. That's a first, in sixteen years: not once have I ever laid a hand on her, except affectionately." She lowered her head to her arms and began to weep.

I stood up, removed the bottle of gin from the table, emptied the remainder of her glass into the sink, and plugged in the electric kettle preparatory to making her a very strong coffee. Normally I wouldn't dream of intervening in anyone's slide into intoxication (including my own), but she'd promised to brief me on some family background that might be useful. And I needed to update her on my investigation into her brother's murder. I especially thought she needed to hear what I'd uncovered about her nephew, William. Perhaps her concern for her wayward daughter had overwhelmed her passionate interest in seeing justice done.

When I set a large mug of black coffee beside her on the table, she raised her head, then straightened up in her chair. She took a big gulp of the coffee. "Thanks, Jane, I guess I need this. I'm sorry for dumping my personal problems on you. I know you came here on business."

"Please don't apologize. None of us have any control over the timing of our troubles."

She reached across the table to squeeze my hand, by way of thanks. Hers was very cold.

CHAPTER 12

THE COFFEE WORKED its miracle. Simone recovered enough to pull some food together.

I briefly met her husband over lunch. She called him in from his workshop in the converted barn where he built musical instruments for a living. We chatted brightly over homemade minestrone, which she served with thick slices of crusty bread, local butter and cheese, fresh tropical fruit. Simone had gone to the trouble of stocking Newcastle Brown for me. She wisely declined Robert's offer to share a bottle of white wine.

Tall, with a heavy-set but muscular build and a receding hairline more than compensated for by a bushy black beard, he was a quiet, serious man. Obviously in love with his wife and his work. I noticed that he and Simone avoided raising the subject of my employment; presumably they had reached some prior agreement about appropriate luncheon topics. Nor was Rebecca on the menu. After dessert he returned to work, Simone and I to the living room.

I sat down on a big overstuffed sofa close to the wood-burning stove.

She began to shake the family tree. "My decision to marry Robert was the *ostensible* reason Charles and I stopped seeing one another."

"Charles didn't like him?" I asked.

"Charles never even met Robert. He refused to. Called him a Jewish hippie, then carried on like my husband didn't exist."

"But Charles was courting a Jewish family to help bail him out of ComTech," I said.

Simone's laugh was tinged around the edges by a bitterness I hadn't detected throughout our first meeting. "I never said he wouldn't *do business* with Jews — or Arabs. He just didn't want them in the family."

I reflected for a moment. "You'd think Charles might have related to the non-WASP members of the corporate world — I mean in the sense that the élite regards them all as outsiders, too, no matter how successful they become. I've heard that some Hong Kong businessmen complain among themselves about their exclusion from the pack."

"That would be true enough for most people, but Charles wasn't most people. He had to be extraordinary. He didn't believe in relating to anybody, or maybe he just didn't know how. He desperately wanted some sign that he had been accepted, but that's as far as it went. Connecting with people in any way apart from money and power fell totally beyond his ken. And, in any case, his rejecting Robert for being Jewish was only a subterfuge for getting back at me for having a different value system. He never forgave me — or his son — for not being blueprints of himself: working-class heroes. He quit school in grade eleven. I went on to get my Masters in Social Work at the University of Toronto. William has a Fine Arts degree from York. Since Robert and I moved here, I've been employed as a social worker with the local Children's Aid. Charles once told me he spent more on lunches than I earn in a year. 'So much for education,' he sneered. He took great pride in being a self-made man."

She paused briefly to light a cigarette. "Yet I think he envied me my peace of mind and my joy in family — things his money could never buy. Charles was the loneliest person I've ever known."

"Were you close when you were growing up?"

Simone nodded. "Yes, closer than most sibs. All three of us kids were — until Pierre died. After the mine accident, Charles pulled himself into a shell. I honestly don't think he let anyone matter to him ever again."

She seemed overly confident about her assessment of her brother's life, considering that she hadn't seen him in years. Or maybe she just assumed that some people are incapable of change and growth, surely a discouraging attitude for a social worker.

"But he got married, didn't he?"

"Sure. He married Helen shortly after Pierre died. But I don't think he cared much for her. And it was obvious after he became successful that her presence in his life actually caused him acute embarrassment. He did seem fond of William, though — for the first few months of his life. Like someone had given him a new puppy. In time, he turned out to be as neglectful of his son as he was of his wife." She shook her head. "Without men like Charles, there'd be a lot less work for people in my line of work."

"Simone, I met with Helen yesterday afternoon. She struck me as a very bitter woman."

"She has every right to her bitterness," Simone confirmed. "But if you're thinking that she might have had something to do with Charles's death, you're on the wrong track. Helen is a thoroughly burnt-out case. Angry, neurotic, humourless — but lacking the energy to do anything but bewail her fate. To my knowledge, she has been totally out of touch with Charles for at least as long as I have."

"When did your final split with him happen?"

"Charles refused to come to our wedding. I converted to Judaism, so Robert and I were married in a synagogue. I saw my brother only once, shortly after my marriage. He told me that if I wanted to continue our relationship, I would have to see him alone, completely leave Robert out of the picture, not even mention his name. He refused to acknowledge Robert's place in my life." She crossed her legs primly, folded her hands in her lap and affected the Queen's public smile. "So I told him to fuck off."

"Did that affect you financially?" I asked, remembering she had mentioned in the course of our first meeting that my payments would be coming out of a trust fund Charles had set up for her.

"Yes. Charles always made sure that people paid dearly for crossing him. About seven years before I met Robert, Charles set up a family trust fund — over which he retained voting rights — as a tax avoidance measure. It included me, his son and later, his second wife. Two weeks after our last encounter, I received a letter from his lawyers informing me that, while the trust fund would remain as Charles had established it, thereby guaranteeing me an annual income, I was no longer a beneficiary of his estate."

"How did you feel about that?"

She shrugged. "Absolutely indifferent. I never had any intention of drawing upon the trust fund, let alone any legacy. As I told you on Sunday, your fees for investigating his murder will be the first withdrawal. Rebecca will inherit the remainder, except for an endowment for the women's shelter. So his cutting me out of his will only struck me as a pathetic slap in the face from a little boy who had picked up his marbles and refused to play the game when he couldn't make up all the rules. Charles was a master manipulator, Jane. Money was his big stick. When he finally realized that I couldn't give a damn about his shekels, he knew he couldn't control me. That must have left him a very frustrated little boy."

And you a newly empowered big girl, I silently appended. "But do you know for sure that you are excluded from his will?" I asked, wondering when the document would be probated.

Simone set her coffee mug down on the table between us and looked directly at me. "No. I have no way of knowing that for sure. But I can assure you that I don't care. In fact, any money he might have left me will only create a hassle: I'll have to decide how to dispose of it without touching a cent. I guess I'd give it all away to worthy causes he would have disapproved of — like more women's shelters, baby seals and rain forests."

I believed her. From the evidence I'd seen, Charles's sister had built herself a very secure life in complete independence of him.

"Jane, please make a real effort to understand me. I *pitied* my brother. Even though I let go of our relationship years ago, I do care about the fact that he was murdered. Call it 'survivor's guilt': deep down, I think I hired you as a sop to my conscience. The social worker in me says that perhaps I should have done more to effect a reconciliation with Charles. You know, try out a few of those conflict resolution skills I'm always encouraging my clients to practise. But I care infinitely more that my nephew is going through hell — *I know William is innocent.* So tell me what you've found out so far. Have you made any progress in clearing him?"

"So far, all I can gather from my police and press sources is that Charles died Friday night some time between seven and ten p.m. from massive head injuries caused by a not entirely blunt object. No new information along those lines is likely to surface until the coroner's report is filed, but I'll keep the pressure on my sources anyway. For the time being, though, the way he was killed certainly doesn't resemble anything like a Mob hit — although that could have been a deliberate subterfuge."

"Do you mean a *professional* killer — someone actually *hired* to murder him?" she asked, incredulous as if I'd just told her that the Pope had been named in a paternity suit.

"That's certainly possible. The idea may strike you as incredible, but five fairly prominent Toronto-area businessmen have died recently in Mob-style killings. In fact, if the person who wanted him dead is someone in the business community, he or she likely would have hired a hitman — or woman," I added, just to cover all the politically correct linguistic bases. (I rather fancy the idea of a hitwoman).

Simone's expression signalled that she was still having trouble believing me.

"Think of it," I continued, "can you imagine Gerald Dawson, for example, knowing how to shoot a water pistol? Or even if he were a skilled marksman, being willing to take that kind of risk? You know, there is an underground placement service for executive hit men. The police think that the best of them — the ones who never get caught — are brought up from New York. They make their hit, then immediately head south again. If their employer wants a message sent out, he arranges to have the guy killed in a gangland trademark style."

She looked discouraged. "If Charles was murdered on a contract, then there isn't much chance of the killer being caught, is there?"

"No, those guys rarely get caught. And when they do, they seldom talk, even when they're promised immunity from prosecution. But for now I'm working on the assumption that Charles knew his killer. I did manage to pry loose one important fact from my police contact— that a book of matches from a gay bar was found in his office. The cop I spoke to wouldn't name the bar, but I found it out soon enough from a lesbian friend who is well connected to the gay scene."

I paused to choose my next words carefully. Simone might not know that her nephew was gay. But she beat me to my script.

"The matches were William's, weren't they? I certainly can't imagine Charles having any other gay acquaintances."

"Yes, they would appear to have been left there by William — which doesn't, of course, necessarily implicate him in his father's murder," I replied.

"What are you suggesting?" Simone asked anxiously. For sure she didn't want to invest any money in proving patricide.

"There are a number of possibilities — apart from the obvious one that William may have inadvertently left them there after he killed his father. And that *is* a possibility. They had a serious argument in Charles's office two days earlier — and William did meet with him again the night of the murder."

She interrupted me. "How do you know that?"

"Give me a minute. William could have left the matches there on an earlier occasion — perhaps to enrage his father by flaunting his sexual orientation. Perhaps he casually discarded them simply because he'd used up all the matches. Even if he did leave them there Friday evening, Charles might well have had another visitor *after* William left his office. Or Charles may have recently discovered that his son was a homosexual and have produced the matches himself by way of proof or challenge. Apparently some activists in the gay community had discussed 'outing' William. Maybe they decided real blackmail would be more profitable." I hadn't thought of that one until I spoke it. It came dangerously close to making me feel too clever by half.

I had been ticking off the possibilities on the fingers of my right hand. I reached my thumb. "Or the matches could have been planted on the crime scene by the real killer in order to frame William. It wouldn't take much digging around to discover that he was gay."

Simone stood up and began to pace back and forth behind her chair. She combed her fingers through her thick hair. "God forbid that William did it. One of my consolations about Charles's death is that now he won't be able to inflict any more pain on our family. And William is the most vulnerable of us all."

She stopped pacing long enough to throw a log on the wood-burning stove and return to her seat. "Please tell me how you know that they had an argument and that they met Friday night."

I summarized what I had learned from my conversation with David Walker at Leather Boys.

Simone looked very troubled. "But what William found out that he thought he could use to pry money out of his father — was it something that incriminated Charles in some way? Some shady business deal, something fraudulent? I'm sure Charles would have done anything to save the corporation or to save face."

"I just don't know, Simone. It could have been something like that, but it could just as easily have been something that

Charles might have found useful in his efforts to salvage what was left of his empire. Maybe it concerned someone else's criminality."

I paused briefly, before asking her something I'd been curious about since the funeral. "How close were you and William? Close enough to tell me if you think he's capable of threatening his father with blackmail?"

"William and I both worked very hard at maintaining our relationship, in spite of Charles's efforts to undermine it. We are very fond of one another. He often turns to me when he is troubled. I guess I play the role of surrogate mother."

She shook her head and looked to be on the verge of tears. "Christ, this whole thing is so sad. I've told you that Charles was a desperately unhappy man. The roots of his misery go back to our parents, of course. A few years before Pierre's death, our father had been retired on a permanent disability pension after his right hand was crushed on the job. After that, Dad just withdrew into a corner and drank himself to death. He never even let on the rest of us were there. Not surprisingly, Charles grew up to be an emotionally distant father, as remote from William as our father was from us. No matter how badly Charles behaved, at home or in the corporate world, no matter how deeply he sank in his son's estimation, William always craved his attention and his approval — so desperately it broke my heart to witness his yearning."

Her words confirmed what David had told me, uncomfortably nudging William forward in the lineup. "So it seems unlikely to you that William might have tried to blackmail him?"

"Yes, it does — unless William had reasons for needing money that I don't know about." I remembered David telling me about the impending loss of the gallery, about needing expensive drugs to treat his AIDS. I decided against telling Simone at this point. Presumably William had good reasons for not confiding in his aunt either about his financial situation or his partner's disease. I didn't want her to clam up at this point. And why give her reason to fear for her nephew's health in the bargain?

"William knew what a mess his father was. Charles was constantly at war with his own demons. His incredible success never diminished that. Because he blamed the bosses at Canco for the deaths of both our father and Pierre, he raged against them for overlooking worker safety. He had a mania for safety on his own construction sites; in fact, he developed an innovative worker-safety program that won him an industry award. But nothing quelled Charles's own yearning for Dad's approval — which, of course, he never got."

"Is it too silly a leap to suggest that Charles's manic pursuit of Establishment acceptance was a substitute for your father's?" I asked.

"Not silly at all. Just tragic — a tragedy compounded by the fact that he inflicted the same syndrome on his son. Twenty years of social-working disturbed kids has taught me that without intervention, dysfunctional families tend to spiral in the same vicious circles for generations."

"Simone, some of what Helen told me about Charles suggests that he might have been manic-depressive. It strikes me as not unlikely. One of the most frequently quoted words his business acquaintances have used to describe his personality is 'mercurial.' 'Volatile' often crops up too. Did you see any evidence of those traits when you were kids?"

She laughed bitterly. "I didn't see much evidence to the contrary. Charles never rested on any emotional plateau for longer than a few days. Some days he'd be flying like a kite for no reason at all. Those highs always terminated abruptly in an explosion of rage over the most petty things, especially whenever anyone crossed him. Then he'd withdraw for weeks, sometimes a month or two at a time, leaving the rest of the family relieved that he wouldn't be destroying furniture or hitting anyone for a while."

"Do you know if he ever saw a shrink or was put on medication?" I asked.

"No, I don't know, but it strikes me as unlikely. Charles was too driven to give anyone — or any chemical — power over his own temperament. But Judith might be able to answer that question. When do you plan to speak with her?"

"Soon," I replied, "but I'd really like to connect with William first. Do you think she might be able to help me with his whereabouts?"

"Again, I don't know. I met her for the first time the day we made arrangements for the funeral. I'd spoken to her only once before that. She phoned me one night about five years ago, sounding very agitated about something. But I never found out what was troubling her. She seemed to lose her resolve as we spoke. In fact, she sounded a bit drunk to me. Perhaps that's how she worked up the nerve to call me in the first place. We wound up chatting briefly about absolutely nothing. To this day I don't know why she phoned."

"From my observation of her at the funeral and at Swindon Path, I have a sense of a woman who could easily be underestimated. I mean, she's obviously set about creating an image of herself as the brain-dead blonde bimbo. But when I watched her circulating, and dealing with William's freak-out, I wondered if the image might not be a smoke screen for her real role — if not the power behind the throne, at least an alternative source of energy and intelligence. The kind of woman who could prop up a man on a disaster course." I suggested this off the top of my head, mainly to get Simone's reaction.

"I think you're right on target there," she said. "But I doubt she wanted Charles dead. I don't know anything about the state of their marriage, but William has indicated that she wanted out. And, when you think of it, she may have been in a better financial situation than Charles — at least on the surface."

I nodded my accord. "Apparently she incurred none of his indebtedness and owns outright their three residential properties — the Swindon Path mansion, a villa in Montreux, and an estate in the Bahamas. Swindon Path alone is estimated to be worth eight million dollars at current real-estate values. So any motive she may have had for killing him likely would have been personal, rather than financial, unless she saw his death as plugging a hole in a leaking bucket."

Simone shook her head. "I really don't think you'll find Charles's killer in the family. And I'm sure it has already occurred to you that, in the police view, one of us would make the easiest — and probably safest — candidate."

"Yes, that has occurred to me," I agreed ruefully. In continuing to point the guilty finger at the corporate élite, was she simply expressing her honest belief — or trying to influence my take on the murder? I told her about Harley's sheared brake cables.

"If you want to drop this now, Jane, believe me, I'll understand."

I chuckled. "I wouldn't dream of dropping it now, at least until I've discovered who hurt my bike! I've already made plans to meet early next week with a man who has some insider information on Charles's bid for Imperial Trust. In the meantime, I want to track down William. And I'll keep you posted on any important developments."

We enjoyed a half-hour walk along the stream running behind the house. I set my helmet on my head and ignited Harley.

CHAPTER 13

FRIDAY MORNING I spent too much time in bed, awake and thinking. Normally I hit the floor as soon as my eyes open, throw on my running gear and trot off to the park with Max. Usually the routine works: rarely does a troubling memory crease my brain until after I've showered and eaten. Then I plunge straight into my research and writing, which concentrates my mind too narrowly for me to hear my heart's uneasy intimations. Late afternoon I emerge from my paper cocoon and go out to a cheap Italian café for supper and a few beers, pick up a video on the way home, and spend the rest of the evening watching it while I read at the same time and quaff another beer or two, sometimes three — depending upon how successful I've been at keeping the dogs of grief at bay. I choose not to truly feel my sadness: the goal of grieving is to let go of the one you've lost. Maybe I'll never be ready to do that.

I don't need Etta to tell me that this is not a healthy lifestyle. This isn't even a life, but it's the best I've been able to manage since Pete died. I've always needed a lot of solitude, but lately I've let myself slip into the kind of isolation that you read about in biographies of depressed women writers who killed themselves. The fact that this doesn't scare me should terrify me, but hey — what's the alternative? Lying in bed long after the sun has risen into a pollution-sullen Toronto sky, picking over emotional scabs?

The lure of money aside, I never should have agreed to work for Simone. She should have listened to me when I warned her that I just couldn't cut the mustard as an investigator. After four days of seeing more people than I normally work into a year, of listening to life stories and *kvetches* about family relationships that would exhaust a shrink's resources, I still didn't have a clue who had paved Charles Durand's premature passage into that Great Corporation in the sky — and I still didn't give a damn.

Some deaths don't disturb me, especially when the deceased's prime function in life had impeded our collective well-being. Maybe God sees the little hawk fall, too.

But blaming a victim for a crime he maybe didn't commit *should* grab my attention. William was the obvious suspect in his father's murder. Yet I had heard enough about his relationship with his father to sympathize with him. From my conversations with his aunt, his mother and his lover I had developed a sketchy, but basically compassionate portrait of the man. Did I really want to uncover anything that might incriminate him? *No.* If I did manage to get my hands on some evidence against him, would I take it to the police? Probably not. In any case, I didn't even know where he was.

Along with my hair, my moral sense seems to take on more and more shades of grey.

Perhaps if I really pushed on with my so-called investigation, I might discover enough to at least exonerate William, if not identify the real killer. At this low point in the morning, I couldn't convince myself that I might unearth enough to cast even a tiny veil of suspicion over anyone else. That is what separates my research for a book from this kind of investigation. Research always yields results, comforting little factual tidbits I can weave into a thesis, shape a narrative around. The investigation was leading me nowhere. I hate facing a heap of random data I can't see any pattern to. Mental chaos terrifies me.

The night Pete died, only Silver's voice penetrated the black hole. She told me that when the Great Mystery lowered us onto Turtle Island, we landed here equipped with all we need to get on with our lives. Since then I've often had occasion to wonder if the Great Mystery dropped me without a medicine wheel. Now that's about as self-indulgent and destructive a thought as any I've had. I forced my bones out of bed.

Max raced across the room to greet my resurrection, reminding me that I am not alone in this vale of tears. As I emptied two heaping cups of Science Diet into his bowl, the phone rang. Before my answering machine could click in, I picked up the receiver.

"Good morning, Jane. It's Lennie."

"Lennie, forgive me for not asking how you are, but I've just gotten out of bed. My brain's not clear enough to register your answer, love."

He laughed. "That's okay, you're one of the few people I know who pauses to listen to the answer. Do you want me to call back later?"

"No, the sound of your voice is bringing me back to something that almost feels like awareness," I replied, wishing I'd had time to brush my teeth. I seem to articulate more clearly when I'm not speaking through moss.

"I'm not entirely sure that's a responsibility I'm prepared to take," he joked. "But I do have some news for you. As soon as I got to the office this morning, I spoke with Michael Diamond — my colleague who worked for Gerald Dawson when Durand made his takeover bid for Imperial Trust. I explained to him that as Durand's official biographer you needed a sound overview of that episode in his life, given its importance in his career. He said he'd be delighted to meet with you."

I smelled a rat. "Why *delighted*, Lennie? I mean, why not just *willing* to meet with me?"

A brief silence ensued. "Well," Lennie resumed in a subdued tone of voice, "I might have mentioned your credentials — and that you are a close personal friend."

"About my credentials: are we talking books or more tangible assets?" Over the past several months, once they felt I'd observed the requisite year of mourning, Lennie and Portia had tried to set me up with various eligible males of their acquaintance. I knew they meant well, but I had to crawl along at my own speed.

Lennie's voice got a bit aggravated around the edges. "We're talking *both* — I always use whatever I have in my arsenal when I'm trying to pull off a tough deal, Jane. The inner circle around the Imperial fiasco, which is in fact a very small, very tight-lipped group, are reluctant to talk about Durand's takeover bid, even now. It's history, it's ugly unbecoming history, and they want to pretend it never really happened, or that it happened the way it did for reasons the media never understood. If you want access to probably the only man who can and will fill you in on the details, I'm not sure you can afford to bitch about how I persuaded him to see you."

I hope I sounded as chastened as I felt. "Lennie, I'm sorry. It's a bad morning. When the phone rang, I had almost decided to stuff this job and take off on the next plane for Barbados."

His voice softened. "That's okay, Jane. I understand. But don't give up now. Hang on at least long enough to hear Michael out. I'm sure he'll give you a lot of insight into the characters and motives of the principal players — as well as a lead or two."

"Tell me something, Lennie. Why do you care whether or not I drop this job?"

He cleared his throat. "I know how much you hate the privileged classes and how much those of us who grease the capitalist engine irk your socialist soul. God knows, we've had enough arguments over the years! But you are bright and honest enough to appreciate that not all of us who spend our lives driving the wheels of commerce are crooks. Jane, there *is* something seriously rotten at the heart of Bay Street — and you just might be the one to dig it out."

I had never heard him get that emotional. In the past, Lennie has argued that my research into corporate crime only hit at local, exceptional violations of whatever ethical code he believed informed the stock exchange. Never once had he intimated that the problem was systemic. Only then did it occur to me that maybe he suspected more than he had let on the other night.

"Now you've got my attention. When can I see Michael?"

He chuckled. "I knew the bait would have to be political. Michael suggested I give you his home phone number. He's expecting a call from you shortly after six tonight to set up a meeting."

"Lennie, if Portia hadn't found you first, I would have jumped your bones for sure. You're a dear. Thanks so much. I'll phone him tonight."

"You're welcome. But before you hang up — don't you want to know what he looks like?"

It was my turn to laugh. "No more than I want to know about Mike Harris's toilet training."

"Jane, your research instincts are slipping. Knowledge of our premier's toilet training might tell us *everything* about why he's intent on closing so many hospitals."

"Probably only about why he can't get off the pot. Bye Lennie." I hung up the phone, grateful that my social isolation hadn't excluded Portia and her husband.

I pulled on one of Pete's sweatsuits, put my exuberant companion on his leash and headed out the door.

When we reached the centre of the park, I let him loose for a run, contrary to city by-laws. I thought I could just sit back in the grass and fret some more about my ongoing role in the Durand case while he meandered. I was wrong.

Max is a border collie. He can't resist the blood-pull to herd everything that moves. Immediately he streaked off at the speed of a laser beam after a clutch of seagulls feeding on a pizza crust. They clattered into the air in raucous protest, leaving my demoralized mutt to sniff out the bases of tree trunks. He trickled his four-drop signature on a Japanese maple, then hared off in pursuit of other victims. Fifteen minutes later, having cleared away enough birds to satisfy his lust to intimidate, he followed me home.

As I released Max into my studio, I decided to have a quick shower and give my investigation a few hours of concentrated work. Mucking around in the detritus of strangers' lives won hands down over introspection.

My homework for my meeting with Michael Diamond involved reading the contents of a file I'd put together on Durand's infamous Imperial Trust takeover bid. Just as I hit the last page, the phone rang.

"Hi, Jane. It's David Walker — William's partner." He sounded agitated.

"Did you think I'd forgotten you already, David? I always remember juice-drinking medievalists."

His voice relaxed a bit. "They don't stock mead at Leather Boys. How are you?"

"So far I've been having the kind of day that makes you wish you'd never gotten out of the sack. And you?" That knee-jerk question takes on a whole new resonance when you're asking it of someone with AIDS.

"Sounds like we're suffering from the same bad karma. But I've heard from William — and he wants to talk with you. He's very scared. I told him I thought you might be a good person to connect with."

First Lennie's call, now this. Obviously some Higher Power didn't want me off the case. "I'm free to meet with him whenever, wherever he finds it convenient, David. And I really hope I can help."

"Thanks so much. Right now we really don't know which way to turn, and you're the only person I feel safe discussing this whole thing with. The police were here at the apartment last night, asking what I knew about William's whereabouts on the night of his father's murder. And they obviously didn't believe me when I told them that I was just as much in the dark about where he is now."

"That doesn't surprise me, David. I didn't really believe you either."

He was immediately contrite. "I'm sorry I lied to you about that — but it was the *only* thing I was dishonest about with you. Please believe me. William made me promise not to tell anyone where he's staying. I lied to the cops about knowing that he did see his father Friday night."

"That's something I can live with. When the real crunch comes, we all have to weigh our conflicting loyalties pretty delicately. I can see why you came down on the side of maintaining William's confidence. But I do think he'll have a difficult time persuading the cops that he didn't kill his father — especially if that's their favourite scenario. At the moment, I have no more reason to think he's innocent, but my gut tells me he didn't do it. Maybe William can help me find out who did or at least point me in the direction of someone whose motivation to bump off Durand-the-Elder was at least as strong."

David's voice reassumed its desperate edge. "Jane, even *I* don't have any hard proof that he didn't do it. And William knows that I won't concoct an alibi for him. I'm willing to conceal what I do know from the police, but I won't write fiction." His voice trailed off. "I guess that sounds pretty shabby from an ethical point of view."

"Shabby's my middle name, so let's get down to how I can connect with William."

"I know this is short notice, but are you free on Sunday?" he asked.

"I don't even have to check my social calendar to confirm that I am, David. Where would he like to meet me?"

"He's been staying at a cottage on Lake Simcoe, near Jackson's Point. Friends of mine own the place, and they understand our need for secrecy. They originally offered it to us when I first got sick, in case we wanted to be together some place out of the city while I recovered. Do you know the area?"

I had to pause to catch my breath. Our first summer together, Pete and I rented a cottage in Jackson's Point. "Yeah, I know it well. Can you give me the address?"

"Sure. It's 25 Lakeside Road — you know, the street that curves around the lake off Main Street? You pass six gorgeous summer homes along the shore, then there's a really dilapidated white frame two-storey cottage with green trim. It looks abandoned. Our friends got it really cheap, but they haven't had the time or money to renovate it," he explained.

"I know the road. I'll have no trouble finding it. When does he want me to arrive?"

"He said any time after nine in the morning would be fine."

"David, please tell him I'll be there around 9:30. And thanks for not reminding me that everything you've told me is in the strictest confidence."

He laughed. "I wouldn't have called you in the first place if I'd thought that was necessary. Thank you so much for agreeing to see him."

"No problem. It may help kick my investigation into gear and, we hope, simplify your situation. If I don't hear from you, I'll assume the time and place are okay."

"Great. Thanks, Jane."

I liked this man very much. "David, before you ring off, do know that you can call me any time, for any reason."

"I think I sensed that already. Maybe we can have a meal together sometime soon? I'm a good cook — in fact, on bad days at the university I think I missed my calling."

I laughed. "Thank both your lucky culinary and academic stars for calling you. I still haven't figured out my mission in life. I'll phone you mid-week to set up a dinner date — and you should also know that I hate radicchio!"

It was clear, at least for the time being, that I was recommitted to the case. Those two phone calls piqued my curiosity.

Talking with William Durand would give me a chance to check out my gut instincts about his innocence and to elicit some more information about Charles from a primary source. I had to remind myself how tainted by disappointment (not all of it stemming from realistic expectations) and pain is anyone's "candid" memoir of a parent.

Perhaps I should have been more cautious about the prospect of flying off to meet the prime suspect in a murder investigation in a relatively secluded spot. But retrospective wisdom is always cheap. Etta told me that I'd had to burn my fingers three times before I accepted her assessment of the stove as hot.

CHAPTER 14

SHORTLY AFTER six o'clock I rang up Michael Diamond. It was, in fact, 6:01. I didn't want to give the guy the correct impression that I was in a hurry to meet him. When a more-than-pleasant, indeed, heart-stopping voice-to-drop-your-jeans-for said "Hello, Michael here," I tried to assume the tone of a research librarian. I didn't want Lennie or this man getting the idea that my interest was anything other than strictly acade-mic. But I could cut myself a little slack and fantasize a bit.

"Hello. This is Jane Yeats calling. Leonard Sherman sug-gested that I contact you to set up a meeting on Monday." As my voice echoed across Ma Bell's line, I couldn't believe how much I sounded like Ernestine, Lily Tomlin's officious phone operator.

"Yes, I was expecting your call. I gather from my chat with Lennie that you'd like to ask me some questions about the Imperial Trust takeover bid," he said, calm as an idle sailboat on a wind-free Lake Ontario afternoon.

"Um, yes," I replied. "I'm grateful you're willing to take the time to talk to me. Are you free for lunch on Monday?"

"Only if lunch is a hot dog grabbed from a street vendor. I usually work right through lunch. I'd prefer to meet with you when I'm not feeling pressured to get back to the office. Could we have supper together?"

If this guy was as hot a source as Lennie claimed, I was willing to meet him at midnight on the Bloor viaduct over a Mars bar. "Sure. Where would you like to meet?" I inquired, less nonchalant than I intended. "I'm sure you'll understand when I say I would prefer that our conversation take place in private. Virtually everything I will tell you must remain confidential. Would you be comfortable coming to my house around seven? I'll bring home some take-out food from my local deli."

I crossed my mental fingers that his desire for privacy truly was motivated by confidentiality. If he was setting up a seduction scene, he was in for major disappointment. But Celibacy Queen can handle bad theatre. "That's very gracious of you. Please tell me how to get to your place."

I didn't need to write down his instructions. The address he gave me was in the Annex.

My final question totally blew my lady-librarian façade. "Can I bring anything — like a bottle of wine?"

"Bring anything you like." His voice could charm a cat away from a captive mouse. This made me hope that he wasn't good-looking. Not that looks are important, as Etta often remarks in the midst of assembling her face.

I parked Harley in the lot behind Sweet Dreams. Most Friday nights Etta stuck around, but tonight Slim wanted to go bowling. With an even bigger dollop of her usual guilt-laden insistence, she'd asked me to show up before they left, so I could meet her new boyfriend. Perhaps she was serious about this one: her normal practice is to change them so often that introductions became highly inappropriate by the time my path crossed theirs.

Mom and her date were sitting at the bar when I walked in, deep in what from the door looked like a pretty intense chat. When I approached them, Slim stood up to grasp my hand. Immediately I knew Etta had lied to me about the bowling. He was built like a Sumo wrestler, but dressed like Tex Ritter. The row of tiny mother-of-pearl buttons that held his black satin shirt closed must have been riveted on. The only way he'd get a ball down any alley was by shooting it out of a cannon.

He grinned. I recognized the teeth. "It's real nice to meet you, gal. Been hearin' all about ya from your ma here."

I smiled and returned his handshake. "It's nice to meet you, uh — " I'd blocked his name.

"Slim," he roared, smacking his belly. "Slim Horowitz."

When I asked him about their recent pilgrimage to Nashville, he launched into a paean that would have done the president of the local Chamber of Commerce proud. Etta, dressed to the nines and going nowhere so far, was looking vexed, her burgundy fingernails tapping out a threatening tattoo on the bar counter. She interrupted him to say they were late already.

"Sorry, honey," he apologized, rising again from his stool far faster than I would have thought possible. If Sweet Dreams ever goes bankrupt, my mother can open up a male obedience school.

Etta didn't bother to say goodbye. I honest-to-God think she was jealous. She just turned to me, directed two mauve-ringed cold eyes at my face and said, "If them two transvestites come in here tonight, make sure they behave themselves. I don't mind them dressing up, but I don't appreciate them getting up on stage and imitating the Mandrell sisters. It's disrespectful." Given the outfits many of her female patrons wore in here on weekend nights, I was tempted to ask her how the hell I'd spot a drag queen.

The buttons on Etta's scarlet blouse were straining across her breasts as much as Slim's over his belly. I've always been embarrassed at how my mother flaunts her glands. I suppose it's envy, really, given that whatever trickled down to me from her gene pool didn't include that munificence. From my father I inherited a flat chest, along with an inclination to despondency which I too exacerbate with too much drink.

Etta was more than a survivor. She had overcome a hard life and triumphed. Her outlook was so upbeat she attracted swarms of good, humorous people who shared her serious pursuit of fun. My father had been a morose son of a bitch who punished his liver until it retaliated by going on permanent strike. Miserable on those rare occasions when he accidentally lapsed into sobriety, Seamus grew mean as a hornet when he was drunk. Etta and I didn't mourn his passing, just his life.

On the spot I decided to try a can or two of that "beer" that has most of the alcohol leached out of it. Kenny-the-bartender raised a dubious eyebrow when I asked for one.

"You must be nursing one hell of a hangover."

"Just this once, Kenny, I'm working on avoiding one."

He didn't look impressed. If the entire east end went on the wagon, he'd have to learn to type.

The evening was uneventful. Etta had booked a good local band that played two lively sets the crowd loved. I did spot the transvestites when they appeared, but they managed to curb their performance addiction. Kenny kept an eye on them, though. If they tried to pick up a weekend cowboy, they might wind up dead if their mark didn't see past the falsies in time to salvage his ego.

As Kenny was opening my third fake beer, he nodded toward the front door. "Looks like your cop friend can't stay away from here. Good thing Etta's not around."

As he walked toward the bar, I noticed that Ernie had taken some uncharacteristic trouble with his wardrobe. I hoped he hadn't come courting. He's such a nice misogynist I wish I could introduce him to a woman who might take the edge off his loneliness. My fondness does not extend to personally undertaking the task.

He sat down beside me. "Hi, Jane. Can I buy you another?" he asked, pointing to my deceptively foam-capped glass.

"No thanks, Ernie. This is my third."

"That must be strong stuff. I've never known you to cut yourself off so soon on a Friday night."

I laughed. "This beer is so impotent I can't imagine swilling a fourth. If the writing on the can speaks the truth, you'd have to down ten of these to equal one of the real thing. I'm on the wagon tonight."

I appreciated his not asking why or making a wisecrack. So I explained, "I was thinking a bit about my dad earlier tonight. If I don't watch it, I'll be headed down the same slippery slope."

He nodded. "I went home from work and drank myself to sleep every night for eight months after Sandy died." Three years ago his twin brother had been killed in a head-on collision with a drunk driver. "Then one morning I woke up and realized I hadn't really *felt* a feeling all that time. It occurred to me that I'd never manage to get on with my life if I didn't get sober and let myself mourn."

I was curious. "Is it better sober, Ernie? Does the pain eventually go away?"

"Even when it's not better, at least I know it's real. And no, the pain never goes away completely — but I wouldn't want it to. I think if it did I'd lose the memories, too."

"You're getting wise in your middle age, sir."

He shook his head. "Not half as smart as I need to be to crack the Durand case."

Oh, oh. He'd come on a fishing expedition. And this time I knew something important he didn't. I had no intention of telling him where William was hiding out, let alone that on Sunday morning I'd be seeing him.

I have some integrity: because I wasn't prepared to play traders, I forced myself not to ask him about the coroner's report.

"We got the report from Forensics this morning. But it doesn't help a damn at this point, because we don't have the murder weapon." He turned on his bar stool and looked directly at me. "I don't suppose it would hurt if I told you a detail or two, given that we obviously can't connect an unknown object with a missing suspect."

I was puzzled. He almost sounded like he was inviting me to pry the information out of him. "Ernie, I'm not going to ask you for anything you're not comfortable giving me."

His voice got angry. "I know that, Jane. This isn't about trusting you. It's about *me*. I'm so goddamn fed up with how the Department is handling the whole thing that I'm ready to toss you a bone in the hope that *you* might come up with something! I'd like to see the guy who killed Durand nailed. We're being discouraged from extending our inquiries beyond the family. And God knows, the man had enemies everywhere he'd ever done business. I mean, maybe the kid did bump off his old man, but at least between now and when we find him we might as well be sniffing under all the carpets."

"What are you saying? That perhaps it's easier for me to sniff under some of those carpets?"

"Yeah. Exactly. What I have to tell you is going to be something of a downer, though. I sure as hell don't know what to make of it."

I reached over and shook his shoulder. "Keep me in major suspense, why don't you?"

"The main finding of the coroner's report seems to be that Durand's skull had particles of talc embedded in it, along with microscopic traces of a few other minerals."

I shook my head. "Great, Ernie. You're saying that Durand was beaten to death with a can of baby powder?"

He laughed. "Our Chief Coroner is something of a scholar, as you know." Last year I'd contributed a profile of Arnold Togawa to a glossy magazine. "After he isolated and identified all the minerals present in the wound site, Arnold added them together, figured out the ratios, and came up with soapstone."

"Shit! An Inuit carving. Inuit carvings are made from *soapstone,* Ernie. And Durand collected indigenous art. In fact, he had one of the best collections in the country."

"Top of the class, girl. His murderer may have sent him off to glory with one of his own *objets.* The office is packed with them. But it's not likely that the perp held on to it any longer than he had to, is it?" Ernie has to be the only cop in the city who tosses words like *"objets"* and "perp" into the same breath.

"No, and it doesn't sound quite like a Mob hit, does it?" I joked.

Ernie picked up on my nervousness. "Have you heard

anything about William's whereabouts?" His timing caught me totally off-guard.

"No." My denial came out in the falsetto tone I veer into whenever I even begin to speak a lie.

"I know there's no point trying to pressure you into breaking your word to someone," he replied, far more reasonably than I had any right to expect. "But promise me this — share your information with me as soon as you're free to?"

I put my hand on his arm. My touch startled him. "I promise you that."

He grinned and patted the top of my hand. "So I can expect a phone call as soon as you stumble across a blood-stained Inuit carving with a tuft of Durand's hair transplant stuck to it?"

"You'll be the first to know. Seriously, though, thanks for your understanding."

His hand was still resting on mine. "Jane, would you like to go out to dinner with me soon? Maybe we could try that new Thai restaurant on Bloor?"

I paused to choose my words carefully. I didn't want to hurt this lovely man. "Ernie, if that's a date you have in mind, I have to say 'thanks, but no thanks.' But please don't take it personally. I haven't dated anyone since — "

He saved me from having to say it. "I guessed that. And it was a date I had in mind." He removed his hand from mine, looking so bloody disappointed I wished I could put my arms around him.

"Ernie, if I asked you to go to a ball game with me, say the season opener — with serious friendship in mind — would you say 'no'?"

"No. I mean no, I'd say yes. I enjoy your company."

When he stood up to leave, I pulled him toward me and kissed his forehead.

I watched him walk toward the exit. His step wasn't as jaunty as when he'd entered the bar.

CHAPTER 15

SUNDAY MORNING shortly after nine I pulled Silver's Toyota into a spot beside Graham's Pharmacy on the main drag of Jackson's Point. A woman on a Harley attracts too much attention in small places. The cottage where William was hiding out was only a five-minute walk away, so I ambled along the street in the opposite direction for the two blocks of stores that defaced the landscape until it reverted back to lake on one side and clapboard bungalows on wide, woody lots on the other.

I felt like I'd stumbled onto the deserted set of an old cowboy movie. Most of the residents must work in neighbouring towns like Sutton and Keswick, or farther afield. There wasn't enough commercial development here to sponsor a bantam hockey team. Several of the stores looked like they only opened up for the cottage season — an arts-and-crafts shop, a windsurfing store, a handmade chocolates place, a hole-in-the-wall bait shop. The Imperial Pagoda restaurant was shut tight, but Betty's Burgers was open. An overweight, middle-aged waitress in a less-than-fresh white nylon uniform was setting a plate of bacon, eggs and home fries in front of an unshaven guy who looked like he'd forgotten to wash for a month. Inside Charlene's Laundromat a young woman in a track suit held onto a kid with one hand while she shoved bunches of wet clothes into a dryer with the other.

I went into the grocery store next to the Unisex Hair Salon and bought a pack of Rothmans and a three-day-old local newspaper. A diminutive boy who had to step up onto a wooden crate to reach the cash register rang in my purchases. As I walked back along the street toward the cottage, I spotted only two other pedestrians, an old woman gingerly inching her way forward with the aid of a walker and a rotund man of indeterminate age who was seriously involved in a conversation with himself. A small sign inside the window of the real-estate office promised that "Jackson's Point offers the metropolitan dweller a real change of pace." Not misleading.

As I approached the fork in the lakeside road leading to the address David had given me, I was surprised to see that a huge corner lot on the east side had been cleared and a three-storey condominium erected on site. The exorbitant cost of Toronto housing has driven a lot of young couples who work in the city out this far in search of affordable shelter; in my lifetime urban sprawl will clear-cut its way right up to Thunder Bay. Three roads, each running one long block north of the main street were dotted with modest wartime houses. The character of the buildings changed dramatically as soon as the street forked along the lake. Beautiful summer residences, all of them recently built or restored, sat on deep, landscaped lots sloping gently down to their own strips of private beach. Further along was a small public beach for the folks who lived year-round in the modest houses. Class-wise you couldn't force a much sharper demarcation if you set an Indian reserve in the heart of Rosedale.

A weathered piece of wood with the number "26" mounted on it was nailed to a tree at the entrance to a cottage so ravaged by time and Canadian weather that it must be driving the upscale owners of the adjoining real estate to derangement. The dilapidated, two-storey building, the back of which faced the road, looked ready to cave in on itself. It had been painted white with dark green trim, probably in the same year Buddy Holly died. Its deep, pie-shaped lot was lined on either side with tall, neglected cedar trees grown so close together that only the tops remained green, their sun-starved lower branches entangled with thick, ropy vines. The screen door at the rear of the building hung on one hinge in front of a windowless door that a squirrel could kick in. The path leading up to it took a major slump on either side, choked with dead tiger-lily foliage.

I could guess where the septic tank was buried.

There was no car parked outside. Cold as it was, the chimney wasn't smoking. William obviously didn't want to advertise his presence. I walked along a dirt path to the left of the cottage. Stained cotton curtains with the colour and pattern bleached out of them drooped inside the windows. The side section of the porch was half missing. The front of the cottage overlooked the lake, its water that brutal shade of blue that puts you in mind of death. I wouldn't have been surprised to see Norman Bates dart out of sight. I walked to the front edge of the property, where it quickly dropped down to the water.

Number 26 was situated midway along the shore of a small bay. The cottages on either side had grassy landscaped lots that inclined gracefully down to the water, new docks and boathouses. This lot had not been cleared or sculpted: a broken wooden staircase zigzagged steeply down to a stony beach through an overgrown rocky bank with some scraggly poplars clinging to it for dear life. Huge sections of broken concrete still loosely connected by rusted reinforcing rods lay like a ruined necklace across the width of the shoreline.

As I turned to face the cottage, I shivered. Toronto seemed a thousand miles away — maybe my love of solitude is conditional on being able to escape it in sixty seconds. The cottages on either side looked like they'd been closed up for the winter. I delicately set my feet down on the three rotting wooden steps leading up to the porch screen door, which was off the latch you might say, the latch having gone missing. I crossed the sagging porch floor and knocked on the main door.

The young man who had been at Helen Durand's side in the Cathedral, who had maniacally sliced up his father's portrait at the wake, who was the chief suspect in his murder, came to the door. He held out his hand. From the neck down he looked to be in fine shape: navy wool fishermen's sweater over a Black Watch plaid flannel shirt, pleated jeans and leather running shoes. But his fair hair was dishevelled, his delicate face etched by fatigue.

"Thanks so much for coming. I really appreciate it. Please come in," he said, stepping aside. When I started to remove my jacket, he added "You might want to leave that on. It's kind of cold in here. I'm afraid to light the fireplace," he explained, gesturing in the direction of a huge, double-sided stone fireplace that stretched to the ceiling. "There's only a small baseboard heater."

As I accepted his offer of coffee, I saw my words momentarily inscribed in the air. He disappeared into the kitchen at the back of the cottage, leaving me in a huge living room with early American chintz sofas and chairs set against both walls. Four large, multi-paned windows, many of them cracked, a few patched with hockey tape, overlooked the frozen lake. The ceiling fixture was one of those plastic wagon wheels Etta is so fond of. The décor was vintage '50s, hand-me-downs from an "I Love Lucy" set. I checked out the worn paperbacks in a small bookrack on the mantel. *Peyton Place,* some Arthur Haileys, Leon Uris's *Exodus,* a Norman Vincent Peale, three Harlequins, a Nancy Drew, Pearl Buck's *The Good Earth.* No Northrop Frye. But no Danielle Steele, either. The library must have come with the furniture.

"I'm sorry about the mug," William apologized, as he placed a piece of chipped green and red *kitsch* with holly on its handle on the coffee table.

I took a warming sip of coffee, which was surprisingly good. Hell, microwaved cat pee would taste fine in this chilly setting. "You must be very frightened to be willing to stay here alone, especially at this time of year."

He laughed nervously. "Yes, you could say I'm very frightened. In fact, I'm scared shitless." He crossed his legs. His eyes widened. "The police actually seem to think I murdered my father. The closest I've ever come to trouble with the cops is getting a parking ticket, for Christ's sake!"

"If it's any assurance, William, I don't think you're being paranoid. From what I can gather, they *are* regarding you as a major suspect."

"Tell me the truth: do you think you can come up with anything that might get them off my case?" he asked.

I forsook comfort for candour. "So far — and keep in mind that only a little over a week has passed since your father was killed — I don't have a shred of anything to point me in any other direction. Nor, I assume, do the police. But maybe they're not as motivated as I am to prove your innocence. So if you're willing to answer my questions, we might come up with something to set me off in the right direction." I was calculating that his fear, as palpable from his body language as the nip in the air, might overcome his reluctance to open up.

His face relaxed. "You just said *in the right direction.* That makes me think that you're assuming I didn't kill my father." He reached for the pack of du Maurier Lights lying beside him on the sofa.

"You're right, but that comes from my gut, not my head. I need you to confirm my instinct about this one," I admitted, reaching into my jacket pocket for my cigarettes.

"Where do you want me to start?" he asked.

"I want you to start with the events leading up to the night of your father's death. David told me that you saw your father on at least two occasions that week."

He nodded, exhaling a quick puff of smoke. "Yes. And that was unusual. Prior to that, I hadn't seen him since I took him to court over my trust fund last spring. But I really needed some money — a big chunk of it — to keep Per/Visions going. Like a jerk, I decided to tell him why I needed the money. I thought if I showed him how carefully I'd been running my gallery, he might respect me enough to advance me a year's operating costs. And I fully intended to pay him back."

I interrupted because I wanted to help keep him honest. "William, David told me that you also needed money to pay for his medical treatment."

This threw him into a tight loop. The muscles of his already crossed legs seemed to contract even further. "David told you that?" Incredulity elevated his voice to the *castrato* range.

"I don't think you should interpret his confidence as a betrayal. He's terribly worried about the pressures you're under."

"Yes, well, I certainly didn't tell my father that's why I needed the money. I mean, after my lawsuit failed, I'd crawl naked from here to China before I'd beg him for a cent — if David weren't sick. Anyway, if the old man thought I'd been within a square mile of anyone who had AIDS, he never would have agreed to see me. If he'd known I was gay, he would have disowned me. But I was desperate."

"How did you set up your meeting with him?" I asked.

"I just phoned his secretary and told her I needed to talk to him about a business matter. She got back to me about an hour later and told me to come to his office on Wednesday afternoon at two. My guess is that he thought I was going to launch another court case. He hated publicity about his private life and would have done almost anything to avoid it — short of coughing up what I had coming to me. And since the corporation got into deep shit, the media were on his tail almost every day. Anyway, I showed up at his office on the stroke of two with all my financial statements in my briefcase, prepared to make the presentation of a lifetime. About five minutes after I launched into it, he started laughing so hard you'd think he was watching *Saturday Night Live*."

William abruptly stopped talking. He sandwiched his trembling hands between his knees.

He resumed talking when he got the shakes under control. "Since the time he admitted to himself that I would never work for his bloody corporation, he refused to take anything else I did seriously. So he really got off on mocking me as I described the gallery's financing. That made me crazy. I mean, here I was trusting him enough to lay bare my pathetic little business to a man who spends more on his suits in a year than I do on my whole operation, and there he was laughing so hard tears are streaming down his face. When I screamed at him that I was taking a big risk by appealing to his respect and his compassion, he just looked at me like I was a creature from another planet. 'Respect for you?' he said. 'I've got more respect for a cockroach who's forgotten a whole lot more about survival than you'll ever know. And as for compassion, I think you mistook me for someone who gives a damn about you.'" Again William couldn't continue.

"Had I been in your situation, I would have murdered him on the spot," I remarked.

He looked up at me. "You know something: if I didn't have David in my life, if I didn't want to be around to take care of him when he gets really ill, I would have strangled the S.O.B. on the spot. My father's death might have screwed up my head — you were there when I freaked out last Tuesday — but I am not sorry he's gone. Mourning him would be like missing a tumour!"

"If it makes you feel any better, I can tell you that I haven't met anyone who is sorry he's no longer in the land of the conniving. But please go on, William. How did that meeting end?"

"Quickly. I gathered up my papers and stormed out. His laughter followed me all the way down the hall." He stared glumly at the cold fireplace.

"I need you to get me from there to your second meeting with him, on Friday," I urged.

"Needless to say, my head was not in a great space when I hit the pavement. I was really screwed up. I needed more than a drink. I needed to snort a few lines." He looked up from the fireplace to meet my eyes. "Did David also tell you that I do coke?" he asked, looking more like a truant schoolboy than a crazed dope fiend.

"He told me that was history," I replied.

"Yeah, I thought it was too — until I got stupid enough to let the old man press one too many buttons. I couldn't get the sound of his mockery out of my head, so I headed straight to my dealer — who just happens to be my father's chauffeur."

The fine hairs on the back of my neck jumped to attention. I think they're connected to my grey cells. "But surely your father didn't know — "

"No. Not that I do coke and not who I bought it from. His chauffeur, Archie Price, is one of the biggest dealers in the city. He was in an ideal position to traffic cocaine. On days when my father knows — *knew* — he was going to be in his office for hours at a stretch, he just contacts — *contacted*, hell, I haven't shoved him into the past tense yet — Archie on his cell phone and asked him to pick him up when he was ready to leave. So most days Archie was free for hours to travel around the city peddling in posh restaurants and hotels around Yorkville, and still be close to Bay Street."

"You are sure that your father didn't know about Archie's — ah — moonlighting?"

"Are you kidding? He would have fired him on the spot! No, he would have reported him to the cops and had him arrested first. My father was a moralist, believe it or not, at least on the subject of substance abuse. You've got to keep in mind that his old man was a drunk. I mean, he wouldn't even go on lithium or anti-depressants to control his mood swings, like his doctor recommended. Anyway, Archie lived in a coach house on my father's estate. So Wednesday afternoon after I left my meeting with the old man I took a chance on his being at home. Sometimes he'd go back there just before he picked up my father — I guess to dump his drugs and money. When I got there I found him shoving his belongings into a few suitcases and garbage bags like he'd just heard a hurricane alert. Here's this guy, who's usually so cool he could stare Caligula in the eye without blinking, so terrified I can't believe it. When I told him I wanted to buy a few lines, he reached into one of his suitcases and tossed me a whole bloody bag of coke. 'Think of it as a going-away present, kid,' he said."

"What time did you get there?"

"I drove straight there from my father's office, so it must have been some time after three o'clock."

"Go on, please."

"So I asked him what the hell was going down. He told me — and all the while he's talking he's throwing stuff into his suitcases — that he'd been caught doing a double-cross on a big deal. He ripped off the Mob for ten kilos and they put out a contract on him. If he didn't get out of the city fast and permanently, he'd be looking up at the SkyDome from the bottom of Lake Ontario. Just as I was walking out the door, he said 'You wanna know the funniest thing of all, kid? Them guys like your father ain't no cleaner than me!' When I asked him what he meant, he said 'You really wanna know how to get some serious bread out of your old man — tell him that Gerald Dawson is in bed with the Mob.'"

He flicked me a disbelieving glance. "When he told me that, I figured he'd really gone over the top. I mean, Dawson is supposed to be the Mr. Clean of Bay Street. So I asked Archie, 'You mean insider trading or tax evasion or something like that?' 'I mean *money laundering,* sweetheart,' he said, 'washing the Mob's drug bucks so clean you could throw them in a collection plate at church.' He sneered, 'I guess you got it right about him being Mr. Clean.' I pushed him for more details, but he was in a real hurry to clear out. Said he couldn't tell me any more anyway, that the little bit he did know he'd picked up from a good buddy, who worked as the money delivery boy between the Mob and Dawson."

"Did he tell you his friend's name?" I asked.

"He only mentioned his first name: Luciano. I remember it because David adores Pavarotti. Oh yeah, he said he was a biker."

What I was hearing just didn't compute. For what possible reason would Dawson, the white knight of the business élite, soil his hands, jeopardize his empire and his reputation, to do the Mob a major favour?

"I don't get it. Why would Dawson get involved in money laundering? What could be in it for him — I mean, to make the incredible risk worthwhile?"

William shrugged. "I can't help you there. I haven't a clue about how the corporate world works — except that they figured out a long time ago how to legitimize what ordinary people get thrown behind bars for doing on a much smaller scale."

"So how does what Price told you connect to your next meeting with your father?"

He jumped up from the sofa to pace the room. "Well, just think about it, Jane. If even a shred of what he said was true — I mean, think about what that information would mean to my father. He *hated* Dawson. He would have sold his soul to get back at him, especially after Dawson screwed up his Imperial Trust bid."

"So you bargained on using what Price told you to pry money out of your father?" I guessed.

William nodded. "You've got it. I didn't have any proof, but I figured that my father could hire a private investigator to do some snooping. Even an anonymous tip to the newspapers might inspire an editor to put a reporter on it. Anyway, I phoned my father Thursday afternoon and told him that I had picked up some incriminating information about Dawson I thought he could use. He immediately agreed to release all the money in my trust fund in exchange for what I knew — if it sounded useful. So I told him most of the rumour. I held back a bit by way of insurance. He said he'd have his lawyer draw up the necessary papers as soon as he got off the phone. Asked me to come to his office Friday evening at seven to sign them.

"The rest is an anti-climax. I showed up Friday night, signed the papers — he'd already had his secretary 'witness' both our signatures in advance — and left."

"What time did you leave his office?"

"It can't have been much later than 7:10, give or take a couple of minutes. As soon as I signed, he really gave me the bum's rush. I didn't even have time to finish my cigarette — or collect my matches," he added ruefully. "The old man was exultant — like three feet off the broadloom — and well, I guess 'restless' is the best word. I think he was in a hurry to leave. I assumed he was calculating how to nail Dawson."

"What did you do before you met David at Leather Boys later that night?"

"I sat all by my pathetic self in a cheesy bar on College

Street and drank myself legless. All I could think was, imagine sinking so low you wind up blackmailing your own father."

"William, if it's any consolation, yours was probably one of his less sordid business deals. And I'm sure your father thought he'd struck a great bargain. Do you have any reason to think that he hadn't already been in touch with Dawson — before you got to his office Friday night?"

William shook his head. "No, I just didn't think he would have moved in so fast. How, at that point, could he have come up with anything to back up the suspicion or even have hired someone to start checking it out?"

"If you're right about his wanting to leave shortly after your meeting with him, then either something interrupted him that kept him in the office longer than he intended — or whoever did kill him may have been in the building already."

I had a scary thought. "William, could his killer have been close to the office when you were in there? Does the office have a private washroom nearby, for example?"

William turned ashen. "Why, yes. I used it when I was there on Wednesday. It's right off the office. The door to it is on the wall to the left of his desk. Oh Christ, do you think someone could have been in there, waiting for me to leave? I mean, close enough to have overheard our conversation?"

"Yes, I do. If someone hid in there before the other offices in the building emptied for the night, he or she could have avoided the after-hours security check. Now think hard: is there a separate entrance from the outside hall to the washroom, so that someone getting off the elevator could get into the washroom without going through your father's office?"

He needed only a moment's concentration before saying, "Yes. I guess it's there so the cleaning staff can get in without disturbing him. But they must keep it locked."

"Wouldn't any visitor first have to go through your father's secretary?"

"Yes, and it wouldn't be easy. That woman is such a bitch. The way she protected him you'd think he'd hired her as a bodyguard. She reminds me of that dreadful old woman in *From Russia with Love* — you know, Kurt Weill's widow — what's her name?"

"Lotte Lenya. She was great."

"Yeah, that's it. But come to think of it, Ruthless Ruth wasn't there when I arrived. Maybe he let her off work early — it was a Friday afternoon. She probably went home to sharpen her nails." I wondered what she had told the police about Durand's appointments and visitors that afternoon.

William returned to the sofa. Immediately his hands started jumping around again like they'd taken on a neurotic life of their own. "I'm trying to remember if we said enough for anyone who might have been listening to figure out that I was the source of my father's information about Dawson," he explained. "Because if he *was* killed by someone who wanted to shut him up, then I'm still alive only because they haven't had a chance to kill me yet." Had he been stranded naked out there on the frozen lake, he wouldn't be trembling more.

My brain had been busy computing its way to the same horrifying conclusion. "That's a possibility, William. But hopefully only a small one. It depends upon a whole chain of events being set into motion in a very short period of time. Your father must have contacted Dawson. Dawson arranged to have him killed. The killer overheard you and your father — "

I trailed off when I noticed that my reasoning wasn't reassuring William. That didn't surprise me. I really wasn't convinced that he was out of danger, yet I couldn't see any point in further escalating his alarm. And the sequence of events I had outlined was all too plausible, allowing for some minor variations I didn't elaborate on. Such as that the killer needn't have been in the immediate vicinity of Durand's office Friday evening to know that William was his father's informant: he could have tortured that much out of his victim before bumping him off.

I stood up, stretched and walked to the window overlooking the lake. A strong wind was pelting drifts of snow into peaks across its frozen surface. Lake Simcoe is famous for its ice fishing, but I couldn't see any huts set onto this bay. Only a lone Skidoo way off shore.

When I turned to face William, he was shuddering so badly I thought he might be sobbing. I crossed the room and put a hand on his shoulder. "I think you should consider returning to the city and contacting the cops. Tell them more or less what you've just told me. If they think you're in any real danger, they'll put you under police protection."

His eyes darted up to my face, astonished. "I can't believe you said that! David told me to trust you. My aunt told me to trust you." Each sentence notched his voice up several decibels. "In return for being honest with you, you are telling me to commit suicide." He jumped up and flung his coffee mug at the fireplace.

I decided to let his anger run its course before I tried to explain myself. This was the second time I'd watched him lose control. Even Simone might admit that he needed to do some anger management work.

"If I tell the cops that I was at the office Friday night collecting my blackmail booty, I'll be handing them a motive on a silver platter! Think about it: they'll have me at the scene of the crime with a reason to kill him if he refused to cough up the money — the murderer probably stole those papers I signed. You don't have to be Miss Marple to figure out that the only thing missing is a weapon." He paused. "What was he killed with? Do you know? Have the police got it?"

I raised my hands, palms outward. "Whoa ... William ... please slow down. I feel like I've been hit by a tidal wave. I can't think straight when I get overwhelmed."

He forced himself to sit down. "I'm sorry," was all he could say, in a small voice finally drained of rage. His feet beat an impromptu tattoo on the floor boards.

I nodded. "That's okay. You have every reason to freak out. Let me try to answer your questions about the weapon. Yes, Homicide does know. The lab report indicates that some-one crushed your father's skull with a soapstone carving —

presumably from his own collection that he kept in the office. And no, the killer didn't leave it behind. But I'm sure they'll have someone making the rounds of the art dealers to help them compile an inventory of the collection so they can determine which piece is missing. Some killers are funny that way — they'll run the risk of keeping the murder weapon because they regard it as a kind of souvenir, a trophy."

His voice grew agitated again. "Then you can see why they think *I* did it. A hitman is hardly going to count on finding some handy blunt object at the scene to kill his mark."

"Unless he wanted to make it look like a crime of passion, rather than a hit," I observed. "Or — unless Gerald Dawson showed up personally, maybe thinking they could cut a deal, lost his cool when your father provoked him or refused his terms, and grabbed the closest thing at hand."

William shook his head doubtfully. "That still doesn't get me off the hook, does it? I can't believe that the cops will investigate Dawson. Even if they caught him in the office with a smoking gun in his hand — I mean a bloody carving — he could still buy his way out of it. He's just too powerful."

I couldn't argue the point. I was remembering that the police had stopped their investigation into the allegations in my book about corruption within the force well short of the executive suite. Remembering that they still handled complaints internally, the same biased way doctors and lawyers are allowed to "investigate" and "discipline" their own colleagues. Remembering, too, what Ernie had told me: that before Charles Durand was cold, the heat was on the department to make a quick arrest — and to keep it all in the family, if possible.

I met William's eyes. "It's my turn to apologize. When I suggested you go to the police, I was scrambling around trying to think of a way to ensure your safety. It wasn't a very creative idea. The police have enough circumstantial evidence to arrest you — maybe to convict you. And even if their case falls apart in court, you could be separated from David for a long time." I added softly, "Too long."

One of the more witty gods must have been keen on getting me the rhetorical devices prize. Just as I finished my sentence, it got fortuitously punctuated by a THUNK that sounded not far beyond the front of the cottage. I stupidly jumped up but was smart enough to scream at William, "HIT THE FLOOR." Before I had time to think about protecting my own bones, something fast as a speeding bullet shattered the glass in one of the lake-facing window panes and whizzed past my face. It must have lodged somewhere on the way to the kitchen. I hit the floor.

I looked across the pine boards at William. He was so still I got scared. "Hey, you're okay, aren't you?"

I could hear him breathing.My antennae were so focused I could have heard a spider mending its abode in the corner.

"Yeah, I'm okay. But I think I've wet my jeans for the first time in twenty years."

"If that's all the damage that comes out of this, we're laughing. Don't move." I didn't know where this take-charge attitude of mine was coming from, but it might have had something to do with the fact that the man lying beside me had just lost control of his bladder.

A third unfriendly missive annihilated the window pane next to the one that got hit a few seconds earlier. Once inside the cottage it shattered more glass, this time a pane in a picture frame hugging a likeness of Queen Elizabeth, years before she had all those family problems.

Unlike my companion, whose kept his chin pasted to the floor, I was more angry than frightened. Not to mention what the humiliation factor was doing to my ego. I began to elbow myself on my belly toward the front wall, which I reached without another bullet making an uninvited appearance on the scene. When I rose to my feet, I was surprised to find that my knees hadn't turned to jelly. I peeped beyond the sun-scorched curtain in time to see the Skidoo I'd spotted earlier heading in some haste for the far shore. The guy who'd been passing his time using us for target practice must have been equipped with a high-powered rifle. From the little bit I could make out of him in the distance he might have been second cousin to an over-ripe Chiquita Banana — skinny, dressed in black, his head covered by a balaclava.

I walked over to William and patted him comfortingly on the shoulder. "It's safe to get up now. Our friend has left."

He rolled over slowly and looked down at his wet crotch. "This is really embarrassing. I mean, in all the scripts we grew up with, guys never did this."

"Sure they did, William, only we never got to read about it because the boys who wrote the books never reported it. Heroes don't have bladders. Their oversized gonads shoved them into extinction."

He went upstairs to change into a fresh pair of boxers and jeans. I took advantage of his absence to root around for the two bullets that had come to rest inside the cottage. I found one lodged in the wall behind Her Majesty. The other had ended its flight in a kitchen cupboard. I dug them both out with a rusted Swiss Army knife suspended from a piece of dirty cord beside the sink. All I could conclude was that they looked nasty. I don't know a thing about ballistics.

William entered the kitchen as I was cupping the deadly pellets in my hand.

"They were probably fired at long range from a high-speed rifle," he said. The deduction restored some authority to his voice. The poor man must be working hard at recouping his masculinity.

"How do you know that?" I asked.

"When we lived in Noranda, my father used to drag me along with him when he went hunting. I loathed it, but he was dead set on making a little man out of me. I remember what the bullets looked like. And whoever was firing at us had to be taking aim from somewhere out on the lake, probably in a direct line to the cottage, for them to have entered at the angle they did. I saw the hole in the wall behind Betty Windsor."

We returned to the living room and had a short conference about what he should do for the next while. I decided that I wouldn't report the incident to the police, which might have necessitated my coming clean about William's whereabouts. In any case, the shooter had scooted off with his weapon, so our ballistics evidence wouldn't help them identify the source of the bullets. I pocketed them as a sop to my conscience; maybe I'd give Ernie a heavy metal necklace for his next birthday.

William was adamant about not returning to Toronto, at least until I'd spent a few days checking into Dawson's possible implication in his father's murder. I didn't tell him how disheartened I was feeling about my chances of uncovering anything substantial enough to force an official investigation into GOD's inner circle.

He finally decided to go into deeper hiding. One of the co-owners of the cottage worked at a new AIDS hospice in Haliburton. He was sure his friend could arrange to let him stay there. He'd be safe. No one would report his presence. The gay community has learned to take good care of its own, he told me. I insisted that he phone his friend before we left. After he made arrangements to travel directly to the hospice from the cottage, I hung around while he flung the few belongings he'd brought with him into a sports bag.

Outside the front porch I quickly located the first bullet and pocketed it. We walked together to a secluded spot off the road where he had hidden his car. Before parting, we agreed that David would serve as our contact person, calling William at the same time every day from a pay phone to pass on any new information I had dug up.

He hugged me shyly before he got into the car.

"Good luck, William. And take very good care," I said.

"At this point, I think *you* are the one who really needs to heed that advice."

As he drove away, I reflected that now his life was as imperilled as his lover's. However irrationally, I felt responsible for their well-being.

A freezing wind hammered my back as I walked to the Toyota, my jacket collar up, my spirits low.

Because I'm so afraid of disappointing people's expectations, I've made a career of avoiding intimate relationships. I drove back to Toronto, encumbered by obligation. I wished Simone had picked up the Yellow Pages to hire an investigator. Apparently there are listings of people who actually do this sort of thing for a living.

How do they get life insurance?

CHAPTER 16

WHEN I HEADED back to Toronto, it was well past noon. On the way home I picked up a McSomething or Other, fries and a chocolate shake and wolfed them down while I drove. A tell-tale sign of my preoccupation: I forgot to buy Max a burger.

I rode the freight elevator straight up to the fourth floor and knocked on Silver's door. She opened it a wedge and eyed me grumpily. Half her abundant hair had escaped its braid.

"Hi. I thought you might want the keys back, in case you had something planned for this afternoon." Why couldn't I bring myself to tell her straight out that I was frightened out of my wits and desperately needed comfort?

"Have you forgotten what day it is?" she snapped.

Oh God, I'm always forgetting birthdays. What the hell, I decided to take a chance. "Of course not," I lied. "Happy birthday, Silver."

I knew I had miscalculated when she briefly pulled the door open wide enough for me to see what she wasn't wearing. "This is my birthday suit, but I don't get to celebrate it until November 30th. Remember— you were at my fucking party three months ago!" I couldn't help noticing that her birthday suit had puckered at bit at the seams.

Two things came back to me: the party, at which I'd gotten more than a little drunk, and the fact that Silver had a big thing about not being disturbed on Sundays before sundown. Her Saturday night frolics often spilled well over into the next day.

I was a bit hurt that she didn't want to hear about my meeting with William. Obviously my need to talk was greater than hers. I handed her the keys and thanked her for the use of the car.

"You're welcome," she said, almost catching my wrist in the door in her haste to close it.

I swiftly inserted my foot. "Silver, who the hell have you got in there — Hillary Clinton?" I was thoughtful enough to lower my voice.

"She should be so lucky." The door slammed shut. I extricated my Doc Marten just in time.

Clog-dancing to the stairwell, I sang myself a chorus of "Friendship."

Max gave me the kind of welcome I deserved, deepening my guilt about returning home empty-handed. I promised him pizza for supper.

Contemplation time. I poured myself a Smithwicks, put on a Gregorian chant tape (pre-dating by twenty years the chart-topping Benedictine Monks of Santo Domingo de Silos, and so enchantingly rendered you didn't even recognize their *Ave Maria*), and flopped down on the sofa.

William's information was affecting my brain like a Mobius strip: no matter how long I stared at the thing, I still couldn't get it. If GOD was the culprit, he must have had a major motive for sending Durand on to premature glory. Did Archie Price's money-laundering allegations have any substance? If they did, GOD would soar to the top of my suspects list. If Durand had threatened him with exposure, I'd have a gilt-edged motive to pin on his rival's lapel.

The killer had reduced his victim's head to hash. Maybe GOD had agreed to meet Durand, hoping to cut a deal in exchange for his silence. Maybe Durand, who had a perverse talent for enraging people, drove GOD to unpremeditated homicide by making him an exorbitant offer he couldn't afford to accept — or by humiliating him the way he had William. More men have killed in defence of their ego than their country. Yet from everything I'd read, GOD had the emotional range of a lizard. Not the type of guy who'd let his feelings get in the way of his calculations. If GOD had informed the Mob boss that Durand could pull the carpet on their cozy arrangement, the Mob could have ordered the hit. And bikers have been known to rapidly facilitate the aging process of people who ran afoul of the Mob — but with an Inuit sculpture?

I kept bumping my head against the improbability of the dean of the Anglo-business élite entering into a partnership with drug traffickers. Hopefully, tomorrow night when I met with Michael Diamond, I would learn more about GOD from someone who had an inside track. I certainly wasn't yet prepared to "interview" the deity himself. Michael was a tax accountant: I could also ask him to fill me in on some of the finer mechanics of money laundering. I'd read a bit about it in the course of my research, but not enough to understand its finer workings.

Meanwhile, I knew I'd be on more secure ground if I could firm up some connection, however tangential, between the Mob and GOD. According to William, Archie Price had been preparing to hare off late Wednesday afternoon. By now he was probably out of the country, permanently. Some careers have a shorter life span than a gymnast's. So forget talking to him.

I was drowning in a sea of "ifs" and "maybes." I groaned. Max moaned sympathetically. Too late to back out now. William's life was at risk; in any case, he couldn't bear a prolonged separation from his lover. And Winston, the bartender at The Sinful Place night club in Bridgetown, had a lovely rum punch waiting for me. I had to push my investigation a step closer to resolution.

I turned my attention to Luciano. Archie told William that his friend ran heavy errands between the Mob and GOD. Luciano was a biker. Hank, the guy who services my Harley, hangs out with The Renegades, who've accepted him as a "friend of the club." Some professor from down East who was researching a book on outlaw bikers travelled all the way to Toronto just to interview him. He knows that much about the subject. Hank wouldn't tell the poor man a thing. Seems he identifies more with the brotherhood than academia. He might talk to me, though. I'd have to wait until tomorrow morning, when he opened the shop.

At this point in my mental perambulations, I didn't feel terrifically confident that I was on the right track. I was about to pursue the *only* track I could see leading out of this thicket I'd so stupidly agreed to enter at a time when I was doubting my writerly vocation — or couldn't get my next book off the ground. Writer's block is a dangerous syndrome.

Perhaps in taking William's innocence on faith, I was merely swimming against the current — the only direction I seem to have recognized since I took that fateful voyage out of Etta. (Even then I was headed the wrong way.) But after spending time with the chief suspect, I was further convinced he wasn't guilty. When you stop trusting your own shit detector, you can find yourself up to your chin in the nasty stuff before you have time to grab a shovel.

On that lyrical note, I hauled my butt off the sofa and made two short phone calls. David Walker's line was busy, but I did manage to get through to Simone. First I inquired after Rebecca, but she didn't seem inclined to update me on the state of her daughter's well-being. I quickly summarized my meeting with her nephew, omitting specific details. I told her I had a few shards of new information that looked promising — in fact, my first real lead in a week — and I reassured her that William was safe. When I refused to divulge his new hideout, she grew quite angry, but I explained that William and I had agreed to confide his whereabouts only to David. Before hanging up, I promised her that I would contact her as soon as I came up with something concrete. She wasn't mollified; perhaps I wasn't meeting some imaginary deadline she'd set me. Story of my life.

When I redialled David's number, he picked up the phone on the first ring. He had just been talking to William, who'd called him from a phone booth in a service centre south of Minden. He expressed his relief that William was in a safer space, but said that they missed one another terribly. I told him that with any luck at all, I might come up with something in the next few days that would shed some light on the murder. I was getting very skilled at dispensing false assurances. We confirmed that he would call his lover from a phone booth every afternoon at 4:30.

David and I agreed to talk later in the week — earlier if necessary. He told me he was keeping busy marking student essays and preparing a paper on some Augustinian monk's translation of a French treatise on gluttony. "I hope the good brother had a tolerant take on the subject. Good vices are getting harder by the day to maintain," I said with feeling. Celibacy sharpens my appetite for alcohol and nicotine.

I didn't feign interest in his research; in my experience, academics too often jump like starving wolves onto an ailing deer at the faintest sign of encouragement. I once dated a guy who would wax passionate about the higher reaches of particle physics — in bed, and to the extent that he totally lost track of what was happening below his navel.

Five minutes later the phone rang, just as I was preparing to order Max's pizza (large, double salami, double cheese, hold the anchovies). It was Portia, asking what I was planning on wearing to Michael's tomorrow night. I told her I'd been torn between my black lace *bustier* and my army fatigues. I thought I'd go for the army fatigues — if things heated up, I could always slip into something less comfortable I'd just happened to bring along in my sports bag. She told me I was hopeless. I told her that depended on what one was hoping for. We laughed. She made me promise to give her a full report. I told her to get her Peeping Tom fixes by watching Geraldo or Oprah.

At nine the next morning I pulled my bike to a stop outside Hank's repair shop. Wanting to catch him off guard, before he had time to think about whether or not it was smart to answer my questions, I hadn't called him in advance.

I found him inside the garage operating on a Honda Nighthawk 750. "You're slumming," I said, gesturing at his patient, a feeble glitter-blue thing covered in macho decals.

He grinned, and retorted: "Most Harley owners know how to keep their own bikes running — even some of the girls."

"Hey, Hank even you know it takes a real woman to ride a Harley."

He walked toward me, rubbing his hands on a greasy rag. "So what got you out of bed so early, real woman? Your bike sick?"

"No. Harley's fine. I'm doing some research for a magazine article I'm writing. It's about the links between organized crime and the business world. I want to spend a paragraph or two on how some of the big Mafia groups in Metro use outlaw biker clubs to manufacture and distribute drugs."

Now, Hank's a wiry little guy, maybe five feet, seven inches. It never occurred to me before to be frightened of him, in spite of the guys he hangs out with. But he was looking at me with eyes suddenly gone glacial. "So who's going to print this article?"

"Oh, *Maclean's*," I lied.

He shrugged. "I don't read nothin' but biker magazines. But I know how the papers always handle stories about the clubs. Why would I want to tell you anything?"

"Why wouldn't you, Hank? I only need enough information for a couple of sentences. I'm not going to use names or anything. I mean, I just need a few details to make it sound like I know what I'm talking about. Hey man, I'm not even mildly interested in causing bikers any grief — it's the guys in suits I'm really out to get, but I can't make much of a case against them without having a few hard facts about who they do business with. These days the lawyers at the magazines pick through every damn word we write, before the publishers even think about going into print with anything they might get sued for. Give me a break, Hank."

His face relaxed a bit. "No names, eh? And you wouldn't tell nobody I talked to you?"

"I'd go to jail before I'd reveal a source."

"Okay, come on back in the garage with me so I can keep

working on the Honda. Owner's coming to pick it up around lunch-time. You can ask me some questions while I fix it." I followed him into his large concrete bunker. Before returning to the bike, he walked over to a Coke cooler at the rear of the shop. He tossed me a can of beer, and snapped the cap off one for himself. I took a swig, surprised at how good it tasted this early in the morning on an empty stomach.

"I've really only got one question. A friend of mine who worked on that documentary the CBC made a few years ago on organized crime in the city —"

He interrupted me with: "So what the fuck is *disorganized* crime?"

"I think it's called politics."

He laughed. "Go on." The tension lifted a whole lot.

"Anyway, this friend mentioned a few names, you know — people their researchers talked to or heard about on the grapevine when they were preparing the film. He thought maybe one or two of them might be willing to talk to me, for a small reward or to settle a score. He mentioned Dominic Ricciutelli, Giancarlo Giovannini — oh yeah, and somebody named Luciano. Do you know who they ride with?" I desperately needed his help: the outlaw clubs are notoriously private, even harder to penetrate than their establishment counterparts.

"I know a Dominic Paoletti, but he got sent down to Kingston for eighteen months. Nope, no Ricciutelli and no Giovannini." He shook his head and concentrated on loosening a wheel bolt. I wasn't surprised: I'd made up their names.

"Uh, what about a Luciano?"

He looked up at me. He was gripping a serious wrench. "You don't have his last name?"

"I think my friend told me, but I've forgotten it. He did say that this Luciano was some kind of courier," I persisted.

"That's Luciano Lombardi — he's with The Bad Men. And he's one mean fucker, is Lucy. You definitely don't want to talk to him. Last summer his ol' lady bad-mouthed him at a party at the club house. He cut her throat so bad I thought her head was going to fall off. Had some of his brothers toss her body in a dumpster. And she'd been his ol' lady for five years." His own head shook disapprovingly at this mode of disposing of troublesome bimbos, but he looked half-impressed.

I shivered and took a deep pull on my Blue. In fact, I emptied the can. "You just made up my mind, Hank. I don't want to talk to him. So maybe you can tell me a bit more about what exactly he does for a living?" I asked hopefully.

"He used to distribute drugs to a lot of dealers on the street, for the Costa-Romeo-Figliomeni family — they're Calabrian Mafia, the 'ndrangheta. Guy named Guiseppe Nicaso is the boss. I heard Luciano got a promotion. Apparently he just runs money now."

"Like between where and where?"

"Between the guys who count the bucks that come in off the street and the guys who toss it in the dishwasher for the Mob." He stood up. "That's it, Jane. I'm not saying another fuckin' word."

I ventured one more. "I guess you couldn't tell me where I could find the dishwasher?"

"Sure, I can. Bargain Harold's. No down payment and three years to pay."

"Thanks, Hank. I appreciate your help. I owe you. And I'll keep my mouth shut."

"Do *yourself* a favour and keep away from Lucy. Even his brothers think he's a bit of a psycho. He'll cut you up finer than fettuccine if he thinks you're snooping."

"About his nickname — Lucy?"

"You'd have to see the bugger to appreciate the joke. Remember those old Popeye cartoons? He looks just like Bluto. Built like a shit house, must weigh three hundred easy, big black beard, greasy hair, beer gut. Got a tattoo on his right arm of a dagger with blood dripping from it onto the word 'Death.' He's gotta be the farthest thing from a Lucy you can imagine."

"Doesn't sound like my type." I put on my helmet, threw a leg over my bike and waved shakily as I pulled away.

CHAPTER 17

MAX EMITTED TWO resonant belches as I rushed past him on my way to the phone. Either his gastric juices were having trouble with the salami or he was issuing a vulgar commentary on my failure to kiss him "hello." I didn't care: my excitement over what I'd just learned from Hank was making my inner parent thick-skinned.

I picked up the phone. It was Sam Brewer, asking me to meet him for another lunch at Delaney's.

"I just got something that may interest Charles Durand's biographer," he said dryly. His voice was low and calm, but I detected an intriguing undertone. I quickly agreed to lunch.

"Sam, could you give me just a hint?"

"Nope," he replied, amiably but conclusively. "You know how paranoid I am about phone lines."

I told him I'd be there at one o'clock, and hung up the phone only long enough to retrieve the dial tone. On the way back from Hank's shop, I had decided to call Judith Durand, ostensibly to set up a date to interview her domestic staff. What I really wanted was to find out how she'd respond to my request to talk to Archie Price. After all, I rationalized, a contemporary mogul's chauffeur must be the equivalent of the trusted British butler — that tight-lipped confidante of aristocratic Englishmen, a veritable mother-lode of information any conscientious biographer would sell her grandmother to mine.

The phone rang only twice before being answered by a woman with a French accent. "Charles Durand residence," she said, in a tone suggesting I'd made an offensive collect call to the Palace of Versailles. I wondered how long she'd be answering with her late employer's name. "May I help you?" She didn't sound the least bit prepared to be helpful.

"Good morning," I replied in my snootiest accent. "My name is Jane Yeats. I would like to speak with Mrs. Durand."

I guess I didn't pass the first screening test. "I'm afraid Mrs. Durand is reluctant to disturb her mourning. May I take a message." She didn't pose the last sentence as an invitation.

For the life of me, I couldn't conjure a mental image of Judith Durand as Queen Victoria in widow's weeds. More than likely, she was sitting naked under a silk robe over a champagne brunch. "I'm sure she'll be willing to come to the phone if you give her my name."

She asked me to repeat my name.

I worked some serious authority into my voice. "Jane Yeats. The Prime Minister's Office."

She almost dropped the phone in her haste to summon her mistress.

"So you've got a real job," Judith chuckled into the phone.

No point telling her that I considered writing a real job: some folks never get the point — and I sure as hell didn't want to risk losing her co-operation. "Sorry about that. I couldn't think of any other way to get past your receptionist."

"Everyone Charles hired is close-mouthed," she said. "Can I do something for you?"

After inquiring about her well-being, I outlined the purpose of my call. While I appreciated that it was much too sensitive a time to ask her to consent to an interview, I did feel that talking to members of the household staff would be very useful — especially while their memories of their employer were still fresh. I explained that I needed their impressions of her husband to fill in my sense of his "personality" and assured her that I wouldn't be asking questions about the Durands' private lives.

She immediately co-operated, even suggesting that I visit Swindon Path on Thursday. I told her that I needed to spend no more than half an hour with each staff member.

"Then why don't you come at nine, and after you've finished your interviews we'll have a light lunch together?" I wondered if her being so obliging stemmed from a desire to be perceived as helpful or from a simple need for company. They say life up there can be lonely. Her late husband, driven by his craving for Establishment acceptance, was denied entrance to the inner circle. That must have placed his second wife, a fashion mannequin of disreputable lineage whom no one took seriously, on the periphery of nowhere in Toronto society.

I thanked her for her assistance. Just before we were about to ring off, I asked as off-handedly as I could muster, "Oh, by the way, I wonder if it might be possible for me to meet with Mr. Durand's chauffeur — um, I think Archie Price is his name — that is, assuming he's still in your employ?"

She paused before replying, "No, that wouldn't be possible. Mr. Price is no longer working for us. You see, I don't need a driver. I prefer to drive my own car. I have a Porsche."

She was too fulsome in her provision of detail. "Do you have a phone number or a forwarding address for him?"

"No, I don't. I understand he was planning on moving abroad somewhere," she said in a voice completely drained of friendliness. I decided to press her no further. We said goodbye.

Her reply didn't jibe with William's story. Why hadn't she told me that he'd done a bunk? She clearly implied that she'd let him go after Durand's death because she had no further need for his services. And there had been a marked change in her manner when I introduced Price's name. Could she have been playing Lady Chatterley to Price's gamekeeper? I've heard rumours that more than a few Rosedale matrons are having it on with the family chauffeur, some with their husband's blessings.

On the other hand, Durand may have confided in Judith — in which case she might know about Price's drug dealing, perhaps even about GOD's Mob connections. Would she have told the police? Or would she have been too scared, maybe having guessed why her husband got bumped off?

A less pleasant possibility scudded into view. William could have fabricated his story — especially if he had reason to believe that no one would be hearing from Price again.

For the second time that day I hopped on my bike. I made it straight east along Bloor to Sherbourne in ten minutes. Inside Delaney's I greeted Frank at the bar.

"Janie, get over here. Your Guinness is getting lonely," Sam bellowed from his corner.

After our usual warm hug, I held the old bear at arm's length. "Something's weird, Sam. Your suit's been dry-cleaned. Fresh shirt. No tell-tale beer stains on the tie — and new shoes! You've got me worried, man," I teased.

He blushed. "Yeah, well, I figured I could do with some tidying up, what with spring coming and all."

I laughed. "I must have seen about seven springs run past your wardrobe, Sam, and all they ever accomplished was to make you retire your crumpled overcoat for six or seven months. Come on, what's up?"

"Drink your beer, for Christ's sake. I'm the reporter, so I get to ask the questions." He paused, and looked sheepishly at the head on his beer. "Actually, I'm interested in a lady." He told me that he had been working up his nerve for months to ask a secretary who worked at the *Post,* a widower like himself, named Sandy, for a date. This morning she agreed to go out with him. I was delighted. Sam's far too nice a guy to spend the rest of his days crying into his beer over a dead wife.

He looked up at me and grinned. "So now it's your turn to start working on a social life, lady."

"I'm not going to make any promises, but if there's hope for you I should be hearing from Richard Gere any day now."

He told me he only had time for one more beer because just before phoning me he got a call from Ernie Sivcoski. Apparently the police had another homicide on their hands. Sam had to write it up for the next edition.

"Nothing unusual about another murder. Metro seems to be averaging at least three bodies a week so far this year. That's not why you called me, is it?" I asked.

Frank brought us a second round. I hadn't knocked my first glass back an inch. "Yeah, it is. This one's definitely in your ball park, so listen up. Ernie said Homicide got a call from the RCMP — the national crime intelligence section in the city — about ten o'clock last night. They got a tip from a 'trusted informant' who led them to a car parked behind a nightclub in North York. There was a body stuffed in the trunk. Looked like he'd bled to death, judging from the fact he'd been stabbed enough times to kill a whole baseball team. It was obviously a contract killing — you know, one of those red flags the Mob sends up when they get cheated in a big way. The guy was curled up like he'd never left the womb, ten times bloodier than if he'd just been born, wearing only his socks. His feet and hands were tied and some kind of cloth was wrapped from his neck to his ankles. Trussed like the Christmas turkey."

"Drop the cliff-hanging, Sam! That makes about six Mob hits in as many weeks — their last victim got dismembered with a chainsaw. So there's a war going on over drug turf. What makes me interested in this one?"

"This one was the late Charles Durand's chauffeur," he said triumphantly.

"Fuck." I actually knocked over my beer. That's something I've never done before, not when I'm sober.

Frank came over, towelled off the table and picked up my mug, which hadn't broken. "If I didn't know better, I'da thought you was pissed. What happened, did the old goat propose to you?" he asked, jerking his thumb at Sam. Frank's been working on his wit ever since he got addicted to *Cheers* reruns.

"You're telling me Archie Price got hit?"

"So you know his name already," Sam said. "You've been doing your research."

I nodded. "Did Ernie tell you anything else about Price — like why they figure he got killed?"

Sam shook his head. "Nah, he wouldn't say another damned word. Promised to fill me in as soon as he could. Said this was being handled *very* sensitively, in view of it maybe being connected to the Durand case — which, as you well know, is 'still under investigation.' So what else do you know about this Price?"

"I'll give you this much, Sam: I've been told that he was dealing, in a very big way. But I haven't had time to check it out."

He was very fast. "Did Durand know?"

"I honestly can't tell you that. But if he did, my source suggested that he only found out recently — like a day before he died."

"So that could be why Ernie was being so careful — maybe they're thinking that Archie is a suspect. Durand could have stumbled on to his dealing and threatened to go to the cops with it. And Price offed him to shut him up. Right?"

I agreed, feeling like I had enough egg on my face to make a soufflé for twenty. All my clever musings hadn't led me along that track: I had assumed that Price did a bunk without ever seeing his employer again. But Durand could have confronted him, demanding to know what Price could tell him about GOD's connection with the Mob — in exchange, say, for keeping quiet about his chauffeur's off-duty job. Price could have killed him on the spot, before he got a chance to tell the cops, figuring he didn't have anything to lose. He was planning a hasty emigration anyway.

"Right — and that script would tidy up the Durand investigation very nicely for everyone concerned, wouldn't it? The Mob could have put out a contract on Price — just in case he got arrested for his boss's murder and decided to testify against them in exchange for a reduced sentence. Sam, you can start drafting your headline: MOGUL MURDERED BY DRUG-DEALING CHAUFFEUR, NOW VICTIM OF MOB HIT." My beer suddenly tasted sour.

"Can you suggest a better script?" he asked.

"I sure as hell could *write* a better one, but it wouldn't hold up in court. Sam, will you phone me as soon as Ernie leaks out a few more facts?"

"Why not?" He gulped down the remainder of his beer and stood up. "In exchange, of course — we'll keep playing traders?" he grinned. "I've got to run."

"Thanks, Sam. Of course we'll keep playing traders. And good luck with that date."

He walked out of Delaney's with a teenager's bouncing step.

Amazing, how some people keep haring after romance.

CHAPTER 18

MAX OBSERVED MY preparations for my dinner meeting with Michael Diamond from his magisterial perch on the sofa. He was working at appearing inattentive by pretending to follow the hectic dance of rainbows cast by the crystal hanging in front of one of my windows, all the while following my progress from the corner of his doleful left eye: that's how I knew he was intensely interested in my efforts to put together a look of unstudied casual semi-elegance.

During my shower I shaved my underarms and legs. This is not something I normally subject my flesh to in winter time, when nobody but Max sees my legs anyway — and I figure he feels more bonded to me when we share the same furred look. Not that anybody was going to see my legs tonight. Sometimes a woman like me tilts slightly in the direction of femininity when she's feeling insecure about something else — like her deductive skills. The Durand case, now maybe the Durand-Price case, was turning out to be a dangerous conundrum. I wasn't sure why scraping the hair off my legs made me feel like a marginally less incompetent accidental sleuth, but it did. I have great legs. One day I might think a bit about why I rarely display them.

Having shed an ounce or two, I stepped out of the shower and towel-dried my hair. Years ago I learned that time spent trying to style natural curls is time wasted. Like a tangle of morning glories, my hair single-mindedly climbs and trails wherever it bloody well pleases. It's bright mahogany red, a colour that looks better on an Irish setter. In summer it competes for attention with my freckles. I could pass for an aging Anne of Green Gables — if I never opened my mouth.

I chose a dark green suit with loose, pleated pants and an unconstructed jacket, a beige silk shirt and a fairly new pair of dark brown suede boots. Long silver earrings in the shape of a fish skeleton that I'd bought one morning when I had my first impulse to diet. No make-up: there I draw the line. Just some lip gloss, so I didn't look too parched between my nose and cleft chin. On good days, when my depression lifts long enough for me to work up a more positive take on my appearance, I fantasize that I could be mistaken for Katie Hepburn in, say, *The African Queen*. Midway down the river. God help me if Michael Diamond looks anything like Bogie.

Before leaving I opened one of the doors of an oak washstand in which Pete used to store the small collection of wines he had started a year before his death. I'd been saving them, not for any particular event, just reluctant to let go of a connection. Perhaps it was time. To cover all the culinary bases, I chose a German white and a French red.

I must have been feeling guilty about accepting Michael's hospitality when all I intended to do was pick his brains about his corporate connections. Perhaps by dressing up a bit I was hoping to mislead him into accepting my contrived professionalism. *Professional what?* I wondered. The closest I've ever been to the high of distinguished performance came the day in grade seven when I placed third in a city-wide poster contest. My prize was a bath mitt and two bars of lavender soap. The experience left me decidedly unmotivated when it comes to the pursuit of excellence.

Max did not run to his bowl when I tossed in a Kosher hot-dog. Nor did he accompany me to the door. Jealousy perverts the soul.

I asked the cab driver to drop me off a block short of my destination. I'm a good socialist: I don't like people to think I have enough money for taxis, when I can be seen to be virtuous riding public transit.

He lived halfway up Howland Avenue. A quiet, tree-canopied street of late-Victorian red-brick houses. The outside of Michael's residence had been modestly restored, rather than modernized. It didn't boast any of those trendy touches that add up to a yuppie semiotics of renovation. I liked that. I announced my arrival with three knocks on a beautiful door with frosted panes. From within a dog immediately set about barking excitedly.

In addition to two bottles of expensive fermented grape juice, I must have arrived carrying some preconceived notion of what a tax lawyer looks like. I was surprised when the door opened on a man in blue jeans, white sweatshirt with a brilliant toucan printed across the front and low-cut red canvas running shoes. No socks. Just as he opened his mouth to greet me, a small rocket hurtled past his legs onto the front lawn. He cursed and streaked off in pursuit. By the time I glanced down the sidewalk, the grey-and-white fur ball had already reached the point at which I had exited the taxi. Then it disappeared in a blur around the corner onto Bloor Street.

I decided to step through the open door into the foyer. Unsure of the protocol of entering one's host's house for the first time in his absence, I left the door open. Fortunately I didn't have to stand sequestered in a hallway wondering what the interior held. All the interior walls on the ground floor had been removed, leaving a single, well-lit room that extended from the living-room window straight through to two large sliding glass doors leading from the kitchen onto a deck and garden. The brick had been exposed on one wall.

I heard a woman's throaty voice singing "Meet Me Where They Play the Blues." Good voice. Interesting song. I traced the music to two speakers set on a bare oak plank floor on either side of the front window, the kind of speakers that constitute art objects. I checked the empty jewel case beside the CD player. Mary Coughlan, *Tired and Emotional*. So far I liked his taste. It seemed to run to female, Irish and depressed.

Only the sumptuous forest green leather sofa and armchairs in the living room looked factory-built. The rest of the furniture — a long, plain dining-room table with six Shaker chairs, sideboard, shelf unit housing a book collection and sound system, kitchen cupboards — was beautifully hand-crafted in fine woods. A few bright carpets relieved the floors of bareness. A single large painting hung over the sofa, a forest landscape by Emily Carr. It was not a reproduction. Three backlit shelves mounted on the brick wall held a collection of Micmac baskets. I recognized them because Silver had given me one on my last birthday. Out of sheer perversity, I reminded myself to buy her a birthday gift.

Just as I was considering the delicate issue of whether it would be in questionable decorum to examine his books, my red-faced host rushed in through the front door, carrying a now-docile bundle of fur which he set down with an amiable snarl — after carefully locking the door. He grinned sheepishly and extended his hand. "I'm Michael. I'm sorry about the puppy from hell. I just got Aphra about three weeks ago and I haven't been very successful at training her, I'm afraid. May I take your jacket?" He was sweating from his impromptu jog. He brushed back the lock of thick black hair that overhung a pair of bright green glasses, then extended his hand.

I laughed and shook it. "Please don't apologize. I was beginning to think you'd wind up in Mississauga before you caught her." I handed him my jacket.

He placed it on a brass hook on the entrance wall. "She stopped outside of Honest Ed's, actually. When I caught up to her she was looking through one of the windows at a display of diapers. Given how her toilet training isn't progressing, maybe she was trying to tell me something."

I shook my head. "More like she's trying to teach you that *she's* the one who does the training. I have a dog who has manipulated me into structuring my entire life around his needs."

He laughed in turn and appreciatively eyed the two bottles I extracted from my leather knapsack. "Do you mind if I open the red?" he asked. I followed him to the kitchen area, where he invited me to sit down at a small pine farm table set under a window that overlooked the side of his property. The tin ceiling had a large skylight cut into it. A hanging terracotta pot of luxuriant rabbit fern hung beneath. The floor and counter tops were covered with large Mexican tiles. He reached for a huge bowl from a deep open shelf containing enough casseroles and copper pots to stock a kitchen boutique. Apparently the man took his cooking seriously. Good-looking, too. Tall, lean, about one hundred and seventy pounds, each one of them falling very nicely into place where Venus has decreed. World-class butt, I chanced to notice as he bent to peer through the oven door. No harm in giving my eyes permission to roam.

I caught myself before I tumbled into a slough of despond thinking about my empty fridge, collection of mismatched chipped enamel pots, and garden-variety butt.

While he assembled a melon salad and prepared some rounds of French bread, we talked about dogs. When he lifted the lid on a casserole he removed from the oven, the suspicion already aroused by my nose confirmed *coq au vin*. He tasted it, adjusted the seasonings and returned it to the oven. Then he topped up our wine glasses and carried the salad bowl over to the dining-room table, which he'd set beforehand.

Throughout dinner our conversation ranged easily through a variety of topics that included Irish music, Emily Carr, kayaking around the Queen Charlotte Islands and cabinet-making. He had made all the furniture I'd been admiring. Incredibly, the *coq au vin* tasted even better than it smelled. Dessert was cold lemon soufflé topped with sinful swirls of whipped cream and finely chopped pistachio nuts.

When we finished eating, he poured us both a brandy and suggested we move to the living room. At this point I was ready to express my gratitude in ways unbecoming a Celibacy Queen. Rarely have I eaten so well and never for free. On the way to the sofa I reminded myself that I was a writer, not a courtesan. I simply thanked him for the fine fare, profusely.

He smiled as he sat back in one of the armchairs. "I suspect you'd like to get down to the reason we're meeting."

After a meal like that, I should need a reason? "How much did Lennie tell you about, um, about the case I'm working on?" I asked nervously.

"Just that you had sort of fallen into investigating Charles Durand's death and were interested in learning more about his relationship with Gerald Dawson."

We were off to a good start. I was relieved — and intrigued — that he hadn't chosen to editorialize about the impossibility of Dawson's implication in Durand's untimely passing. I didn't need anyone else amplifying my own perplexity. "Yes, I'd really appreciate your telling me what you know about Dawson's role in blocking the Imperial Trust bid. Lennie told me you worked for him at the time."

He leaned forward and compelled my eyes to meet his. They were attractive enough to compete for my attention with his butt, and that's a good thing: I could scarcely have asked him to spend the better part of the evening crouched in front of the oven door.

"I'm prepared to tell you everything I know — on the strength of your friendship with Lennie and Portia, and on the even more considerable strength of my respect for your writing. I think *Unfair Exchange* is a terrific book. In fact, that's really why I was willing to talk to you in the first place. I wanted to meet the writer." He stood up and walked over to the bookcase. To my surprise he removed a copy of my exposé of insider trading on Bay Street. When he shyly asked me to autograph it, I felt foolishly proud and graciously consented.

He returned to his chair after setting the book on the coffee table. "I really do need your assurance, though, that you won't go into print with anything I tell you. That could ruin my career — and I'm still a few decades away from retirement."

I told him that I was interested only in understanding what underlay the toxic relationship between the two moguls. "You seem to be familiar enough with my work to be aware that I have a fairly good outsider's knowledge of the corporate world. What I'd like to hear from you is what really went on behind the scenes when Durand set his sights on Imperial."

He frowned slightly, rubbed his forehead and brushed the wayward fall of hair from the top of his glasses. As he began to speak, his manner became slightly professorial. He started at the beginning and economically ran me through a potted history of the bid, sticking close to the facts as he knew them. I learned a lot about this unsavoury chapter in Canadian business history that had never reached the papers — or by the sound of it, the Ontario Securities Commission ...

"In April of '89 I was working as a tax lawyer for Imperial Trust. At the time Imperial's president and CEO, Timothy Richardson, was just a few months short of retirement. He was a crusty old bugger and disliked Charles Durand as much as the rest of the Establishment did — maybe even more than most. Remember that Imperial is the monolith of Canadian financial institutions, the country's largest trust company and biggest real-estate brokerage firm. Its head offices were originally in Montreal but in the late '70s, when it began to look like Quebec might separate, it relocated to Toronto — along with a lot of other companies that got the jitters. They brought with them most of the old Westmount Gang, who came here with a real hate-on for francophone entrepreneurs.

"Durand approached Timothy Richardson in mid-April with a $500-million cash bid for 100 per cent of the company. Before he even spoke to Richardson, he had tied up 10 per cent of Imperial's stock through a deal with ATM Financial Corp. He offered $20 a share for common stock and $30 for preferred shares, conditional on his obtaining 51 per cent which, of course, would give him majority voting power. It was a good price: Imperial shares were then trading in the $15 range. On the spot, Richardson reacted as if Durand had just threatened to rape the Blessed Virgin! The very thought of the reviled outsider owning Imperial made him crazy. He said he'd do everything in his power to stop the bid — on the grounds that no one person should have absolute control of a large financial institution serving the public. He may have believed that, but his subsequent actions proved, at least to me, that his outrage was really fuelled by his personal dislike of Durand. He actually ordered a security guard to remove him from the building.

"Richardson was smart enough to know that he wasn't smart enough to lead the campaign against Durand. So he went straight to his old friend Dawson who, as head of Titan Corp., presides over the largest agglomeration of economic power in Canada. Titan owned a lot of Imperial stock, and three Titan directors, including Dawson, also served on the Imperial board. Apart from being the most influential man in the business élite, Dawson is respected even by his enemies as a brilliant tactician.

"After calling an emergency meeting with the Imperial board to organize their defence, Dawson immediately started holding top-secret meetings with the heads of some of English Canada's most powerful banks and companies. He asked me to attend all of them, to advise the parties on the legal and tax aspects of their various options. After rejecting the idea of a friendly merger with another company or of launching an unconditional counterbid for the Imperial stock, Dawson decided on an informal strategy. He worked all his contacts and friends, several of whom then formed an alliance they dubbed 'the angels.' In the three weeks the shareholders had to tender their stock, the angels managed to get close to 64 per cent of Imperial shares locked up in their allies' hands. Dawson persuaded major shareholders to pledge not to tender; others entered the market and bought up available shares to their 10 per cent ceilings. Although they were all aware that when the Durand bid failed, the value of their Imperial stock would quickly drop, these companies wilfully jeopardized millions of dollars by holding on to it. That will give you an idea of how badly the Old Boys wanted to keep Durand out of the club!

"As the deadline approached, Durand was still in the dark about the cabal, but he was aware of the heavy trading. He complained to the Ontario Securities Commission, who agreed — reluctantly, I'm sure — to investigate the weird stuff happening in the market. This made one of the big banks, a major shareholder, really nervous. They were already uneasy about the prospect of becoming a minority shareholder in a company commanded by Durand. When they and two other big shareholders threatened to tender, Richardson met with the three and gave them his personal assurance that 64 per cent of the Imperial Trust shares were locked up. He even told them the names of some of those who had bought shares.

"Presumably that was the only way the three executives could be kept onside, but Richardson's disclosure of material facts — without disclosing the same information to *all* Imperial's shareholders — was a blatant case of 'tipping.' That's why the Ontario Securities Commission later found him guilty of acting improperly.

"But it worked: by the deadline, only 24 per cent of the Imperial shares had been tendered to Durand's bid. By then, of course, he had figured out what the group had done. And he knew that Dawson had masterminded the whole operation. He couldn't have derived much satisfaction from the Commission's ruling. Richardson got his trading rights suspended for sixty days. Four months later he retired. Apparently Dawson made a hefty contribution to his pension fund. Business returned to normal on Bay Street."

Michael smiled wanly across the room. "And thus endeth that obscene chapter in the Book of Free Enterprise. May I get you another brandy, or some more coffee?"

"No thanks. May I ask you a few questions?"

He nodded. "Shoot."

"Do you have any concrete reason for believing that GOD was motivated to block the bid for purely personal reasons?"

His brows knit in concentration and he was silent for a minute before replying. "I don't think his actions had a damned thing to do with business ethics! *He is not an ethical man.* But I'm not sure I would describe his motivation as 'personal.' Let's face it: nobody liked Charles Durand. The man had no friends — even his own son took him to court. He was singularly without charm, even when he was trying. He was a brilliant entrepreneur, but he was also several sandwiches short of a picnic when it came to engaging people's affection. There always seemed to be something in his mistrust that came close to paranoia, like he thought the whole world was conspiring against his every move."

"But he sure as hell did have real-world enemies, Michael."

"True. And GOD was the leader of the pack. Look, apart from the Imperial bid, his path and Dawson's never directly crossed, but their mutual enmity bonded them like Crazy Glue. Dawson's the last of a passing breed. Like the British aristocracy, he and his kind of corporate wizards are nearing extinction. In the last decade or so, it's become increasingly obvious that their old, inbred ways of doing business are growing obsolete. The truth of it is, they no longer know how to manage effectively. They're losing their grip and they know it. Durand symbolized a new, almost renegade style they despise mostly because it threatens them. They wanted to keep him on the margins as long as they could — ostracize him socially, kill the Imperial bid, whatever. I think Dawson got off on flexing his corporate muscle by pulling together his friends in a dazzling display of what old money can do. It was a massive ego trip."

I interjected. "It went even further than that, don't you think? … I mean, Durand reacted so wildly to his defeat, he really drove the coffin nail in on himself. For the first time in his career, he started making deals like a megalomaniac — bad deals that eventually pushed him to the brink of bankruptcy."

"You're right," Michael agreed. "You didn't have to like the guy to have felt a bit sorry for him. You know, rumour had it that he was really emotionally unstable."

I laughed. "So am I. I guess it's a good thing I never have more than a few hundred bucks in my savings account."

His smile was wry. "I'm not sure that's a compelling argument for poverty, but if it gives you strange comfort …"

"I've made a lifestyle of strange comforts!" Ouch. Strange disclosure on my part, so early in a conversation. Time to shift gears. "So Dawson got an even bigger pay-off for his dirty work. Afterwards, all he had to do was just sit back and watch Durand shoot himself in both feet until he fell flat on his face."

Michael leaned forward. "I'm not sure that GOD has been laughing too hard lately — if the rumour mill is correct. Bay Street insider speculation has it that Titan Corp. may be in deep shit."

I jumped up from the sofa in excitement. If Titan were in a crisis, Dawson might have been open to doing business with the Mob — if it promised him huge infusions of critical cash.

"What? The very idea of guys like GOD going broke seems incredible!"

"A lot of people said the same thing just before the crash of '29, and many more are saying it now," he dryly remarked. "You know that the Titan empire was built mainly on resources. About twelve years ago, Dawson diversified into commercial real estate, first in Toronto, then in New York and Europe. Five years ago he started the $3-billion Pacific Shore development on Vancouver Island. Back then the bankers were throwing money at him on the strength of his name alone. Now they're meeting behind tightly closed doors to figure out just how deeply they've buried themselves. Over the past year, the Titan portfolio has been losing about $5 million a day."

"How in hell did that happen?" I asked.

"Well, add the cash drain created by the vacancy rate at Pacific Shore to sagging stock prices and a worldwide slump in property values and commodity prices, and you've got the deadly recipe. The daily interest alone on Titan's debts is phenomenal. So that's the big scoop: Titan is in the throes of what

Bay Street euphemistically tags a 'liquidity crisis.' And so am I," he said, glancing at the empty snifter in his hand. "Are you sure you won't have another brandy? I'll drive you home if you're worried about the time," he offered.

I glanced at my watch. It was twenty past the witching hour. I declined the liquid part of his offer, but accepted the ride — prompted, of course, by the safety factor. Take back the night, indeed.

As I slipped on my jacket, I was scheming how to set up another meeting with Michael. I was still clutching a string of unanswered questions. *Is it conceivable that Dawson is in bed with the Mob? Do you have a lover? Is there any way of ascertaining how serious Titan's troubles are? You're not gay, are you?* (The thought had crossed my mind, what with the décor, the cuisine and his unlikely bachelorhood.)

We chatted amiably while he drove me home. As we neared my neighbourhood, I realized that I couldn't return his dinner invitation unless I enrolled in cooking-immersion school first thing in the morning.

He solved the problem at my front door. "I've enjoyed this evening very much. Could I phone you soon?" he asked.

"Sure," I replied, faster than a speeding puppy. "Thanks so much for your help, and a gorgeous meal. I enjoyed too." He smiled, and navigated the world-class butt back to his car.

No harm in giving my eyes permission to roam when I could keep my feelings on a leash.

CHAPTER 19

TUESDAY MORNING I woke up in an uncharacteristically cheery mood. I discharged the extra calories I owed to Michael's dinner by jogging, rather than crawling, twice my usual distance through High Park. Max distinguished himself by sniffing vigorously at the heels of an older woman who was striding toward Grenadier Pond as if she were late for an assignation with Tom Jones. After two unsuccessful efforts to fend him off verbally, she swatted him on the flank with an oversize handbag. I hate violence. He decided against biting her and returned to my side, his tail no longer rampant. I pretended not to have witnessed his humiliation.

All through the park massed yellow and purple crocuses were pushing their brilliant heads through winter-seared grass. It must be due to the return of spring, this sudden lifting of my spirits. *Don't let yourself think for a second there might be any other reason,* I cautioned my battered heart. Still, I did have to see Mr. Diamond again soon, for business reasons.

I like doing my mental stock-taking in the open air, while I'm on the move and companioned by the consoling notion that I can outrun any thoughts I don't care to pursue. However, no amount of running was going to shake loose one red flag that kept rearing its impertinent head: I had been avoiding contact with Simone who, after all, was subsidizing my lunatic venture into the shoals of amateur detection. My last phone communication with her had left me unsettled. She had seemed impatient, almost angry with my lack of progress — especially with my refusal to divulge her nephew William's whereabouts.

As soon as I got back to my studio, I picked up the receiver, then promptly set it back in its cradle. With any luck at all, Simone might be even crabbier with me this time around. Maybe she'd fire me. As long as she paid my outstanding expenses, which really only amounted to a few gas bills, I'd be happily out of this maze.

That was fear and insecurity speaking. Actually I was eager to get on with my investigation. The prospect of exposing Dawson as a money launderer, as well as a murderer, warmed the cockles of my vindictive heart. In order to firm up my case against him, I needed access to Titan Corp.'s financial records, but I didn't have a clue how to get my eyes on them. Oh well, I needn't tell Simone that. Probably I'd uncovered sufficient new information since our last conversation to keep her happy for the time being.

In spite of my long run, the studio was making me stir-crazy. After months of hibernation and claustrophobic thinking, spring sunshine was luring me outdoors. I decided to bike up to Simone's instead of phoning her. I'd sooner explain to her face to face the complexities of the possible links between her dead brother, GOD, Archie Price and the Mob.

Because I hit the roads well past morning rush hour, it took me only fifty-five minutes to reach the Goldberg house. Stepping off my bike, I felt exhilarated: Zen and the art of speeding through an awakening countryside on a Harley.

Rebecca answered the door. Her pale face was devoid of make-up and expression. Blonde dreads fell over the shoulders of a T-shirt with a green tree frog splayed over her chest. Blue jeans, seriously frayed at the knees, hugged her long legs.

"Hi, I'm Jane Yeats. You must be Rebecca," I said.

My smile didn't elicit any reciprocal warmth. "Yeah." She looked past me at Harley. "Cool."

A voice came from inside. "Who's at the door, dear?"

She grimaced and ignored Simone's question. "Like, does your mother call you 'dear' — even when you ride a hog?"

"You don't want to hear what my mother calls me — especially when the subject of my bike comes up."

Simone appeared behind her. "Have your manners completely deserted you, Rebecca? Please come in, Jane."

Rebecca stepped aside with a snort. Manners clearly weren't high on her agenda.

I was hoping Simone would ask Rebecca to join us for coffee. Maybe I'd better understand their relationship if I had a teenager. Recalling my own passage through those turbulent years makes me feel relieved that I've never generated a creature who even vaguely resembles me.

Rebecca followed us into the kitchen and slouched against a counter, peering at me curiously.

"Don't you have something to do, dear?" Simone suggested.

"No. You're the one who always needs to be doing something."

"Then find somewhere else to do nothing, Rebecca. I'd like some privacy."

Taking twice as long as necessary to stroll out of the kitchen, Rebecca muttered in my direction, "Like, does your mother ever make you feel totally unwelcome?"

I laughed. "Only when the plumbing in her bar is working. The rest of the time, I think she finds me really useful. Maybe we'll have a chance to chat another time, Rebecca." Negotiating one-way conversation through the tension of this mother-daughter land mine was stressing me out.

Simone closed the door behind her. "I'm sorry if I seemed in a rush to get her out of the room, Jane, but I was. I've had about as much of her as I can take."

Perhaps her exasperation was genuine. Or maybe she wanted to cut short my communication with Rebecca. Oh well, Simone wouldn't be the first mother to feel that I mightn't be an appropriate role model for her daughter. I know Etta feels the same way.

"I have some new information for you and I decided on impulse to deliver it personally. It's such a beautiful day," I explained. Hopefully she wouldn't get off track again and start moaning about filial misdemeanours.

"That's fine. You're a welcome distraction. Please let me know what you've learned."

Over coffee, I summarized my findings to date, focusing on the possibility that Durand may have taken his suspicion about GOD's money laundering for the Mob to his rival, hoping to bleed some money from Dawson into the ailing Durand Corp. When she queried me closely about the likelihood of my obtaining any evidence of GOD's implication in the murder, I told her I thought it far more likely that sufficient suspicion about the money laundering could be raised to force an official investigation into Titan Corp. Perhaps then the police would be obliged to check into whether or not Durand had tried to blackmail Dawson — especially after they received an anonymous tip from me. When I added that I'd just found out that Archie Price had been murdered, she asked if I thought he might have killed her brother. Based on what William said he knew, I told Simone it seemed more likely that Price, having already arranged his getaway, wouldn't have wanted to add murder to his drug dealing, thereby ensuring that the cops, as well as the Mob, would be on his trail. And if he had wanted to nail the Mob, he'd already dropped a flea in William's ear that could take a life-threatening bite out of their operations.

She asked me what I planned to do next.

I tried not to let my voice betray my uncertainty. "At this point, Simone, I don't have a shred of anything convincing enough to take to the police. Everything I know is simple hearsay — and who I heard it from wouldn't exactly convince the cops of their veracity: William, the gay son, who has taken his own father to court and is a suspect in his murder; Price, the dead drug dealer from whom he got his information; and a motorcycle mechanic with strong biker friendships. The only way I can think of to firm up the money-laundering allegation is to try and get access to the books at Titan Corp."

"And how in hell can you manage that?" she asked.

"I don't know how, but I think I know *who* I can ask to help me. I've just met a man named Michael Diamond. He used to be a tax lawyer with Imperial Trust. I'm working up my nerve to broach the subject with him, but I'm not too optimistic about getting his co-operation. After all, the only way an outsider could access the books would be illegal."

Simone grinned for the first time. "It seems more than a little out of character for you to suggest that a lawyer is above breaking the law!"

I laughed. "I couldn't agree more. Almost every scam known to the business world involves the connivance of a lawyer or two — and quite a few of them have been caught working their own shady scams with their clients' money. But Michael struck me as one of the honest ones."

"Perhaps if you're already on a first-name basis, you might charm this honest man into bending his principles a bit, especially in the service of nailing a crook," she suggested.

"I would never use my meagre charms to persuade someone to break the law!" I retorted. Even as I spoke, I nearly retched at my self-righteous indignation — especially because en route to Simone's my mind had been busily occupied scripting various scenarios to entrap Michael into abetting my investigation.

Her silence made the kitchen air fibrillate with tension.

"Actually, I'm intending to do precisely what you suggested. I seem to be having some difficulty acknowledging my own capacity for sleazy behaviour," I confessed.

"This makes you different from the rest of us?" she asked.

I shrugged. "I give myself a lot of grief when I fall spectacularly short of my own standards. Perhaps it's time I admitted what a dirtball I'm prepared to be when I can't find any alternative." If I kept this up, I'd soon be rivalling Max for exhibitionist displays of contrived shame.

She rose from the table and came over to pat my shoulder. "But just think of the satisfaction you'll get if you are instrumental in bringing GOD to court. And think of the book you'll be able to write!" She was seductive as Satan during his forty-day joint tenancy of the wilderness. Certainly the first prospect was more than a little beguiling.

I agreed to keep her posted. Just before leaving, a curious thought struck me. "Simone, Rebecca seems to be reacting so strongly to her uncle's death. I mean, it couldn't have anything to do with her decision to drop out of school, could it?"

Her response was in place almost the instant my question sounded. She swiftly shook her head. "Oh no. Rebecca didn't know Charles. She's never even met him. I'm sure whatever she's going through is completely unrelated. Anyway, her academic troubles started months before he died."

I wished her luck with her daughter. She warmly thanked me for my concern. As Harley roared to life, it occurred to me that she hadn't asked about William. Probably she was too distracted by the tensions within her immediate family circle.

I glanced up to the second floor. Rebecca was waving from a window. I banged my right hand on the top of my helmet and swept it into a clenched-fist salute. Her delighted grin illuminated that gut-wrenchingly vulnerable young face. For her benefit I sprayed some gravel as I took off down the drive.

I hate how the tiny, maniacally blinking red light on my answering machine beckons me as soon as I enter my studio. On my return from Simone's, I got hit by six blinks. Like an automaton, I walked toward the machine and put it out of its misery and into mine by pressing PLAY. She-Who-Suckled-Me-and-Therefore-Can-Not-Be-Denied flooded the first two bites of ear-time:

> Hi dear it's your Mom. You shoulda been in here last night *[raucous laughter collapsing into hacking cough segueing into click of her Bic].* You know them two girls who used to be guys— call themselves Gypsy Rose and Foxxie and come in here all the time? I can't imagine why when there's bars for them types. Who knows, maybe they like cowboys. Anyways last night in struts Gypsy Rose — the one with so much orange hair she makes Dolly Parton look like Sinéad O'Connor. She's

flaunting a diamond big as the SkyDome with — are you ready for this — Foxxie beside her, except Foxxie's now dressed like a man and they announce that they're celebrating their engagement, for Christ's sake. I mean I thought they had their tools cut off and them foam cushions put in! So how do you figure they do it? Slim says he don't know. Anyways we had a real good party for them even though I can't make any sense out of it but maybe you don't have to, you know what I mean …

Sweet Dreams' answer to Dr. Ruth got rudely terminated in full verbal sail by my tape's two-minute recording limit. Next message, of course, is Etta resurgent, albeit her spirits now modulated into a minor key by the constraints of verbal economy:

Anyways I was calling to see how you are and ask if you'll do me a real big favour and babysit the bar tomorrow night that's Wednesday because my bowling league is havin' our annual Knock 'Em Down Banquet and you know I don't trust no one but you to keep an eye on the joint. Oh yeah, Slim says howdy. See you at seven eh? …

The next three callers were more economical. Portia called with the inevitable sweet query into how last night had gone. Ernie Sivcoski left a gruff message asking me to contact him at Homicide. David Walker phoned to say William was well, but anxious to know if I was making any progress. All of my body hair, beginning with the ones on the back of my neck, jumped to attention like Grenadier Guards at the fifth voice that "was hoping you might be able to set Friday night aside to go to a play — that is, if you enjoy theatre." Hell, I was prepared to sit through *Man and Superman* for a guy who could cook like Michael (the world-class butt being strictly incidental). Immediately I felt guilty for my sinful thoughts. I was still Pete's woman, wasn't I? Getting emotionally involved with another man was *not* on the agenda.

I returned all their calls, in the order in which they were electronically queued. YES to Etta, NO not being within the realm of choice.

"Michael and I enjoyed a wonderful evening — I think I'm pregnant, so start knitting," I breathed heavily into Portia's machine.

I got through to Ernie, who informed me I'd be happy to hear that he had the Durand investigation "damn near wrapped up." Sure enough, the official script would read: Durand murdered by drug-dealing chauffeur after threatening to turn him in to police; Price snuffed in Mob hit for pulling drug double-cross. Both murder cases totally unrelated. Not much chance of nabbing hitman, but in the official version cops would be "pursuing their investigation." Rough justice seen to have been done. Ernie asked me out for a beer. I didn't want to give the guy any more scope to gloat; nor did I want to give him a chance to read the disbelief and contempt scrawled across my face. I said I'd take a rain cheque.

David was delighted when I told him that, given the Homicide Squad's conclusions, I saw no reason why William couldn't return to Toronto immediately. He said they would call me as soon as William was back. I agreed to come over for dinner to join their celebration, deeply moved that words like "celebration" remain part of the instinctive vocabulary of a young man with AIDS. Contact with people of his spirit was putting me in guilty touch with the self-indulgent aspect of my sorrow. I've buried two years of my own living in drink and depression, all the while taking for granted my right to commit slow suicide.

I paused to invest an inordinate amount of time in preparing Kraft Dinner for two. Max always loves it when I grate a hunk of aged Cheddar over the top. Actually I was delaying returning Michael's call. He might by then have arrived home from work. The raw truth of it was that I was frightened even to mention my need to see GOD's books. That considerable fear paled beside the realization that, during our time together last night something had clicked, a small, remote sound telling me that this man just might become one of the few who mattered. I chose to interpret that sound as a warning. A few months ago, my shrink told me I should get an award for scripting worst-case scenarios. *What does she know?*

I dialled Michael's number. His easygoing manner massaged a knot or two from my shoulders.

"Hi, Jane. I called you from work this afternoon in the midst of a boredom fit. I was thinking about how much I enjoyed talking to you last night."

What planet had he fallen from? I simply can't fathom creatures who speak their feelings so forthrightly. What cocoon insulated him from fear of rejection?

"Oh," I croaked back, articulate as a toad.

He laughed. "I'll take that as a sign of encouragement. Are you interested in doing something with me Friday night?"

"Actually, I'm interested in doing something with you sooner than that," I blurted. Immediately upon realizing what I'd said, I offered up a silent prayer that he wasn't into sexual innuendoes.

Silence on the line. He must have been waiting for me to clarify my desires. "What I mean is, I do want to ask you to help me with something — something related to the Durand thing that will take a bit of explaining. Tomorrow night I have to babysit my mother's bar from seven to closing time. Would it be convenient for you to meet me there, or for me to pick you up?"

"If you pick me up we can save on fossil fuel at the same time we enjoy one another's company. Should I know anything about the dress code at Sweet Dreams?"

"No suit. Anything else goes — including a blonde wig, if you've got one in the cupboard."

"Great. I'll be ready any time after 6:30. I look forward to seeing you, Jane."

I hung up the phone very carefully. *Please God, don't let him own a blonde wig. I can't afford to pay that dear a penalty for being a smart-ass.*

Before taking Max out for his evening relief, my environmentally conscientious exercise in stoop-and-scoop, I cracked a beer and sat down with this morning's paper, which I'd left unread in my haste to get to Simone's. With its usual detailing of the past day's murders, rapes, abductions and fears of another serial killer on the loose on the home front, amplified by drought, famine, terrorism, war and pestilence abroad, the first section provided no hopeful fodder for a recovering depressive. Unless you think of the report about the priest in Buffalo who got arrested at a pro-life demonstration for waving a plastic bag containing a human fetus as an absurdist sidebar. The Fashion section brutalized me with feminine fabric follies modelled by the eating-disordered straight from the vengeful minds of woman-hating designers. The Life section instructed me on how to deal with a dying parent. The Classifieds tormented me with Progressive Positions light years beyond my grasp. The Food section offered up cunning tricks on how to whip together a four-course dinner for six in the microwave I don't own. The Wheels section reminded me that if Harley had another two I'd be a car owner.

Then a few paragraphs in the Business section ignited my interest. Under the headline "Titan Corp. backs away from commercial paper" was a quote from an unnamed spokesman for the company denying rumours about its financial ill-health:

> There is no accuracy whatsoever to the rumours that Titan will file for bankruptcy protection from its creditors. Like most companies, we have been severely squeezed by the recession. Firm plans are in place to meet our financial obligations by selling our stake in one or two of our resource firms.

So the giant was beginning to bleed in public.

CHAPTER 20

M ICHAEL DID NOT answer the door sporting a blonde wig. Nor did he bat an eye when I handed him a full-face helmet and escorted him to Harley. He was passing all the tests. I wondered how he'd react when he met my mother inside her temple to country kitsch.

Etta gave him no time whatsoever to orient himself. As soon as we entered Sweet Dreams, she honed in on her target, fearless as a Stealth missile. I hadn't given her advance warning that I was bringing along a male companion, which would have elicited a dozen unwelcome questions I wasn't about to answer, truthfully or otherwise. Years ago I gave up battling to change her social behaviours, even her shamefully transparent efforts to connect me with an eligible man. (Etta gives "eligible" a loose definition: anything in pants who hasn't yet received his hundredth-birthday telegram from the prime minister. By contrast, my shopping list is so long and picky it guarantees me spinsterhood through several reincarnations.)

She had Slim in tow. For the Knock 'Em Down Country Bingo Banquet, both were identically costumed in black Stetsons, fringed scarlet satin shirts, black stretch jeans and red bowling shoes. Etta yanked Michael's hand into her iron grasp. Soon he'd be handcuffed to a pillar while she called in a priest. She didn't wait for me to introduce him; indeed, she barely acknowledged my presence.

"I'm Etta, Jane's mother and the owner of this juke joint. And this here is Slim," she effused, grabbing Slim's arm with her free hand and tugging him forward. I prayed that her boobs wouldn't burst the mother-of-pearl buttons straining to contain them under a stressed layer of gaudy satin.

"Howdy — I mean hello," stammered Michael, blushing a tone deeper than their shirts. Etta released his hand long enough for him to extend it toward Slim, who shook it with enough vigour to separate a pair of copulating porcupines.

Etta slapped her thigh. "Shit, honey, you've nabbed yourself a shy one!"

Tell me, God, how did I screw up? You could have given me a mother who was president of the PTA, who sang in a United Church choir, even a holy roller. Instead I get a geriatric bimbo cowgirl.

I made an heroic effort to banish matricidal thoughts. "Michael is here to help me with some business, Mom." I tried to catch her eye, hoping she might register my tactful sub-text: *one more goddamn provocative word outta you and I'll tear your face off.*

"There's a whole lot of people in this world who know how to get a little *pleasure* outta their business, dear," she replied. "And you're sure as hell lookin' at two of them." She nudge-winked Slim. "Anyways, we better get goin'. I promised Louella I'd help her out with the food. Hope everythin' stays quiet in here tonight."

She slapped me on the shoulder and, Goddess forfend, planted a kiss on Michael's cheek. This left a waxy carmine impression of her big mouth across the side of his face. *May there be no jukeboxes in heaven, Etta. May there be no men.*

I watched her sashay out the back door, her stretch-denim-swathed bum thumping a lively two-step to the rhythm of her sassy gait. I turned to face Michael, surprised to find him still there.

He was grinning. "She's terrific!"

My tension exploded into laughter. "Yeah, she is. But sometimes I catch myself wishing she was somebody else's terrific."

I asked Michael to get us a table in the corner while I went to the bar and pulled two pints of Upper Canada Rebellion. Last month Etta told me nobody but me and some yuppie who came in once a month drank the stuff. I threatened to revoke my pub-sitting services if she removed it. I won that round.

I set a mug in front of Michael, without even checking to see if he drank beer. He immediately raised his mug, smiled and said, "Cheers."

"It looks like a slow night, so I shouldn't have to do much of anything — unless the plumbing rebels. Etta keeps a plunger with my name engraved on it in the basement," I observed.

"Then why don't you get right down to explaining how I can help you?" he suggested.

I guiltily recalled that I had responded to his invitation to a theatre date with a request for more information. "I'm sorry I was so abrupt on the phone. I guess I'm obsessed with getting this job out of the way. I never really wanted to take it on in the first place and it's suddenly grown a lot bigger than I think I can handle. What I'm trying to say is — I also wanted to see you again, whether or not you can help me." I delivered my message to the table, rather than his eyes, unable to believe what I had just said.

When I ventured to look up, I met another smile. "Good, the desire was mutual." His tone grew businesslike. "We left off Monday night with me suggesting that the only safe way you could really confirm that GOD might have his hands in some dirty laundry was to cop a look at Titan Corp.'s financial records."

I nodded. "There is another route, though. I could try to locate this Luciano character — the guy who allegedly runs the cash to the laundry. But I don't think I stand a chance in hell of tracking him down and, even if I did, the most co-operation I could expect from him would be a knife between the ribs. I'm not a hard-boiled private eye. I'm a writer. Toronto is not Chicago, but it's still got its share of mean streets and psychopaths. One of my sources tells me that Lucy is definitely trouble."

Michael frowned. "I'm assuming that you're too bloody intelligent to have seriously considered pursuing that route! And I agree, it could only lead to a dead-end anyway — pun fully intended. So let's take a look at what's likely to be involved in getting our hands on GOD's books." He paused to sip his Rebellion.

I stared at him incredulously. "Did I just hear you say *our* hands?"

"You did."

"Were you speaking hypothetically?"

"No."

Something that had nagged at me during his Monday evening narration of the Imperial Trust affair surfaced: perhaps he was not an honest lawyer. The possibility threw me into conflict. In some obscure corner of my heart, I wanted him to have integrity but, if he did, he surely wouldn't consent so readily to being my accomplice in crime.

He interrupted my struggle around phrasing my next question. "Let me guess what you're thinking, Jane. *This guy is one of the dirty ones.* No, I am not. In fact, that's precisely why I came here prepared to help you. I told you that I sat in on the early meetings GOD orchestrated right after Durand put in his bid for Imperial. I advised the angels on the tax and legal implications of each of the various strategies they proposed. When it became clear to me that Dawson and his cohorts were planning to subvert the takeover by adapting means that I regarded as downright unethical, if not illegal, I advised him against that course of action — on *ethical* grounds. He told me that he didn't get rich sweating ethics and I wouldn't get far on Bay Street preaching them. He was as good as his word. When the whole affair was over and the Securities Commission handed down its pathetic ruling, he suggested I look elsewhere for my pay cheque. I already had another job, but I'd been holding onto my resignation from Imperial, just waiting to see if he'd sack me."

"Has he done anything since then to hurt your career?" I asked.

He shook his head. "Not that I know of. In any case, why would he? He already had what he wanted — my silence," he said bitterly. The lines between his furry eyebrows deepened. His shoulders tensed under his corduroy shirt. "Some of that Imperial dirt stuck to me, Jane. I'd be the first one to stand up and cheer if GOD got exposed as the white-collar thug he is."

"Then you won't be horrified when I ask if you think there could be any conceivable connection between him and the Mob?"

"Hell, no! I've read almost everything you've published, so I'm probably safe in guessing that capitalism is *not* your political flavour of the century. It is fundamentally unjust — the way wealth doesn't get distributed. But it is the system and there are a lot of decent business people out there who work honestly within it. And then there are the deviants like GOD, who bend every rule to their own advantage, then step right outside the game to pull off deals that the law doesn't sanction. Lots of countries were open to doing business with South Africa during apartheid. Some of our big corporations are into clear-cutting forests, devastating the environment, wiping out the traditional livelihoods of aboriginal people. Last week I heard that a big Canadian resource concern is going after permission to slice the top off a bloody mountain in B.C. so they can mine the copper — and poison the ground with sulfur dioxide in the process. When we talk business ethics, Jane, we're really talking shades of smut. A lot of the time, I honestly can't see that much difference between the Mob and the Suits."

I couldn't help laughing. "You've just delivered the kind of rant that I put my friends to sleep with! So how do two avenging angels set about getting their virtuous hands on the incriminating evidence?"

Kenny came over to the table with a couple of fresh pints. He looked dolefully at my half-full mug. "What's wrong, doll? Forgotten how to swallow?"

"No, Kenny, it's just that I don't have time for AA meetings these days. They really cut into a girl's schedule."

"Wouldn't know," he grunted, wiping his hands on his bar apron. "Sooner go to church than AA. Oh yeah, lady just come up from the basement. Told me the can won't flush." He walked away a happy man.

I shrugged resignedly at Michael. "Sorry, with any luck it should only take me a minute or two."

Half a dozen plunges did the trick.

When I returned Michael quipped, "I should have offered to help you with the plumbing, but a guy can only take so much romance in one evening. So before our next interruption, let me tell you what's likely to confront the avenging angels."

He told me that the books would be on a computer in the head accountant's office at Titan Corp. For security reasons, this computer was unlikely to be connected to a network — they could be really inaccessible. Savvy corporations now transfer all their sensitive financial information onto removable cartridges that they store in office safes. If Titan followed such a procedure, we were out of luck. However, it was more likely that they simply used some type of data protection software, probably high-end stuff. If we could get into the computer, past its electronic security and copy the files we needed onto floppy disks — and make a discreet getaway, then Michael would sit down and do some serious forensic accounting.

When he finished I got hit by a tidal wave of dismay. "So all we have to do is get past the security guards, through the building's electronic surveillance, past the computer security and out again. Michael, when I lock myself out of my studio I can't get back in again without collecting my spare key from my friend upstairs."

"Oh ye of little faith," he countered. "I have a plan."

"You have a plan, already? I think you're in the wrong career!"

"So do I, but that's another conversation. Listen up. I know a guy, Gordon Spender, who runs a small computer systems service business. He specializes in database and spreadsheet users. He's the best in the field. Our company has used him for years — and so does Titan Corp. In fact, my recommendation to Titan's chief accountant got him their contract. So he owes me a big favour."

My obstinate mind kept throwing up obstacles. "But you'd be asking him for a favour that could land him behind bars. And even if he were foolhardy enough to try it, wouldn't we have to wait until he gets called into Titan when they have a problem with that particular computer?"

"No to both your questions. I honestly don't think the risk factor would be very great. Because he would already be into the computer and be able to access their files, it wouldn't take him long to transfer what we need onto floppies or a cartridge. Even if someone noticed him doing it, they probably wouldn't think it peculiar: they'd probably assume he was doing a back-up. And we wouldn't have to wait. Everyone in the computer world who's networked currently has a problem. You must have heard of the Kafka virus that's threatening to infect hard drives across the globe on April Fool's Day. Gordon has been going crazy — and getting very rich — trying to keep up with the demand for his services. These days all of the corporations have virus protection for their computers, but it has to be constantly updated in order to detect the latest strains. He promised to safeguard my computer before he took on his other customers; in fact, he did the job for me the end of last week."

"But what makes you think he hasn't already been to Titan? They must be his biggest account."

He stood up abruptly and reached into his jeans pocket for some change. "Where's the phone, Jane?"

I led him over to the hot-pink phone Etta had stashed on an upper shelf under the working side of the bar. He riffled through the phone book, then dialled. Unable to stand the suspense, I returned to our table. About three minutes later, he set down the receiver and raised his arm in a victory salute. He almost broke into a run getting over to me, all the while grinning like he'd just discovered the cure for baldness.

"Can you believe it? He's booked Titan for tomorrow afternoon — and he's agreed to come by my office for a 'briefing' before he goes there!"

Michael stayed with me until closing time. We passed the remaining hours in relaxed chatter about non-corporation related subjects. When I dropped him off outside his house, he promised to phone me as soon as he heard from Gordon Spender. He also suggested that I set aside Friday evening to keep him company while he dissected the hoped-for Titan financial records.

I drove away invigorated by his optimism — and the simple ease of our connection. Because our conversation at Sweet Dreams had tapered into some fairly personal stuff that seemed to be drawing us past Stage 1 Intimacy, I thought he might kiss me good night. He did not, leaving me to wonder if: (1) he was too much of a gentleman to attempt sexual contact after only two encounters (such courtliness would place him in a school of one these days, when a lot of single women stride into bars with condoms in their purses); (2) he didn't find me particularly attractive; or (3) he did not find women in general appealing. The first speculation intrigued me; the second depressed; the third left me wallowing in irony — I was prepared to lower my defences for a man who might sooner be chasing a different set of glands.

Another possibility eased my passage into sleep: perhaps like me, Michael was one of the walking wounded, half-reluctantly clinging to celibacy as a security blanket. Settling for friendship with such an agreeable man could scarcely be reckoned a booby prize. Just a tragedy of grand dimensions.

Still, I knew I could keep my feelings on a leash.

CHAPTER 21

THURSDAY MORNING shortly before nine I braked Harley to a gravel-spinning stop outside the gatehouse to Charles Durand's exercise in instant château gratification.

The same Tom Cruise-cloned security guard Portia had finessed the day of his master's wake popped predictable as a cuckoo out of its clock and approached my bike.

"Delivery, sir?" he asked, before I had time to remove my helmet and definitively (I hoped) assert my gender. *May you be found dead in a black garter-belt,* I silently cursed.

I decided to leave the helmet on and try raising my voice an octave by way of compensation for the missing visual cue. "No delivery, madam. My name is Jane Yeats. I have an appointment with Mrs. Durand."

He scowled, then checked on the intercom connecting him to the mansion, presumably to verify my claim to an audience with Pope Judith. "Just drive your … um … vehicle up to the front entrance, ma'am. You can park it yourself."

He returned to the gatehouse and punched some keys on his computer console. When the two ornate wrought-iron gates slipped noiselessly into their stone sheaths, I accelerated Harley up the birch-lined avenue and executed another impressive stop-on-a-dime brake feat right in front of the main doors. Prick my class antagonism and I revert to behaviours unworthy even of a rebellious teenager.

This time round no liveried retainer approached to open the car doors I didn't have. Judith Durand herself greeted me at the door, without the intervention of a butler. Was the chatelaine cutting back on staff because her assets were temporarily frozen, or did a wench on a bike simply not merit the servants' attention?

With a big grin on her face, she ushered me into the foyer. I couldn't help noticing that not all her assets were frozen. Her version of widow's weeds was beguiling: a long black double-breasted jacket with leopard-print buttons over leopard-print stretch leggings. She looked like she was having fun when she took my helmet and leather jacket. I followed her lead into the first-floor room where she'd taken William after he slashed Daddy's jewels the afternoon of the funeral.

She must have seen the surprised admiration in my face as I looked about the sunlit room. From what I'd seen of the mansion on my earlier visit, I had assumed that the whole place would be repro Louis you-choose-the-Roman-numeral. Instead my eyes roved over a bright, energetic and creative décor that Georgia O'Keeffe might have devised. In fact, a gorgeous O'Keeffe hung over the fireplace: a sinfully lush tropical plant, its creamy infolded petals redolent with subliminal suggestions of delicate labial traceries.

Her soft voice broke into my thoughts. "This is *my* room — the one room in the entire palace Charles allowed me to decorate. Do you like it?" Her voice sounded a tad anxious, as if she cared what I thought of her taste.

"It's beautiful. I like it very much."

"And the painting?" she wondered.

I stepped back to gaze at it again. When I turned to answer, her eyes met mine directly — and held on. "If I didn't know better, I'd think Georgia had something other than botany on her mind!"

She smiled elusively. "Yes. I've just finished reading a new biography of her. Apparently she always denied giving her work any erotic implications — but, then again, don't most of us?" She was sitting on a richly patterned hand-woven carpet, her legs drawn up in the lotus position. As if to reinforce her bimbo-Buddha impression, she raised her hands into an elegant, imploring arc.

So there was more to Durand's second wife than rumour suggested. This lady was no mere clothes rack. And her question was not rhetorical. Behind it I sensed some odd pressure to reveal myself. Fat chance.

"I don't know. When it comes to erotic intentions, I can only speak for my own." And I wasn't about to. Was I imagining that I could actually *feel* this stunning woman's hot breath as it wafted across the room, settling on my neck as diminutive, intriguing Dior-scented clouds? I was confused. She seemed to be teasing me, almost seductive. Perhaps I just can't penetrate the semiotics of idle rich women. Whatever sexual tension was or wasn't blurring the lines of our peculiar exchange, I channelled my thoughts to my purpose in being here.

Her laughter tinkled mysterious as Chinese wind-chimes. "I'm sorry. I was being mischievous. If you follow me into the kitchen, you can begin your interviews." As she effortlessly rose to her feet, she reached into her jacket and extracted a small piece of lined paper. "I've written down the names and the positions of our household staff, in the order in which they'll be talking to you." She handed it to me.

"Thank you very much. It was thoughtful of you to organize things for me."

She shrugged her shoulders. "Don't mention it. Frankly, I haven't had much else to do this week. I'm hungry for diversions."

She wouldn't be long finding them. I took a seat at the refectory table.

"I've left a fresh pot of coffee and some pastries on the counter," she said. "Please help yourself. I'll ask Susan to come in first. And, by the way, don't hesitate to ask the staff whatever the hell you like. I don't give a damn what you write about Charles."

I thanked her for the permission (which I would have taken without her go-ahead), and glanced down at her list. At the top was "Susan Henshaw, cook." This was followed by

"Annie Morgan, housekeeper; Colette Dubois, social secretary; and Archie Price, chauffeur." The last name had been scratched out. Because I didn't for a moment think that any of these people could materially assist my investigation, I worked my way through her crew shortly and efficiently. I asked each of them a few questions about her duties and her relationship with her employers, pretending to garner first-person nuggets that would help me flesh out my portrait of the deceased.

It's a good thing I don't do this for what-you-might-call "a living." I gleaned from Susan the cook, a six-foot-tall anorexic, that Charles Durand hated broccoli, beef, lamb, pork and quiche, while Mrs. Durand favoured salads with low-cal dressing, brown rice, lentils and peas. Rich people can afford to like the kind of shit poor folks were forced to consume, she commented. What could I say?

Annie Morgan, gentle as a ferret, delivered her sentiments in a volume that would put a heavy metal band to shame. She told me that her job description was a load of crap: she was really the cleaning lady and did all the laundry. Although her boss had been a nice enough man, she wasn't sad he had croaked. As far as she was concerned, he changed his shirts, boxer shorts and socks far more often than was necessary — even for a man in his position.

Colette Dubois, uptight, prim and dressed like she was auditioning for the lead role in *The Prime of Miss Jean Brodie,* made sure that she didn't tell me anything — except that Susan had been having it on with the chauffeur. I could not work up a mental image of any guy settling his bones on Susan's without cracking them. Ms. Dubois pretended to throw in this bit of gratuitous information as though she were describing the wallpaper when, in fact, it was obvious that she harboured some nasty grudge against the cook. Perhaps she had nursed a crush on the late-lamented Archie, so recently summoned into a celestial livery.

After the inappropriately monikered Colette left the kitchen, I recalled Susan. I wasn't quite prepared for her response to my question about her amorous relationship with Archie. I mistakenly thought she was too skinny to expend much energy on rage. My impression was misleading.

"That fucking bitch!" she screeched, jumping up and down on the marble tiles like the Wicked Witch of the West. "It was Colette who told you me and Archie was lovers, right? That fucking bitch. I'll put rat poison in her goddamn soup." Her homicidal threat was impressive: as she spoke it, she set about chopping up a green pepper with a Chinese meat cleaver, an instrument that seemed to me slightly excessive to her purpose. But what do I know of techniques culinary? The closest I've ever come to Cordon Bleu is the instructions on a box of Kraft Dinner.

I assured her that I had no interest whatsoever in her private life, but that I had been interested in talking with Archie — prior, of course, to his untimely demise. I lied when I told her that I had vainly tried to contact him last Thursday. My mendacity was rewarded when she told me that he had flown the coop the previous afternoon, without bothering to make any farewells with his employers. She knew he was a dealer. "That don't make him no worse than the rest of us," she observed. Whoever said Canadians make poor philosophers?

Before telling Judith that I had finished interviewing her staff, I reviewed my meagre notes. God didn't put me on this planet to be a biographer. I think I can live with that.

Leading me into the dining room, Judith apologized for its grandeur. "I wish we could eat some place cozier, but there isn't one," she said.

"Hey, I'm prepared to digest good food in the Taj Mahal," I reassured her.

She turned to me and beamed a look direct as mid-day sunlight. "Maybe, but would you want to live there?"

I shook my head. "No. I live quite modestly — and I'm happy that way," I said.

She looked at me earnestly. "You may not believe this, but I'd be too."

A sharp rap on the door preceded Susan's entrance with a dinner cart. She set down artichokes vinaigrette, roast fillet of beef Dubarry and château potatoes, and a bottle of red. She'd even brought in the dessert, oranges in caramel with brandy snaps. Given the venomous dart she shot me on exiting, I wished for a slave to test my food for extraneous toxins. Susan would have done nicely.

Judith wasn't cool enough to wait at least until the oranges before she carried on. "I'm here because I thought that marrying Charles was the fastest way to get out of where I was. I grew up with a manic-depressive mother and an alcoholic father who routinely beat both of us. Once I got access to Charles's money, I guess I learned what every unhappy soul learns *after* she moves to lotus land: a woman can be miserable anywhere." She whirled around. "Do you want to know what's so pathetic about this place? Charles built it to impress the Establishment. The poor bastard never did clue into the fact that they only impress one another — and not with their homes or cars or clubs. They impress just by being *born* to it. That's the only real entrée, and you can't buy it."

"You're telling me, among other things, that your marriage wasn't a happy one?" I ventured.

She laughed. "I've never seen a 'happy' one — at least not close up. Neither Charles nor I expected our marriage to make us delirious. Ours was what wiser people call a marriage of convenience. He got the attractive young wife a powerful man needs to window-dress his social image, and I got …" She paused, leaving me to wonder if she was trying to remember her compensation.

"I got respectability, freedom from money worries — and a good cover," she itemized.

"Cover for what?" I wondered what she had to conceal.

"Is this conversation off the record? I mean, you won't use what I'm about to tell you in anything you publish?"

Given that my future plans never had included writing a word about Charles Durand or any of his relations, business or personal, I could honestly assure his widow that whatever she was about to tell me would never escape any word processor, including my lips. I simply nodded.

"You might not believe this — given how I present myself," she ventured, running her hands down her leopard-patterned thighs. "But I am a lesbian." She paused long enough to give me time to process her revelation, and maybe to give herself time to ponder her own sagacity.

I shrugged. "I hope you're not expecting me to be shocked or something. All the hoopla surrounding Ellen DeGeneres coming out on her own TV show probably has Oprah wishing she were gay. Look, Judith, when I'm not working at being celibate, I seem to fall — in terms of my own sexuality, that is — somewhere between Mae West and Gertrude Stein. Gender doesn't constrain me. When I sleep with someone, it tends to be whomever I'm feeling connected to at the time ..." I trailed off, amazed at my own candour. There was something disarmingly unpretentious in this woman's self-presentation that seemed to invite intimacy. I was curious, though, about how her late husband had reacted to her sexual proclivities. "But I'm not married. Do you mind if I ask you if your husband knew about your lesbianism?"

"I don't mind at all. He knew — right from the first night we went out together. I'm not out of the closet in the way that groups like Queer Nation think people like me should be, but I'm also not into being so secretive that I can't get on with living the way I need to. I've been lovers with the same woman for eight years ... and I did not intend to give up that relationship when I married Charles. He agreed to that — so long as I remained discreet about it, of course."

I couldn't resist asking the obvious. "But what about your sex life with him? Didn't it bother him at all, that you were with another woman?"

"Not a bit. It suited him perfectly. Charles had no — and

I do mean *no* — interest whatsoever in sex. He wasn't the least bit sexual. My being a lesbian relieved him of the pressure to perform that sleeping with other women laid on him."

Her response didn't really satisfy me. Human sexual drives are so complex, so perverse and insistent, I just can't believe that not attending to their imperatives somehow magically erases them. God knows, even nuns and priests are not exempt, simply because they committed to not practising.

"Judith, I have no problem getting my head around your end of the arrangement. Charles put no sexual demands on you and you met your own needs with your lover. But what I'm having trouble figuring out is what *he* did with his needs."

"That would have been a problem if he had any of those sorts of needs," she said. "Look, he was driven by something far stronger than sexual desire, much more urgent than our need to get it on or off, or whatever. Charles needed other people to confirm his *life*. He couldn't even believe that he was in the world if the Establishment didn't prove to him that he existed! The fact that I didn't demand anything of him in bed came as a huge relief. That's what made that stupid accusation so ridiculous!" she added, almost as a footnote.

I may not be a biographer, but I was born with an investigative reporter's instincts. "What accusation?" I gently queried.

"A few years ago, Charles bought some horses and joined a posh Equestrian Club — Grasmere Stables. He kept a mental checklist of what the right people do in order to maintain their credentials. One of the things he discovered they do is ride. He did develop a genuine love of horses, though. Anyway, just last fall some girl complained to the owner of the Club that Charles had tried to molest her in the stable. Apparently there was a bit of a kerfuffle — mind you, not a word escaped the place — then it died down. It was such a joke! I mean, the very notion that he could have come on to a teenager, when he had about as much interest in getting laid as a castrated bull. Charles resigned on the spot, just to avoid any scandal."

I pretended to accept her reckoning of the absurdity of the girl's accusation. But quite unwittingly, she had opened up a new avenue of investigation — that is, if Durand's sex life could give fresh direction at this point to my inquiries into the circumstances surrounding his murder. Still, I found it difficult to dismiss the notion as readily as she had — maybe because I was sexually abused as a kid: first-hand experience makes it hard to pretend that being molested doesn't matter. Probably it wasn't germane to this case, but try telling that to my head.

We finished our lunch in amiable chatter about other topics, none of them related to her husband's death. I found myself enjoying her company. When she suggested that we get together again, I happily consented.

Harley and I sped past check-point Cruise. My head was turning like a kaleidoscope, amazed at the utter unpredictability of human nature, the startling new takes each fresh twist presents.

CHAPTER 22

I'D BEEN BARRELLING north of the city for about five minutes when I pulled Harley to a stop in front of one of those phone booths Ma Bell generously drops like Easter eggs into the midst of nowhere. Some aspiring terrorist had severed the phone cord, but the Yellow Pages were still there to let my fingers do the walking. I needed to know where my bike was pointing me.

Under the listings for "Stables" I found a box ad for the Grasmere Riding Academy. *Dressage and Hunter Instruction — Equestrian Boarding Facility — Large Indoor Arena and Lounge — Tack Shop — Corner of Major Mackenzie and McCowan.* I decided not to call in advance of my arrival. The proprietors were unlikely to welcome a stranger who wanted to inquire into allegations of sexual misconduct on the part of one of their members (so to speak).

Less than half an hour later, I turned onto the unpaved road leading into the Grasmere Riding Academy. Not wanting to frighten the horses, I parked my bike just inside the entrance, behind an elegant sign. As I strode womanfully up the gravelled road, I observed gently undulating grassy hills divided by spanking white rail fences, three one-storey red-brick stables, a ranch-style frame bungalow prissy enough to serve as the set for *Anne of Green Gables*, horses munching about, groomed to show standards.

I walked past a row of parked cars — BMWs, Mercedes, an Audi, a Rolls etc. — and three horse vans toward the first stable. The moment I entered, the keen ammonia scent of horse piss, not absorbed by new hay, creased my nostrils. The interior was clean, elegantly appointed and spacious enough to house a sizable clutch of street people. A bevy of pubescent girls attended the inmates, currying them down, settling saddles and harnesses onto their gleaming bodies, chattering back and forth as they worked. I asked the first girl I encountered where I could find the owner. She shook her blonde hair in the direction of the bungalow, not missing a beat in her devout grooming of horseflesh.

The front door was answered before my third knock had time to register. A woman of Wagneresque proportions and an imperious manner stood before me. I felt like I'd come in response to a bondage-and-discipline ad from the back of *NOW* magazine. I worked strenuously at passing as a sanctimonious mother, hoping that she hadn't seen me pull up on a Harley-Davidson.

"Yes?" inquired the woman, dominant in tan jodhpurs and high black boots.

"My name is Joan van der Feld," I said, extending my hand. "I've come to inquire about enrolling my daughter Tiffany in one of your riding programs."

Evidently Brunnhilde mistook mendacity for the scent of money. Her face, hitherto as welcoming as a gargoyle's, crinkled into a semblance of civility. "Ah, yes," she replied, drawing my hand into a vice. "I'm Ilsa Vonnegut. Do come in." The way she pronounced "do" made it sound like the wet stuff that settles on your grass in the early morning. I followed her into a living room so stuffed with horsy memorabilia I developed an allergic reaction on the spot.

She settled herself into a capacious armchair. "May I offer you some tea, Mrs. van der Feld?" This caught me unawares: I'd been expecting oats.

"No, thank you. I can only stay a few minutes," I replied, glancing authoritatively at the nude spot on my left wrist where my Swatch would have been strapped had I remembered to don it after this morning's shower. "I'm due back in the city shortly." I tried her trick of pulling words up through my nose before releasing them, but succeeded only in making myself sneeze. "I'm sorry," I muttered across my sleeve, "I must be allergic to horses."

Our conversation went smoothly enough, as she enthusiastically informed me about all the equine services Grasmere could offer my imaginary daughter. Then I tossed something as unsavoury as a steaming horse-bun into her sales pitch by mentioning that I had no hesitation whatsoever in writing her a cheque on the spot for Tiffany's enrolment — except that I had heard a rumour from a close friend that some of Grasmere's girl pupils had been "bothered" recently by one of the male members of the Club. The room grew so quiet you could hear a horse hair settle on the carpet.

"From whomever did you hear such a thing?" she asked, her right eyebrow levitating.

"Oh, Evelyn Eaton cautioned me just last week when I mentioned that Tiffany was developing an interest in horses and had heard about your establishment. We bumped into one another at that annual charity ball for the Differently Abled at Casa Loma, you know."

She nodded her head in acknowledgment of a non-existent woman at a non-event on the social calendar. I guess she had trouble keeping up, what with cleaning out the stables, mowing the grass, and all.

She was expert at recovering control. "I can assure you, Mrs. van der Feld, you needn't worry about your daughter's safety on these premises. Even if the gentleman in question had been guilty of what those girls accused him of, he is no longer a member of this club."

"I understand that he is no longer a member of the human race," I remarked somberly.

She ran her palms along her thighs, presumably to wipe off the sweat. "Ah, true enough. He died recently — shortly after resigning from Grasmere." She made it sound like cause and effect; evidently Grasmere was the centre of her mental cartography.

"Yes," I said, "and he met an untimely end — indeed, rather a violent one, I gather."

Obviously I had set my investigative steed down a byway she didn't want to follow. "Well then, there can be little point in one worrying about it," she said dismissively.

I wasn't about to be diverted that summarily. "Do you know if any of the girls' parents planned to lay charges against him?"

She shifted her ample butt on the chair, uncomfortable as that fabled princess who discovered a pea under her mattress. "Not to my knowledge. One has got to be very careful about jeopardizing a man's reputation on the basis of what some foolish girls fantasized about him. Adolescence seems to be such a peculiar phase."

Instead of strangling her on the spot for a remark I regarded as unconscionable, I took the route of dumb persistence. "In my experience, men seem to find their sexuality a peculiar phase."

This angered her. I was relieved when she raised only her voice. I had anticipated a whip. "Mrs. van der Feld, whatever did or did not transpire on my property is no longer of any concern to any of us. Do I take it that you are still interested in enrolling Tiffany at Grasmere?"

"Oh yes," I replied, keen as a stage mother whose kid has just been offered the lead role in *Annie*. When I produced my chequebook, she rose and walked over to a file cabinet cunningly disguised as a sideboard at the side of the room. She handed me an application form. "Would you be so kind as to fill this out? We ask it of all our prospective members, of course. One's got to be very careful about who one lets in — as you can imagine."

I set about filling in the blanks on her form with poetic licence, fabricating all the responses — except for the names of my two references. I entered "Portia Sherman" and "Mrs. E. Yeats."

Ilsa excused herself to answer a knock at the front door. I

took advantage of her absence to whip over to the sideboard and examine the papers on the shelf from which she'd taken the application form. Close by that stack I found a mimeographed membership list and a schedule of classes. I borrowed them.

When she returned to the room, I had reseated myself and stuffed the purloined papers into my knapsack. She glanced perfunctorily at my completed application, then rose to her large flat feet. "Do you ride, Mrs. van der Feld?," she inquired as she led me to the front door.

"Oh yes," I smiled. "A Harley-Davidson. She doesn't eat much and she never farts."

Visibly unimpressed, the dear lady shook my hand like it was a dead carp.

Anxious to eyeball the Grasmere papers, I drove back to the city at well over the speed limit. I needed to know if Durand had, indeed, been molesting one or more of the girls. A cursory survey of the membership list, dated January, confirmed that Durand was no longer a member. I turned to the schedule of classes for the winter session and found that Junior members were slated for instruction on Wednesday afternoons and Saturday mornings. The instructor was Miles Cahill. Seven other girls were included in the Wednesday group class; two of them, and an additional six, were on the Saturday roster. I returned to the membership list, which was conveniently divided into Adult and Junior categories. I found the addresses and phone numbers of all thirteen girls.

The phone rang as I was pondering my next move. I picked it up, glancing guiltily at the message display. Three calls.

"Hi, Jane. It's Michael." His voice was excited and impatient. "I'm so glad you're in. I've called three times in the last hour." Not wanting to exceed my newly imposed quota on wisecracks, I resisted asking him if his toilet was blocked.

"I'm sorry, Michael. I just got back and I've been a bit distracted."

"Wait 'til you hear my news — it will focus you, for sure! Gordon Spender phoned me at the office just after five. Mission complete: he managed to get what I asked him for and he's coming over here tonight to give me the disks."

I was delighted. "That's wonderful. When do you think you'll get a chance to look at them?"

"First thing tomorrow morning. As soon as I knew, I asked my secretary to cancel my appointments. I'm taking the day off work to indulge myself in forensic accounting," he said. "Are you free to come by?"

"Probably not until later in the day. Something came up during my chat with Judith Durand that sent me haring off on another trail. That's why I was late getting back. I think I should spend some time tomorrow checking it out." I found myself not wanting to tell him what particular worm was eating away at my brain.

"Do you want to tell me about it?" he asked.

"Not really — at least not tonight, Michael. It's really only a detail, a possibility that's nagging at me. I haven't had time to think about what it might mean, if anything. I just don't like loose ends when I'm researching something."

"No problem, then, as long as you assure me that whatever you're snooping into won't put you in any danger. Don't forget that researching a book is not the same thing as investigating a murder. I've never heard of anyone being shot at in the stacks of the Metro Library."

"Perhaps not, but I've almost died of boredom there on several occasions," I quipped.

The line was silent. "Are you still there?" I asked.

"Of course I'm still here," he snapped. "I was simply waiting to hear how many wisecracks you could weave around a serious topic before you got real again."

"I'm sorry. That's a bad habit of mine, especially when I'm nervous. I really do appreciate your concern for my safety, but

I honestly don't think I'm in any danger at all." I was glad I hadn't told him that some spook had sheared the brake cables on Harley just last week, that I'd spent a few stressful moments Sunday morning dodging bullets. His concern touched me, but I had turned myself into such a paragon of self-reliance I didn't know what to do with a protector.

"Apology accepted. I wasn't offended, Jane. It irritated me to listen to you being so cavalier about your own well-being. Why don't you phone me when you're free tomorrow?"

"I will. I really appreciate your taking the time to do this for me."

"Thank me if I manage to hand you some useful information about Titan Corp. I'm not at all confident that I can figure my way into getting past the data protection that's bound to be in place. I'll look forward to your call."

I hung up the phone feeling displeased with myself. Avoidance had driven me into my smart-ass routine. I didn't want to make the phone calls I knew I must — and I was fighting my galloping attraction to Michael. Hell, I'd just reached the point in my therapy where I was beginning to acknowledge that Pete didn't intend to betray me by dying. It made no sense at all to lay myself open to fresh pain by letting another man get close. I kept reminding myself that slugs managed to expand their territory by deciding to go shell-less in the world. Probably because they didn't think too much about their evolution.

I've never mistaken lust for love. Lust lets you keep your shell.

Short of getting drunk, which was beginning to strike me as one of my less creative cures, I could think of no way to shut down my unhappy brain. I went to bed early.

CHAPTER 23

SOMETHING DARK and formless hovered at the edges of my dreams, disturbing sleep. When I couldn't summon the energy to play fetch-the-stick in the park at the crack of dawn, Max got crabby. On the way home, I grabbed a take-out breakfast and a carton of orange juice at my local greasy spoon, resolved to take moderately better care of myself.

I decided to phone the homes of the thirteen girls who took riding lessons at Grasmere. I briefly rehearsed my patter. I planned to introduce myself as Amanda Marsh, a concerned mother whose daughter had her heart set on enrolling at the Riding Academy. I'd say that Ilsa Vonnegut had kindly given me the names of a few parents I could contact as references for the Academy. I preferred to speak to the girls' mothers, simply because I knew I'd be more comfortable raising such a gender-sensitive issue with another woman. I would confide that I had heard an unpleasant rumour I was anxious to dispel prior to going ahead and enrolling my child, and ask if she knew anything about it.

I knew that my calls could damage Ms. Vonnegut's horsy enterprise. I didn't give a rat's ass: in the interest of maintaining respectability and her bank account, the woman had neglected to pursue a very serious allegation. Some people get their priorities so skewed they forfeit their right to compassion. I easily excised Ilsa from my list of people whose well-being engages me.

Two hours later I was ready to give it up, having left messages on four answering machines and with three housekeepers. The daughters of two of the women I did get through to hadn't belonged to Grasmere when Charles Durand was a member. One of the women for whom I'd left a message phoned when I was between calls. She quickly denied having heard any such rumour and got off the line before I could thank her. Her tone of voice told me that the very suggestion of sexual impropriety on a member's part had affronted her.

On the tenth call I struck gold. I reached Nancy Hawkes, who confirmed that last year her daughter Katherine had mentioned "something that was bugging her" about a man who rode at Grasmere. She said it wasn't the sort of topic she was comfortable discussing on the phone and, in any case, she was late leaving for a weekend at the family ski chalet. I knew I'd probably get much more information from her if we could meet in person. Before ringing off, she agreed without reluctance to meet me for lunch on Monday. She suggested the members' dining room at the Royal Ontario Museum.

I persevered until I reached the bottom of my list. One mother, who grew very agitated when I asked her about the rumour, remained civil long enough to say that another student's mother had passed on some such "gossip," but she quickly forgot it after making sure that her own daughter hadn't been "bothered" by anyone. She terminated our exchange when I asked her to give me the name of the gossip-monger. I was beginning to sense that I'd touched on a conspiracy of silence. Maybe it was only upper-class decorum rampant. Whatever the root of this reticence, it was extremely irresponsible. Helps you understand, though, why so many perverts get a long lease on their sexual practices.

On my final call, I got through to a man who turned out to be a single custodial father. He knew nothing about the allegation, but assured me that he'd slice the dick off of any bastard who ever tried to do anything weird to his girl.

Why was I surprised to hear a bank president express himself in the vernacular? Non-abusive fathers are known to be intensely sexually protective of their daughters. Some women conceal the fact of their children's abuse from their husbands, terrified that the dark knowledge might provoke them to homicide. I remembered the case of a grief-crazed father who shot his daughter's rapist/murderer to death right in the court room, just *after* a guilty verdict had been handed down. He was later acquitted by a jury.

I needed time to relax and clear my head before going over to Michael's. I ran up the stairs to Silver's and persuaded her to go out for lunch with me. I had caught her standing in front of a blank canvas, where she said she'd been glued for an hour with artist's block. She wasn't a bit reluctant to take a break — especially for food.

Fifteen minutes later we were seated in a nearby East Indian restaurant. Before we set foot in the place, we had agreed on what dishes to order. Yet Silver insisted on studying the menu. When the waiter returned to our table, she looked up at him innocently and asked for the beaver tail and beans.

"Could you please tell me again what you are wanting, madam?" he asked.

I darted her a warning. "Don't even think about repeating it, Silver."

She smiled sweetly and got on with asking for chicken tikka, lamb masala, dry mixed vegetable curry, biryani rice and two stuffed parathas.

"You can do a reasonable imitation of a normal person when you really set your mind to it," I chastised her after the waiter scurried off to the kitchen. "You know, if I thought there was a goddamn beaver in the neighbourhood I'd trap the thing and make you eat it."

She grinned. "They probably taste dreadful. But maybe if you tossed in some coriander, a little cumin …"

"And don't forget the *soupçon* of bullshit," I added.

"Since when did you, of all people, get touchy about someone else's twisted sense of humour?"

When I tried to shrug, I realized that my shoulders were clenched. "Sorry, Silver, I guess I'm kind of stressed out."

"Well, it can't be your love life, because we both know you don't have one — although some of us addicts break into a cold sweat just at the thought of celibacy! So I'm probably safe guessing that it's this girl-detective thing you're doing. Right?"

"Right." I lit up a Rothmans. "You didn't order us anything to drink, did you? I need a beer."

"Nope, I didn't. The fact that you need a beer is a good reason for not having one. I'm going to order two of those yogurt shakes when he brings the food. I want to know why you're so uptight."

I started filling her in on what I'd been doing. When I got to the Jackson's Point episode, she exploded. "You mean to say some asshole with a rifle was using you for target practice and you never told me? Lady, you are putting some major strain on this friendship."

"I think I intended to tell you when I came to your door to return the car keys. But, as I'm sure you will recall, you were preoccupied with something else." Nothing like tossing a little guilt into the pot when you're on the defensive.

"I don't put such a high priority on answering the call of the wild hormones that I wouldn't have taken time out to talk to you, for Christ's sake! Don't ever walk away again without telling me you got something to tell me. I mean, that shooter's probably still out there tracking you."

I tried to assure her that I was certain William had been the target. I explained that there was a strong possibility that his father's killer wanted to silence the son too. If William went to the police with the rumour about GOD's link to the Mob — and the fact that he had passed that information on to his father, who intended to blackmail Dawson — the police would be obliged to investigate Titan Corp.

Silver reminded me about the sheared brake cables. "Maybe you could have written that off to some asshole who was getting his rocks off that night by imagining bikers smashing themselves into concrete walls after he'd done his dirty work, but when you put it together with what happened at the cottage, I just can't see how anyone who's getting paid to be a detective could think they're unrelated." She was very exasperated.

I nodded. "Okay. I did think a bit about it. But even if Dawson has heard that I'm researching a book about Durand, he still wouldn't have any reason to suspect that my work might lead me to suspect his involvement in any sleazy dealings. After he blocked the Imperial Trust bid, he and Durand had no further business connection — at least that anyone else could confirm."

"Apart from the fact that the same person who sheared your brake cables, or another hired gun, could have been tailing you and followed you up to Jackson's Point! He'd only need a pair of binoculars — or a telescopic sight on his rifle — to identify who you were meeting at the cottage. GOD or the Mob could have wiped out two birds with one hitman," she concluded, her voice dripping with irony.

"Right, that's a possibility. But I'm still more inclined to think that whoever was behind both attempts — whomever they were intended for — only wanted to terrify me and William into keeping quiet. A contract killer could easily have blown me away in the parking lot behind Leather Boys and made a safe retreat. Remember how dark it was back there? Same goes for the cottage. The shooter could have made his way from the shoreline right up the hill without being seen. The whole lakefront was deserted that morning."

Silver conceded that I had a point, but extracted a promise from me that, beginning now, I would not leave my studio without informing her of my itinerary and that I would check in with her as soon as I returned. As we ate and sipped our non-alcoholic beverages, I told her about how Michael had gotten his hands on Titan's books or, rather, the disks that held the files.

"So what's this guy like?," she asked, deftly scooping up some vegetable curry with a paratha.

"Oh, he's very bright. I'm sure he's very good at his job."

She just stared at me until I volunteered that he was also a very nice man.

"*Nice*? I didn't think that word was in your vocabulary! *Nice* is how you describe Pat Boone, or Anne Murray or Michael Landon or somebody's aunt. Now I know you've got the hots for this guy." She look pleased with herself.

"Michael Landon's dead."

"I only keep track of the Indians."

I didn't succeed in keeping a poker face. "Ours is strictly a business relationship — but I will admit to a lascivious flash or twenty. However, impure thoughts do not have to land a girl in bed."

"No, but you can always pray, honey," she laughed.

Before we parted, she suggested that I start sleeping over at her place until I was out of danger. I hate sleeping anywhere but in my own bed, but I agreed, just to avoid an argument I knew I'd lose. I was feeling guilty about having supplied her with an edited version of events. I'd left out the Grasmere sub-plot — mainly for reasons of self-protection. My anxiety levels were high enough without skyrocketing them into a full-featured panic attack by forcing myself to discuss a topic I still have difficulty even thinking about.

CHAPTER 24

MICHAEL OPENED the door looking as though he'd walked a straight line from bed to his computer early that morning. His face was flushed, his hair tousled, he was barefoot and wearing a cotton sweatsuit. Excitement obviously over-rode any self-consciousness he might have been feeling at my showing up without notice.

I stepped in quickly, in case the fur ball-from-hell was at the post. Michael took my jacket and helmet and started babbling.

"Jane, you won't believe it, but this is turning out to be a lot easier than I could have dreamed. In fact, in an hour or two I might be able to give you a rough analysis of Titan's current financial status. Do you know how lucky we are? I mean, how much do you know about computer security? Oh God, I'm sorry. I haven't even asked you if you'd like something to eat or drink! Would you?"

I burst out laughing. "Michael, your brain is off and running faster than your dog. You look like you're the one who might need some nourishment. I bet you haven't even eaten today."

"You're right. Just an apple and a coffee first thing this morning. I haven't been able to tear myself away from the computer. Come, let's go into the kitchen."

He jumped at my suggestion that I prepare him a meal while he sat at the table and talked. I was relieved to discover that I could assemble a nourishing cold plate from the contents of his well-stocked fridge.

"Security turned out to be no problem at all. Titan's chief accountant — his name is Ronald Jordan — took what is probably the simplest and most effective route to keeping unauthorized people from snooping into his confidential files and from stealing the data. First of all, his computer wasn't on a network, so nobody could tap into it from another computer. Second, he stored all his data on removable cartridges, which he simply had to pop out of the hard drive and lock in a safe when he wasn't using them. There was only one level of protection in place, and my guess is that he had it installed in the event that he might be called out of the office briefly and didn't want to bother shutting down and locking up — or in case someone managed to steal the cartridge, which he'd keep at least one backup copy of stored in the safe. So he used an encryption program to protect his sensitive files."

I interrupted. "Please slow down a bit, Michael. Computerese is not my first language. What's an encryption program?"

He brandished a slightly tarnished celery stick. "Oh, sorry, I guess I got carried away. It's a nifty little bit of software that allows you to scramble a document's data so no one can view it without supplying a password. If a user can't supply the password, an encrypted document is useless. Essentially it's like coding a message. These programs automatically ask for the password, and encrypt, decrypt, and re-encrypt protected files as you save, reopen, and close the files. You never need to worry about accidentally leaving a file unprotected."

"But surely this Jordan would just have memorized the password or kept it in the safe," I remarked.

He nodded. "You're right. But Gordon, bless his larcenous heart, figured I'd be needing it. So he did something really clever. Do you know about PRAM?"

I shook my head. "I know about SPAM — Etta fries slices of it when she's in a festive food mood. If this PRAM is a kissing cousin, I don't want to hear about it."

"Your wit just might be the cure for my intensity," he laughed. I was relieved to hear that he had at least two takes on my sense of humour. "PRAM is just a small bank of battery-powered memory that stores user configuration choices after you switch the power off. Gordon temporarily installed a program on Jordan's hard drive that secretly stores passwords in PRAM. After he upgraded the anti-viral program — which he'd been called in to do in the first place — he asked Jordan to enter his password, open the encrypted folder, and check to make sure that his accounting program was functioning properly. He explained that installing virus protection occasionally corrupts a file or two. He left the room, of course, while Jordan did exactly what he asked. When he returned, he pretended to perform a final check on the computer, while he was in fact retrieving the password and removing his own bit of outlaw software."

I clapped my hands. "Fantastic! Just out of curiosity — what is the password?"

Michael grinned. "Even GOD's chief accountant genuflects before the master. The password is JEHOVAH."

"Congratulations. Let's hope we can change it to NEMESIS. What's next?"

"Just before you arrived, I was printing out the financial statements. So now we have to make a fine-tooth analysis of them. What we're looking for is a clear, deliberate pattern of fraud that is probably embedded in a whole series of transactions. If illicit funds are being laundered through Titan, we have to track them," he said, sounding much more confident that I thought the circumstances warranted.

"Have you spotted anything yet to suggest that Titan is doubling as a Maytag washer?" I asked.

"I haven't examined the statements — that's what you can help me with — but I can already tell you that we're probably on the right track: Ronald Jordan has been keeping *two* sets of books. So we'll find the official version that he prepares for Revenue Canada and the shareholders and, I suspect, we may discover the original version, the real set — before he entered his creative revisions to produce the official one. You see, there's no legitimate reason to keep two sets of books."

His excitement was contagious. "But what can I do to help you?" I asked. "God knows, I'm no accountant."

He smiled. "That's okay. In fact, I'm glad you're not! What we need to do first is bring all the spreadsheets I've printed out down to the dining-room table, where we'll have lots of room. I'll work from the original statements, and you'll have the official ones in front of you. I want you to read out the figures I ask you for from your set. That will save me a lot of time."

We worked flat out for four hours, pausing only to refill our glasses of Perrier. The routine we established reminded me of the time I'd helped a friend who was in graduate school. Her thesis required that she compare the manuscript version of a novel with the first edition. She read from the manuscript while I followed in the printed version, interrupting her every time I spotted a difference between the two. As Michael read from a balance sheet, for example, I would follow my version for the same time period, carefully marking every revision. For the first couple of hours, our progress was very slow and nitpicking. Then Michael began to hone in on a few key documents and line items. He seemed particularly interested in Titan's income statements for the past six months.

A few minutes after seven, he suddenly banged his fist down on the table, which by now resembled the bargain stationery counter at Honest Ed's. "I've got it! I think I've got it!" He jumped up and pulled me into an enthusiastic hug. He let go of me too soon — or just in time, depending on the outcome one desired. I wasn't sure.

"Look, I'm starving, and in even greater need of the shower I skipped this morning. Can we break for a bit? I'd like to take us out for supper. There's a great little Hungarian restaurant just around the corner on Bloor. I feel like eating something really substantial, and washing it down with some red wine. I'll explain what I think may be going down at Titan over a Black Forest Platter. Are you game?" he asked.

Five more seconds of hug and I might have been game to share the shower, too. "I'd love that. Would you like me to take Aphra out for a short walk while you shower? She's sitting at the door with her back legs crossed."

He tossed me her leash before heading up the stairs. As I snapped it on the dustmop's collar, I tried not to visualize him slipping out of his sweatsuit.

I tried.

By the time we were biting into the apple strudel, I had learned that, prior to six months ago — when Jordan began to keep his second set of books — the balance sheet confirmed that Titan was, indeed, cash-starved. In fact, Michael estimated that had the corporation continued to bleed at the same rate over the next quarter, they would have been forced to work out a lot of fancy re-financing strategies and probably sell off their deadwood. Even those measures would have staved off the inevitable only for a few more months.

However, the records for the past six months put a whole new — and startlingly rosy — complexion on Titan's public face. The monthly income statements showed several huge infusions of money. Suddenly, cash was flowing through the corporation's veins like water over Niagara. Income from the retail outlets swelled; a number of generous loans were recorded; cash payments for major commercial real-estate transactions appeared with increasing frequency. The bottom line was that Titan was now in a much better position to borrow money and to attract investors.

But based on our purloined paper evidence, I didn't see how we could prove that any of the new income, which Michael estimated ran in the ballpark of four hundred million dollars, was not legitimate.

"From what you've told me, it's damn near impossible that all this mystery cash came from kosher sources. But how do we get closer to knowing where it really originated?" I asked.

"To a trained eye, the statements for the past six months at least raise enough questions to interest the police forensic accountants. They can start asking questions, checking out who's at the other end of these sales and deals. Isn't that all you need — to force them to start an investigation in earnest?"

I sipped my coffee. "No. I seriously doubt that they'd venture into GOD's territory without some *very* blatant evidence of major fiscal wrongdoing — and even then they might turn a blind eye. And I need something concrete to link Dawson to the Mob. Without it, I won't be able to tie him to Durand's murder. I mean, if I went to Ernie Sivcoski with what we have now, he'd laugh in my face! Michael, we are assuming that Dawson is laundering huge sums of money, probably drug profits, for the Mob. It gets delivered to Titan, the accountant records it as a legit transaction, but it still has to be deposited in the bank. How does a corporation get away with depositing millions of dollars, probably in relatively small bills, without attracting the attention of the bank? Those guys are supposed to be on the lookout for unusual banking activity — like heavy deposits."

"You're right, they are, although Canadian banks are much more loosely regulated than American ones. They aren't even required by law to report large deposits. It's well known that organized crime now has a firm foothold in the financial community; in Canada, marriages between the Mob and the white collars are fairly common. In fact, the most successful money-laundering operations use existing systems and are fully taxed. On the white-collar end, it requires a creative accountant like Jordan to fiddle the books, a crooked lawyer to fabricate the legal documentation — and a bank official who's willing to be bribed. The only way we might nail Titan is to check further into the tell-tale transactions. I can check out the real-estate sales and see whose names they're registered in …"

I interrupted. "And my friend Lennie Sherman can look into some of the stock purchases. He's a genius at analyzing market activity." I shook my head. "But you know, I'm not convinced that any of that will get us very far. Think of it, Michael: Titan even controls a small trust company, so Dawson wouldn't even need to bribe a bank official. And don't these money launderers use all kinds of sophisticated layering techniques and things to cover their tracks?"

Michael looked glum. "Yes, they do — and the RCMP's Anti-Drug Profiteering Section estimates that they're successful at least 80 per cent of the time. They figure that about ten billion dollars in annual drug revenues fall through the net."

I racked my brains. We'd come so far I couldn't let go at this point, when all we had was a wicked hypothesis. "Wouldn't GOD keep track of what belonged to whom? After all, the Mob isn't handing him that money as a gift. Sure, he must be getting a big chunk of it as his reward for laundering the dirt — and the income sure improves his cash flow, but only temporarily. There must be a record somewhere of the dates and amounts of each transaction, and where the money eventually wound up. Did you print out everything that was on the disks Gordon gave you?"

"I printed out the spreadsheets and all the financial statements, everything that had been created in Lotus, yes." He paused. "There was something else — a folder that held a few word-processed documents. I figured it was just correspondence. I didn't even open them up; Jordan is hardly going to hang himself in a letter. That's not how these guys communicate."

I stood up. "Let's pay the bill and head back to your place. If Jordan was such a security freak, he may well have entered his notes on the computer and shredded any incriminating paper. You said that even if someone had managed to steal one of his cartridges, it would be useless without the password."

As soon as we walked out the door of the restaurant, we broke into a run. Michael turned to me as we paced one another along Bloor Street. "I hope you can pray and run at the same time," he said.

"As well as you just proved you can eat and think at the same time."

. . .

An hour later we settled onto the sofa, one giant tantalizing run closer to the goal post. I was feeling particularly happy at having kicked the ball forward this time. When Michael and I viewed the contents of the word-processed documents on screen, we encountered what appeared to be routine accountant's notes — except for a three-page file named "Good News" that consisted of dates and figures arranged under two columns.

When I'm writing the first draft of a manuscript, my word-processor allows me to record voice annotations, a quick and easy way to insert brief comments about facts that need checking, awkward passages in want of major surgery and so on. At a later stage, I can locate any annotation by its speaker symbol and play back my comment. These symbols can be hidden.

Just for the hell of it, I went to the Tools menu, chose the Preferences command, then the View category; under Show, I selected Hidden Text to display any annotation symbols. Instantly a number of entries in "Good News" sprouted a small speaker symbol.

Michael screeched, "You're a genius!"

We listened to Jordan's annotations, which provided the basic data we needed to identify the precise points at which the dirty money entered the system and where it ended up with no rings around its collars. Michael cross-checked and found that the numbers corresponded to the suspicious new infusions of revenue. What had been a skeleton now had flesh and a wardrobe. But who was wearing it? Who was GOD's anonymous benefactor?

We sat in silence, thoroughly exhausted but unwilling to stop just yards short of the goal post. "*Good News* — who brings good news?" I turned to Michael, whose head had slipped onto his right shoulder. He was sound asleep.

Careful not to disturb him, I went upstairs to fetch a

blanket to cover him with before I left. As I nudged him onto his back, his eyes opened. "Jane, you look as tired as I am. Please don't drive home. Will you sleep in the guest room?"

I was wiped out — and scared about returning home so late at night. Some of Silver's fear for my safety had rubbed off. I called her and told her not to expect me back tonight. She snickered.

Like two weary campers, we made our way to our separate bunks.

I was awakened shortly after six. My face was being licked. Alas, it was Aphra my right eye opened onto.

"Michael," I hollered. "Michael."

He was in the room in a flash, clutching a bunched-up sheet to his waist. He rushed to the bed, where I was sitting bolt upright.

"Jane, what's wrong? Are you all right?"

I stared at him. "*Good News* — who brings good news to Dawson's cash-starved corporation? I should have seen it right away: GOOD NEWS — GN— it's his initials — Guiseppe Nicaso. The Mob boss!"

Michael flung both his arms toward the ceiling in a victory salute. The sheet covering his loins travelled in the opposite direction. He looked down. I looked across. Then our eyes met.

"I'm sorry," he said.

"I'm not." I stretched out my arm. When he took my hand, I tugged him onto the bed.

Aphra had the wits to scurry from the room. No one was paying her any attention.

CHAPTER 25

WHEN WE STEPPED out of the shower shortly after noon, Michael said he had a great idea. I listened to it very attentively. Over the past few hours I'd learned that letting him exercise his creativity yielded delightful side effects. Cooking was but one of his talents.

He suggested that we drive up to Muskoka and spend the remainder of the weekend at a country inn he knew, where we could relax around a fireplace, make love, cross-country ski, hot tub, make love, eat sumptuously, make love …

I almost refused. My inner Puritan nagged at me that taking time out for a romantic interlude in the country while I was in the midst of a murder investigation was not terribly professional. And I was still recovering from the aftershock of having seduced Michael. Actually, you couldn't claim he'd been unco-operative, once I'd tugged his naked body in my direction. It wasn't really my fault: two years of celibacy had pushed my hormones right off the top of the Richter scale. I could but follow.

Lust, I reminded myself, is one thing — emotional intimacy quite another. I'd managed to let go with my body, but I still needed to keep a tight rein on my heart. Although two years had passed since I'd watched Pete's coffin being lowered into the ground, part of him still hadn't released me. And a big part of me clung to him fiercely as ever.

Was I letting my resurrected sexuality prolong denial, the way booze and overwork had?

Thirty minutes later we were in my studio. Michael offered to walk Max while I flung some clothes into a bag. I was astonished that my dog didn't object. So much for the territorial imperative.

While they were gone, I ran upstairs and asked Silver to babysit Max until the following evening. She consented, delighted to play a modest role in facilitating my return to sex. Then I phoned Etta to say that I wouldn't be available to pinch-hit for her at Sweet Dreams that night.

"I was counting on you," she snapped. "What's so goddamn important you desert your own mother on night like tonight?"

I swiftly sidestepped her question. "What's so special about a night like tonight?"

"I've got a private party booked, for Christ's sake! Slim's band has got a new record out and the record company is launching it here. I need you to help out with the bar."

"Etta, you've got a list as long as your tongue of guys you can call in to do bar duty. Just this once, don't hassle me. Something's come up I have to do. Okay?" I was starting to whine. How is it that mothers can reduce children on the cusp of middle age to eight-year-olds?

"My regulars expect you to be here. Anyways, you're the only one I really trust when the joint's crowded, eh? I mean, what if the john backs up or something?"

I was getting angry. I didn't want Michael returning in time to overhear my end of this ridiculous exchange. "You gave birth to a writer, not a plumber. I know that's been a terrible disappointment, but maybe it's time you learned to live with it. Look, Mom, I have to get off the phone. I'm sure you'll manage splendidly without me."

"And I hope you'll manage splendidly without your mother when she's gone. I could change my will, you know. Slim would love to inherit Sweet Dreams."

I exploded. "If he also inherits the bag of guilt that goes along with the dump, I won't give a damn."

Just as I was about to bang down the receiver, Etta said "I hear you. Maybe I did go too far this time, but I would have been a whole lot more understanding if you'd answered my question in the first place. What's so goddamn important you desert your own mother on a night like tonight?"

I did not chill out. "Sex, Etta, sex. S-E-X. I'm going up to Muskoka for an orgy of SEX, SEX, and more SEX. Do you get it?"

She burst out laughing. "So why the hell didn't you say so right off the top? Hey, I won't have any trouble getting someone else to do the bar. Have a good time, eh dear?"

"Thanks, Mom. I'll phone you Monday." I hung up feeling like I'd just completed the triathlon.

Thirty-two hours later Michael pulled his car up outside my building. We'd had such a glorious time together, I was anxious to part company. I needed time out to let it all settle into place. Even so, I couldn't resist asking him up for coffee.

As we approached the door of my studio, I reached into my jeans pocket for the key.

"Jane, forget your key," Michael said so abruptly I turned to him. He gestured at a note stuck to the door with masking tape.

I immediately recognized Silver's hand. She'd written with a thick black felt pen: "JANE, DO NOT ENTER! COME STRAIGHT UP TO MY PLACE. THIS IS URGENT!"

"Let's just do what she asks," Michael suggested, taking my elbow.

I ignored him and banged on the door. There was no response. "Oh shit, something's happened to Max. He should be barking his head off."

I took the steps two at a time and hammered on Silver's door. "Silver, it's me — Jane." I recognized Max's excited yelp before she got to the door.

My friend was not smiling. I rushed past her to hug my dog. I heard her and Michael introduce themselves. I looked up. Silver, who is usually very comfortable meeting strangers, was standing awkwardly beside my new lover, watching my reunion with Max.

I gave Max another squeeze, then rose to my feet. "So what's the note about, Silver? I thought something had happened to Max."

She looked at me sadly. "Will the two of you please sit down? I'll get us some Cokes."

We seated ourselves side by side on her sofa. She set three cans of Coke on the coffee table and lowered herself into the tatty chair facing us. "Nothing happened to your dog, as you can see. But that's probably because I brought him up here yesterday evening. After I walked him, he moped around your place like he'd been abandoned." She shifted uncomfortably. "But something did happen to your studio, Jane."

"What are you talking about?" I asked, in a moderate state of panic.

She set down her Coke and looked directly at me. "This morning after Max walked me, I went to your studio to get his food. The door was locked, so I wasn't expecting to see anything unusual. But someone had broken in during the night. Came up the fire escape, smashed a window close to the door, and reached in to unlock it. The whole place has been trashed. I'm sorry. I was going to try to clean it up before you got back, so it wouldn't be so shocking, but then I figured you would want to see how it was left — like maybe you could figure out what the asshole was looking for, or something," she said apologetically. "And I didn't call the cops because I figured you probably wouldn't want them to know."

I just sat and stared at my feet, willing myself not to cry. After all, Silver and Max were unharmed; the rest, I told myself, was only material possessions. All I really valued was Pete's stuff and my research files.

Michael kept his arm around my shoulder as we went down the stairs to inspect the damage. Although Silver had prepared me to expect the worst, I wasn't ready for the devastation that confronted us when I turned the key in the door. The interior looked like the aftermath of a combined earthquake and hurricane. The space I had so lovingly constructed as my safe haven after Pete's death had been violated to the extent that I scarcely recognized it as my own. I guess it wasn't mine any more. Perhaps Pete didn't live here any more. Could memory harbour us now?

My impulse to cry gave way to rage when I saw my cherished photo of me and Pete on a sailboat in Cuba lying on the floor in a broken frame. Shards of glass had incised white scars across the face of our happiness. That's when I lost it. I picked up a huge quartz paperweight and flung it through a window. I fell onto my knees, crying "fuck, fuck, fuck ..."

Silver ran to my side and held me in a tight embrace until the shudders subsided. As she patted the back of my head, she asked Michael to boil some water for tea. He returned from the kitchen area and reported that the stove had been smashed and all the cupboards emptied onto the floor. He couldn't find any tea bags.

I sat on the floor, with Max on one side of me and Silver on the other. Michael sat cross-legged across from me, looking deeply concerned and confused. When I tried to organize my thoughts and decide what to do next, I came up empty. My mind was in a state of chaos. I was inarticulate with rage and grief. It hadn't occurred to me yet to be scared.

Michael suggested that we return to his place and try to sleep on it. I looked at Silver. She intuited my fear: I was already anxious about how quickly this gentle man and I had connected. If I accepted his offer of protection during a crisis, our bond would deepen more than I was ready to handle.

"Perhaps it would be simpler if Jane spent the night at my place, Michael," she said softly. "We'll call you first thing in the morning."

Michael was sensitive enough to pick up on my nervous vibes. "That sounds like a better idea. Are you sure you'll both be safe, though?"

Silver rose to her feet and stood proud as an Amazon.

"Fuckin' tank couldn't get through me, man. And, if it makes you feel any better, I've got a gun up there — little souvenir from the stand-off with the cops at the rez," she explained. "Tonight we'll sleep safer than the president of the United States — and with a cleaner conscience."

Michael allowed himself a grin. "Already I'm feeling sorry for anyone who's even thinking about bothering you! Please call me at work. I have to go in for a meeting in the morning, but I'll ask my secretary to put you through."

Before leaving, he kissed my cheek. I was still staring at my ruined photograph.

CHAPTER 26

MONDAY MORNING I woke up before the sun. I rolled to my right side and looked toward the west end of Silver's studio. My friend was curled up like she hadn't been born, snoring enough decibels to get her into the *Guinness Book of Records*. Max, the infidel, was flopped over her. He, too, wheezed the deep sleep of the innocent.

When I saw the gun beside Silver's head I felt dirty. Clumps of GOD's criminality were clinging to me, stubborn as dog shit between the grooves of my Reeboks.

Rage is a complicated emotion. Hold onto it too long and it becomes corrosive. But in the short term it often confers astonishing clarity. As I lay there fretting about how my involvement in the whole Durand miasma had spilled over onto my friend's life and Michael's, two things became clear: I was onto a transgression that smelled worse than a barbecued sardine, and some deadly nutbar suspected that my investigation was about to do major damage to a few bespoke suits. Harley's sheared brake cables, the shooter up at Jackson's Point gunning for me and William, and the trashing of my studio were like a Wagnerian *leitmotif* threading its way through the opera, repeating itself with variation, echoing, linking all those strands into an ultimately meaningful orchestration of the original theme. Problem was, I couldn't get it.

Sure, it had taken some serious smarts to work my way through the wormy maze that began with Charles Durand's head flopped in a bloody pulp on his mahogany desk, then slimed a path through to the destruction of my cherished photograph. But I now needed a strategy, some cunning trick whereby I could get to Them — GOD and his mates in the Mob — before they wiped out more than my abode.

All this rapid-fire thinking held one consoling spin-off. Since Pete's death, I'd spent a lot of time dousing depression in beer, unconsciously hastening my progress into wherever he was hanging out. That slow suicide was over. I just plain did not want to die any more — certainly not on GOD's schedule. Period.

So I lay there staring at Silver's latest painting in progress. It was a rude assemblage of thickly laid strokes of primary colours, suspended somewhere between abstraction and therapy. I focused all my powers of concentration on a slash of crimson outlined by yellow reaching for the upper right-hand tip of the canvas. I couldn't see any bridge that would connect GOD's money laundering to Charles Durand's murder. Price, the chauffeur, was one of the links, but Ernie Sivcoski had already concluded that his murder was a Mob hit for a drug double-cross — and William had confirmed that Price had, indeed, screwed the Mob. Although Michael and I had reasoned our way through the two versions of GOD's books, I was still no closer to meeting my contract with Simone.

Saturday night over brandy, lying in front of the promised fireplace, Michael had tried to persuade me to hand all the documents in the Titan paper trail over to Ernie. I resisted on the grounds that such a move would forewarn GOD, give him time to cover the paw prints leading to Durand's body. Sure, he'd still be left holding a steaming bag of corporate shit that would destroy his reputation and put him behind bars — but Durand's murder would remain unsolved.

Before pulling myself out of bed, I resolved to meet with Sam Brewer, show him the Titan books and explain the interpretation Michael and I had developed — all in exchange for his promise to pass the documentation on to Ernie after he'd written up the story for the *Post*. To conceal the fact that Michael and I had conspired to steal the Titan files, Sam could claim that he was the unwitting recipient of an anonymous gift. Whether or not Ernie believed him, as a reporter he wouldn't be obliged to disclose his sources. If the police brass tried to suppress an investigation into Titan Corp., Sam could use his considerable journalistic heft to force the issue. I would remain on the sidelines, the mystery catalyst.

My reasoning fell short of devising a way to flush GOD out of his homicidal bushes. It might come down to confronting him with what I knew, once I'd safeguarded myself by giving Sam the Titan documents.

In the meantime, I had a lunch date with Nancy Hawkes. Given what Michael and I had sniffed out about Titan, I wasn't sure why I was bothering to pursue the shadowy possibility that Durand was a child molester.

Still, it was one of those itches you have to scratch.

I made my way past throngs of school children lined up outside the Royal Ontario Museum to see the dinosaurs. I took the elevator to the fourth floor and was led to a table by the long windows overlooking Bloor Street. A woman draped in floral-patterned silk rose graciously to take my hand.

"I'm Nancy Hawkes. I'm glad you came." She paused. "Hell, I'm glad I came!"

I relaxed and sat down. After we had ordered a carafe of white wine and the poached salmon, I elaborated a bit on why I had asked her to meet me. Right off the top, we established a working rapport. She informed me that one afternoon on the drive back from Grasmere Riding Academy her daughter mentioned, in that deflective way teenagers do, that some man had come on to one of the other girls while she was cooling down her horse after class. Nancy had told her daughter to do everything she could to persuade the girl to report the incident — first to Mrs. Vonnegut and her own mother, then to the police if neither one of them seemed serious about pursuing the allegation. A week later, Katherine told her mother that the girl wasn't bothered about it any more. Apparently the man had diverted his attention to another girl.

"Did you ask Katherine who the other girl was?" I asked.

"Yes. She told me she didn't know: the girl who told her didn't mention her name."

"And the man? Did you find out who he was?" I held my breath.

Mrs. Hawkes speared a moist chunk of salmon. "Oh yes. Katherine said it was Charles Durand. She recognized him from a photo in the newspaper."

Much as I had already warmed to this woman, I was growing exasperated. "Did you do anything with your daughter's information?"

She put down her fork and stared me in the face. "Of course I did! I phoned Ilsa Vonnegut and told her I'd blow the whistle on her whole damn operation if she didn't get to the bottom of it. A few weeks later Charles Durand was dead." She shrugged her shoulders and resumed eating. "So who knows, maybe there is a God."

Although it was only half-empty, I pushed my plate aside. The conversation had suppressed my appetite for any pink flesh except a chunk out of somebody's butt.

"But Nancy, didn't it occur to you that there might be some connection between Durand's murder and the fact that he may have been molesting young women? I mean, why didn't you go to the police at that point?"

Her eyes widened. "When I read about his death, I figured he'd gotten his just desserts, sort of at random, probably for some other reason entirely. Take it from me: men in high places have a lot of enemies, including one another — not to mention their wives! I'm unhappily married to one of the S.O.B.s, so I know. And look, Jane, I have to admit: even if it had occurred to me to connect his murder and the alleged abuse, I probably still wouldn't have gone to the police. In the first place, I'm not particularly interested in helping them make a case against an aggrieved parent — let alone a mere girl! My notion of what should be done to child molesters would shock even Amnesty International. And second, what would have been the point in exposing his victim to all that nasty questioning?" She shrugged again, as elegantly as the ex-prime minister who had refined the gesture into a rhetorical sculpture. "In any case, you don't really believe that anyone would actually resort to murder to revenge child abuse, do you?"

Maybe not according to her lights; presumably her childhood lights hadn't been dimmed by a pedophile. I was reading from a different script. Motives for murder must be as various as the people who provoke and commit them. But in my damaged books, sexual abuse constitutes one legitimate cluster.

I thanked her for seeing me and quickly excused myself. My guts were flapping so badly I thought I must have swallowed the salmon live.

As I re-entered the splotch of sunlight bathing Queen's Park outside of the Museum, something indigestible kept eating away at my guts. It wasn't the *Béarnaise* sauce. I decided to walk south and think upon it.

Clumped flakes of wet snow melted on contact with my head and shoulders as I trudged past the McLaughlin Planetarium, mulling over what Nancy Hawkes had told me. Her willingness to pass on the allegations must have served as a sop to her conscience: she had transferred the moral baton to me. She was right about one thing. Had Durand been cultivating an unhealthy appetite for girls, his death terminated any further abuse. But I couldn't accept as glibly as she that the worm came so simply to rest.

I gave my flowchart another pass over my brain. Michael and I had verified Dawson's involvement up to his genteel armpits in money laundering for the Mob — and we had the incriminating paper trail. I believed William when he told me that he had taken the rumour to his father. I further suspected that Charles Durand wasted no time leaping upon the opportunity to blackmail his old rival. But I had nothing substantial that connected Durand's murder to GOD's money laundering

— and therefore no hook upon which to hang GOD for killing him. And that's what I'd been hired to do, to find the murderer.

In return for my inconclusive efforts, I'd had my Harley sabotaged, been shot at and had my beloved sanctuary reduced to the kind of rubble that Californians fear from the Big One. In order to maintain my shaky hold on sanity, my mind had been busy caretaking me by blocking the obvious. Someone assumed I was on to something threatening enough to risk tossing another corpse or two into the ring.

Resigned to squeaking out of the whole mess by laying the goods on Sam Brewer's desk and hopping the next flight to Barbados, I stepped onto the street. Screeching brakes brought a Honda Civic to a stop inches from my body. Badly shaken, I apologized to the driver. If she'd been equally preoccupied, I'd be a spreading stain on the road.

The rancid red herring about Durand's alleged nasty sexual proclivities flopped back into my awareness. Now I was confronting a serious ethical dilemma: what to do with what I had learned … more precisely, how to tell Simone that her brother may have had sexual designs on girls.

I followed the sidewalk as it curved west along Hoskin Avenue. Suddenly my mouth filled with acid. I quickly turned my body toward the pollution-black face of Trinity College and threw up into the grey slush. I kicked some wet snow over the mess and trudged along. My guts were wrenching my brain out of denial.

I was angry. In fact, I was in a towering rage. A mother lode of wisecracks, booze and cynicism couldn't smother my compulsion to declare war on what was pissing me off. The anxiety and depression that had dogged my every waking hour and, if my nightmares are a reliable witness, also most of my sleeping ones ever since Pete's death seemed to be undergoing a strange metamorphosis. I felt this irresistible need to channel all that thwarted energy and desire into destroying whoever had recently enlisted himself in the service of sending me off to glory faster than my self-destructiveness could ever do.

As I continued to walk on automatic pilot, my footsteps kept leading me westward toward the site of my devastated studio. Yet I knew I wasn't ready to undertake the restoration of my physical space; that would have to wait until I had pulled myself together. I could think of only one route back to emotional composure. I took charge of my feet, turned on my heel, crossed the street at Bathurst and hailed a cab in the opposite direction. I was preparing to confront what really ailed me, and I needed my mother. GOD was a carbuncle — no, worse than that — he was a tumour and I was going to excise him from the body politic. Free of cost to the public. Not that I was about to let Etta in on my mission. I just needed her bizarre, reassuring presence prior to girding my loins.

CHAPTER 27

I THRUST A TEN-dollar bill over the seat at the cab driver and hopped out without waiting for him to execute the first steps in the strange dance that begins with him returning part of your change and waiting for a serious reward, while you calculate 15 per cent of exorbitant less what he'd already screwed you out of.

When I walked into Sweet Dreams, Happy Hour had just begun. The place was half-empty, the folks there not unhappy to be caught between work and going home to dinner with the spouse and kids — mostly because they had neither the job nor the nuclear family.

Behind the bar was the Happy Hooker, my mother, Etta Yeats, dispensing good cheer and her own peculiar brand of "don't worry, be happy" to her customers. She was wearing a purple T-shirt and white jeans.

By the time I reached the bar she'd pulled me a pint of draft Rebellion and set it on the counter. "What's up, doll?" she asked. "I ain't used to seeing you show up when I didn't even phone ya."

I took a long pull on my beer. "Nothing's up, Etta, not the Dow Jones, not the sun, not even Mick Jagger's pecker. Certainly not me."

Ignoring my declaration of global impotence, Etta set about mixing herself one of those non-alcoholic pink frothy things that winds up looking like it should be sent straight to the Department of Health for toxic analysis.

She picked up her glass and nodded toward the rear corner of the room. "I only got about twenty minutes, girl. After that

I got four broads showing up to audition for a spot on Saturday night. Call themselves the Meno-Paws. Slim seen them open a show for k. d. lang a while back."

I'd describe the grin that followed her declaration as sheepish, if one could legitimately describe anything that crosses a shark's face as sheepish. "Now, you know I ain't no fan of k. d. lang's," she continued, "but ever since she come right out and said she's queer, I've been listening harder to her music. Right?"

And here I'd been wasting away thinking that she despised k. d. because her vegetarianism hurt cowboys. I was just too caught up in my own wretchedness to give pondering the evolution of my mother's eclectic belief system any further energy. I simply nodded my head, like it all made sense.

"Anyways, Slim says these Meno-Paws is worth a listen. But so are you, girl. So what's happening in your life?" Four fuchsia fingernails tapped an impatient tattoo along the side of her glass.

For some reason too complex and murky to comprehend, buried somewhere back when I thought blue Popsicles were the closest you could get to heaven, today I had migrated to this dump like it was home. After my lunch date and long walk in the snowflakes, I felt dirty, confused, incompetent, muddled and eight years old. I needed my mother.

Five sodden minutes into my spilling out my latest escapade, Etta eyeballed me fierce as an eagle. "The scariest thing about being your mother is that you're always wandering off into some strange space where I can't follow you. And this time you're really freaking me out. That nice Indian friend of yours, Silver, called earlier and told me what had happened to your studio. Look," she implored, pausing to suck up a full two inches of her flamingo-pink drink, "sounds to me like you got yourself into some kind of shit that's real dangerous. I don't like it one bit. What scares me the most is you could be drowning and you'd pretend you was just paddling around if anyone was watching you. Some folks don't have the smarts to scream for help when they really need it."

Etta paused to contemplate the ring of lipstick smearing her cocktail straw. "I must have told you about the time when you was only two years old and I took you up to a cottage on Lake Scugog and you just jumped right off the end of the dock like God was gonna teach you to swim before you hit the water?"

To her credit, she paused to check out whether or not I'd already heard this story. Truth is, I was weaned on it. The sequel was that her sister jumped in to rescue me, I almost drowned Aunt Kath, but both of us got saved thanks to the intervention of a Labrador retriever who had more smarts than God gave the two of us. Etta always told this story like it was some kind of morality play about me having been reckless since conception. Good thing she never stayed in school long enough to have heard the story about the renegade son who made himself a pair of wings and flew too close to the sun. I'd still be picking the wax out of my teeth.

She stood up. "If you'll excuse me for a minute, I got a business call to make." Before flouncing off, she picked up my empty mug. "I'll be back in two minutes with a refill, kid."

I watched my mother walk toward the phone behind the bar. If it's possible to have a brave butt, Etta's got one. Age has not wearied her, nor have the years toned her down. I reminded myself not to *kvetch* so much about the old girl. While we still haven't learned how to narrow our communications divide, when it comes down to the crunch she always manages to find a way to keep the lines open.

Half an hour later I was nursing my second pint with Etta beside me and the Meno-Paws strutting their sassy stuff on stage. The quartet of young women were boogying and belting out tunes about this middle-age rite of passage, their shaved scalps wrapped round with mini pads in the fashion of sweatbands.

Michael appeared at the table. As he lowered himself onto a chair, Etta vacated hers in a rare show of diplomacy.

"These broads are terrific. I'm going to sign them up. Excuse me." My mother departed the scene she'd set up.

Michael glanced at the Meno-Paws and winced. I looked at him with the obvious question in my eyes. So who invited you?

He grinned nervously. Could it be because I was seeing him in a suit for the first time? "Your Mom phoned me just as I walked in the door from work."

"What did she want — a date?" I was feeling more than a bit hostile. I mean, if I had felt that I needed to see this man, I would have phoned him myself. Anyway, I was having my usual trouble relating to a suit. I liked his tie, though, very sexy flowers on fine silk.

Michael reached across the table to take my hand. I pulled it away faster than a barn cat's paw.

His scowl of displeasure augmented my resistance to male authority (of which suits are the signature tune). "Look, all your mother said was that she thought you really needed someone to talk with and she didn't feel like she was the right person. If she was wrong, or if I'm not the right person, just tell me that — and I'll be out of here."

An edge of hostility embroidered his offer. Who could blame the guy? Ever since I'd first heard his voice over my phone, I'd been beaming him push-pull messages that would discombobulate an air traffic controller.

To my shame, I managed to suppress any overt signals of actually feeling ashamed. "I'm feeling kind of edgy, Michael." I was about to inform him that he wouldn't be on the receiving end of my distress if he hadn't put himself in my face, unsolicited — at least by me. Then I made the mistake of making eye contact. I should have known better. This man's eyes were more mesmerizing than Max's.

I resisted the impulse to fetch myself another pint. "I came over here after lunch with Nancy Hawkes — the woman I told you about on Saturday. She confirmed what I'd already suspected: our working-class hero did seem to have a heavy interest in getting it on with girls." I nudged my empty mug aside and fiddled with the cardboard coaster.

Michael made an ineffectual gesture at flipping his hair away from the upper rims of his glasses. He shook his head like he hoped it would clarify his thoughts. "I don't know what conclusions to draw from that, Jane. Someone prematurely transported Durand to the one piece of real estate he really deserves." He blinked. "You're not beginning to think that maybe GOD isn't responsible for his murder?"

My next lapse into eye contact totally undid me. "I'm not thinking. For once, I'm feeling. And what I'm feeling has got me so freaked I lost my cookies all over the lawn in front of Trinity College." When I saw the concern in his face I added, "And don't even think about telling me what to do next."

"The notion of trying to direct your actions hasn't creased my brain, Jane, not once since we met." He stopped right there, just as I was beginning to hope that he'd slip into his Superman suit, sweep me up into his arms, take flight and show me how the world made sense from five thousand feet above ground.

Relating to him was becoming one weird chess game.

"I guess it's finally sunk into my stubborn skull that I had better cut my losses and hand the proof of what I know over to Sam Brewer," I said. "I hate like hell giving up on this case before I've really sewn it up for Simone, but I value my bones enough not to risk them again." I figured I had better stop while I was ahead, before Michael realized I was lying through my teeth.

He observed a full minute of silence before it dawned on me that he had no intention of saying anything.

"I'd sleep more soundly tonight if I could get all the Titan paper into Sam's hands before I go to bed," I commented, "along with copies of the disks. Is that asking too much of you, Michael? I mean, I'll go back to your place for the stuff and arrange to meet Sam here later on."

He reached under the table for his briefcase. "I brought

everything with me. And I left copies of it all in my safe at the office. If you'd like me to stay while you hand it over to Sam, I'll do that happily. He might need some help finding his way through the books and interpreting some of my notes before he writes his article. I'd like to ask you, though, if you plan to attach any conditions to your 'gift' — after all, you're about to hand him the story of the year. Maybe you should make sure you safeguard yourself in the bargain."

His sweet logic had the effect of forcing me to organize my thoughts. He hadn't mentioned the fact that he had put his career at risk in persuading Gordon to steal Titan's books. "Thanks, Michael, very much, for your foresight in bringing the stuff with you and for offering to meet with Sam and me. I would like you to stay."

He smiled his acknowledgment. "Let me run this past you," I continued. "In return for my 'gift,' I plan to inform Sam that two things are not negotiable. One, he must never reveal his sources to anyone, not even if the cops put a cattle prod to his *cojones*. And I promise you, he will be very insulted when I deliver that condition: his integrity as a journalist is unparalleled. Two, he has to promise me that he won't submit his copy to the paper for twenty-four hours." I glanced at my Swatch. "That should give the *Post* just enough time to get it to press for the Wednesday morning edition."

As I rose from the table to head for the phone, Michael looked up at me. "May I ask why the twenty-four-hour delay? I'm nervous about what you plan to do in the interim. Not," he quickly added, "that I plan to persuade you to step onto the next plane for Bridgetown. But you'd put my chauvinistic heart to rest if I knew you weren't about to do anything dangerous. In case you haven't noticed, *I give a damn*." He was blushing.

How long after he discovered I had lied to him would he continue to care? That was a risk I had to take. I had one or two outstanding items on my agenda more imperative than my need for a long-term lover, especially the caring kind.

"Michael, after we've connected with Sam, I plan to go straight upstairs and crash on Etta's sofa bed for at least ten hours. Then I plan to drive out to Simone's and fill her in on what we unscrambled about Dawson's dirty dealings with the Mob — and how they might connect him to her brother's murder. She can do whatever the hell she wants with the information. After that I plan to check into a downtown hotel, go out to some mindless movie, head back to the hotel and sleep the night away. Very early the next morning, I will jog to the nearest newsstand and buy several souvenir copies of the morning *Post*."

I wasn't surprised to note that he looked wounded; nothing in my schedule included him and I hadn't acknowledged his *I give a damn*. Later, he'd find out why.

"Sounds fine," he said through very tight lips. "Why don't you make your call?"

Two hours later we had concluded negotiating what would probably turn out to be the big breaking story in Sam Brewer's career. I'd never seen the man so excited or so grateful. He couldn't figure out why I wouldn't write up and sell the story myself, even when I told him how dirty the whole Titan mess made me feel. But, then again, I was telling him only half of why I felt like I had filth clinging to my soul. I was relieved to see that neither he nor Michael seemed to have clued into the real motive fuelling my benevolence: I was buying some very valuable life insurance on the cheap.

I prayed to the patron saint of mendacious souls that I'd live long enough to collect the dividend.

CHAPTER 28

A T 2:31 A.M. I was crudely awakened out of a deep sleep rampant with erotic images Madonna couldn't top — or bottom. I knew my dream was heavily sexual because a diminutive Etta, who had sprouted wings and a halo, floated cherubically across the top of the screen delivering a sermon on safe sex to the tune of "Stand By Your Man." I knew the precise time because my Swatch glows gangrenous in the dark, like my eyes when I'm blasted out of slumber.

What had awakened me was lying close to the sofa bed. I couldn't quite make out what it was, but some lout had tossed it through Etta's living-room window. My nose immediately began to twitch to the noxious odour of fumes reminiscent of only one fluid in the world: Nikos's homemade ouzo. Could it be that the proprietor of The Last Temptation next door was trying to summon my mother to an early morning tryst? I could hear him screaming like the Greek equivalent of a banshee from the sidewalk below. As I raised myself on one elbow, seriously contemplating murder, a second smell assaulted my nostrils. Then my lungs. It was smoke. When I blinked, my eyes felt like they'd been bathed in Javex.

I hit the floor and broke into a sprint for the bathroom, where I grabbed a towel, ran cold water over it, flung it over my nose and mouth and beat a path for my mother's bedroom, all the while screaming: "MOM. ETTA. SHIT. FIRE."

Etta's bedroom had already filled up with smoke. I had trouble seeing my way to her bed, but no difficulty at all hearing her mutter, in a slow, sullen voice like she was drugged, "So is it shit or is it fire?"

"FIRE, Etta, it's FIRE," I managed to bellow before a drift of black air hit my mouth. I dropped the wet towel over her face and scooped her and her blanket up into my arms like a cocooned baby. Staggering like I don't after eight brews, I made it through the kitchen to the back door which opens onto a fire escape. Still cradling this precious, magnificently irritating old cowgirl, I managed to jiggle open the two locks and set her down on the top landing of the fire escape.

As she steadied herself on her feet, I noticed that she was clad in a scrap of black lace too small to discreetly cover her head for Mass. "Just hold onto the railing and make your way down to the backyard, Mom."

She grabbed me by the neck of my T-shirt and screamed, "I ain't goin' nowheres without you. Where's your goddamn brains, girl?"

For a few seconds I tried to locate them. All that was computing in my adrenaline-drenched mind was getting back into the living room to retrieve my jeans and knapsack. It was my American Express Gold Card I was really concerned about. That had taken real creativity and fraudulent form-filling to obtain.

Etta slapped me across the face so hard my grey cells kicked back in.

When we reached the ground Nikos was there to greet us, flapping his arms like a berserk scarecrow and screaming in Greek, his face streaming tears of what I took to be gratitude to all the gods of the pantheon for Etta's salvation.

She gave him a big hug and shouted into his face — in Greek! And here I always figured her mother tongue was still posing a challenge. He switched to English. "Oh ladies, thank God, you are safe. I was just coming back from my meeting with my brother Cypriots when I see a guy throw something through your front window downstairs. Next thing I'm seeing fire. So I run into my place and grab a bottle of my precious ouzo and throw it into your window upstairs which I will replace tomorrow. That's how much I care about you, Mrs.

Etta. That was my second last bottle of last year's — and it's my best year — ouzo."

"Later I'll find a way to thank you, Nikos," she promised. From the way he was staring at her swatch of lace, I could guess his preferred method of payment. "But right now, I need to know if you also phoned the fire department."

His black eyes widened. He threw his arms up to the sky. "Mrs., you think I'm some kind of ass and a fool? Right after I throw the precious bottle, I run back in to my restaurant and phone them. I call 911 — right? Mrs., you insult your neighbour."

I heard sirens. Just in time, too. I couldn't see into the bar through the thick, frosted glass pane in the back wall, but the interior sure as hell was lit up as if a forest fire were raging inside. I thought of all that barn wood lining the walls.

I quickly made my way along the alleyway and reached the street in time to see the first fire truck brake to a stop. Four more quickly followed, trailed by an ambulance. Sirens and flashing red lights gave the street a frenetic, almost festive air. I told the first guy who hopped off that no one was inside. In a few seconds, they'd smashed in the front door and were dragging a hose into Sweet Dreams. Only then did I step back and notice the shattered window through which the arsonist Nikos spotted must have tossed his destructive missile.

A thick white-furred protective arm around her shoulders, Nikos escorted Etta round to the front of the street and ushered her into The Last Temptation. When I noticed the fire inspector's eyebrows rise as he took in her black lace, I decided to delay claiming ownership of the woman.

Much later, after the inspector assured me that the fire was out, I went next door to check on my mother. I shouldn't have worked up so much concern. She and Nikos were partying, boogying like Zorba the Greek on acid to the deafening strains of "Never on a Sunday" issuing from a tape deck behind the bar, and sipping away at a shared glass that must have been poured from his sole extant bottle of ouzo. It was 4:30 in the morning, I was exhausted, strung out and smelling like a dead campfire. I couldn't handle a love scene stickier than a plate of baklava.

Perhaps if she'd had the grace to thank me or feign even moderate embarrassment, I might have resisted saying: "Shouldn't you be dancing to 'Ring of Fire,' Etta? Your place of business — which is also your home — just got the guts burnt out of it. And you're celebrating? Did you pay someone to torch the dump so you could collect on the insurance and fly off to Athens with Nikos?"

She clutched her bosom, tragic as Phaedra. "So what am I supposed to do? Stand out on the Danforth half naked in the middle of a freezing winter night boo-hooing while the joint burned? Wasn't nothing I could do, Jane."

Glass of ouzo in hand, she tottered belligerently over to me. Nikos was hanging back on the fringes, the way all of Etta's men quickly learn to do. The old lady was on a roll. Nothing like a pyre to clean out the cobwebs. "I'm sick and tired of you acting like you was my mother, instead of it being the other way around. The place was insured — you know that. And anyways, I was getting bored with the décor. Now I can get it all redone at Allstate's expense and have a bit of a holiday while it's being renovated. I did not arrange to have that fire set. You and I both know that's probably got a whole lot more to do with the kind of people you mess with than anybody I know. So what's to cry about?"

She stuck one of her hideous acrylic fingernails so close to my face I would have bitten it off if I had a dental plan. I got real mean. "Hank Williams's famous hat, you know the one you built a shrine for, the one folks as besotted as you travel up from Oklahoma to see? That's what to cry about, Etta. It's gone the way of all the lonesome cowboys."

She crossed her arms over what she could of her boobs and smirked. "And happy trails to it, as far as I'm concerned. If you had half the brains God gave a parakeet you'd have guessed a long time ago that I picked up that piece of felt shit at the Hadassah Bazaar ten years ago. I got a special rider on my insurance policy to cover anything happening to it that should pay for an extra week's holiday for me and Slim or Nikos or somebody …" she trailed off.

I lied to myself that my mother was behaving in such an unseemly way because she was repressing her grief and fear. Or maybe she was, as the self-help movement instructs us, *in denial.* Deep down, I knew the truth: Etta was so far from feeling that she had anything to deny, if you cloned her the whole movement would be out of business in the flash of a crystal. On the spot I decided to cut my losses and salve my bruised soul elsewhere.

"I'm out of here, Mom. I just checked in to make sure your back wasn't going into spasm or you weren't pitching a heart attack or anything. You've reassured me." I turned on my heel. "Send me a postcard from you and the lucky winner. And never forget, Etta, no love without a glove."

As I stormed out the door her calm voice followed me. "I'll phone you later this morning, dear."

I drove my bike down to the lake along a route Harley must have memorized, because my brain wasn't clear enough to lead me a secure step in front of my nose. For a quarter of an hour I hunkered against the trunk of an ancient maple tree, staring out at the deathly cold waves lapping against the shore. I stood up, stretched, collected a few flat stones and skipped them out into the water. Then I jogged along the wet sand until my lungs were ready to go the way of a mature milkweed pod. As the sun broke over the horizon, I headed back to my ruined flat.

Max was still upstairs bunking with Silver. I psyched myself up before putting my key in the lock and programming my head for a towel search as soon as I opened the door. I stood for ten minutes under the shower head, five of them scalding, five of them freezing. Wrapped in Pete's thick terry shower robe, I sat cross-legged on the floor facing the windows in front of a bowl of burning sweet grass. I wafted its purifying smoke over my body as I meditated my next moves. Calm, fixed in my mission as the letters chipped into a tombstone, I rose and dressed.

Clean, snug blue jeans — no fancy pleats, cowboy cut and worn to thin milk-blue at the knees. Braided leather belt. Tight black cotton T-shirt. Wool hockey socks. Shit-kicker boots. No bra. Just a tantalizing hint of musk behind the ears. A single earring (right lobe): silver fish skeleton. Black leather biker's jacket.

Before heading off, I briefly contemplated writing a few notes — to Etta, Silver, Portia, Max, Michael and Pete's ghost — but decided against it. If my guardian angel was on duty, the notes would be redundant anyway — and I'd wind up feeling pretty silly, having put all that love and despair down on paper, for all my small world to see.

CHAPTER 29

FIFTEEN MINUTES LATER I pulled Harley into a parking spot on the north side of King Street just east of Jarvis. There's something about a woman knowing she can manoeuvre a few hundred pounds of metal between her own strong thighs that gives her a fresh take on empowerment. I pushed a quarter into the meter. It was 9:05 a.m.

The executive suite of offices for Titan Corporation was wittily housed in a gutted Gothic grey stone Anglican church. The original rectory just north of the church now served as the central office. Dawson's thought-control centre was based in the church itself. I wondered what kind of deal he had worked with the Bishop of Toronto to get title to the property. Christ would have given his holy eye teeth for a chance to desecrate this renovated shrine to Mammon's moneylenders. I entered it as his self-appointed deputy.

I'd only read descriptions of the interior in flattering newspaper and magazine profiles of the High Priest of the old Canadian Establishment. I tugged open the oak entry doors. Stained-glass guys looking stupidly astonished by their own holiness stared down from the east and west walls. Even though all the appurtenances of sanctity had been removed, I still wasn't prepared for the high-tech reception area facing me. A receptionist sat behind a huge curved oak work station that hinted sanctimoniously at recycled pews. Something about her retro-beehive hairstyle whispered that this was no vestal virgin. Her eyelids strained under a thick coat of collard-green mascara as she looked up at me. I watched the contours of her left blushed cheek alter as she shifted her wad of chewing gum to her back teeth. Her style caught me by surprise; I guess I'd been expecting someone with a touch of class, like Maggie Smith between movies. Maybe what passes for sex appeal in soft-core porn had a hold on GOD's pretence to gentility.

She didn't manage to contort the relevant muscles into a welcoming smile. "May I help you?" She paused. I removed my helmet and shook out eighteen inches of hair.

"Yeah, you can," I snarled. "I'm here to see Gerald Dawson."

She shook her bottle-black vacuous head. Not a spritzed strand of hair responded. "I'm afraid that Mr. Dawson is available only upon prior appointment." Business-speak. She conspicuously glanced down at a leather-bound appointment book. "And I see here that he doesn't have any appointments scheduled for this morning." She ventured a look at me, without bothering to throw any serious energy into appearing regretful.

I reached over the top of the console and grabbed her book. "I'm happy to confirm that you've got that much right," I said, after perusing the blank lines. "So much the better. I know your boss will make time for me." I wrenched my countenance into a shark's grin.

She looked like she didn't know whether to shit, type or send her tongue off in search of her bubble gum. "And who should I say is here … um, madam?"

"As you may have guessed, I'm not the Avon Lady. Tell him it's his conscience calling. We have a long overdue appointment to reconcile our books, you might say. So just mention that it's Medusa from Sweet Dreams."

As the Greek fabulists have it, Medusa was one mean lady, with snakes where other girls have hair. Apparently her face was so nasty that just looking at it turned a guy to stone. GOD would be lucky if our surprise meeting didn't shove him well into the quarry.

I wouldn't have wasted all that energy getting through to the man had I known the precise location of his office: I didn't want to risk getting tossed out by a zealous security guard as I kicked my way through the place.

SuperSecretary levitated her body onto a pair of three-inch heels and headed to the back of the building. Less than two minutes later she reappeared. "Mr. Dawson will see you now. Just follow me."

I followed her down a short corridor. She swung open a massive oak door on decorative iron hinges and removed herself from the scene.

Gerald Oliver Dawson's executive suite looked like a storeroom at Sotheby's. I couldn't spot a piece of anything designed for a garden-variety office. Subdued shades of brown on the walls, lush Oriental carpets, an Adam sideboard, a leather sofa and chair off to one side, a crystal chandelier, bits of chinoiserie tossed like wedding rice here and there, built-in shelves housing calf-bound books, a scatter of sailing trophies, some duck decoys that actually improved on nature. A squash racquet that showed no sign of even minimal wear-and-tear leaned into a corner. A small art collection that (reading clockwise from above his august head) began with a hunting scene and ran a safe aesthetic gamut through a cozy Krieghoff winter landscape studded by worthy habitants, an indifferent Group of Seven-derivative pine tree on a wind-swept rock struggling harder for survival than a bonsai, and a Morrice watercolour of a sailboat adrift on waters far south of here. The only contemporary painting was a large flower thing that so faultlessly colour co-ordinated with the wallpaper I could easily deduce which was the chicken and which the egg. The kind of safe stuff that makes me thirst for a nice plaster bust of Elvis.

No Inuit soapstone carvings were on display.

About a half city-block west of the entrance door sat GOD, resplendent in a purple leather swivel chair behind a huge Chippendale desk. He smiled up at me like he was the Governor General receiving the plebes on New Year's Day. The liver-spotted, faultlessly manicured white hands resting on top of the desk belied his youthful face. His lapel sprouted an orchid. He nodded his silver head and gestured me in the direction of a chair somewhat less splendid than his, situated just to the right of the desk. He did not stand up.

I would have preferred the strategic advantage of refusing his command and maintaining the height differential, but my bones were too weary to keep me standing and thinking at the same time. And what the hell?, I figured as I lowered my jeans into the chair, why not appear to co-operate? I needed to talk turkey to this sweetheart who'd opened his corporation to the Mob, jeopardized my life, done major damage to my studio, torched my mother's bar — and probably murdered Charles Durand. I figured I had enough ammunition in my belt to hold the advantage in any power shift he tried to swing. Even so, it couldn't hurt if for once I repressed my attitude about men in authority.

Maybe I could turn this unsolicited opportunity into a learning experience for him. Maybe I would even live to reap the fruits of my teaching. Etta always says I should have gone to hairdressing school. For the first time in my adult life, I saw her point. Who ever got killed for screwing up a perm?

I organized my face into an expression that demanded: *so who let you in?* and beamed it on Gerald Oliver Dawson. He smiled through perfect caps. His slate-blue eyes, cold as this morning's waves down at the lake, cruised me like they were mounted on a crocodile's head, alert to my dress, calculating every nuance of my body language, searching out any visual clue that might betray a weak spot — or my motive for so rudely bearding the lion in his corporate den. He said nothing.

He must have been in the Drama Society at Upper Canada College about half a century ago. My thespian skills paled beside his. "May I offer you a beverage, Ms. Yeats?" he finally asked. For a moment I thought I was watching Russell Baker introduce Masterpiece Theater.

"Only if it's a beer," I replied, smugly presumptuous. Why was he offering alcohol this early in the morning? Was he highlighting my dipsomania, providing a cover for his own or trying to disarm me?

He opened a small bar fridge and extracted a Newcastle

Brown. He poured the contents of the can down the side of a pilsener glass. From a cut-glass decanter he helped himself to something the colour of single malt, spritzed it with water. When he passed me my beer, I considered flinging it at his three-piece suit. Respect for fine fabric stayed my hand. His hand had trembled. Parkinson's or nerves?

I stared down at my favourite ale. Hey, I had to credit the guy for doing his research.

He opened his lips into a dazzling smile that told me some dentist had retired early on the proceeds. "I've always believed in capitalizing on happy coincidences. What brings you here?"

"What happy coincidence led you to crawl into bed with Guiseppe Nicaso?" Call me vulgar.

The smile evaporated. "My consultants were right: you have a way of getting straight to the point. I like that — even when it comes packaged as a woman." It had only taken him four seconds to recover his charm.

"Forgive me not mistaking this for a date … and, just for the record, I don't give a shit for your tastes in femininity." I leaned back in my chair and put my biker boots on the Chippendale. "I think we've both agreed to cut the small talk. You've doubtless gathered that I'm hoarding some information you'd sell your wife's body for — if it isn't already mortgaged."

His left hand grasped the fabric of his suit leg and gave it a slight tug above the knee, prior to crossing it over the other leg. I must have struck a vital nerve. He was shielding his balls.

"We agree then, Ms. Yeats. We have some business to conduct." His tone of voice told me I was trying his patience.

I wasted not a word as I briefed him. His listened with polite attentiveness, as though I were reading the Morning Lesson from *The Book of Common Prayer*, and did not interrupt. By the time I finished, his facial expression and body language had slipped into a more characteristic mode: deal-making. By my reckoning, this man hadn't done an honest day's work in his life. He did deals. Mountains of paper — very expensive paper — got shuffled according to his dictates. He could pick up the phone and watch his words inscribe trajectories across stock markets in Toronto, New York, London and Tokyo. His financial whims dictated the course of lives numerous enough to populate a small country. In a post-Christian age, this guy was indeed a god.

I reminded myself that I wouldn't be sipping the free beer if I didn't have something he needed. Desperately. That was my high card, my only card, and I had to play it with deadly accuracy.

"Ms. Yeats, I've always been interested in acquiring … shall we say … valuable properties. Of course, prior to your visit, I'd already been reliably informed that you may be in possession of some valuable information and … um, *documentation* … that I'm prepared to offer you a very handsome sum for." The words flowed from his lips like greased peas. The menace underlying his speech insinuated itself very subtly, subtextually you might say.

He looked at me for confirmation. Had he reckoned me stupid or scared enough to jump in and name my price? Hey, he was fishing, I was fishing. I stared at him across the top of my glass, like he was speaking Swahili.

"Perhaps I'm not willing to part with it," I remarked. "You must be aware that what I'm holding onto puts me in a seller's market. You'd be a fool to assume you've got the upper hand here — and that must be a real learning experience. I have the edge in this negotiation, Mr. Dawson. And let me tell you something you need to know: you've probably never encountered the likes of me before. I would sooner die a slow and painful death than let you get away with humiliating me any more than you've already managed to. So don't even think about pressing any ivory buttons and summoning your bouncers. Do me a favour: make me an offer I can't refuse, damn fast!"

He looked at me with reptilian eyes. "I began by telling you that I have reason to believe you may be in possession of some information I don't want circulated. Look, I'll be honest:

I have no sure way of knowing how much you know about certain of my business dealings, but I do have reason to believe that your research could do me a lot of damage. Since Charles Durand's untimely death, you have been passing yourself off as his official biographer. If you agree to suppress everything you've uncovered in the course of your work — if you agree, in short, to drop the whole Durand project — I'm prepared to compensate you far beyond anything you might have contracted for to work on the Durand thing."

I shifted my boots on the table and crossed my arms over my chest. "I won't say I'm not interested. In a good year, I probably earn a fair bit less than your chauffeur. But give me a reason to live. Here's what you'd be buying: I know that Durand intended to contact you concerning a rumour he had picked up about Titan Corp. doing serious laundry work for the Mob. I also know that he intended to use that rumour as leverage to blackmail you into bailing him out of bankruptcy. And I can confirm that information from sterling primary sources — your own books. Both sets of them. I think they might give the police serious motivation for checking into your operations, especially if the press also had its hand on the scoop. So what kind of deal are we talking about here?"

"We're talking say, seventy-five thousand dollars a year for a four-year contract. You sign to ghost-write my autobiography — which you can write according to my dictation or not write at all — and your freelance cheques will be deposited to your account every month, along with all the royalties, should you choose to write the book."

I let his offer hang in the air. I didn't want him thinking I'd sold out without a least a minor skirmish with my conscience. "Just to put my mind at ease, Mr. Dawson, there are a couple of things I need to know before we negotiate any further. I mean, if I accepted your offer, how could I get on with enjoying my new-found income if I couldn't relax enough to … say, ride my Harley without fear of the brakes failing, visit a friend at his cottage without fear of getting shot at, return to my studio knowing that it's still in one piece, sleep overnight at my mother's bar without getting my toes toasted? In fact, now that I think of it, maybe you should be offering me a compensation package as well."

He grinned. "You're a tough negotiator. Okay, I won't shit you. Yes, I was behind all of those unfortunate circumstances. But think back. You must see that none of them was intended to *kill* you. They were meant simply to warn you off. Obviously, they weren't effective. If you accept my offer, clearly there will be no outstanding reason to threaten you in any way."

I nodded. "Right. And I can make sure of that by giving my favourite crime reporter a sealed envelope containing enough information to send you off to Kingston for the remainder of your tacky existence, with instructions that it be delivered to the press should anything untoward happen to me. Which I've already done," I added, glancing down at my Swatch. "In fact, if we don't reach an agreement real soon, your face and smeared reputation will be all over the front page of Wednesday morning's *Post.*"

"Fair enough," he snapped. "We're agreed, then?"

"We're agreed, my silence in exchange for one hundred thousand dollars a year for five years — on one condition," I replied.

"I'm not sure that you are in any position to be laying on additional conditions but, just for the fun of it, what is it?" I had to give it to him, the guy had a certain cheesy grace under pressure.

I threw down my wild card. "Can you prove to me that you didn't kill Charles Durand — or that you didn't hire someone to do the job? My lapsed Catholic conscience can stretch itself thin enough to let you buy my silence on your sleazy financial shit, but it can't stretch far enough to provide a cover for murder."

He raised his palms to the gods. "You must be of *Irish* Catholic stock. Your lot never learned how to separate piety from politics. I'd sooner deal with Jews."

"And I'd sooner watch Alfred Hitchcock undress than listen to your racism."

He let that one go the way of autumn leaves. "Look, I'm sure you think I'm capable of doing anything to advance a deal, to save my shirt. And you'd be right, with one exception. Believe me on this: I am not a murderer, nor do I sanction killing. I had nothing to do with Charles Durand's death — although I do not mourn his premature passing, as I'm sure you've guessed."

I glanced at my watch again. "If we don't bring this meeting to a sharp close, I won't make it home in time to catch 'The Young and the Restless.' So convince me you had nothing to do with his death."

"Short of handing over the killer — and I can't do that because I don't know who killed Durand, there's no way I can prove that I'm not connected to his murder. But I can tell you this much. The day before he died, Durand contacted me. I even accepted his phone call — it was a boring afternoon. He didn't even hint at having anything on me. Said he just wanted to set up an appointment. When I told him that he and I had nothing to discuss, that I wouldn't do business with him even if Titan were going the way of the Titanic, he said that he felt otherwise, that he wanted to make me an offer I couldn't refuse. I cut him off by telling him to send me a fax. Next thing I knew he was dead."

"Did you receive a fax from him?" I asked.

"Hell, no! And even if I had, you can be sure there'd be a record of it at his end. The police would have been on to me by now."

That much was probably true, but I had no way of knowing whether or not the police had contacted him — or whether they would have, even had they known he and Durand had been in recent communication. "So why is Archie Price dead too?" I wondered aloud.

"Archie Price is dead because he pulled a fast one on the Mob," he said.

"How do you know that?"

"I know that because I read the newspapers," he smirked.

"So what got you on to my case?" I asked.

"Before he killed him, the hitman the Mob hired to silence Archie Price persuaded the poor bastard to admit that he'd told William Durand about my money laundering. So they put a tail on Durand's faggot son. That led them to you, chatting up his boyfriend in a leather bar, biking up to his aunt's house, meeting the queer himself at a cottage, sharing beery lunches with one honest hack from the *Post* and another from the police department, shacking up with a tax lawyer who used to work for Imperial Trust. One thing led to another. The picture added up to you pushing dangerously close to my arrangement with Mr. Nicaso. We didn't know how much you knew, but we figured you were getting close enough to do us some damage. So we threw at a few warning signals at you." He smiled and drained his glass. "Obviously you didn't get the message. But I do assure you, neither I nor my colleagues had anything to do with Durand's murder."

I shrugged. "I'll consider ours a done deal. I guess you know where to send my cheques — same place you sent the S.O.B. who trashed the place. And while I'm thinking about it, you might consider adding some sugar to our agreement by sending over a few folks to repair the damage to my studio and to rebuild my mother's bar."

"Ms. Yeats, I think it important that you have a comfortable ambience in which to write the story of my life. And that your mother enjoy the same in her golden years. Please have them both repaired, decorated and furnished at my expense."

He extricated his hand from the empty whisky glass and extended it to me.

I looked sourly at his lily-white palm and shook my head. "Sorry, too many nasty social diseases are making the rounds these days."

I slowly dragged my heels off his desk, set my Pilsener glass on the carpet, and rose to my feet.

Three steps short of the door, his voice reactivated the microcassette recorder in my jacket pocket. The man just couldn't resist over-playing his hand.

"Should you ever, Ms. Yeats, allow your pretty head the luxury of indulging a single thought about tearing up our contract, take a few seconds to remind yourself that old women have very brittle bones. Surely you've already subjected your dear mother to an inordinate amount of stress."

The man made a big mistake. My sanity snapped faster than an octogenarian's hip bone. I went straight to the far edge.

"Me?" I shrieked, poking my right thumb at my chest, "me — allow myself the luxury of *thinking*? Listen up, you foul shard of moose shit, you desiccated prick, you pompous piece of trash: sooner than the stock market blips you're gonna have so much free time on your hands you'll be sending out for knitting patterns and a Scrabble board!" I moved as I ranted, straight for his Adam sideboard, where I'd earlier spotted a jeroboam of Château Mouton-Rothschild on vulgar display. I grabbed it by the neck and glanced at the label.

"Nineteen twenty-nine. A very good year for grapes, if not for the economy." I raised it to a point just above my right shoulder and brought it down on the edge of his desk. He stood up and watched approximately three litres of eight-thousand-dollar antiquarian grape juice soak into the carpet.

I figured that the green shard clutched in my hand would serve my purpose as well as the neck of a bottle of Bright's bottom-line plonk. I advanced around his desk. The stupid bugger's glazed expression alerted me that my breach in decorum had driven him catatonic. As my left hand grabbed a bunch of expensive fabric at the side of his chin, my right pulled the jagged glass to a point just south of his left ear.

"The skin on your flabby neck is a whole lot thinner than my mother's bones, you tacky imitation of a human being. And at this precise moment I don't give a sewer rat's shitty ass for your life." I pressed the bottle neck into his throat, just enough to draw a bead of blood that wasn't blue. "If you do anything to cause my mother one more second of grief …," I said very calmly, as I sketched a fine arc from my original entry point to the centre of his chin, "… I will personally carve you up from the top of your enterprising scalp to the bottom of your scabrous feet — slowly and with great pleasure."

I paused to examine my handiwork. A fine red line decorated his chalky throat. Itzak Perlman couldn't have done it with more finesse. I glanced down. His body hadn't moved, but his bladder had. A big wet patch was darkening the crotch of his Savile Row trousers. Urine traced a dark trail right down into his Guccis.

"You've lost control, man — of your bladder, of your corporation, of your whole fucking life. You're ruined. It's all over, Mister Gerald Oliver Dawson, gone the way of Madonna's virginity. The old order is dead. Your Establishment is extinct. And there are no hunt clubs in hell."

As I hit the pavement beside my bike, I began to retch.

What was making me infinitely more nauseated than my own near-murderous behaviour was the fact that I believed GOD when he told me he had nothing to do with Charles Durand's murder.

I still had miles to go before my head hit the sack. And I had to get there before the cops hit on me for assaulting one of the planet's lesser gods — or before my heart exploded, whichever came first.

Dawson's vile blood had already dried on my hands as I gripped them around Harley's handlebars. I kick-started my bike with a force strong enough to knock the ghost of Malcolm Lowry into sobriety.

CHAPTER 30

STOPPED ONCE en route, to replenish Harley's "Fat Bob" fuel tank, but took a pass on grabbing a burger at the service centre's sandwich bar. I couldn't rest until my adrenaline-pumped brain shot me to my destination.

At the very moment I'd begun to etch that delicate ruby necklace across GOD's throat earlier this morning, my mind had clamped onto something nasty. Nothing as sharp as a fact, nor as intricate as a theory. A sensation, dark and instinctive, worming its way out from under the flat rock of my unconscious, playing havoc with my sanity. I had to stay in motion until it shook loose.

Harley chewed up the miles separating me from my target. I suppose the wind slashing my body was corpse-cold, the sky above that washed-out shade of blue that's just decided it's easier going grey, the melting snow on the surrounding fields dirtier than my conscience. My mind was busy making baroque notations more critical than weather. The ticking of what I thought was my Swatch surprised me over my bike's dull roar, until I realized my pulse was beating a bloody tattoo in my eardrums.

Maybe my sense of urgency derived from feeling like my soul needed a good scrub. I wanted to dump this case right back in Simone's lap. Summarize my findings about GOD's money-laundering scam and Durand's foiled attempt to blackmail him. Then I'd leave, after apologizing for not having discovered who killed her brother — and refusing any payment for my incomplete work of detection. Maybe one day in the far-distant future I'd find it hilarious that en route to *not* solving the crime I'd been hired to, I had totalled the career of a bigger corporate crook. Simone might encourage me to continue looking into Durand's murder, but my gut told me that would not be a good idea. I didn't have the emotional stamina to examine what lay beneath any more flat rocks. That her brother was a perv in addition to all his other sins I would have to tell her, but even thinking about pursuing the implications gave me a migraine.

Writer's block had led me into this malignant folly in the first place. Maybe to pay the rent I should set up one of those personal hot-sex phone lines you see on late night TV. I could video Portia in a bikini on a tropical beach for the conservative guys, Silver in a wet suit on the shores of Lake Ontario for the even more exotically inclined, Etta resplendent on satin sheets in her black lace for the Golden Agers. I could set myself up as a phone-in spiritualist, reassuring all my callers that their dearly departeds were drinking champagne in chauffeur-driven limos in the sky, benevolently presiding over their survivors' lottery picks.

Some nasty gremlin whispered in my ear that I was losing it.

I was still on automatic pilot when I ground to a stop outside Simone's house. Without a clue as to what I was about to say or do, I pounded on the door with the presumptive authority of a storm trooper. No one answered. I walked around to the converted barn her husband used as his workshop. The huge double doors were padlocked. No car was in sight. Returning to the front door of the main residence, I checked the lock for pick-ability. The door simply opened as I turned the knob, sparing me the humiliation of attempting to exercise a skill I don't possess.

I stepped into the foyer, pausing for a minute to see if my entrance activated the alarm system. Oddly, it didn't. In a politely earnest voice that sounded too much like a Greenpeace worker soliciting donations for endangered large things that swim, I asked if anyone was home.

I was not surprised when no one replied. Only the dead could have ignored my relentless pounding at the door. Christ — *only the dead ...*

Rather than yield to my urge to flee, I began a frantic room-to-room search: nothing thorough, just a glance into each room to make sure that a corpse wasn't strewn across a bed or carpet. I couldn't start worrying about bodies propped up against closed cupboard doors.

My check only confirmed what I already knew — *other people actually do housework*. I returned to the main floor, and left a note for Simone on the kitchen table, telling her I'd dropped by and checked out the house (after "noticing" that the front door was unlocked) and asking her to call me as soon as she got in.

As I headed through the living room toward the front door, something caught my eye in a sectional bookcase to the right side of the fireplace: an entire row of books with the word "horse" printed on their spines. Resting across the tops of several of them was a folded sheaf of papers. I raised the glass-fronted door and extracted it.

Just as I opened it up and recognized the logo at the top of the first page, a voice behind me demanded, "So when did you figure it out?" Totally mesmerized by my discovery, by its possible consequences, I hadn't heard a car approach or anyone entering the house.

I spun around guilty as a kid caught masturbating. Simone was standing in the doorway. This was not the sane and gentle woman who had appeared at my studio shortly after her brother's murder. Not only was she violating her own dress code, but her eyes signalled that she had migrated to the margins of self-control. Today's version of Simone looked manic enough press the trigger of the gun she was now holding pointed at my chest, with no further provocation.

Talk about needing to choose your words carefully. Cops who negotiate with hostage-takers take special training to prepare themselves for similarly strained conversations. I decided to wager on the truth. "You're not going to believe this, Simone, but I haven't figured out anything — at least I haven't figured out who killed your brother."

She icily eyed me with total mistrust. "So why are you

poking about in my bookcase?"

If she didn't lower the gun, I'd soon be looking to borrow a dry pair of panties. "I said I hadn't figured out who killed your brother — but in the course of trying to find out who did, I stumbled upon a huge money-laundering scam that's going to shake a lot of rotten fruit off the corporate vine, including GOD. And I'm pretty sure that your brother was aware of the scam and that he intended to blackmail Dawson. Isn't that motive enough for murder?"

Her kelly eyes held mine, which are always tempted to wander when I'm playing fancy riffs around the truth. "The need to silence Charles is a good motive, but was it his killer's motive?" she asked.

I couldn't think of a safe reply, so I just stood there, paralytic, mute and flustered, still clutching the sheaf of papers. She gestured the gun at me, like I was a shy pupil in need of encouragement. "But was it his killer's motive? Answer me!" Her voice had tipped over into hysteria.

No matter how carefully I pulled my verbal punches, I couldn't control this situation. "No, Simone. No. It wasn't his killer's motive. I don't believe that the guy who laundered millions for the Mob killed your brother. In fact, I don't think your brother even got a chance to blackmail him or squeal on him, or whatever the hell else he intended to do. Fate, you might call it, intervened and did GOD's dirty work for him. Someone else killed Charles."

"And you know it was me," she shrieked. In the interval before she acted, I calculated my chances of distracting and somehow disarming her. The thin line separating her from complete insanity had to be as taut as a violin string. Suddenly she drew her right hand back behind her head and let the gun fly with a velocity that would have brought Blue Jays' fans to their feet. It shattered its way clear through the window. Her leg bones went into melt-down, and she crumpled onto the carpet.

My emotional passage from terror to relief was not smooth. Miss Manners hadn't dealt with this one yet.

ME: *I'm standing in front of an unarmed self-confessed murderer who seems to be having a nervous breakdown. What should I do?* P.S. *Oh yes, we're both women.*

MISS MANNERS: *Given your peculiar postscript, I would recommend tea and sympathy.*

Hastily refolding the papers, I filed them in the back right pocket of my jeans, then helped her to her feet. Supporting her by the arm, I got her into the kitchen and settled into a chair. She sat there unseeing and said nothing until I placed a slug of brandied tea beside her hand. Then she made urgent eye contact, as though she'd resolved to pull herself together and come clean with a full confession.

"Before you say a word, Simone, please remember that I'm not the police. You don't have to tell me anything; in fact, if you do, I could be called upon as a prosecution witness. And that's not a role I want to play."

My caution scarcely grazed her ears. "Then think of what I'm about to say as a rehearsal, not a confession. I'll phone the police later. If you'd had time to look through those papers, you'd already have guessed why I killed Charles. But I'd sooner tell you myself. Throughout your whole investigation, I've been dishonest with you. It's an odd thing: my conscience is clean around murdering my own brother, but I feel really guilty about having misled you." She paused to sip her laced tea. "Maybe you'll understand how I could have been so calculating when I tell you why I did it."

What she divulged over the next fifteen minutes about her relationship with her late brother certainly clued me in to her state of mind at the moment she said she had grabbed the Inuit carving from his desk and reduced the side of his head to chopped liver. Hers was an oft-told woman's tale, but one that didn't lose its poignancy in the retelling. When she was ten, Charles began using her for sexual practice. "I was his first commodity." Being a clever little entrepreneur even back then, he also hired out her services to his friends. They each got a turn for a quarter. He didn't have to buy her silence or even threaten her with what he'd do if she told on him: she knew her mother wouldn't believe her and, anyway, it must have been her fault. Such dirty things didn't happen to other little girls, she was sure of that. A few years later, at the very time their older brother had been killed in the mining accident, Charles lost all interest in her.

All these years, she had kept her secret to herself, never even privately confronting her brother with his transgressions. Then in February, after Rebecca dropped out of school and started getting into trouble, Simone searched her bedroom for any clues that might explain the girl's uncharacteristic misery and misconduct. Expecting to find drugs, booze or birth control pills, instead she discovered a diary. As she read the entry describing her brother's rape of his own niece, she began to formulate her retribution. She said nothing about her plan to her husband or to Rebecca. That Friday night, she went to Charles's office not clearly intending to kill him, but fully aware that her rage wouldn't burn itself out until he had at least admitted what he'd done. She went without a weapon.

"Charles secured his own fate when he sneered at me. He taunted me, asking me if I was jealous of my young, prettier daughter. He said no one would believe me anyway. Why had I waited so long to say anything? And hadn't this 'false memory' syndrome proven that a lot of innocent men were being victimized by neurotic women? He told me my accusation wouldn't even make it to court: surely I didn't want my daughter dragged through a nasty trial. Had I even thought about the defence he could buy — like *Greedy menopausal mother alleges sexual assault in million-dollar law suit?*"

Simone paused to finish her tea, looking like she was ten minutes into a twenty-four-hour hot flash.

"Years of working with troubled adolescents has taught me not to place much faith in the criminal justice system. So I grabbed that soapstone carving from his desk and bashed him with it until I was sure he was dead — several times *after* I was sure he was dead, actually. And however much this may shock you, Jane, I felt more like an instrument of divine retribution than a killer." She looked at me steadily, awaiting my reply.

Her grim narrative had a lot of emotional authenticity, the dialogue was good, the action certainly compelling, and I didn't doubt that Durand had abused both mother and daughter. But the entire account lacked a single concrete detail concerning how she had managed to get in and out of the building without being seen — especially out, given that she must have been splattered with blood. Perhaps she found the "means and opportunity" aspects of her crime less compelling than her motivation, but the police sure as hell would be interested.

My chest tightened. "Simone, you started out by saying that this was more of a rehearsal than a confession. If you want the cops to believe it, you're going to have to flesh out your story with some convincing details, like how — "

She cut me off in mid-sentence. "What do you mean, *if* I want the cops to believe it? Why wouldn't they?" She looked bewildered, as though some illogicality had escaped her.

Assured that her gun was lying impotent somewhere on the front lawn, I no longer felt the need to pick through my words like some of them might be land mines. "Because they'd still be looking for a suspect … and you would have inadvertently pointed an incriminating finger straight at the very person you'd die to protect."

Her face crumpled. Her right hand drew ineffectual circles in the air, as though she were summoning her muse for renewed inspiration after delivering an unconvincing first draft of her plot.

"If I were you, Simone, I wouldn't even bother trying to get my story straight. Under police interrogation, you'll never be able to fill the potholes in your script."

A menacing voice sounded behind me. "Maybe I can fill in the potholes."

Rebecca, she of the Botticelli face, entered the room. Her right hand clasped the wayward gun.

CHAPTER 31

MY PHYSICAL RESOURCES were nearly exhausted. Just as I'd decided that I would use my residual energy bleeding to death with dignity right there on the tiles, I realized that Rebecca hadn't even raised the gun.

She was staring at her mother. "What the hell was this thing doing on the front lawn? Who threw it through the window?" She carefully placed the weapon on a side table.

Simone moved toward her, then checked herself. "I did. I went crazy a few minutes ago — when I realized that Jane had figured out that I killed your uncle." Her eyes bored a *just go along with this* message into her daughter's.

Rebecca responded in that tone of exasperation teenagers reserve for their impossibly thick parents. "Drop the crap already, Mom. I was listening outside the door when she told you that the cops will know your confession is total bull. You can't cover for me any more."

"Rebecca, shut up this very moment and go up to your room." Simone gestured ineffectually at the doorway.

"You know, if you were social-working any other kid, you'd be counselling her to take responsibility for what she'd done and helping her to deal with the consequences." Although Rebecca's entire body was shaking, her voice had grown in strength.

"You are not *any other kid*, my darling," Simone cried. "You are my daughter — and I love you so very much."

Rebecca rushed over to embrace her mother, who stood several metres away, stranded on an island of maternal grief. "Sometimes during the last few months when I was acting so crazy, I thought you must hate me, Mom. I'll never doubt your love again: you were ready to take a murder rap for me. Like you could have spent the rest of your life in jail — that is, if Jane revised your story before you told it to the cops." She looked at me over her mother's shoulder, managing a wink through her tears.

I reached into my jeans pocket and extracted the papers I'd removed from the bookcase: Grasmere Riding Academy membership list and class schedules for September. Simone turned to me, looking so desperate I wanted to do what little I could to ease their way into the next phase of their blighted lives. "I want you both to sit down and listen carefully to what I have to say. Simone, you must have become very familiar with the Young Offenders Act in the course of your work, but it might help if I run it past you both right now. Friend of mine's sister got busted a few years back, so I know it almost by heart."

They sat down side-by-side. As Simone took her daughter's hand in her own, I began my recital, hoping it would give them some time to compose their thoughts and to consider a fresh course of action. "In this country, anyone between twelve and eighteen years old who commits murder gets a maximum sentence of three years. Youth Court hearings are open to the public and the press, but the press can't publish the offender's name, address or photograph. Five years after the sentence has been completed, the records are destroyed if the young person remains free of any criminal activity during that period. Under exceptional circumstances — which include murder — the Crown attorney may apply to have the offender transferred to adult court. But given the circumstances in your case, my guess is that Rebecca would be tried in Youth Court and that she would be detained in a psychiatric institution where she'd receive appropriate treatment."

Simone spoke first. "I hear what you're saying and I'm grateful for the reminder, but I haven't any idea what I should do next — and, frankly, I don't have the nerve to ask you for any more help." She shook her head in complete perplexity.

"But there is one thing I want you to know for sure: when I was pointing that stupid gun, I never would have shot you. I just grabbed the damn thing — my husband keeps it handy to scare away the groundhogs — because I had to slow things down. Do you know what I mean?"

She probably could have taken the life of her brother, though, an exemplary candidate for extermination. Reaching across the table, I clasped both her trembling hands in mine. "Simone, just this morning my own rage at Dawson — my rage at the whole world — drove me right over the edge. I came very close to killing a man as loathsome as your brother. Most of us would do anything to save or defend someone we love. So yes, I do understand why you pointed a gun at me. And whether or not you feel entitled, you can count on my help. But first I need to hear what really happened the night Durand was murdered. Then we can consider your options."

My request for disclosure triggered her to shriek despairingly, "Options — what options? They really boil down to phoning the police and turning in my own daughter, don't they?"

"If you take the initiative, speak to a lawyer, then contact the police *before* they get around to sorting out this whole sorry mess by themselves — well, it can't hurt. And you won't be betraying Rebecca. I'm sure she's been nearly catatonic with fear and guilt ever since the murder. So she needs some kind of resolution. Anyway, she's already made it clear that she would never stand by in silence while you got charged for her crime." Rebecca nodded her confirmation. "After she's told us her side of the story, I'll give you the name of a very good criminal lawyer who will accompany you to the police station. If you want, I'll also call the cop in charge of the investigation before you go. He's an old friend of mine and he's a very decent man."

I looked directly at Rebecca, hoping that her mother wouldn't caution her again to remain silent. Her range of choice was so limited and all of it no-win. I wanted to give her some space to articulate her pathetic options for herself.

Autonomy struggles for breath in such narrow passages. She wiped her eyes and glanced at Simone, who wearily nodded her head.

Rebecca turned her face to me, achingly vulnerable, looking for direction. Tendrils of blonde hair hung in fine dreads over her slumped shoulders. Her young eyes had absorbed far more experience than they should have at sixteen. My head screamed *how ever could he?* as my voice urged her to tell me, as best she could, about the events leading up to his murder.

One Saturday afternoon last November she had met her uncle for the first time, shortly after she'd finished competing in an equestrian competition at Grasmere Riding Academy. Hearing Rebecca's name announced just before she rode into the ring, Durand had realized that the beautiful young woman must be his niece. At first she had politely tried to extricate herself from a conversation she knew her mother would not approve of, but he pressed her to talk with him over dinner at a nice restaurant.

I interrupted to ask if she hadn't been warned off him by the other girls he'd come on to. No, she replied, she hadn't heard any rumours about her uncle. She hadn't even known he was a member of the Academy. From her parent's "cheap" car, the school she attended and the fact that she didn't own her own horse, the other girls had quickly figured out that she didn't share their privileged background. Also jealous of her superior equestrian skills, they shoved her to the margins of their circle, never letting her in on the gossip that enlivened their conversations.

Durand insinuated his way into her reluctant trust by pleading for her advice on how he could best go about healing the rift with her mother. Finally she agreed to go to the restaurant and phoned her mother to say that she'd been invited to a girlfriend's house to have dinner with her parents and watch the video of *Pulp Fiction*.

Over dinner at Giancarlo's, an upscale restaurant in Little Italy, he'd warmly reminisced about his childhood. He told her how much he'd always loved his "baby" sister, how the "misunderstanding" that had led to their alienation had tortured him for years, how in middle age he longed to be reunited with her, how grateful he'd be for any help his niece could give him. Rebecca, her wits impaired by the two glasses of wine from the expensive bottle he'd encouraged her to share with him, was touched by his story. She had even wondered if her mother hadn't treated her brother a bit harshly. And she was flattered by how Uncle Charles treated her like a grown-up, attentive to her every word and appreciative of her "mature" insight into sibling issues. After dessert, he asked her to accompany him to his office, where he kept a family photo album. She was intrigued: her mother had never shown her any images of her youth.

In spite of her upbringing by two parents who scorned materialism, Rebecca was impressed by the evidence of her uncle's wealth embodied in his monument to himself. After parking his Mercedes in a special, secluded bay in the underground lot beneath the Enterprise Tower, they rode up to the penthouse office in his private elevator. He used a plastic card to access the elevator, remarking that he refused to have surveillance cameras tracking him in his own building. Special guests like Rebecca, he remarked, he could buzz into the elevator from a console on his desk. She wondered at the time why he carried on like a secret agent, but figured maybe famous businessmen attracted stalkers the way Hollywood celebrities did.

Rebecca swiftly summarized what had ensued. In an eerily detached voice that suggested the events she was narrating had all happened to some one else, she sped through the bare bones of her nightmare. She accepted the glass of wine he pressed on her. Drinking had become a badge of her new sophistication. After groggily listening to him natter on about how he was going to crucify the only man in Canada who had been stupid enough to get in his way, she asked to see the photo album. She discovered that it didn't even exist: it had been a ruse to lure her into his lair. When she abruptly stood up to leave, almost losing her balance, he shoved her onto the floor. He yanked her sweater over her arms, left it hanging around her neck, unzipped her jeans and tugged them off. Dazed and weakened by the wine, pinned to the carpet by his knee in the pit of her stomach, she watched in horror as he tore open his fly to reveal his erection.

"Then he raped me. It hurt so much." Her words were barely audible.

In the brief pause before she resumed her story, her mother sobbed as though she was being forced to watch her daughter slowly being tortured to death. The echo of her own childhood abuse by the same man added tragic resonance to the horrific plot.

I decided to terminate Rebecca's revelations then and there. To hell with my own ignorance about the facts of the murder. I could still help this devastated pair by contacting a lawyer and the police.

Rebecca turned her head, staring at a point somewhere beyond my left shoulder. When she finally connected with my eyes, I witnessed a look of determination that told me she needed to finish. "The next morning, after faking to Mom and Dad what a good time I'd had at my girlfriend's, I realized that I couldn't have done anything to stop him from raping me. But I also knew that I could find a way to make sure he didn't do it to me again. The following Saturday after I finished my riding lesson, I saw his car parked at the bottom of the driveway at Grasmere. I walked over and told him that if he ever bothered me again I would call the police and have him charged. I said that I'd started seeing a therapist and she had encouraged me to confront him. Actually, I was too scared and guilty to tell anyone about what had happened, but I hoped that he wouldn't know that. By the time I finished ranting at him, he looked more scared than me. He just took off in the car and I never saw him again." Her hands began to shake uncontrollably. "At least not until the night I murdered him."

I placed my hand over hers until the trembling stilled.

"Rebecca, you don't have to go on with this, you know."

She looked at her mother, transformed by suffering into a new representation of the *pietà*. "I know it's harder for Mom to hear than for me to tell."

Simone only whispered, "if it helps you to get it all out, just keep talking, love."

Rebecca held her hands to her face. "I tried really hard to keep it together after that, but everything just fell apart. I couldn't do my schoolwork, I couldn't even think about riding ever again, I felt so dirty that I thought people would *know* just by looking at me, I couldn't even fathom how to talk to people any more. It was like I had lost my personality or something. I couldn't be with Mom and Dad without thinking how ashamed they'd be if they knew what a slut I was. So I was sort of glad when they enrolled me in boarding school. None of the teachers or other kids knew me from before, so they wouldn't recognize how weird I'd become. But then I started noticing some changes in my body, like my stomach seemed bigger and my breasts were tender. I told myself it was just stress, but after I missed my second period I knew I must be pregnant."

She hurriedly turned away and stared out the window, making direct contact only with her own tortured memories. "What was so horrible was that I didn't know *who* the father was. Just a couple of months before I got raped I started sleeping with my boyfriend, Mark. Like we used condoms most of the time, but neither of us worried about STDs because we hadn't been with anybody else that way. But sometimes we got careless. Maybe deep down I even wanted to have his baby, I don't know. It was the first time I had ever been in love and I couldn't think straight about anything. Like I was so totally caught up in thinking about him all the time — and feeling so guilty about deceiving Mom and Dad — that I couldn't keep my mind on school, or anything. Things that used to be so important to me just didn't seem to matter much any more and a whole bunch of other things took their place.

"Anyways, when I got scared about being pregnant, I was

so desperate I confided in one of the older girls at school. She'd been sent there because she was so wild. Caroline told me that I better get an abortion fast — like before I was twelve weeks gone. Maybe if I'd known for sure that it was Mark's baby, I would have told Mom. But the thought that it might be my uncle's baby made me feel like I had some kind of horrible tumour growing inside me. So I phoned Uncle Charles and told him I really needed to see him. I couldn't figure out how else I could get the money for the abortion and, anyways, I thought he should have to pay something for what he'd done to me. The way he laughed when I spoke to him, it sounded like he thought I wanted to let him rape me again. He told me to come to his office at six that Friday night."

She had left school early and driven there in Caroline's car, more frightened by the act of driving unaccompanied on a new licence than by the prospect of confronting her uncle.

Durand hadn't received the pleasure he anticipated. Rebecca told him she was pregnant and let on that she had been a virgin prior to his violation of her; paternity was not an issue. She demanded money for the abortion. He pulled out his wallet and placed five one-hundred-dollar bills on his desk. As she reached for them, he tried to pull her into an embrace. She managed to shove him away, only to unleash a torrent of filth. "You are your mother's daughter. A stupid little slut, no more skilled at sex than she was." He went on to say that there couldn't be any harm in "one final fuck" between them — given that she was already knocked up. She grabbed the Inuit sculpture and ground his head into the desk.

Afterwards, she functioned like a homicidal robot programmed to cover its tracks. Removed her bloody clothes, stuffed them in a plastic bag inside her sports bag — along with the weapon, showered in his private washroom, changed into fresh jeans and a sweatshirt she'd packed in her bag, and left the building undetected via the same route she'd learned the night of her rape. Undoubtedly she'd left behind fingerprints and bits of trace evidence, but the homicide cops couldn't be blamed for not thinking of placing her at the scene. She stopped her car several blocks north of the Enterprise Tower to toss the plastic bag in a municipal garbage bin.

"I was terrified. Twice I almost crashed the car. But somehow I felt way cleaner than I had after he raped me."

A week later, Simone had heard Rebecca screaming in the bathroom. She found her daughter sitting beside the toilet bowl, its contents crimson with the miscarried product of Durand's abuse — or Rebecca's first love.

Simone extricated her hands from Rebecca's clasp. "Jane, that Thursday morning you rode up here to fill me in on your progress — I was in such a horrible state because I'd just discovered that Rebecca was pregnant. We had an awful fight. She told me she'd been running around behind our backs with some boy we'd never met. When I found her diary that night and realized that Charles had raped her, I knew I'd never forgive myself for hurting her so."

The penny dropped. "So at the time you hired me, you really didn't know that Rebecca had killed him," I remarked.

She shook her head. "No. After recording the rape, Rebecca never made another entry in her diary. When we fought over her pregnancy, she still didn't tell me that my brother might be the father. But right after the miscarriage, I took her straight to the local hospital to make sure that she'd had a complete abortion. On the way home, she was dazed and exhausted, almost in shock. That's when she told me everything — about the rape and that she had murdered Charles. The next time we spoke, you were hot on the trail of another suspect. I knew that if I called off your investigation at that point, it would raise too many questions. So I just let you get on with it, even hoping that somebody else would get wrongfully convicted."

I shrugged. "My prime suspect has committed enough other serious crimes to land him in jail for the rest of his life anyway. A murder conviction wouldn't have changed his future prospects. We don't hang people any more; the system rehabilitates them all! So don't get your knickers in a twist fretting about your own culpability in regards to anything that might have befallen Dawson if he'd been found guilty of killing your brother. I think you should be sweating about the big stuff right now."

Through her tears, she forced a grim smile of gratitude. As she rose from her chair, her body took on a new, authoritative posture. "May I phone you after we've reached a decision? Afterwards, I'm sure we'll want to talk with your lawyer and police friends."

My knees were weak as I rose from my chair. "Yeah … I'll be waiting for your call. Now, if I don't get some sleep real fast, I'm going to have to check myself into rehab."

She pulled me into a powerful hug. "There's no way to even begin to thank you, especially after how I've deceived you …"

I cut her short. "Yes, there is. Say no more. Just put all your resources into taking care of yourself and your family … and God bless."

Rebecca gave me a wan smile. How could she summon such bravery after such agony?

I hoped it would carry her through the long years ahead.

CHAPTER 32

ARRIVED BACK AT my studio knowing that if Simone didn't notify the cops, I wouldn't. I was too tired and too confused to play God. My mind would never be clear enough to make such judgment calls — which is why, I suppose, God takes more than the occasional snooze. If all the events leading up to Charles Durand's murder were ultimately meant to assume the shapeliness of a morality play, then someone forgot to deal me the appropriate cue card.

Max slobbered a bucket over me when I fed him a T-bone. As he wolfed it down, I stumbled through the rubble and fell on top of my duvet, fully clothed. My other relations were vastly more complicated than my affair with my dog. I'd take care of them later.

Just after seven the next morning, I was awakened by persistent pounding at my studio door. As Max raced to check it out, he set up an unholy chorus. He stood snarling through bared teeth, ready to launch himself at our rude caller. He didn't even look like my dog; he was doing some atavistic shtick that recalled wolfy ancestors.

As soon as I opened the door, his canine civility returned. Uniforms can have that effect. Ernie Sivcoski was standing there, framed by two of Toronto's finest boys in blue. Their eyes widened as they took in my towering beer-carton sculpture. They widened much more when they surveyed my ruined abode.

I tried to comb my hair with my fingers, but stopped

when they got caught in a tangle two inches from my scalp. I tightened the belt around my bathrobe, calculating that the illusion of a waistline might distract. Ernie just stood there, scowling stern as granite.

"I suppose I should ask you gentlemen in," I said. "After all, I do have an image to maintain in this neighbourhood."

"You got a hell of a lot more to worry about than your image," Ernie barked as he and his cohorts entered the studio. I would have offered them a seat on my sofa, but it was upside-down. Anyway, I got the impression this wasn't a social call.

"Would you get dressed and come down to the station with us?" inquired my old drinking buddy.

I get riled when people try to pass off commands as requests. "Why don't you tell me why I'd want to accept your invitation, Ernie? Am I under arrest?" I asked, thinking that the very absurdity of the notion might snap him back into remembering we were friends.

"Not yet. But I'd bring your lawyer's phone number with me, if I were you."

"For God's sake, Ernie, tell me what this is about."

"Gerald Dawson has been found dead in his office. His receptionist told us a woman had forced her way in there yesterday morning and provoked a violent fight with him. She gave us a description of a woman that fits only you. Now, let's get a move on."

Not once did he look me in the eye. He kind of shoved me through the door. "I won't ask what happened to your studio until we get to the station. I know you're a slob, but that mess takes the cake."

Twenty minutes later, the interview began at No. 12 Division. It didn't end until early afternoon. My initial shock at hearing of the death of GOD turned to mere panic when I realized that Dawson hadn't slowly bled to death through a scratch to his throat. He'd taken the express route to glory, blowing away a sizable chunk of his head with a gun you wouldn't expect to find in the hands of a businessman. The tart-on-heels receptionist had left the office at five, after having checked in on her boss before hitting the happy-hour trail to the singles bars. She remembered him looking upset, but definitely still breathing and as close to warm as any reptile gets.

He'd been discovered about three hours later, by a beat cop who heard a gun go off inside the building just as he was checking the door on the east side. Dawson left himself in an uncharacteristically messy state, but apparently had put his more urgent affairs in order prior to pulling the trigger. A terse, factual suicide note was displayed on his computer screen. A hard copy of it sat on his desk blotter. The signed note recorded his complicity in the money-laundering scam — and cited me as a source for the documentation that would back up his confession. And it ended: "I have no reason to conceal the truth about anything else. I am guilty of many things, but I am not willing to die with the suspicion of murder further blackening my reputation. I did not kill Charles Durand." Beside the note was an white envelope with my name typed on it. When Ernie took the liberty of opening it, he found inside a cheque made out to "Jane Yeats" in the sum of seventy-five thousand dollars.

Only after I'd told Ernie about how I'd figured out the money-laundry thing (omitting all reference to Michael), and how I'd confronted GOD in his office, did he tell me about the note and the cheque. He also enumerated enough of the insurmountable problems facing GOD — prior to my unsolicited visit — to assure me that I was not responsible for his suicide. GOD's wife had left him two weeks ago, having sniffed several dead rats under the Persian carpets. Soon he would have been facing a shitload of lawsuits, civil proceedings and legal judgments against him. He was about to be ousted from his own company. *Yeah*, I thought, *from the golf club too*. Life at the top gives a guy one hell of a long way to fall. GOD had chosen his peculiar descent from Everest, the sole remaining action he could control.

In exchange for absolving me, I even told Ernie that it might be useful for the coroner to know that GOD hadn't tried to cut his own throat with a shard from a broken wine bottle before blowing away his head. Ernie was so pissed off, I got high on the sudden hope that he might stop trying to date me. Even though he was relieved to have the Dawson suicide tied up so quickly, he hadn't forgotten that the Durand case was still festering.

When he looked at me like he'd sooner be interviewing Paul Bernardo, I knew it was safe to conclude that he'd lost all romantic interest in me. "Moving right along, Kinsey Millhone," he snarled, "what do you know about who killed Charles Durand?"

I tossed a skittish grin his way. "Actually, if you'd let me make a couple of phone calls, I might be able to give you a lead on that one, too," I said cheekily. He gave me the defeated look that used to cross Etta's face about three decades ago when I haggled to stay up well past my bedtime for "The Alfred Hitchcock Show."

About an hour later, I was out of there with a promise to make sure Ernie had every shred of the Durand paper trail on his desk within an hour, so he could pass it on to the forensic accountants. He also insisted that I make myself "immediately available upon demand for at least the next seventy-two hours." I was happy to comply. Hell, I even offered to throw in a few floppy disks — and the tape of my fateful conversation with GOD!

I raced out of the building. Cop shops nudge funeral parlours off the top of my "most hated sites" list. I did not hop in a cab and head straight for Michael's, although GOD's death must have hit the news hours ago.

CHAPTER 33

I WAS LYING IN bed listening to Big Mama Thornton belt out "Just Like a Dog, Barking Up the Wrong Tree" from her "Hound Dog" CD. Figured the old blues shouter might help me sort things through prior to calling Michael.

The phone rang. I picked it up by the third insistent summons: I'm working my way through a twelve-step program for telephone avoidance.

It was Etta, ever redolent of roses after falling into a bucket of shit. Given my inner therapist's promptings that my mother is the root of my addiction to answering machines, fax machines and e-mail, I chose to regard this direct connection as a learning experience.

"Honey, I just read the *Post,* eh? And sayin' I'm proud of ya would be like sayin' I *like* men — one of your serious understatements, right? Anyways, you know how weird getting all sentimental makes me feel …"

I had to interrupt, before she wandered too far down that happy trail. "*You* feel weird getting all sentimental? Am I talking to the woman who played 'Will the Circle be Unbroken?' at her husband's funeral?"

"Only because the damn priest wouldn't let me play 'Your Cheatin' Heart' or 'Don't Come Home A Drinkin,'" she snapped. "And just in case I never told you before, I hate it when you put me down. All it proves is that you ain't got the manners God gave a magpie. Anyways, I was calling to invite you to a shindig but if you don't get more polite real soon, I could change my mind."

I loathe these turns in her monologues, the points at

which she's humming "I want to be seduced" in the background. My inner therapist advised a fresh response.

"Please, Mom, you know how much I love your parties." In a fair world, daughters would not have to tell egregious lies to placate their mothers.

Mendacity worked its usual transformations. "Well then, dear, I'm inviting you and that new boyfriend of yours to a party Nikos and me are throwing this Saturday."

I did not ask: "What about Slim? Have you invited Nikos's wife?" Etta has no patience for petty details. Before I pried myself from the phone, I extricated the time and place from she-who-must-be-listened-to.

Prior to dialling my "new boyfriend's" name ten minutes later, I spoke briefly with my Higher Power. Last night after leaving the cop shop I fell into bed after leaving a hurried message on Michael's machine that I was fine, but did not want my sleep disturbed for at least twelve hours. I just didn't have the stamina for another interrogation.

I invited him to Etta's party, refusing to discuss yesterday's events until he accepted. He immediately insisted on meeting me within the hour — at his place. I agreed. Playing hard-to-get only works when you are. Was he lusting for information or for me?

Twenty-four hours later, I left his bed to buy a dress for the shindig. I felt utterly debriefed.

Etta loves to quote that old line "I never fell in love, but I think I stepped into it a few times."

As soon as Michael and I entered Nikos's *taverna,* I could tell that she had stepped into it again. Shortly after ensuring that all their guests had a tumblerful of his homemade ouzo from Hades, the grizzled proprietor toasted my mother, his "new Helen of Troy." *Right. The battleship that launched a thousand faces.* Then he announced that they were leaving the following night for a two-week cruise of the Greek Islands. Call it *Love Among the Ruins.*

When I managed to elbow my way through their festive circle of friends, neighbours and regulars, Etta was chattering on about the free cell phone she got for booking their trip. God help me: I'd always felt some safety knowing that the umbilical could stretch no further than her phone cord. I congratulated her on the cruise anyway. In her peripatetic imagination, it's a short hop from Tennessee to Thermopylae.

Simone had phoned me the previous day to report that the police had treated her family with incredible solicitude; Rebecca's lawyer was confident of the best possible outcome. Her forced optimism did nothing to alleviate my despondency.

The party provided some comic relief. Sam Brewer brought his new lady. He kept repeating how grateful he was that I had given him the story of his career. Silver got along famously with William Durand and David Walker, but almost left in a huff when I told her I'd kill her if she hit on Portia. David was still hard at work on his thesis. William was working creative riffs on keeping him healthy, much encouraged by a new three-drug treatment.

The new lovers had solved the cross-cultural problem by hiring a country group, and playing Greek melodies from Nikos's jukebox whenever the band took a break. I couldn't believe my eyes when I saw Portia and Lennie line dancing. They left the floor, though, when the Tush Push was called. Silver jumped up and danced it with Judith Durand's girlfriend.

Ernie Sivcoski, whom I didn't think would show his face, came in shortly after two a.m. As he accepted a glass of *ouzo,* he half-heartedly asked Nikos if he knew it was illegal to be serving drinks at that hour. Etta retaliated by asking him to dance.

Judging by the amazed look on Michael's face as he observed the goings-on, he must have suffered a normal life until he met me. How long could we stay close? I feared that soon he, too, would withdraw from my life. If I was lucky, he'd give me more warning than Pete had.

I grabbed myself a bottle of Blue from Nikos's tacky selection of beer and carried it with me through the back door onto a depressing makeshift patio, its tawdriness exacerbated by moonlight. Maybe it looked better in June – maybe everything would look better in June.

Propped on a mildewed white plastic chair overlooking the laneway, I subjected my brain to the kind of checklist no woman in her right mind would compile after the witching hour.

Life only imitates TV if you spend too much time watching it.

There couldn't be any tidy wrap to a crime that began when Simone was a child and culminated in her own daughter's vindication of them both. Maybe I should be talking Greek tragedy instead of TV, about how evil works its slow stain through successive generations, until one can scarcely distinguish perpetrator from victim, or know foe from family.

The country had lost two of its legendary gods of commerce, but I wasn't convinced that their untimely passages to glory would serve as exemplary tales for the next litter of weasels. GOD's malignancy was systemic: it had metastasized into all the organs of the body politic. His suicide excised only one tumour.

Durand's perversions were as old as Mammon. Incest and sexual abuse permeate our culture. His murder was not the cure.

Although Simone had lost a brother, and Judith Durand her husband, some girl-instinct told me their collective tears wouldn't wet a shamrock. It didn't take a crystal ball to predict that Rebecca would stand trial in Juvenile Court and receive a compassionate sentence: yet nothing could erase the scars. Her mother's faith in counselling was misplaced.

Chugalug. Shuddering in the chill wind that bounced off the concrete block wall sheltering the incinerated remains of Sweet Dreams, I sucked in a deep breath and flung my beer bottle at it.

Justice is not the lady performing a balancing act with her scales. Justice is a crapshoot.

Good night, Pete, wherever you are.

LIZ BRADY, an editor for twenty years, has a Ph.D. in Virginia Woolf from the University of London. She is the author of *Tintype* (Fiddlehead Poetry Books) and *Marian Engel and Her Works* (ECW Press). She is currently at work on her next Jane Yeats novel and a non-fiction work on women writers and alcohol. Apart from the fact that they both live in Toronto, Liz Brady refuses to divulge which attributes she shares with her sleuth.